Secret Affairs

NATALIE ANDERSON
SARAH MAYBERRY
CHANTELLE SHAW

MILLS &
BOON

Published in Great Britain 2015
by Mills & Boon, an imprint of Harlequin (UK) Limited,
Eton House, 18-24 Paradise Road, Richmond, Surrey, TW9 1SR

SECRET AFFAIRS © 2015 Harlequin Books S.A.

The End of Faking It, *Her Secret Fling* and *The Ultimate Risk* were first published in Great Britain by Harlequin (UK) Limited.

The End of Faking It © 2011 Natalie Anderson
Her Secret Fling © 2010 Small Cow Productions Pty Ltd.
The Ultimate Risk © 2011 Chantelle Shaw

ISBN: 978-0-263-25201-9
eBook ISBN: 978-1-474-00380-3

05-0215

Harlequin (UK) Limited's policy is to use papers that are natural, renewable and recyclable products and made from wood grown in sustainable forests. The logging and manufacturing processes conform to the legal environmental regulations of the country of origin.

Printed and bound in Spain
by CPI, Barcelona

THE END OF FAKING IT

BY
NATALIE ANDERSON

Possibly the only librarian who got told off herself for talking too much, **Natalie Anderson** decided writing books might be more fun than shelving them—and, boy, is it that! Especially writing romance—it's the realisation of a lifetime dream kick-started by many an afternoon spent devouring Grandma's Mills & Boon® books...

She lives in New Zealand, with her husband and four gorgeous-but-exhausting children. Swing by her website any time—she'd love to hear from you: www.natalie-anderson.com.

For my awesome daily support structure:
Dave, Mum & Soraya.
You guys helped with the heartache of this one
especially. Am so happy to be returning the
favour now, Soraya!

CHAPTER ONE

ANOTHER two minutes couldn't possibly matter—late was late and this was too important to leave.

'Come on, Audrey,' Penny muttered softly. 'Let's keep you all healthy, huh?' She scattered the plant food and put the pack back in the top drawer of the filing cabinet. Then she picked up the jug of water.

'What are you doing?'

Her fingers flinched and she whirled at the sound of deep, accusing anger. She saw black clothes, big frame, even bigger frown. Striding towards her was a total stranger. A tall, dark, two hundred per cent testosterone-filled male was in her office, late at night. Not Jed the security guard, but a hard edged predator coming straight for her—fast.

She flung forward, all raw reflex.

He swore as water hit him straight in the eyes. She lunged again, hoping to knock him out with a Pyrex jug to the temple. Only halfway there her arm slammed against something hard, whiplash sent shudders down her shoulder. Painfully strong fingers held her wrist vice-tight. She immediately strained to break free, twisting skin and muscle. He sharply wrenched her wrist. She gasped. Her fingers failed and the jug tipped between them.

The shock of the ice-cold water splashing across her chest suffocated her shriek. She recoiled, but he came forward relentlessly, still death-gripping her wrist. The drawer slammed as she backed up and banged against it.

'Who the hell are you and what are you doing in here?' he demanded, storming further into her personal space.

Shock, pain, fear. She couldn't move other than to blink, trying to see clearly and figure a way to escape.

But he moved closer still. 'What are you doing with the files?' Pure menace.

The cold metal cabinet dug into her back. But he wasn't in the least cold. She could feel his heat even with the slight distance between them. His hand branded her. Her scream couldn't emerge—not with her throat squeezed so tight and her heart not beating at all.

He pushed back his fringe with his free hand, also blinked several times—only his eyes were filled with the water she'd thrown at him, not tears like hers. He actually laughed—not nicely—and his grip tightened even more. 'I didn't think this was going to be that easy.' He looked over her, scorn sharpening every harsh word. 'You're not screwing another cent out of this company.'

Penny gaped. He was insane. Totally insane. 'The security guard will be doing his rounds any minute,' she panted. 'He's armed.'

'With what—chewing gum? The only person going to the police cells tonight is you, honey.'

Yep, totally insane. Unfortunately he was also right about Jed's lack of ammo—the best she could hope for was a heavy torch. And it was a hopeless hope because she'd been lying anyway—Jed didn't do rounds. He sat at his desk. And she was ten floors up, alone with a complete nut-job who was going to…going to…

Jerky breathing filled her ears—as if someone was having an asthma attack. It took long moments to realise it was her. She pressed her free hand to her stomach, but couldn't stop the violent tremors. Her eyes watered more, her muscles quivered. Dimly she heard him swear.

'I'm not going to hurt you,' he said loudly right in her face.

'You already are,' she squeaked.

He instantly let go of her wrist, but he didn't move away. If anything he towered closer, still blocking her exit. But she could breathe again and her brain started sending signals. Then her heart got going, pushing a plan along her veins. All she had to do was escape him somehow and race down to Jed on Reception. She could do that, right? She forced a few more deep breaths as both fight and flight instincts rose and merged, locking her body and brain into survive mode.

'Who are you and what are you doing here?' he asked, a little quieter that time, but still with that peremptory tone, as if he had all the authority.

Which he didn't.

'Answer that yourself,' Penny snapped back.

He glanced down to where the jug lay useless on the floor and, beside her, where the plant's tub sat. 'You're the cleaner?' He looked from her toes back up to her face—slowly. 'You don't look like a cleaner.'

'No, who are *you* and what are *you* doing here?' Now she could see—and almost think—she took stock of him. Tall and dark, yes, but while the jeans and tee were black, they were well fitting—as in designer fitting. And it wasn't as if he was wearing a balaclava. Not exactly

hardcore crim kind of clothing. The intensely angry look
had vanished, and his face was open and sun-burnished,
as if he spent time skiing or sailing. The hard planes of
his body, and the strength she felt firsthand, suggested a
high degree of fitness too. On his wrist was one of those
impressive watches, all masculine and metal with a million little dials and functions most people wouldn't be
able to figure out. And now that the water was gone from
her eyes she could see his were an amazing blue-green.
Clear and shining and vibrant and…were they checking
her out?

'I asked you first,' he said softly, putting his hands
either side of her to rest on the top of the filing cabinet.
His arms made long, strong, bronzed prison bars.

'I'm the PA,' she answered mechanically, most of her
attention focused on digesting this new element of his
proximity. 'This is my desk.'

'*You're* Penny?' His brows skyrocketed up and he
blatantly checked over her outfit again. 'You definitely
don't look like any PA Mason would have.'

How did he know her name? And Mason? Her eyes
narrowed as the gleam in his grew. Heat radiated out
from him, warming her blood and making her skin super-
sensitive. No way. She wasn't going to let him look at her
like *that*. She sucked up some sarcasm. 'Actually Mason
really likes my skirt.'

He angled his head and studied it yet again. 'Is that
what that is? I thought it was a belt.' He smiled. Not a
scary psycho-killer smile, more one that would make a
million hearts flutter and two million legs start to slide
apart—like hers suddenly threatened to.

It was that powerful she had to consciously order her

lips not to smile right back at him like some besotted bimbo. 'It's vintage Levi's.'

'Oh, that explains it. You didn't realise moths had been at the hem?' His face lit up even more. 'Not that I'm complaining.'

Okay, the denim mini was teensy weensy, the heels of her shoes super-high and her curve-clinging champagne-coloured blouse off the shoulder. Of course she didn't wear this to work. She was all dressed up for dance-party pleasure. Yes, she'd dressed in case there was that other sort of pleasure to be had as well—just because she hadn't found a playmate in a while, didn't mean she'd given up all hope. Only now the pretty silk was sopping, plastered to her chest, revealing far more than she'd ever intended. And she was not, *not*, feeling any kind of primal response to a random stranger who'd all but assaulted her. 'Before I scream, who are you?' Not that there was any need to scream now and she knew it.

'I work here,' he said smoothly.

'I know everyone who works in this building and you don't.'

He reached into his pocket and then dangled a security card in her face. She quickly read the name—Carter Dodds. It didn't enlighten her in the least; she'd never heard of him. Then she looked at the photo. In it he was wearing the black tee shirt that he had on now.

Amazingly her brain managed the simple computation. 'You started today.'

'Officially tomorrow.' He nodded.

'Then why are you here now?' And how? Jed might be slack on the rounds but he was scrupulous about knowing who was still in the building after hours. And surely

Mason wouldn't have let a new recruit have open access to everything with no one around to supervise?

'I wanted to see what the place was like when it was quiet.'

'Why?' Her suspicions grew more. What did he want to see? There wasn't any money kept on site, but there were files, transactions, account numbers—loads of sensitive investor information worth millions. She glanced past him to Mason's open office door, but could hear no gentle hum of the computer.

'Why are you watering the plants at nine-thirty at night?' he countered.

'I forgot to do it earlier.'

'So you came back specially?' Utter disbelief.

Actually she'd been downstairs swimming in the pool—breaking all the rules because it was after the gym's closing hour. But she wasn't going to drop Jed in it. 'New recruits don't get to grill me.'

'No?'

His smile sharpened, but before he could get another question out she got in one of hers. 'How come you're here alone?'

'Mason wanted to get an early night before we get started tomorrow.'

'He didn't tell me you were starting.'

'Does he tell you everything?'

'Usually.' She lifted her chin in defiance of the calculated look that crossed his face, but he missed it—his focus had dropped to her body again.

'Mason buried his heart with his wife,' he said bluntly. 'You won't get any gold out of him no matter how short your skirt.'

Her mouth fell open. *'What?'*

'You wouldn't be the first pretty girl to bat her eye-lashes at a rich old man.'

What was he suggesting? 'Mason's *eighty*.'

His shrug didn't hide his anger. 'For some women that would make him all the more attractive.'

'Yeah, well, not me. He's like my grandfather.' She screwed up her face.

'You're the one who said he likes your skirt.'

'Only because you couldn't drag your eyes from it.'

'But isn't that why you wear it?'

She paused. He wasn't afraid to challenge direct, was he? Well, nor was she—when she could think. Right now her brain had gone all lame. 'I don't believe you're supposed to be here now.'

'Really? Go ahead and ask your boss. Use my phone.' He pulled it out of his pocket, pressed buttons and handed it to her.

It rang only a couple of times.

'Carter, have you already found something?'

Penny gripped the phone tighter as she absorbed the anxiety in Mason's quick-fire query. 'No, sorry, Mason, it's Penny. Not Carter.' She stuttered when she saw Carter's sudden grin—disarming and devilish. 'Look, I've just bumped into someone in the office.'

'Carter,' Mason said.

'Yes.' Penny winced at the obvious. Had the sinking feeling she was about to wince even more. 'He's given me his phone to call you.'

'Penny, I'm sorry, I should have told you but Carter thought it should wait until he got there.'

Thought what should wait? Why was Carter the one calling shots? What was going on?

'Carter heads up Dodds WD in Melbourne. I asked

him to come to Sydney for a couple of weeks. I need his help.'

'What for?'

Carter knew he was still standing too close but too bad. In fact he put both hands back on either side of her. That way she couldn't readily escape. He was certain she would, so he made sure she couldn't—by holding a position that was only a few inches away from intimate.

He was having a time shutting up the temptation whispering that he should lose those few inches. He pushed his hands hard on the cool metal and watched as she pressed the phone closer to her ear and turned her head away from him.

The colour ran under her skin like an incoming tide and Carter couldn't contain his amusement. Mason was his grandfather's best friend. He'd seen him every few months all his life and he was on the old boy's speed-dial to prove it. This was the first time Mason had asked him for help—and help he would. But just this moment?

Distraction. Capital D.

'Of course.' Penny had turned her head even further away, clearly hoping he wouldn't hear whatever it was that Mason was saying.

Carter didn't give a damn what the old guy said right now. He was too lost in looking at her. She had the biggest, darkest eyes he'd ever seen. They drew him in and sucked him under—like sparkling pools that turned out to be dangerously deep, the kind of eyes that you could stare into endlessly—and he was. Peripherally, bits of his body were absorbing the detail of hers and the back of his brain drew rapid conclusions.

A skirt that short, a shirt that sexy, a body that honed, lips that slicked…

This woman knew how attractive she was, and she emphasised all her best assets. Everything about her was polished to pure, sensual perfection. She was no shy, shrinking secretary. She was a siren. And every basic cell in Carter's body wanted to answer her summons. So, so badly.

'Hello?'

She was holding the phone out to him and he'd been too busy gawping to notice. He grabbed it and started talking.

'Hi, Mason, sorry to bother you so late.'

'It doesn't matter. It's great you're onto it so quickly. I can't thank you enough.'

'So Penny's your temp PA?' Carter kept looking at her, still struggling to believe that conservative, eighty-year-old Mason had ever hired such a blatant sex bomb. 'She's working late.'

'She always works late.' Mason sounded pleased. 'She's an angel. I get in every morning and everything is so organised, she makes it a breeze.'

An *angel*? Carter's suspicions sharpened again. Penny wouldn't be the first attractive young woman to turn an older man's head. Carter knew exactly how easy it was for an avaricious, ambitious female to use her beauty to dazzle a fool old enough to know better. He'd watched not one, but two do that to his dad. Despite her outraged reaction, who was to say that wasn't what was happening here? 'How long has she been with you?' He couldn't not ask.

There was a silence. 'Since after the problem started.'

Mason's voice turned arctic. 'I thought I'd made this clear already.'

Yeah. Mason had mentioned his fabulous PA more than once—but not her hotter-than-Venus factor. Not mentioning that didn't seem natural.

'You tell her what's going on,' Mason said sharply. 'I should have already. Carter, she's not who you're looking for.'

Carter stared at the temptation personified before him. Her mouth was as glossy and red ripe as a Morello cherry—and he wanted a taste. That was the real problem. Hell, he was off on a tangent before he'd even started. He owed Mason better than this. 'You're right,' he said brusquely. 'She's not.'

Penny watched him pocket the phone. He didn't seem to be any happier about the situation—offered no laughter or light apology. If anything he looked as angry as he had when he'd first interrogated her. What was he here to do exactly? Mason hadn't elaborated, just told her to help him if he asked her to. They hadn't advertised a new job—she was the one who placed the ads so she'd know. So this was cronyism, some old boys' school network thing. But he was hardly a fresh-faced graduate getting his first contract courtesy of his father. 'You know Mason personally,' she said baldly, annoyed by the fact—annoyed by him—and his attractiveness.

'Have done for years.' He nodded.

Yeah, that was why the job, whatever it was, hadn't been advertised. Mason had probably made something up for him to do. Still smarting from his gold-digger slur, she let her inner bitch out to taunt. 'You don't look like you have to pull favours to get a job.'

'Don't I?' he answered too softly. 'How would you know? Is that what you do?' He leaned closer and whispered low, as if they were intimate. 'What kind of favours do you pull to score a job, Penny?'

Okay, she'd crossed the line a little, but he'd just leapt it. 'What sort of favours do you think I *pull*?' she fired back before thinking.

His eyes flashed, the pupils expanding so fast the piercing colours became the thinnest of circles around the burgeoning black. Riveted, she watched the myriad greens and blues narrow out. He really did have it— perfect symmetry, angular jawbones and hair that just begged to be ruffled and then gripped tight.

The palms of her hands tingled, heated. Only it wasn't just his hair she imagined pulling close, no, now she was pulling on hot, silky hard skin, stroking it faster and faster and—*OMG where had that come from?*

She gulped back the insanity. She couldn't be thinking that. She looked down and clamped her mouth shut, swallowing both literally and mentally, overly aware her breathing had quickened to audible—basically to panting. Again.

Oh, please don't let him know what she'd been thinking. She glanced back up at him. All the blue had gone from his irises leaving nothing but thin rings of green fire around those huge, black pupils. Dusky red tinged his cheekbones. She could relate. Blood was firing all round her body, pinking up all sorts of parts—her face included. But at least he wasn't panting like some dog in heat, which she, unfortunately, was.

He said nothing, she said nothing. But she could see it shimmering in the air between them—razor-sharp attraction. Urges at their most basic. Urges almost uncontrollable.

'There's a problem in the accounts—someone in the company is skimming,' he suddenly said roughly, jerking his head up.

'What?'

'I'm here to check through all the files and find out who and how.'

Someone was stealing? And Carter was here to catch him? Mason had said he headed up some company in Melbourne, so was he some kind of CEO/forensic accountant or something?

Actually that didn't seem to fit. Not when he wore jeans and tousled hair so well. He looked as if he had too much street cred to be a number cruncher.

'The only people who'll know the real reason I'm here are you, Mason and me,' he continued. 'We'll spread it 'round the company that I'm a friend of Mason's who's borrowing an office for a couple of weeks. Which I am.'

The fiery green in his eyes dampened to cold blue serious. The sensual curve of his mouth flattened to a straight, hard line. Penny stared, watching him ice over, as she absorbed that info and the implications.

Then she realised. 'You thought it was *me*?' She basically shrieked, her temperature steaming back up to boiling point. She might be many things, but a thief wasn't one of them. 'I'm the best damn temp in this town. I'm hardworking and honest. How dare you storm in here and throw round your gutter accusations?'

'I know.' His expression went very intense. 'I'm sorry. Mason already told me it couldn't be you.'

He sucked the wind right out of her sails and disarmed

her completely with a sudden flash of that smile. It cracked his icy cover and let the heat ripple once more. But she refused to let her anger slide into attraction. 'You still thought it,' she accused.

'Well, you have to admit it looked…it looked…' His attention wandered—down. 'It looked…'

Her body—despite the freezing wet shirt—was burning. Okay, that attraction was impossible to stop—simplest thing now would be to escape. 'Well, now that you've done your looking,' she said sarcastically, her eyes locked on his, 'are you going to step back and let me past?'

'Not yet,' he said wryly. 'I'm still looking.'

Penny's nerves tightened to one notch the other side of screaming. His lashes lowered and his smile faded. She looked down too. Now her silk shirt was wet it was both skin colour and skin tight and she might as well not be wearing anything. Even worse, she was aching…and horrified to realise it was completely obvious.

'You're cold,' he said softly.

Yeah, completely obvious.

'The water in the jug was from the cooler.'

'So that's the reason…'

All she could do was brazen this out. She tossed her head and met his eyes direct. 'What other reason could there be?'

His lips curved. In his tanned face, his teeth were white and straight and perfect. Actually everything in his face was perfect. And in the dark tee shirt and dark trousers he looked pretty-boy pirate, especially with the slightly too-long hair. The intensity of his scrutiny was devastating and now he'd fixed on one thing—her mouth.

She saw his intention. She felt it in her lips already—the yearning for touch. But even for her that would be insane. She didn't like the way her pulse was zigzagging all over the place. She didn't like the way her body was so willingly bracing for impact.

'Don't add another insult to the list,' she said, trying to regain control over both of them. But the words didn't come out as forcefully as she'd intended. Instead they whispered on barely a breath—because she could barely move enough to breathe.

'How can appreciating beauty be an insult?'

Penny's pulse thundered. She was used to confident men. They were the kind she liked—pretty much bullet proof. But this was more than just superficial brashness; this was innate, absolute arrogance. He stood even closer, filling all her senses. Her blood rushed to all her secret places and left her brain starving of its ability to operate.

His smile suddenly flashed brighter—like how the flame flared on a gas hob when you accidentally twisted the knob the wrong way. His hand lifted and he brushed her lips with a finger. She shivered.

Shock. She was in shock. That was the problem. That was why she wasn't resisting....

His expression heated up all the more. 'You okay?'

'Mmm.'

His traversing finger muffled the words she couldn't speak anyway. She was too busy pressing her lips firmly together to stop herself from opening up and inviting him in. But somehow he got that invite anyway because he lifted his finger and swiftly replaced it with his mouth.

Oh.

It was light. A warm, gentle, coaxing kiss that

promised so much more than it gave. But what it did give was good. He moved closer, not threatening, but with a hint of masculine spice and just enough pressure to make her accept him. To make her want more. Surprised that it wasn't a full-throttle brazen burst of passion, she relaxed. Her eyes automatically closed as her body focused on the exquisite sweetness trickling into her. It had been a long time since she'd felt anything so nice—a subtle magic that melted her resistance, and saw her start to strain for what she knew he was holding at bay.

Her lips parted—she couldn't deny herself. His response came immediate, and powerful. She heard his sound of satisfaction and his hands moved from the steel behind to her soft body. She trembled top to toe as he swiftly shaped her curves, pulling her against him. She had to grab hold of his shoulders or she was going to tumble backwards. The kiss deepened again as she felt the wide, flat planes and hard strength of him. Her neck arched back as he stroked into her mouth. She lifted her hand, sliding her fingers into his thick hair. He showed no mercy then, bending her back all the more as he sought full access, kissing her jaw and neck and back up again to claim her mouth—this time with confident, carnal authority.

She shuddered at the impact, felt him press closer still. Sandwiched between him and the cabinet, she was trapped between forces as unyielding and demanding as each other. Yet she had no desire to escape, not now.

The arrogance of him was breathtaking. But not anywhere as breathtaking as the way he kissed. It was as if he was determined to maximise pleasure for them both and the control she usually held so tight started to slide as her own desire mounted.

He was silk-wrapped steel and she wanted to feel all of him against her, slicing into her. She wanted him. Wanted as she hadn't wanted anyone in a long, long time. Okay, ever. Hungry for his strength and passion, she kissed him back—melting against his body, delving into his mouth with her tongue, so keen to explore more.

And he knew. He lifted his hand from her waist to her breast and, oh, so lightly stroked his fingers across her violently taut nipple.

She felt the touch as if her skin were bare. And it burned too hot.

She jerked back, ripping her mouth free from his. Their eyes met, faces inches apart. A flare of something dangerous kindled in his—different from the earlier fury but just as frightening for Penny. She pushed as far back against the cool metal cabinet as she could, breathing hard. She shook her head, the only method of communication she could manage. While he stood, rock hard, and stared right back at her.

A million half-thoughts murmured in her head—desperate thoughts, forgotten thoughts, *frightening* thoughts.

Carter Dodds wasn't the kind of man to let a woman stay on top—Penny's only acceptable position, metaphorically anyway. He'd just demonstrated he'd always ultimately be the one in charge—his almost pretty-boy packaging disguised a total he-man with all masculine, all dominant virility. He'd made his move that way—lulling her into a sense of sweet security before unleashing his true potency and damn near swamping her reason. She liked sex—enjoyed the chase, the fun of touch, the fleeting closeness. But she never, ever lost control. *She* had to be in charge—*needed* to be the one who was wanted—even if only for that little while. She was very careful with whom she shared her body because she would always walk away. She ensured that a lover understood that. Commitment wasn't something she could ever give. Nor was complete submission. So the sensations now threatening to submerge all her capacity for rational thought were very new. And very unwelcome.

But there was a logical explanation. Less than five minutes ago she'd thought she was being attacked. Her heart hadn't had a chance since to stop its manic stuttering and it was still sending 'escape now' blasts through her blood.

'Well, that was one way to burn off the adrenalin overload.' She totally had to act cool.

'Is that what you were doing?'

'Sure. You know, I was still wired from the fright of you assaulting me in my own office.'

He stepped back, taking his heat with him. But his scrutiny seemed even more intense than ever. 'Oh. So what was it for me?'

She hazarded a simple guess. 'Normal?'

His mouth quirked. 'Not.'

Cool just wasn't happening but she had to scrape her melting body back together. She wasn't afraid of taking fun where it could be found, but there wasn't fun to be had here. Anything that hot eventually had to hurt. And any emotion that intense scared her. In ten minutes with Carter she'd already run the gamut of terror, fury and lust—way too much of the latter. So she turned away from the challenge in his eyes.

'I need to get going. I'm late as it is.' The sooner she got to the bar, the better—she had to burn up the energy zinging round her body like a demented fly trapped in a jar. Fast and free on the dance floor for the next eight hours might do it.

'Hot date?'

'Very.' She lied, happy to slam the brakes on anything between them by invoking her imaginary man friend. She opened up her gym bag; she'd straighten up her appearance and then her insides. But those insides shrieked— she breathed choppily, her heart jack-hammered—so the hairdryer's cacophony was completely wonderful. It muted her clamouring nerves.

Carter took a couple of strides to get himself out of physical range so he could get a grip on the urge to haul her back against him. He didn't know what had got into him. He'd just kissed a complete stranger. A stranger who he'd initially thought was Mason's cheating thief.

He should probably apologise. But how could he be sorry for something so good? Except for a second there she'd looked at him as if he'd struck her, not snogged her. She'd looked shocked and almost hurt, almost vulnerable.

And then she'd blamed that chemistry on adrenalin? Who did she think she was kidding? And now she was apparently late for her *date* and she had her hairdryer blasting. But it wasn't her hair getting the treatment. It was her shirt. She held it out from her body, blowing the warm air over the silk. Then she lifted the nozzle and aimed it down her neckline—what, so she could dry her soft, wet skin? Not helping his raging erection subside any. Nope, that just yanked it even tighter.

A light flickered on her desk. Her mobile. He glanced back up; she was still focused on her shirt. He picked up the mobile to hand it to her, his thumb hit the keypad and, oh, shame, that message from Mel just flicked up on the screen.

Where r u? Kat & Bridge already on d-floor & lookg tragic. Need yr expertise.

Her hot date was with Mel, Kat and Bridge? A bunch of women out on a mission—on a Monday night. That shouldn't amuse him quite as much as it did. He walked up, took the dryer from her hand and pointed it at his wet hair. Immediately he jerked back from the blast of air. 'It's freezing!'

The pink in her cheeks deepened.

'Yeah,' he teased, the sparks arcing between them again. 'I thought you were feeling hot.'

'It's malfunctioning,' she said sulkily.

Carter fiddled with the switch and then aimed the dryer at her like a gun. 'Or maybe it's because you had it turned on cold.'

Boom—even more red blotches peppered her creamy skin. She snatched the appliance back off him and switched it off.

'Here's your phone.' He bit the bullet and handed it over.

She looked at the screen and frowned. 'You read my text?'

'It flashed when I picked it up.' He shrugged almost innocently.

'You didn't need to pick it up.'

'But I like picking up pretty little things.' Even less innocent.

Blacker than black eyes narrowed. 'I'm sure you've had plenty of practice.'

'Well, that does make for perfect performance.' Yep, wickedly sinful now.

'Is that what you think you offer? Perfection?'

He grinned at her tone. She made provocation so irresistible. 'You don't think?'

Her eyes raked him hard and, heaven help him, he loved it. 'I think you could do with some more practice.'

'You're offering?'

She turned away from him, retrieved the jug from the floor and marched to the water cooler to refill it. What, she was literally going to douse the flames again? But, no, she poured the water around the base of the monstrosity that was supposedly an office plant.

'What is it, some kind of triffid?' He reached up to the branches overhanging the cabinet. 'If it grows any more, there won't be room for anyone to work in here.'

'She belongs to Carol and she'll be here when she gets back. All healthy.'

'You think that's really going to happen?' Carter knew Mason's long-time assistant had a cancer battle on her hands. She'd been off for months and Mason was paying her full salary out of his own pocket. Which was why finding the person stealing from him was a priority. He was paying for two PAs. He was a hardworking, generous employer who deserved better than some skunk skimming and putting the entire company in jeopardy.

'Of course she's coming back.' Penny banged the jug back on top of the filing cabinet and finally looked at him directly again. The flames were still there. 'Is someone really stealing from him?'

Carter nodded. 'I think so.'

'But Mason's one of the good guys. He gives so much to charity. He doesn't deserve that.'

'That's why I'm here.'

Her appraisal went rapier sharp. 'Well, you'd better lift your game.'

'Hmm.' He nodded agreeably. 'I was thinking that too.' But the game he meant was the one with her. And he didn't miss the warring desire and antagonism in her expression.

He walked alongside her down the corridor, rode the lift in silent torture. The space between them was too small but he wanted it even smaller—to nothing but skin on skin. Like a tiger, he was ready to pounce. At least his body was; his brain was frantically trying to issue warnings—like he didn't have time for this, like he needed to focus.

The security guard leapt up from his desk to get the door. 'Goodnight, Penny.' His smile widened as he watched her walk across the foyer towards him. That smile faded when he glanced behind her and registered Carter's frown. 'Goodnight, sir.' Suddenly all respectful.

Carter made himself nod and smile.

'Hope Maddie's better when you get home,' Penny said lightly.

'Me too.' The guard's smile spread again. 'See you tomorrow. Not too early, you understand?'

She just laughed as she went through the door.

'Have fun, Penny,' Carter drawled softly as they hit the pavement.

She turned and fluttered him a look one eyelash short of do-me-now. 'Oh, I plan to.'

So she couldn't resist striking the sparks either. And he knew the kind of fun girls like her liked—the eat-men-for-breakfast kind. He smiled, happy to play if she wanted, because experience had made him too tough to chew. She could learn that if she dared.

She walked away, her legs ridiculously long in that sexy strip of a skirt, her balance perfect on the high, narrow heels. Her glossy brown hair cascaded down to her almost too-trim waist. He bet she worked out in the pursuit of perfection. Not that she needed to bother. She nailed it on attitude alone.

Testosterone—and other things—surged again. So did his latent combative nature. That vulnerability he'd seen upstairs when he'd startled her, and again after he'd kissed her? A mirage—she'd been buying time while assessing her position. For Penny the PA knew how to play men—the slayer look she'd just shot him proved it. Mason thought the world of her. The security guy was falling over himself to help her. She'd want to bring Carter to heel like every other man she knew. Yeah, he'd seen her vixen desire for dominance. She thought she could toy with him as some feline would a mouse.

She was so wrong.

But he could hardly wait for her to bring it on.

CHAPTER TWO

PENNY winked at Jed as she walked back into the building just over nine hours later—three of which had been spent dancing and six sort-of sleeping.

'Too early, Penny.' The security guard covered his yawn, clearly barely hanging out the last half-hour before clocking off.

'Too much to do.'

First in for the day, she wanted to get ahead and be fully functioning by the time Mason showed. Definitely by the time Carter Dodds rolled in. The super-size black coffee in her hand would help. But she'd barely got seated when there was movement in her doorway.

'Thought I'd bring this up before I left.'

Jed walked in—well, from the voice she knew it was him. His body was completely obscured by the floral bouquet that was almost too wide to fit through the door.

'They just arrived,' he puffed.

'Not more?' Penny shrivelled deeper into her seat. She knew who they were from. Aaron—a spoilt-for-choice playboy type with several options on the go—the kind of guy Penny always looked for when she needed some company for a while. Only the spark was missing. Last week she'd told him no and goodbye—thought she'd made it clear—but the flowers continued to prove otherwise.

'Thanks, Jed,' she said as he offloaded the oversize blooms onto her desk. 'Have a good sleep.'

'Not me who needs it.'

Penny held back her sigh. She'd take the bunch back down to Reception again but she'd wait 'til Jed had gone for the day—he was exhausted after the night shift and had to go home to a sick preschooler. He didn't need to be hauling flowers back and forth for her.

She picked up her phone and hit one of the pre-programmed buttons.

'SpeedFreaks.'

'Hi, Kate,' Penny said. 'I've got a floral delivery please.'

'Penny? Another one?'

'Yeah.' She tried not to sound too negative about it. It was pretty pathetic to be upset by having masses of flowers delivered; most women would be thrilled. But cut flowers didn't make her think of romance and sweethearts, they made her think hospitals and funerals and lives cut way too short. 'Can you pick them up as soon as possible?'

She heard a movement behind her and turned, smiling in anticipation of Mason. But she forgot all about Mason, or smiling, even the flowers. Only one thing filled her feeble mind.

Tall, broad shoulders, dark hair dangerously leaning towards shaggy—she shouldn't be thinking shag anything. But she was. Because his eyes were leaning towards dangerous to match. She half waved with her phone hand to let him know she was occupied. But he didn't go away and she really needed him to because her head wasn't working well with him watching her like that. She pointedly looked past him to the corridor—didn't he know to come back in a few minutes?

No. He just thudded a heavy shoulder against the doorframe, becoming a human door—blocking her exit and anyone else's entry to the room.

And he smiled. Not just dangerous—positively killer.

She tried to look away, honest she did. But that ability had been stolen from her the moment her eyes had met his.

'Can you get them picked up asap?' she asked on auto, her brain fried by Carter's perfectly symmetrical features. Other parts of her body had gone on quick burn too. Thank heavens she still had her jacket on, because her boobs were like twin beacons screaming her interest through her white blouse. Memories of that gentle stroke last night tormented her. 'They'll be at Reception.'

He was even more handsome in the morning light. Even more now she wasn't blinded by fear and her senses weren't heightened by a surge of adrenalin. No, now it was some other hormone rippling through her body making her shiver.

He stared back as if he were mentally undressing her as fast as she was him. There were no black jeans and tee today, it was suit all the way. Dark, so understated it actually stood out, its uniform style showing off the fat-free frame beneath. Penny's heart thundered.

She turned back to her desk, her voice lowering. 'Thanks, Kate.' She wanted off the phone.

'Are you sure you don't want them? Or him?' Kate didn't pick up on Penny's need-to-hang-up vibe. 'He must be loaded to keep sending you these massive bouquets. And he's obviously dead keen.'

Penny winced. Then winced again as she realised Carter would be able to hear Kate too—the phone volume was too loud. She glanced over her shoulder and jumped. He wasn't in the doorway any more. He was about three inches away—at the most.

'No. I'll spell it out in single syllables.' But Penny tensed. She didn't know how more obvious she could be. She'd thought Aaron would be fine with a few dates' fun before saying goodbye. Only they hadn't got anywhere near that far. She figured the over-the-top floral attention was just him not being used to hearing 'no' and now he was determined to make her change her mind for the boy sport of it. But she couldn't be sure. And because she couldn't be completely sure, she couldn't be completely harsh. Not ever again.

'Where do you want them to go?'

'What about the hospice? But send them to the staff-room. Those guys work so hard.'

'Sure.'

Carter had his ultimate weapon loaded again—that smile was amused now, curving his full, sensual mouth. The green-blue eyes were bright and clear, but the clarity itself seemed to be shielding secrets within. Like a mirror they reflected the surface—and blocked access to the depths behind.

She replaced the receiver and turned to face her shameless eavesdropper full on. She ran her hands down the side of her skirt, pretending to smooth it but really trying to get rid of the clammy feeling.

'You don't want to keep them?' He was far too close

in this spacious office—why couldn't he stay on the far side of her desk?

He inspected the behemoth bunch and looked at the card—the millions of miniature red hearts on the cover obviously showed it was a romantic gift. Somehow him knowing that annoyed her all the more. And he already knew she didn't want them, he'd heard the courier conversation.

'I'm allergic,' she lied through a clamped smile. She wanted to get rid of both the flowers and him. How was she supposed to concentrate when her desk was covered with strong-smelling blooms and a man more gorgeous than the latest Calvin Klein model was making the room shrink more with every breath?

His gaze narrowed. 'Really?'

'Sure.' She blinked. 'I need to get these to Reception.' She reached out to pick up the flowers and escape. But in her haste she scraped her finger against one of the green stems, scratching it. 'Damn.' She looked at her skin and watched the fine white scratch flood with red. Then she glared at the bunch. 'I hate them.'

'Let me see.' He sidestepped the flowers and had her wrist in his hand before her brain could even engage.

Her pulse shot into the stratosphere. 'It's fine. A little plaster or a tissue will stop it,' she babbled faster than a Japanese bullet train rode the rail. Every muscle quivered, wanting him to draw her into a closer embrace.

'Suck on it.' His gaze snared hers. 'Or I will if you want.'

For half a second her jaw hung open. Oh, he was every bit as outrageous in the morning as he was at night. And she was dangerously tickled.

'It's fine.' She snatched her hand back, curling her fingers into a fist. 'I need to get these out of here.'

'Hey.' He frowned and reached out again, pushing her wide gold bangle further up her arm. His frown super-sized up as he stared at the skin he'd exposed. 'Did I do that?'

'Oh.' She glanced down at the purple fingerprint bruises circling her wrist. 'Don't worry about it. I bruise easily.'

He looked back to her face, all the erotic spark in his expression stamped out by concern. 'I'm really sorry.'

'Don't be.' She shook her head quickly. 'Like I said, it's nothing.' Honestly, his contrition just made it worse. She *did* bruise easily and his switching to all serious made him all the more gorgeous. And now he was ever so lightly touching each bruise with a single fingertip.

'It's not fine.'

Penny swallowed. With difficulty. Did he have to be so genuine? She needed to get out of there before she did something stupid like puddle at his feet. That gentle stroking was having some kind of weird hypnotic effect, making her want to move even closer. Instead she turned to the flowers.

'I'll take them.' He picked up the massive bunch with just the one hand.

Okay, that was good because he'd be gone and she'd have a few minutes to bang her head and hormones back together. She should be polite and say something. But she didn't think she had a 'thank you' in her this second. The sensations still reverberated, shaking her insides worse than any earthquake could.

'Penny—'

'Mason should be here any minute,' she said quickly to stave off any more of the soft attention.

'No Mason today,' Carter answered. 'He's working from home. He'll have sent you an email.'

She frowned. Mason never worked from home. He might be eighty but he was almost always first in the door every day. 'I'll take what he needs to him there.' Truthfully she wanted to check on him.

'That would be great.'

Their gazes collided again, only this time the underlying awareness was tempered by mutual concern.

'I'll find out who's hurting him,' Carter said, calmly determined.

Penny nodded.

He cared about the old man, that was obvious. Something jerked deep inside her—the first stirrings of respect and a shared goal.

'I'll be back in a minute.' He swept out of the room.

Penny just sank into her chair.

Carter carried the oversize bunch of blooms down to Reception. Taking the stairs rather than the lift used a bit of the energy coiled in his body, but not enough. Like an overflowing dam he needed a runoff to ease some of the pressure.

Penny had got under his skin faster than snake venom got into a mouse's nervous system. He'd thought about her all night instead of getting his head around the company set-up. Seeing her again today had only made it worse. She looked unbelievably different. The clubbing vixen had vanished and in her place was a perfect vision of conservative and capable. An, oh-so-sensible-length skirt simply highlighted slim ankles and sweet curves, a virginal white blouse was covered by a neatly tailored navy jacket. Hell, there'd even been a strand of pearls at her neck. With her shiny black hair swept back into a plait and her even blacker eyes, she'd looked like the epitome of the nineteen-forties secretary. No matter what she wore, she was beautiful.

Ordinarily Carter wasn't averse to mixing business and pleasure. When business took up so much time, it was sometimes the only way he could find room for pleasure. So long as the woman understood the interest was only ever a temporary thing, and that there were no benefits to the arrangement other than the physical. He didn't generally mix it with someone directly subordinate to him, but someone in one of the offshoot companies or satellite offices.

But he shouldn't mess with Penny—not with only a week or two to find the slimeball ripping Mason off. But he didn't think he was going to be able to work without coming to some kind of arrangement with her, because her challenge was enough to smash his concentration completely. Fortunately he figured she was a woman who'd understand the kind of deal he liked, and the short time frame saved them from any possible messiness. He just had to ensure she understood the benefits—and the boundaries.

In the privacy of the stairwell he opened the card still attached to the flowers.

Hoping to see you again tonight—Aaron.

Carter's muscles tightened. Had she seen him last night? Maybe she had had a hot date after meeting up with the women. Had she gone to this Aaron with the taste of Carter still on her? Because he could still taste her—hot, fresh, hungry.

He wasn't in the least surprised to think she'd go to another guy having just blown hot for him; he was well used to women who manipulated, playing one man off against another. His ex had done exactly that—trying to force him into making a commitment by making him jealous. It hadn't worked. And he sure as hell wasn't feeling jealous now. The aggro sharpening his body this minute was because of the threat to Mason. Not Penny.

He stalked out to Reception and put the flowers on the counter. 'I think a courier company is coming to pick these up.'

The receptionist grinned as she looked at them. 'Penny sent them down?' She shook her head. 'That's the third bunch this week. She's mad not to want them.'

The third this week? It was only Tuesday. Yeah, she would like holding the interest of multiple men. His long-held cynicism surged higher—there was no doubt Penny was as greedy and needy as every other woman he'd known.

It was almost an hour before Carter reappeared, a piece of paper in his hand and a frown creasing his brow. 'Penny, I need you to—'

He broke off as her phone started ringing.

She shrugged an apology and answered it. 'Nicholls Finance, Penny speaking.'

'Did you get the flowers?'

'Aaron,' she whispered, inwardly groaning. She darted a look at Carter, then turned away on her chair so he wouldn't see the flush rising in her cheeks. She already knew he was rude enough to stay and listen. Her best option was to end the call asap. 'It really isn't convenient to talk right now—'

'Did you get them?'

'Yes, I'm sorry, I should have called but it's been a busy morning.' And she could hardly let him down without some privacy. 'Can I call you back?'

'The roses reminded me of you. Stunningly beautiful but with some dangerous prickles.'

Yes, she'd encountered one of those real prickles. She shrank more into her chair. 'Look, it was lovely of you but—'

'Dinner tonight. No excuses.'

She breathed in and tried to stay calm. 'That's a nice idea but—'

'I've already made the reservations. It's my only night off this week and I want to spend it all with you.'

'Aaron, I'm sorry but—'

The phone was taken out of her hand.

'Look, mate, don't bother. She has a new boyfriend and she's allergic to flowers. She's already sent them on to the hospice down the road.'

Penny stared as Carter leaned across her desk. She couldn't hear what Aaron said in response— she could hardly process what Carter had just said so complacently.

'Yeah, I know. Save your dough. It isn't going to happen.' Carter hung up the phone and then looked at her coolly. 'So, I was saying I need you to track down some files for me.'

For a moment she was too shocked to fully feel the rising fury. But then it truck-slammed into her. *What* did you just do?'

Carter met her gaze with inhuman calm. 'Solved your problem. He won't bother you again.'

'How could you do that?'

'Easily. And you should have done it sooner already. Your body language said one thing, your mouth another. You looked like you wanted to hide under your desk for fear he'd appear, but you were brushing him off too gentle. A guy like that doesn't get subtle, Penny. You need the sledgehammer approach.'

'I didn't need you to be the sledgehammer.' She shook her head. 'That was bully behaviour.'

'It was man talking to man,' he argued with an eye-roll for added effect. 'And more honest than the drivel coming out of your mouth.'

'I was handling him,' she said defensively.

'You were *playing* with him.' Now he didn't sound so calm. Now he sounded that little bit nasty.

Her hands shook as she brushed her hair behind her ear. She hadn't been playing with Aaron, she'd been trying to be nice.

'Three bunches of flowers this week already, isn't it, Penny? You're not even honest enough to tell him you don't want *them*, let alone that you don't want *him*.'

Because she didn't want to be rude. She never wanted to hurt anyone. Never. Horrified tears prickled her eyes as she panicked over Aaron's reaction to Carter's heavy-handedness.

'Why are you so upset?' He stepped closer, his eyes narrowing. 'Oh, I get it. You liked to leave him hanging? Was it good for your ego? You like getting all the flowers and attention? You're a tease.'

'I'm not.' She jerked up out of her chair, beyond hurt at the words he'd just used.

'You are,' he argued. 'Why else wouldn't you cut him free sooner?'

'I tried.' She snatched the paper off him and marched

to the filing cabinet, hauling the drawer open with a loud bang.

'That wasn't trying.' He followed and faced her as she rummaged through the files. 'You're not stupid, Penny. You could have flicked him off much sooner.'

'Maybe I'm not as arrogant or as rude as you are.' She slapped files on the top of the steel. 'I don't like trampling on people's feelings.'

'You don't think it's worse to string him along so your ego can be inflated some more?'

'That wasn't what I was doing.' She crossed her arms in front of her chest.

'Oh, don't tell me you really liked him?' He looked stunned. 'Were you just making life hell for him? Playing with him so he'd do anything you ask him to?'

'Of course not!' She clenched her teeth. 'I was trying to make it clear that nothing was going to happen. I thought I had already. But he didn't deserve your kind of in-your-face humiliation.'

'What he doesn't deserve is you screwing him up and spitting him out only when you're sick of chewing him over.'

Breathing hard, she glared at him as fury burned along her veins. 'Wow, you think so highly of me, don't you, Carter?'

His shoulders lifted in a mocking shrug. 'If you really wanted rid of him, you needed to be cruel to be kind.'

'Well, I'm not cruel,' she said painfully. 'I won't ever be.'

He glared right back at her—for what felt like hours. Slowly she became aware of their isolation in the office, the smallness of the space between them. They were just about in exactly the position they'd been in last night.

'How about honest, then, can you manage that?' he asked quietly.

'Not if it's going to really hurt someone,' she muttered. Utterly honest.

'No.' He shook his head. 'That's the coward's way out.'

Well, what would he know about anything? For all his cruel-to-be-kind cliché, she'd bet her last cent he'd never hurt anyone the way she once had.

She blinked back her sudden tears, focused on his eyes instead. Close up now she saw even more colours in them—not just green and blue but shots of gold as well. All of a sudden she was trying really, really hard not to think of that kiss and how incredible she'd felt. Trying really, really hard not to notice how his mouth looked fuller today.

The atmosphere changed completely. It seemed he'd forgotten his anger too. But there was no less emotion in the air—it just transformed and intensified as it swirled around them. Somehow it made her feel even worse than when he'd been so rude on the phone. Somehow she was more afraid. She couldn't move, couldn't speak.

'Do you want me to kiss you again, Penny?' he asked. 'Is that the real problem here?'

That brought her voice back. 'You are so conceited.'

'So you really can't do honesty,' he jibed.

She bent her head and fished for the last few files, needing to find her moxie more than the damn data. He so easily tipped her balance, she needed her defensive sass back. But all she could manage now was the silent treatment.

'So what should that guy have sent you—a big box of Belgian chocolates?' His tone lightened.

'I don't eat chocolate,' she said shortly, not looking up.

'Maybe you should, smooth off some of those sharp edges. Isn't chocolate better than sex?'

'You're obviously not doing it right if the women you know say that.'

He yelped a little laugh. 'Throw out a challenge, why don't you?'

She slammed the file drawer shut.

'And now you're backing away from it again. See, you *are* a tease. You just like having men want you.'

She faced him full on, to put him firmly in his place. Oh, so arrogant Carter Dodds could definitely cope with that—he wasn't exactly crushable. 'You wanting me is not a compliment.'

'You don't think?' He grinned. 'Well, I'm not going to chase after you with a billion flowers or calls. If you want to follow through on this, just let me know.'

'And you'll come running?'

He shook his head. 'I don't run after any woman.'

'Because they all fall at your feet?'

'Much like the men do at yours, darling,' he murmured. 'But I already know how much you want me so maybe I'll make you beg for it.'

'Cold day in hell, Carter.'

'Don't protest too much, you'll only regret it later.'

She held a breath for a sanity-saving moment. 'You always get everything you want?'

'I already have everything I want. Anything extra is purely for fun.' His lips curved so slowly and his eyes twinkled with such a teasing expression she fought hard not to let her lips move in response. They wanted to smile all of their own accord. To mirror the magic in his smile. How could she want to smile when she was mad with him?

Because the fact was, he was honest—and, yes, more honest than her. He might be teasing but he wasn't saying anything that wasn't a bit true.

'Admit it, you love the fun of it.' Both his eyes and voice invited.

'The fun of what?'

'Flirting.'

'Is that what you're doing?'

'That's what *we've* been doing from the moment we saw each other.'

'Oh, please.' This wasn't *flirting*, this was a full-scale, high-impact, brazen sexual hunt. There was nothing subtle about it.

'You can't deny it,' he said. 'You like what you see. I like what I see.'

She dropped her gaze. Yes, that was all it was. A superficial animal attraction—based on instinct and what the eye found beautiful. They were each a pleasing example of the opposite sex with whom to practise procreation.

'That doesn't mean we should do anything about it. You need to concentrate, you've got a job to do here.' And she needed him to give her some breathing space.

'And I'll do it well. Doesn't mean I can't have a few moments of light relief here and there.'

Light relief was all she ever did. But she didn't think Carter would walk as lightly over her as she would him. 'You don't think this is a distraction?'

'I think it's more of a distraction not to give in to it.'

'Oh, right, so really I should be saying yes for Mason's sake.'

He chuckled. 'You should be saying yes because you can't keep saying no—not to this.'

He had the sledgehammer thing down pat.

She'd known many cocky guys. Had heard many lines—hell, she'd even delivered a few herself. But while Carter was confident, she could also tell he meant every word—and not in some deluded way. He really wanted her. And the truth was, she wanted him too—but to a degree too scary. This kind of extreme just couldn't be healthy.

He leaned a little closer and, despite her caution, Penny couldn't help mirroring his movement. She had to part her lips just that tiny fraction—to breathe, right?

He smiled wickedly and lifted his head away again, his eyes dancing with the delight of a devil. He picked up the files she'd thumped on the top of the cabinet. 'I'll see you at the bar later.'

'You're going tonight?' She whirled away to hide the sudden rush of blood to her face. Oh, yeah, all her blood rushed at the thought of him being there.

'Good opportunity to meet and mingle with the staff socially.'

She could hear his smile as he answered. But she frowned, forgetting her feelings about spending social time with him and thinking of Mason instead. 'I can't believe any of them could be stealing.'

'Greed. You never know who has what addiction, what need that'll push them past moral boundaries.'

'But it's not William.' It was the analyst's last day; he was heading overseas to take on the financial markets in Singapore. 'It couldn't be him.'

'I'm checking everyone,' Carter answered, suddenly cool. 'As he's leaving, I'm checking his deals first.'

Penny went straight to the bathroom and spent several minutes touching up her face—pressing powder over her forehead, cheeks and chin with deliberate, dispassionate dabs. She concentrated on her lipstick, not letting her mind think of her mouth as anything other than a colouring-in challenge—certainly not a hungry bundle of nerve endings yearning to feel the pressure of Carter's mouth on hers again.

But then she stared at her surface-repaired reflection. Was he right? Had she been stringing Aaron along? She hated the way Carter had spoken to him but had she been any better? She could have made it clearer—interrupted him and spoken firmly. Only she had that memory, when she'd inflicted so much pain. It was why she was always so careful to establish the ground rules before she entered any kind of affair now. It was why her affairs were so few and far between and super-brief. She had to be careful because she couldn't handle anything more than easy. Anything more than carefree. No pain, just frivolity and superficial pleasure. She enjoyed sex. She didn't have it anywhere near often enough despite her many nights out dancing, preferring to keep safe in all kinds of ways. But this attraction to Carter was the most extreme thing she'd ever experienced.

He'd offered all she wanted—only the physical—no strings, no messiness. There was certainly no fledgling friendship there, not when he obviously thought she was a manipulative tease. She saw how he looked at her, as if she made him as angry as much as she turned him on. Well, she knew exactly how he felt.

But her reaction to him was too strong to be safe. When emotions were out of control, people got hurt. She wasn't hurting anyone or being hurt ever again. That was her one hard-and-fast rule. And this attraction threatened every ounce of control she had—therefore was too dangerous to engage.

But he was absolute temptation.

She shook her head, overruling her warring instincts. He wasn't *that* overwhelming. Her attraction to him was simply a case of it having been too long. Of course she swooned for tall, dark and handsome, any other red-blooded female would too. Except Carter didn't just have those three attributes, he also had a carefree lack of cut to his hair, wicked brilliance in his eyes and the devil in his smile....

Ugh. She turned her back on the mirror and walked out. He was just incredibly over-confident. He probably wouldn't even deliver on the promise he exuded. Because in truth, for Penny, no man delivered.

CHAPTER THREE

'CHAMPAGNE please.' Nine hours of work and thirty lengths of the pool later, Penny had changed into her clubbing gear, heel-tapped her way into the bar and been served ahead of eight people already queued there.

'So you're friends with the bartenders.'

'And the DJs.' She took her glass and turned to face Carter. 'And the bouncers,' she added with just that little bit of emphasis.

His grin flashed. 'Really? I thought you didn't like bullies tossing people out of your life.'

He was dressed in the dark casual again. The edginess suited him better.

She sipped the champagne and pretended she had all the chutzpah she'd ever need. 'There's always the exception, Carter.'

'Oh, that there is.' His brows lifted as he looked over every inch of her second-favourite-ever skirt and then her shirt. 'So this is your hunting ground.' He glanced dispassionately at the dance floor. 'Little loud, isn't it?' He grinned evilly. 'How can you get to know someone properly when you can't hear them talk?'

She sidled another inch along the bar and whispered

in his ear. 'By getting close.' She quickly pulled back when she felt him move.

His hand did lift, but all he did was deposit his glass on the bench behind her. Empty already meant he'd been there awhile and he hadn't had trouble catching the attention of the bar staff either.

Penny searched and spotted her workmates over near their usual corner, some already on the dance floor. Safety in numbers. 'Coming to join the others?'

'If I must.'

She deliberately misunderstood his reluctance. 'You don't like to dance?'

He shrugged.

'You've got no rhythm?' she asked totally overly sweetly.

He took her glass from her and sipped carefully. 'I can hold my own.'

'Really.' She didn't try to hide the dare in her tone.

He turned to face her. There were probably over a hundred and fifty people present, but suddenly there was only him. 'I'm happy to watch for a while first. That's what you want, isn't it? To be watched? That's why you dress like this.' His fingers brushed the hem of her skirt and slipped onto her bare skin.

She took her glass back off him. 'I dress like this because I don't like to get too hot. And so I can move easily.'

'Yeah, real easy.' All innuendo.

Swallowing some sweet fizzing bubbles, she smiled. 'Not jumping to all the wrong conclusions again, are you?'

'No, I'm examining the details and evaluating in a reasoned manner.' His finger traced slowly back and forth over a two-inch stretch of her thigh and, despite the heat of the late summer night and the press of too many people, goose bumps rose.

'Like you did last night?'

'I admit my naturally suspicious instinct overruled my usual close observation. At first.'

'So you admit you were wrong?'

'I already have. And I already apologised. Last night. Stop trying to milk it—we can move on, you know.' He took her glass from her again. 'Or are you too scared to?'

She bit the inside of her lip as he smiled and sipped more of her champagne, intently watching her reaction. He wasn't kidding about the close observation.

'You know we want the same thing.'

'Maybe, maybe not,' she hedged.

'Definitely.'

'All I want right now is to dance.' *With him.* But she had to hold some secrets close.

His grin flared. 'Precisely my point.'

She turned her back on him, positively strutted to where half the others from the office were already getting their groove on. That was one of the things she liked about the company—the really healthy party scene that went with it. They worked hard and played every bit as hard and, despite those thirty lengths already, she still had too much energy to burn. William and some of the other guys joined in and the floor got crowded. Her blood zinged. Yeah, this was what she needed; easy-going freedom and fun.

The music *was* loud—which she liked—the beat both fast and steady. But it wasn't long before she turned her head. Because it wasn't one-way traffic—she wanted to watch him too. She met his stare full on across the floor. For that split second she saw how easily he read her— piercing right into her head to find out exactly what she wanted.

He walked straight towards her.

And, yes, that was exactly what she wanted.

Carter and William were a similar height but Carter drew all attention away from the other man. His aura and his physique commanded it. Broader in the shoulders, bigger, stronger—yes, she was totally going cave-girl, her body instinctively turning towards the male who seemed likely to offer the best protection.

His smile wasn't exactly safe, though. And other instincts were warring with her basic sexual ones—shrieking that getting closer to Carter would be no protection at all. But that look in his eyes mesmerised her again. She couldn't move—like prey frozen in the path of the predator. Not safe at all. But then, at this moment, she didn't want to be.

His hand slid round her back and he pulled her against him, his head descending so quickly she didn't even have a chance to blink. But there was no kiss for her hungry mouth; he was too clever for that. It was the slightest brush on her jaw, so quick and light she wondered if it had just been her desperate imagination. Her breath escaped in a rough sigh of disappointment and then she inhaled—all excitement again as he pulled her that bit tighter to him. Now she was wholly in his arms, her chest pressed to his, his hand wide and strong splaying across her spine, his other lifting to stroke down her plait, tugging at the end of it to tilt her face back up to his.

But she avoided his all-seeing eyes. Turned to look over his shoulder instead. Her workmates' eyes were bugging out. She was definitely breaking a few conventions tonight; she didn't ever dance this close to anyone in the office. But then Carter wasn't officially on the payroll. And in less than a second she didn't care what they were thinking anyway because the impact of his proximity hit her and *she* could no longer think. She couldn't do anything but move with him.

He said nothing, didn't need to, merely moved his hands to guide her where he wanted—natural dancer, natural leader, natural lover. All easy rhythm. And she turned to plasticine just like that.

Chest to breast, hands to shoulder and waist, thigh brushing thigh—but eyes not meeting. The need to deny the madness built in her chest. But he was totally taking advantage of the flickering lights and the crowd of people to crush her closer still. His sledgehammer style—steamrolling over her caution just by being himself.

The feelings intensified. She wasn't comfortably warm any more but unbearably hot. She couldn't breathe either—he always made her so damn breathless, made her heart beat too fast, made her brain go vacant.

She wanted to rest her head on his shoulder for a moment, wanted to escape the crowds and the claustrophobic feeling choking her. She wanted to move slowly with him. Even more she wanted time to stop—to leave her pressed mindlessly against him with no pressure of the past to bear on her.

But that was impossible. And this discomfort was so wrong. Dancing was where she felt the best, the most free. She liked it fast and loud, but now it was only his heartbeat she could hear—strong and regular and relentless—and it scared her. Her own heart thundered, scaring her.

Why was she stumbling, why were her eyes watering, blinded by the flashing lights?

She had to escape. Pushing away from him, she took a deep breath to try to stop from drowning in the sensations. She listened for the beat again. She needed to be alone and unrestricted—alone in the crowd.

She turned, saw William only a couple of feet away. She moved towards him, welcoming the break from Carter. Breathing deeper, more calmly. Yes, she needed recovery time to get her grip back.

William was a handsome guy, easily the best-looking man in the office until Carter had arrived, but there was none of that crazy swimming feeling in her head that she had when dancing with Carter. She had no trouble breathing, or thinking or staying in control of her own body. This made so much more sense.

Manageable.

She breathed deep again and smiled at him. William smiled back. This was better.

Carter stood on the dance floor and watched her spin in some other guy's arms. William. The guy whose work he'd just spent the afternoon cross-checking—and it was all clear. That didn't stop the surge of hatred from rising. Despicable, unwanted, violent.

His fists curled. There was no hope of recovering his calm, not now he'd felt the way she moved against him— all fluid grace and perfect rhythm and soft freedom. All he could think of was her supple body sliding against his as she danced with him intimately. Every muscle ached for the intense release they'd share.

But there she was going from him to another in a heartbeat. Any other woman and he'd roll his eyes and walk away. He made it a rule never to care enough to be bothered by a woman's games. But he had to get out of there before he punched that William guy in the face. And it wasn't even his fault. Penny was the player, not him.

Carter wasn't into violence and the wave of aggression he felt made him even more angry—with himself. He'd punish his own body instead, take it out on the rowing machine or the treadmill or the punchbag that were in the gym down the stairs from his serviced apartment. He'd go there and sweat it out right now.

Raw lust was his problem, and he'd felt nothing like it in his life. So what that she was attractive? There were millions of pretty women in the world—that didn't mean his body had to start acting as if Penny were the only one that could switch him on. It had been a while, that was all, too many hours on the job and not enough off socialising. But maybe seeing her in that half-wet top last night had put some spell on him, because all he could think about was getting her naked. Her and only her.

Well, he'd get over it.

He walked out of the bar, knowing he'd probably just caused a massive stir and a ton of gossip, given he hadn't bothered to speak to any others on the staff. Still, better for them to be gasping over his sex life than his real reason for being there. It provided good distraction in terms of his cover.

But for him, it was an absolute nightmare. Penny's accusation this morning had been on target. She was more than a distraction, she was catastrophic for his concentration, and he couldn't let sexual hunger affect the job he was doing for Mason. He'd commandeered an office on the floor below so he wouldn't even see her during work hours unless it was absolutely necessary, but it wasn't enough. Not when he was hunting her out at night. There was only one way forward—he had to forget her and just get on with the job. She could toy with that other guy. He damn well didn't care.

CHAPTER FOUR

PENNY felt as if she'd overdosed on no-doze. Her heart hammered, she fidgeted. Hyper-alert, she watched every second, hoping he'd hurry up and come say hi. But he didn't. Minutes dragged like decades. Mason had emailed in again to say he'd spend another day working at home. Maybe Carter was with him. Or maybe he was locked in his office down the stairs. She wasn't going to go see. She wasn't going to waste another minute wondering where he was or why he'd done the vanishing act last night. And she certainly wasn't going to regret the fact that he had.

Eventually she went out for a power walk. Fresh air might help her regain her equilibrium and stop her from doing all those things she'd told herself she wasn't going to do.

Twenty minutes later she walked back into the building, even more hot and edgy. As the automatic door slid shut behind her Carter stepped out of the lift. He didn't hesitate when he saw her, just strode straight across the foyer like a man possessed.

'Did you enjoy the rest of your night?' he asked, still ten paces away.

'Yes,' she said brightly. She'd hated it. She'd danced

and danced until she couldn't fake it any more and gone home to stare at the ceiling.

'Really?' Now he looked angry and he lengthened his stride even more.

A rabbit in the headlights, Penny failed to leap out of his path. And all of a sudden he did what she'd wanted him to do less than twelve hours ago—yanked her close—one hand round her waist, his other pulling her plait so she was forced to tilt her head back. Not that he needed to force it, because she melted right into him. For hours in the early morning she'd lain half asleep, dreaming of this. Now she wasn't sure if she was still dreaming—and only by clinging, by putting her palm to that sharp jaw could she be sure that he was real and kissing her hot and rough and right in the middle of Reception.

Her groan caught in her mouth as he plundered. How could she ever say no to this? She was lost to it, utterly lost.

But just as suddenly he pulled away.

'You're still hungry.' His words whispered low and angry.

Stunned, she stared. And by the time she got herself together enough to say something, he'd already gone out of the door behind her.

Her anger hit. What the hell did he think he was doing, carrying on like that in public? Thank heaven no clients had been waiting for appointments. Only the receptionist was there, though that meant everyone in the company would know about it by now—she'd have emailed them already. Not that they'd be surprised after the dirty dancing display last night. Penny ground her teeth. Yes, it was a good thing she was going soon because things

were getting more than a little untidy. She marched up
the stairs and felt even more hot and furious by the time
she got to the top.

Files, she'd sort out the wretched files. She stomped
over to the cabinet and slid the drawer open, pointlessly
checking all the contents were in the right order. Which
they were—but the perfectionist in her just had to be
sure.

'Got you some tea to calm your nerves,' Carter said
smoothly.

She whirled fast to face him. Stepped so close, so
quick, he actually took a step back and deposited the
steaming cup on the nearest flat surface—the top of the
cabinet. She moved closer still, keeping the scarcest of
centimetres between them.

'I don't fool around at work, Carter.' She furiously
whispered in his face, using anger to hide both the turmoil raging inside her and the desire he'd roused so ef-
fortlessly. 'Don't embarrass me like that again.'

His hands whipped round her, pulling her flush
against him. Letting her know how lethally he was turned
on. Her nerves shook beneath her skin, her muscles
melted—only to reform even tighter and aching to feel
his impression.

'You liked it, Penny.' His hand firmly cupped her butt,
pulling her yet closer against his thick erection. 'You
liked it as much as I did.'

She had and she did nothing to deny it now, did nothing to pull away from the searing embrace. If anything
she melted that millimetre more into him. There could
be no denying the force of it. She gasped as he thrust
his hips harder against her—his expression told her he
knew it all. But he was angry too.

'Who was it who ended that kiss, Penny? Who was it who pulled back?' His smile was a snarl. 'If it had been up to you we'd be sweaty and catching our breath right about now. If we'd been alone you'd have let me do anything. And you'd just about be ready to go for round two.'

Her blood beat through her with such force she felt dizzy. 'Well, then, what the hell were you thinking making that move *there*?'

He held still for a moment, and although his body remained rock hard she felt the anger drain away from him. The next second he actually laughed. 'I wasn't thinking. Isn't that obvious?'

Shaking his head ruefully, he looked up above them. 'Here we are again. I'm starting to think this plant is like some kind of magic mistletoe.'

'You always have the urge to kiss me when you're under it?' The urge to flash him a look was irresistible.

'I always have the urge to kiss you, full stop.'

Admittedly he didn't sound that thrilled about it, but even so a spurt of pleasure rippled through her. It was good he wanted her like that. It evened the score. She leaned back against the filing cabinet and looked at him, feeling as if she'd done her warm-up and was ready for the race—excited, a little nervous, full of anticipation.

Carter stepped forward, closing the gap until he was fully pressed against her again. His blue-green gaze devoured her features. She wished he'd just hurry up and kiss her. She put her palm to his jaw again, unable to resist just that small touch.

'Go on, Penny.' Ragged-voiced, he dared her. 'Deal with me.'

Their mouths hovered, barely a millimetre apart, hot

breath mingling with even hotter desire. How could she possibly resist? She opened her mouth that little more.

'Well,' a deep voice sounded. 'Looks like I finally get to meet him.'

Penny leapt a clear foot, or she would have if Carter hadn't had such a grip on her—a grip that suddenly tightened.

'Matt,' she squeaked. Wide-eyed, she stared past Carter at the tall figure standing beside her desk.

'I've heard so much about you but I didn't think I'd get to meet you.' Matt walked closer, his too-intelligent eyes nailing Carter and then flicking to her. 'Penny, you didn't tell us he actually worked with you.'

She was still trying to wriggle out of Carter's grip but he'd tightened it even more to pinch-point. 'Yes,' she managed to say softly but Matt didn't hear her.

'You're him, right?' Matt asked Carter direct. 'The "man" she keeps emailing about—the one who dines and dances and takes her away every weekend.'

Penny wanted the world to open up and suck her under right this second. Because what would Carter think about that lot of detail? What would Matt think when he found out the truth?

She looked into Carter's eyes, saw the blues and greens and ice-cold anger out in equal doses. She pressed against him just that little more, softening herself in the hopes he'd also soften. Okay, she was pleading as she, oh, so slightly nodded her head at him, all but begging with her eyes.

But Carter felt as if he were made of rock as he rubbed one fist across his lips. He seemed to see into her soul with his bleak, penetrating glare. She waited for the axe to fall. Carter wanted her but he didn't think much of her, she knew that. So he wasn't about to come riding to her rescue now.

And Matt, impossibly tall and grown-up Matt, was waiting for an answer.

'Yes,' Carter finally said. 'I'm that man.'

In shocked relief Penny softened against Carter completely, but felt every one of his muscles flinch.

'I'm Matt Fairburn, Penny's brother.' Matt flashed one of his rare smiles and held out his hand.

An infinitesimal hesitation and Carter reached out too. 'Carter Dodds, Penny's man.'

It was a firm handshake, Penny could tell. It went on that half-second too long, as if they were testing each other's muscles and manliness or something. Which was ridiculous, because last time she'd seen Matt he'd still been half-boy, half-man. The intense student too focused and serious for his own good. But now he was...different. Now he was assessing, and judging—just as he wanted to do in his career.

She took the opportunity of their formal introductions to extricate herself from the rock and the hard place she was literally squashed between. Emotionally, she was even more caught.

'What are you doing here, Matt?' She summoned a big smile as she asked, because she had a fictional happy life to live up to.

'Coming to make sure you'll be around to have dinner with me. Has to be tonight because I've got a conference for the next couple of days.'

She hadn't known he was in town. Why hadn't he emailed to tell her? 'Of course I can do dinner,' she said brightly.

'No other plans?' he asked.

'None I can't change.'

Matt's brows lifted. 'What about the man?' He turned to Carter. 'You'll come too, right? I want to grill you. Being the only one in the family to meet you so far, I've got responsibilities to those back home. Namely Mum.'

He spoke casually but Penny understood the undertone. Her kid brother was checking up on her. She tried to make her muscles relax but her smile felt superglued on. 'Carter has to work tonight. Sorry, Matt. He has a meeting.'

'Actually, honey, that one got cancelled.' Carter tucked a strand of her hair behind her ear as if he had all the rights of such casual intimacy. 'That's what I was coming to tell you only I got…distracted.' He looked from her eyes to her mouth in a blatant sensual stamp and then he turned. 'I'd love to be there, Matt.'

All Penny's internal organs shrank. 'But—'

'You can let me know for sure later,' Matt broke in, his expression impassive. 'I have to see your flat too, Penny. More of Mum's orders.'

'You should have warned me.' Penny laughed. 'I'd have tidied up.'

Matt answered with a quick rare smile again, but Carter wasn't smiling at all.

'I'll walk you out,' Penny said quickly, wanting to take charge of the plans without Carter listening in. She manufactured more brightness as she led him to the lift. 'Why didn't you tell me you were coming sooner? I could have made some plans.'

'Wanted to surprise you.'

Yeah, he was checking up. She hated that he felt he had to do that. Her little brother had had to grow up too soon and he'd got all paternal and protective on her. It was her fault. He should be out there having wild times of his own, not worrying about her or carrying the burden of their parents' worry for her. And that was her fault too. She'd tried to ease it—hence her stupid, overly imaginative emails.

But now she smiled and gave him a hug. 'It's so awesome to see you. I'll text you with details of where to meet, okay?'

'You mean you actually have my number?' Matt asked dryly. 'I wondered.'

Yeah, it was only the occasional email that she sent. She rarely texted, and never talked. It was easier that way. She'd never said she was brave. And she was feeling beyond cowardly now. She went back into the lift and reluctantly pushed the button for the top. Droplets of discomfort sweat slicked her skin yet she felt chilled to the bone.

Carter stood by the windows in Mason's office, looking down at the street scene below. She closed the door behind her and waited.

After a moment that made her nerves stretch past break point, he turned.

'Just how many men have you got on the go, Penny?'

She shook her head. Glad his desk was between her and him. Because he was looking more than a little angry and she needed all four feet of solid wood between them.

'Tell me about him.' Carter's voice lifted. 'He's some sugar daddy you spend the weekends with?'

Her flush deepened. 'No.'

'No?'

Penny swallowed the little pride she had left. 'I made him up.'

Carter blinked. 'Pardon?'

'I made him up. In my emails home, I invented a relationship.'

For the first time she saw Carter at a loss for words—momentarily. His eyes narrowed and he took a couple of steps closer. 'You're telling me this "man" doesn't exist? You don't actually have a real boyfriend.'

'No.'

'And there's no one you're dating, or sleeping with, or friends with benefits or whatever you care to call it.'

She held his gaze. 'I'm not seeing anyone at the moment. No.'

He nodded slowly. 'When were you last seeing someone?'

'It's been a few months.' She was flushed with heat—anger, embarrassment and the burning need for him to believe her. For some stupid reason it was important he understand. 'I don't remember exactly how long.'

'But Aaron doesn't count?'

She lifted her chin and answered pointedly. 'A couple of kisses don't count.'

Carter's jaw went more angular. 'So how many kisses haven't you counted in the last few months?'

Her brows shot up. 'Aaron. Another guy. You.'

'My kisses don't count?' he asked softly.

'Definitely not.'

His devil grin flashed. 'I've figured it out.'

Penny blinked at his suddenly bright demeanour. 'Figured what out?'

'How to tell when you're lying.'

She jerked. 'What? How?'

He shook his head and laughed aloud. 'Not telling because then you'll stop doing it.'

'Stop doing what?' She sighed and gave up, knowing he wasn't about to spill it. Besides, there was something more important to know. 'You do believe me, don't you?'

He went serious again. 'Yeah, I do.'

She was absurdly relieved. She'd been a complete fool with the emails and he knew it, but oddly that didn't matter so long as he believed her when she told the truth.

He walked around his desk, picked up her hand and ran a light finger over the bruises still marking her wrist. 'You know I just said that about coming to dinner tonight to wind you up...make up whatever excuse.' He gave her an ironic glance. 'You've got the experience. Your brother might not know your little giveaway.'

Penny frowned and pulled her hand free.

Dinner with Matt. She'd half forgotten it in her need to clear up the confusion with Carter. But now she thought about it, she was dreading it already—the questions, the search for conversation, all the anxiety... She just didn't want to face it. She'd spent years not facing it.

Actually maybe it would be a good idea to have someone with her. With extra company she could present the happy façade for the night, no problem. And she really was happy. It was just that she'd added an imaginary gorgeous man to give the picture a fully glossy finish. Companionship without complications—she had enough complications inside already. It had been so long since her last real, short-term gorgeous man, she'd invented one.

Now she looked at Carter. Handsome, charming, socially expert Carter.

'I think you should come with me,' she said.

His brows shot up.

'No, I mean it.' She stepped in closer to him. 'Come to dinner. After all, Matt's expecting you now.'

His attention dropped to her body and back up. 'Well, isn't that your problem for misleading him in the first place?'

'But you played up to it. The least you can do is follow through.'

Carter leaned back against the edge of his desk, a small smile tweaking his mouth.

Really, the more Penny thought about it, the better an idea it was. Matt could maybe learn a few things from Carter—social smoothness for one. And Carter would deflect the attention off herself. She didn't know how well she could maintain the façade on her own. Most importantly, the conversation would stay in safe waters. Matt wouldn't drag up the past with Carter present.

'I've seen you talking with the guys who work here… And the girls.' Her gaze narrowed. 'You're good socially.'

Too good actually. Every woman looked at him as if he were the biggest honeypot to hit the town in a decade or forty—and they all wanted a taste.

'Is that a compliment? Because the way you're talking I'm not sure…' He studied her slyly.

She couldn't hold back her smile. He was a charming wretch and he knew it.

'Come to dinner with me,' she leant forward to whisper. 'Be my pretend man.'

Carter's blood was still burning from the horror of

seeing her dance with someone else last night. He wasn't a hypocrite—he didn't expect women to have less experience than him, but the thought of her being in bed with another guy had made his stomach acid boil. The foreign jealousy rotted him from the inside out and he badly needed to ditch it. He'd spent all night awake wondering if she'd taken William home. And despite his vow to forget her, when he'd seen her in Reception this afternoon the urge had hit. He'd had to touch and find out—something, anything—like an animal scenting out a threat. So completely caveman and so unlike his usual carefree style.

And now, now the relief in knowing she hadn't was making him positively giddy, because here he was about to say yes to the most stupid suggestion he'd heard in ages. But he was too intrigued not to. 'Why did you make him up?'

Her gaze dropped. 'I wanted everyone back home to think I'm happy.'

Was she not happy? 'And you have to have a boyfriend to prove that?'

'No,' she said quickly. 'I have a great life—great job, I travel lots. But the man was the icing for them. I know they worry I'm lonely.'

Which she wasn't, of course. She had thousands of adoring suitors. She could have a man every night of the week if she wanted. But it was interesting that she didn't want that. It was interesting that she wanted to kiss *him*.

'So you want me to be the icing?' he croaked. Because if that meant she'd use her tongue on him, he was so happy to oblige.

She tossed her head back. 'It's what we're all supposed

to want, isn't it? Someone who cares, who holds you, who's there for you. Companionship, commitment. Happy ever after. That whole cliché.'

She thought wanting a life partner was a cliché? Hell, where had she been all this time? Because he didn't want a life partner either. He just wanted some uncomplicated fun. 'But that's not what you actually want for yourself?'

He could see the goose bumps on her arms as she recoiled. She really only wanted a lover for a night or two? That was fine by him—although he might have to push for a few nights. 'So what did you tell them about your man?'

'I never named him, always kept everything very vague.'

'How long have you been mentioning him?'

'Only in the last couple of months. They've been putting on the pressure for me to visit home and he was my excuse for saying no. Because we've been doing lots of little trips away.'

She didn't want to visit home? 'How long since you've been back?'

She looked away. 'A few years. I've been travelling a lot.'

But there were thousands of planes crossing the globe daily. She could go to New Zealand for a visit and be back the same day. It was obvious there was more she wasn't saying. Did he really want to know what it was?

Actually he was a little curious. But clearly she didn't want to share and he respected her for that. Better than getting a massive 'emo and drama' dump as his ex had always done. But even so, he couldn't let it go completely.

'I still don't really see why you had to make up a whole relationship,' he said. 'And why you want me with you so badly tonight.'

She froze. Carter's radar screamed louder. She was totally hiding something. And he was only human. So he waited, making her reply by pure expectation.

'The truth is I was one of those fat wallflowers as a teen.' Her head bowed as she mumbled.

Carter gritted his teeth to stop his jaw falling open.

'Overweight, acne, rubbish clothes.' She turned away from him. 'Total pizza face. The worst you can imagine.'

Her self-scathing tone rubbed him raw, making him feel an emotion he couldn't quite define. And he couldn't imagine actually. She had the smoothest skin—not a single scar marked her flawless features—and she was so slim—borderline too thin with a tiny waist and tiny wrists and tiny ankles. But she still had some curves that made his blood thicken.

'I wanted to be a whole new me—fit body, jet-set life, great job, gorgeous guy.'

He sighed and reached out to stop those curves escaping from him altogether. So she wanted to look good with a suitable male accessory. He should *not* be flattered about being a good enough accessory for her. That should *not* be pleasing him the sick way it was. But he couldn't help feeling for her. No wonder she was always so beautifully finished—the taunts of teenage years had obviously gone deep. But didn't everyone have scars from those turbulent times? He sure as hell did—it was thanks to the women in his life then that he'd put the Teflon coating on his heart.

'Okay.' He pulled her close and tried to tease her smile

back. 'What do I get out of it? What are you going to offer me?'

Her lashes lifted and the black pools glittered at him. 'You want me so much you'd sell yourself like some sort of escort?'

He was glad to hear her vixen tongue again and he leaned forward to reward her, whispering so close his lips brushed her ear. 'You have to agree that we kiss like nothing else. I'm very interested to see what it'd be like if we did something more.'

'If you wanted something more then why did you walk out so fast last night?' she breathed back.

'Why did you go dance with someone else?'

'That bothered you?' She leaned away and watched his face as he answered.

'I don't do commitment, Penny,' he said honestly. 'But I do do exclusive. And I do respect.'

She drew in a deep breath. 'Ditto.'

He watched her just as close. No sign of the super-quick double blink that happened when she was doing a Pinocchio. Interesting. 'All right, then, I'll come with you tonight, if you agree to stay well away from any other men in the next week.'

'I guess I can handle that,' she said casually. But he could feel her pulse racing.

'You better be sure.' He grinned as her gaze stayed true.

'I'm not promising anything else.'

'We both know that's not necessary,' he drawled. 'It's already a given.'

'This isn't going to get complicated, Carter.'

He really shouldn't feel that as a challenge. Anyway, he thought things were getting that touch more complicated with every passing second.

CHAPTER FIVE

PENNY hadn't seen Matt in just over a year. She'd been in Tokyo then, slowly working her way back to the South Pacific after her years in Europe.

He'd changed—made that final step from boy to man. And he'd almost caught her out in her web of lies. She knew why he was here—it was the start of even less subtle pressure. Her parents' wedding anniversary was coming up soon and they wanted a big celebration—one at home in New Zealand.

She couldn't possibly attend.

She was hoping to save enough money to fly them to her for a holiday. They could afford it themselves of course, but she wanted it to be a gift from her. She wanted that to be enough because she didn't want to have to go to them. The memories were brought to life there in that big house with their ancient, abundant orchard. The wall of trees linked their home to the property next door—Dan's parents' place.

She tried not to think about it and usually, on a day-to-day level, she succeeded. But Matt arriving out of the blue made everything flash in her head movie-montage style. It was almost seven years ago but sometimes felt as recent as yesterday. The darkness of those last few months at home encroached on her vision. And she remembered the estrangement from her family and friends as she'd got mired in a pit of grief and guilt.

She was out of it now. She was strong, she was happy, she was healthy. But the distance from them was still there—literally, emotionally. She didn't think the bridge could ever be rebuilt. In truth, she didn't want it to be.

And in her mind she saw him—as she always did—the day before he'd died. She swiftly blanked the images, focused on pleating the square piece of memo paper she had in front of her. Her fingers neatly folded and creased, working on a displacement activity designed to restore calm.

Because she hadn't coped with what had happened. It had impacted on the whole family and she'd made it worse. Bereavement had shattered the bonds and only by going away had she been able to recover. She needed them to know she was okay. But she couldn't front up to them and prove it in person. Not there. She didn't think she could ever face that place.

Carter couldn't concentrate on the damn transactions. He kept wondering, wanting to know more. In the end he went upstairs and pulled a chair up next to hers. 'We need to work on our story. For dinner tonight.'

She looked completely blank. She hadn't thought this through that far, had she?

He leaned forward and angled for more information. 'So how did we meet? How long have we been dating?'

She turned towards him, her eyes huge. 'I don't know. Can't you make it up?'

'You trust me to do that?'

Beneath her eyes were blue, bruised shadows. 'Sure.'

He stared, on the one hand stupidly gratified, on the other uneasy. What had happened this afternoon to make her look so hurt and exhausted? He glanced at her desk. It was bare, save a folded paper crane—which was unexpected and frankly intriguing.

'Okay, I'll come up with something,' he said, bitten by a random need to reassure her. 'An elaboration on the truth. We met at work.'

She nodded.

'And there was an instant spark.'

She nodded again.

'We were powerless to fight it.'

Her nod was slower that time.

'And we've been inseparable since,' he muttered.

She gazed into his eyes. Hers were so dark he couldn't tell where her pupils ended and her iris began. Black with longing. Right? He leaned closer, feeling unrestrainable longing himself. He wanted to kiss her. Had to. And never stop until she was right back with him. Right here.

Because the sadness in those deep, secretive eyes was unbearable.

He'd seen the attention she got from other men. He wasn't the only one to notice her combination of hotness and vulnerability. She unleashed both passion and protectiveness with just a look. And if they had any idea how she kissed, she'd need a posse of bodyguards to fight them off. Was it just her attention-grabbing trick? He grimaced ruefully; he didn't think so, because she already had him on a three-inch leash.

'Penny with the perfect plait.' He slipped his fingers

into the tight, glossy braid at the back of her head and massaged gently. 'Relax. I'll be the perfect boyfriend. Attentive, caring, funny…'

Why he was saying that he didn't know. He was supposed to be the perfect investigator. He was supposed to be in his office right now working through all the files and finding the point when the discrepancies occurred. Not planning how he was going to spend the evening pretending to be her lover. But she still looked so anxious and he ached to reassure.

'We can laugh and make small talk. Wow the brother and then leave.' He liked the leaving idea. He liked the idea of dressing up with her, going dancing and then dancing some more in private. Yeah, he was a complete fool.

He dropped his hand and stood—a little test of his own strength. 'Are you going to swim first?' He'd learned that was her routine.

She shook her head. 'No time.'

'You want to go home and change?'

'I've got something here,' she mumbled.

'You always have a party-going outfit with you at work?'

She looked surprised he'd even asked.

He went back to his desk for the last hour but all he did was think about her. She was nervous. Why? He didn't think it was because of him—in fact she was relying on him to carry her through this. So why? What was the big deal about her brother? That prickle of protectiveness surged higher. Why hadn't she been back in such a long time? It clearly was a long time. He couldn't wait to go and get some answers.

* * *

Penny stood under the hot jet in the gym shower until the warmth finally seeped into her skin. Over and over she reminded herself that it was going to be okay because Carter was coming and he'd keep it social.

She met him in Reception. He was back in black and another tee that skimmed his hot frame. Pirate Carter. How little she knew about him. How much she wanted to find out.

'You really don't have a girlfriend?'

'Do you think I'd act like this with you if I did?' His expression shut down. 'I don't cheat, Penny. One on one. I expect the same from you.'

She swallowed. 'But this is just for tonight.'

His grin bounced back. 'Oh, sure, you can think that if it'll make you feel better.' He took her hand as they walked along the street, the summer sun still powerful on their backs.

Penny hated public displays of affection. She hated being touched unless she was in a bed and the instigator or lost in the crowd on a dance floor. But Carter ignored all her unsubtle body language. He wouldn't let her pull her hand back, he measured his stride to match hers, drawing her close enough for her shoulder to brush against his arm as they walked. But she tried once more to slip her fingers out of his.

He stopped walking and jerked on her hand so she stumbled near him. His other hand whipped round her waist and his lips caught hers in a very thorough kiss.

She jerked her head back and glared at him. 'What—?'

'If you keep trying to get out of holding my hand, I'm going to keep kissing you. If you want me to act like your boyfriend, I'm going to act like your boyfriend. That includes lots of touching.'

'No, it doesn't,' she hissed.

'I'm an affectionate lover,' he said smoothly. 'I like to touch.'

'Kissing in public is exclusive, rude behaviour.'

'Passionately snogging for hours in front of everyone would be. So you'd better let me hold your hand, then, hadn't you?'

Otherwise he'd passionately snog her for hours? She so shouldn't be tempted by that. 'Don't tease.'

'Why? Did you think I was here to make this easier for you?'

'Of course that's why you're here,' she said completely honestly. 'Be charming, will you?'

'You think I can be charming?'

'You know you can.'

'Why, Penny—' he ran the backs of his fingers down her cheek '—thanks for the compliment.'

'Stop playing with me,' she begged through gritted teeth. 'Please come and talk nicely to him.'

But as they walked closer the cold feeling returned. Until the only warm bit left of her was the hand clasped inside Carter's.

Already seated at the table, Matt watched them approach—correction, he watched Carter.

'Hi, Matt,' Penny said.

Her brother took his steely gaze off Carter and he looked at her. He almost smiled.

An hour or so into the evening, Carter was wondering why she'd been so insistent about his attendance. And why she'd been so anxious. It didn't seem as though her brother was about to bite. If anything he'd looked fiercely protective when he'd greeted them, as if he'd take a piece out of Carter if he made the wrong move. He'd totally given him the 'Big Brother is watching' look. Which was a bit of a laugh, given he had to be the best part of a decade younger. And then he'd started a less than subtle grilling about Carter's background and prospects. Carter had really felt like laughing then, but Matt's questions were astute and intelligent and in less than two minutes he was on his toes and respecting kid brother for that. And he'd gotten no help at all from the woman he was here to socially save. She'd stared intently as he'd answered. She'd probably learnt more facts about him in those minutes than she had in the past couple of days. He'd like to do the same.

So now he willed time to go by triple speed. It refused—in fact he was sure it slowed just to annoy him all the more. Because he wanted to be alone with her. Alone and in his apartment. But there were the mains to be eaten, and more conversation.

'So what do you do, Matt?' Too bad if he should have known already.

'I'm based in Wellington. I've just finished my law degree.'

'So you're going into your first law job?'

'Matt's going to work as a researcher for the judges at the Supreme Court for the year,' Penny interrupted. 'They take three honours grads. Only the best.' Her pride for him glowed.

'I've deferred the law firm job for the year.' Matt shrugged off the accolades.

So he had his future mapped.

'You want to specialize in criminal law?'

'That's right.'

Yeah, that explained the cross-examination he'd just survived. Carter hoped Matt hadn't scoped out the lie right in front of him. Although it wasn't a total lie—Carter did want to be Penny's lover. Just not for ever as 'the man'. He'd settle for just the night. Tonight. Now.

But he forced himself to listen politely as the conversation turned to home and Matt caught her up on the happenings. She was interested, asked a tonne of questions, making him wonder all the more why she hadn't visited in so long. What was so awful about the place when her brother made her laugh about some woman who ran the annual floral festival in their small home town?

'I saw Isabelle the other day.'

It took Carter a moment to register the total silence. The temperature must have dropped too because he could see goose bumps all over Penny's arms again.

'Did you?' she finally answered, her voice more shrill than a rugby coach's whistle. She reached for her water. 'How is she?'

'She's okay.' Matt had stopped eating and was watching her too. 'She's working at the city library.'

Carter had no idea who Isabelle was, but what he did know was that Penny had totally frozen over. Icing over to cover up—what? He tilted his head and looked into her obsidian eyes.

Misery.

Absolute misery.

And she was trying too hard, her smile about to crack. He shot a glance at Matt to see if he'd registered Penny's sudden brittleness.

Yes, he had. He had the same dark eyes as his sister

only now they were even blacker and fiercely focused on her.

She clung on—just—all smile and another polite question. But the façade was as fragile as fine-spun glass. He felt the pressing edge of the knife, waiting for it to slice and shatter.

'You okay?' Her brother ignored her irrelevant question and asked her straight out.

Her lashes lowered and the pretence fell with them. She didn't look at either of them. Carter slung his arm across the back of her chair. She needed a moment of support and that was why he was here. And he wasn't inhuman; his innards twisted at the sight of her.

'Of course,' Penny answered, so brightly it was like staring straight into a garish neon light. 'I'm having dessert. Are you?'

She waved the nearest waiter over and ordered the triple chocolate mousse.

'Excuse me for a moment.' Under cover of the stranger's presence, Matt escaped the underlying tension, shooting a look at Carter as he did.

Penny sat back in her seat after he'd gone and Carter twisted in his to look at her properly. She was even paler now and in her lap her fingers visibly shook. Her mouth parted as if she was working harder to get air into her lungs. Full lips that he knew were soft and that clung to his in a way that made his gut crunch with desire.

She looked terrified. Carter knew there was a big part of this picture that he was missing. But he'd get to that. All that mattered now was bringing her back—bringing back the sparkle, the fight and fire, the gleaming promise that usually filled her.

'Penny?' He slid his arm from the back of her chair to

around her shoulder. Barely any pressure but she turned in to him. Her chin lifted and he saw the stark expression in her eyes.

'You okay?' he muttered as he moved closer. It was pure instinct, the need to protect. To reassure. To make it better.

He couldn't not kiss her.

For a moment she did nothing, as if she was stunned by the touch. But then she kissed him back. Her mouth was so hungry. But then her hunger changed, the tenor of her trembling changed. It wasn't distress any more but need. Her hands clutched his shoulders, pressing him nearer. He wanted to haul her closer still, wanted to curse the fact they were in such a public place.

Her hands tightened round the back of his neck, her fingers curling into his hair. Her breasts pressed against his chest. He wanted to peel her top from her, he wanted to see her as well as feel her. He wanted to touch her all over. He was wearing only a tee shirt and that was too much. He wanted her hands to slide beneath it; he wanted them to slide down his body.

Instead he had to pull back and he had to pull back now.

She didn't move. But her gaze had sharpened, focused. Colour had returned to her cheeks and her lips were redder than they'd been seconds before. She breathed out; he felt the flexing of her shoulders—as if she was shrugging off whatever the burden had been.

Just like that she was back to her perfect image. As if that moment of terror had never happened. As if that shattering kiss hadn't happened.

Carter hadn't felt so rattled in all his life.

There was only one way to deal with it. There was no

going back now. In truth there'd been no going back from the moment he'd laid eyes on her. He'd be her lover for real. He'd see her flushed and on fire and alive. And for someone who'd said kissing in public was rude, exclusive behaviour, she'd been doing pretty well.

Matt noisily returned to his seat and lifted the carafe of water, not meeting Carter's eyes but refilling everyone's glasses as if they all needed cooling down. Carter sure as hell did.

A couple of minutes later Carter was surprised to witness Penny enthusiastically tucking into the chocolate mousse. He'd thought she didn't like chocolate. He thought she worked hard to maintain her figure.

He looked up and saw Matt watching her with wide eyes too. And then Matt looked across at Carter and grinned, the vestige of a wink thrown in. As if he was completely pleased to see his sister putting it away like that.

But because she was so busy dealing with the rich goo, it was down to Carter and Matt to pick up the conversation. Carter darted a suspicious look at Penny. Yeah, she was spinning out the way she was swallowing that stuff—and actually taking the tiniest of forkfuls. In fact he figured she was totally faking her enjoyment of the stuff. Good actress, and calculating minx. But he played along, keeping the conversation safe and saving his questions for later when they were alone.

Only she foiled him.

'Matt can give me a ride home,' she said brightly after Carter had dealt with the bill. 'He wanted to see my flat, remember? And you had to work on those files—you don't want to be too behind tomorrow.'

Carter tried not to bare his teeth as he grinned his way

through acquiescing. He'd been neatly set to the side. But he'd extract a little price of his own.

As Matt went forward to request a taxi Carter pulled her into his arms, so close her body was squashed right up against his. Not as close as he wanted, but it was better than nothing. And as he was staring down the barrel of a night of nothing, he needed a little sweetener. He kissed her, softly, until she opened up for him. Then he slipped his hand up discreetly, quickly rubbing a thumb across her breast. He knew exactly how sensitive she was there. Sure enough he felt her instant spasm, her mouth instinctively parting more on a gasp. But he couldn't take advantage and go deeper. Reluctantly he relinquished his hold on her.

All the wicked thoughts that were tumbling in his head multiplied as he saw her flush and angry sparkle. Yes, it was going to be mind-blowing. But not soon enough.

'Great to meet you, Carter.' Matt walked back from the taxi rank, extending a hand and a bright smile.

So protective little bro wasn't going to throw any punches despite seeing Carter paw his sister? Carter felt smug. He must have the approval, then—on that score at least the night was a success. And he'd claim his reward—tomorrow.

Penny loved her brother but there was only so much she could handle. She yawned and pleaded tiredness. He seemed to understand, getting the taxi to wait while he did a lightning inspection of her flat so he could report back to the parents when he got home.

She stood in her doorway to see him off, thinking she'd got away with the last ten minutes with her nerves intact. Only he turned back, one leg in the taxi already. 'I'm sorry if mentioning Isabelle upset you.'

'Oh, no.' Penny shook her head, swallowing quickly to stop her throat tightening up too much. 'It was so great to see you, Matt. It was a really nice night.'

Aside from that one moment.

'You should come home and visit,' he said, suddenly awkward and emotional. 'You should bring Carter.'

Her throat thickened and tears stung her eyes. Blinking hard, she nodded and stepped back indoors.

Isabelle was Dan's twin and Penny's best friend from age one to seventeen. They'd been closer than sisters. They'd joked about becoming sisters for real when Penny and Dan had gotten together. But then that relationship changed everything—and every other for Penny.

For her, the impact was always there—a weight she carried and could never be relieved of. That was okay, because, as much as she didn't like to think of it, she also never wanted to forget. And her burden was nothing on Isabelle's, or Dan's mother's or his father's.

For so many reasons, Dan's death was the defining moment of her life. The experience and subsequent aftermath were the bases from which she made all her decisions. She wasn't being hurt like that again. More importantly she wasn't hurting anyone else either.

Now she knew life was for living—she would travel, experience and see the world. And always keep her distance.

And that meant distance from Carter too. Especially him.

CHAPTER SIX

'SLEEP well?' Carter stopped by her desk.

'Sure,' Penny lied.

'I didn't either,' he said, eyes twinkling. 'And I blame you for that.'

She didn't rise to his teasing banter. It wasn't entirely because of the memories that had been stirred last night—her instincts had been warning her off Carter from the moment she'd first seen him. She needed to listen to them. He meant danger—not the physical kind, like when she'd thought he was some psycho attacker, but a danger to her head, hormones and heart.

In short, he messed up all her insides.

If she thought she could control it, it would be fine. But she couldn't. Carter wouldn't ever cede dominance and he sought total response. That was fair enough, but it wasn't something she could give.

She wanted to run. That was her usual answer to everything. Only she couldn't. She'd let Mason down if she did and he'd been so good to her and he had troubles enough. He didn't deserve more disloyalty or seeing people flee what could be a sinking ship. If investors got any hint of trouble they might stop the money flow. And in the current economic climate, that was bad news for even the most ancient, venerable financial institution.

So she was stuck here for another month or so. And Carter was only here for a week more. Once he was gone she'd be okay again. She could be strong and stick it out—of course she could.

'What, now I've helped you out with your brother you're ignoring me?' Carter bent and eyeballed her.

'I just think it's better if we keep this on a professional level.'

'Honey, we've never been professional with each other.'

'We're adults, Carter. We can try.' To prove the point, she glanced at him very briefly and offered a tight smile. Then she went straight back to her computer screen.

'Why do women always have to play games?' He sighed. 'Blow hot, blow cold.' The amusement in his voice shouted out his disbelief. 'If I kissed you now, you'd be ten seconds to yes.'

'I'm not playing, Carter,' she said frostily.

He laughed aloud at that.

But she didn't see him again the rest of the day. She worked late, ignoring the lump in her throat and the disappointment that he'd taken her at her word. Slowly the office emptied but she couldn't relax. She really wanted a swim—alone, which meant after hours. It was the only way she could think to ease the aches her muscles had earned from holding her urges in all day.

Jed was on duty tonight so she was in luck. She grabbed her gym bag from her cupboard. She'd log off her computer and collect her purse and jacket later; right now she just wanted to dive into the cool water.

She went via his security station to let him know.

'I shouldn't be that long.' She smiled at the guard. 'Half an hour tops.'

'Sure. I'll lock up in forty, then.'

'Thanks.'

She changed in the small women's room. Kicking the bag under the bench, she took her towel out poolside.

She dived in. The cool water felt fantastic on her hot skin. She stretched out and floated on her back for a while, closing her tired, scratchy eyes. Then she pulled her goggles down and did several lengths. It took longer than usual to get into the rhythm, longer still to try to settle her mind. She was so tired yet she had so much painful energy she didn't quite know what to do with herself—but this wasn't working. Finally she stopped and trod water at the deep end—furthest from the door. Damn it, she'd get dressed and go dancing instead.

She pulled herself up out of the water and turned to reach for her towel. Only someone was there reaching for her instead. Someone who pulled her fast into hot, strong arms. And as she thudded against the wall of masculinity the shrieking fear transformed into sick relief.

'Why do you always have to sneak up on people?' She tried to yell at Carter but it came out like a strangled whisper, her throat all tight with terror.

'Sorry.' His hands smoothed over her shoulders, gently rubbing away her trembles. 'I didn't mean to scare you.' He looked back down at the dim room. 'You're not supposed to be in here.'

'Neither are you,' she snapped. 'Why are you here?'

'Isn't it obvious? I'm looking for you. Why are you here?'

'Isn't it obvious?' She was swimming, for heaven's

sake. She was trying to work him out of her system by exhausting herself.

His grip tightened and he pulled her closer. Her senses were swimming even crazier now. Yeah, the work-him-out hadn't worked.

'You're getting wet.' She put up one last, pathetic defence.

'I don't care.'

'Carter...' she muttered as his mouth descended.

'You don't want me to kiss you?' His lips grazed her temple. 'To touch you? You don't want to touch me?'

Of course she wanted that—she ached to touch him. It was way less than ten seconds to yes.

He laughed, pulling her dripping wet ponytail down the way he liked to, tipping her chin up to meet his mouth. But the laughter died as the kisses deepened and steam rose in its stead.

It was as it had been that first night—a gentle tease to begin with. Until she couldn't resist opening and he immediately went deeper, pushing for more. She lifted her hand and combed her fingers through his silky, thick hair.

His hands slid down her arms, sweeping the droplets from her skin. The hard heat of him burned through his wet shirt. All steel male—with unmistakable purpose.

She managed the first couple of buttons, but he had to do the rest, until she could spread the two halves of cotton and sweep her hands across the hot planes of his chest. Beautiful, hard and hot for her. He saw the look on her face and suddenly tumbled her to the floor, claiming dominance as she'd known he would. The cold tiles were welcome on her burning skin, helping her see straight for one moment of sanity.

'Stop.'

He lifted his head and looked at her.

'You're a player, right, Carter?' she muttered breath-lessly. 'This doesn't mean anything.'

He brushed the back of his fingers along her jaw. 'Not if you don't want it to.'

'Just fun.' She rocked, desire making her body move instinctively against his. All she ever had was just a little fun. Nothing more. This had an elemental undertone of something serious that she wanted to eliminate, but the need to have him was beyond necessity now. That big black hole deep inside her had been ripped open and demanded some good feeling to fill it. Like the good feeling she got when kissing Carter.

And then he did kiss her. She closed her eyes as he moved over her—slowly nibbling across her shoulders, his hands working to peel her tight swimsuit down, ex-posing her breasts. He kissed down her sternum, down to her stomach and then looked back up at what he'd bared. His hands lifted and he cupped her. She shivered at the touch, insanely sensitive there. He rose swiftly, his mouth hot and wide as his tongue swirled around one nipple.

She arched violently, pushing her heels down hard on the cool tiles to get her hips higher—hoping he'd just grip them and surge into her. She wanted it to be powerful and fast. She wanted him to be there now.

But damn him he was slow and toying and touching her all over. His hands slipping into soft parts that she usually held reserved. She tried to guide him back, tried to move her own into dominance—to distract him—but he was focused on his own determined exploration. And it was undoing her completely.

Her whole body broke into a sweat. It was as if she'd

walked into a steam room—suddenly she was so hot, and she couldn't get any of the burning air into her windpipe. She writhed more beneath him, trying to make him move faster—move over her and take her swiftly. She needed it to be finished, because she couldn't cope with heat.

All she wanted was him inside her, riding her, releasing his strength into her. Her mind and body fixated on that one thing—*his* possession, *his* pleasure. Not hers. She got hers from his. That was what she wanted. Not this searing way he was playing with her.

'Carter!' She gasped as his fingers stroked against the strip of her swimsuit between her legs and then slipped beneath the stretchy material. She twisted, suddenly trying to escape him as the strokes grew impossible to bear.

She was drowning, drowning, drowning in the intolerable heat. She couldn't breathe, couldn't think, couldn't control anything. Her fingers dug into his shoulders as the sensations become so strong they scared her.

He lifted his lips from her damp skin. 'Relax.'

How was she supposed to relax? Her toes curled as she flexed every muscle she had, trying to wring the tension from her. But it wouldn't leave her. Instead it worsened.

He sucked her nipple into his mouth and slid a single finger inside. The agony was too complete and she jerked violently—*away* from the source of that frightening intensity. Wrenching herself free from his hold and scooting back on the tiles.

He swore. 'Did I hurt you?' Rising sharply to his knees, his chest heaving, he stared across to where she now sat half a metre away.

She shook her head, breathing hard and shivering as

the sensations still scudded through her. But they were weakening now, becoming manageable.

'Penny?'

'I just needed a second.' Panting, she moved back towards him. Wanting to get the situation under control. She wanted *him* under control. And she knew how—to hold him, kiss him, suck him in deep and squeeze him hard.

Both her mouth and sex were wet with that want. But it was her mouth that wanted first—to lessen his potency. She'd pleasure him enough to make him tolerable for the rest of her, to make him speed up. She wanted him quivering beneath her. She'd be in control again and watch him ride the wave; she wanted to witness the orgasm rippling through him. She wanted to be the source of that pleasure.

Because that was the pleasure in it for her.

Silently Carter watched her crawl back towards him. Still he said nothing as she knelt in front of him. But she felt his ragged breath when she ran her hands down his chest. She spread her palms wide on his thighs, and then she narrowed in on her target. Oh, yes, she loved the size of the erection that greeted her. Her fingers twisted, searching for the zip so she could free him. But all of a sudden he grabbed her hands and stopped her.

She looked up at him. 'Don't you want me to?'

He stared hard into her face—from her mouth to her eyes. 'The setting isn't working for me,' he said. 'We should get out of here.'

She sat back on her heels and swallowed. Suddenly cold. Suddenly aware she was half naked. She wriggled her breasts back into her cold wet swimsuit with absolutely no dignity whatsoever. Not able to look at him again until she was as covered up as she could be, with the towel like a tent around her. By the time she did look across at him he'd fixed his own clothing and was standing waiting for her.

He held out his hand. 'Come on.'

She couldn't refuse his offer of assistance. But as soon as she was on her feet he dropped her hand. He was careful not to walk too close. She was careful not to stare at his strained trousers. She really wished he'd let her do something about that. She really wanted to, wanted *him*, but it had to be her way. Only, as she'd suspected from the first, Carter wasn't one to let that happen.

They got to the door and Carter turned the handle. It didn't move. He twisted it again. Then the other way. It still didn't move.

'It's locked,' Penny said. 'Did you lock it when you came in?'

'No.'

Penny frowned and tried the door herself. Then she looked through the small window to the darkened foyer beyond. 'Jed must have locked it.'

He must have had a quick look in and seen the empty pool—and not seen their entwined bodies in the dark corner at the end of the room. He thought she'd gone so he'd locked it up for the night.

'So we're stuck in here?'

'Looks like it.' She swallowed and drew the damp towel closer around her shoulders.

'We could bang on the door, he'd hear us, right?'

She shook her head. 'He's up one floor and he listens to his iPod.'

Carter rolled his eyes and cursed under his breath.

'Don't make trouble for him,' Penny said quickly. 'I talked him into it. It's my fault really.'

'Why do you come here after hours? Why not when it's open?'

'I like having the pool to myself. It gets really busy before and after work.'

'You don't think it's dangerous?'

'I'm a really strong swimmer. And Jed knows I'm here.'

'He's useless at his job, though, isn't he? He doesn't know I'm in here too.'

'He'd have heard the lift you were in and thought it was me going back up. He probably thinks I left the building while he was down doing the lock-up.'

'Don't try to make excuses for him.'

'He has a young family, he doesn't get much sleep and he needs the job, Carter. Leave him alone.'

'Well, if you really care about him staying in employment then you should stop getting him to break the rules.'

'Okay, fine.'

He sighed and glared back at the deep blue water, and the big still space. Then he looked back at her. 'You can swim in the pool in my apartment complex. It's big and private and hardly anyone swims there.'

'Do you?'

'Yes, but in the morning. You can have it all to yourself at night. And I'll watch.'

'I'm not going to be there at night.'

'Oh, I think you are.' He stepped closer and put his hand on her shoulder. Even through the damp towel she could feel the sizzle. 'You should get dressed.'

She braced for his reaction to this last pearl of info.

'The only way to the changing rooms is through that door.'

'You're kidding,' he snapped, immediately trying the door one more time.

She shook her head.

Carter leaned forward and banged his head on the wood. They couldn't even get to the changing rooms where there might have been a condom machine on the wall. He'd hoped anyway. Because they had no cell phone, no condoms, no couch, no cushions, nothing to cover them in what was going to be a long, cold, frustrating night. He frowned as he felt her shivering beside him.

His clothes were damp and freezing. The whole place was freezing. And all she had on were wet togs and a wet towel. 'What time do they open up in the morning?'

'Six o'clock,' she answered. 'I think the gym attendant gets in around quarter to.'

Just under eight hours away. Eight hours alone with her mostly naked and he couldn't even take advantage of that fact.

'Come on, then, let's try and get comfortable.'

He walked back down to the far end of the pool. Foam flutter boards weren't the softest things in the world, but they were better than cold concrete. He scattered a couple by the wall, gestured for her to take one and he sat on another himself. She cloaked the towel around her and avoided both looking and talking.

Carter tried not to stare at her too obviously while he attempted to work out what had happened when she'd pulled away from him so abruptly. He didn't think he'd hurt her; he'd been being gentle and taking it slow. Well, kind of slow. But it was as if she'd suddenly freaked out—and he'd thought she was so close. She *had* been so close. Right on the brink. Was that the problem? She hadn't wanted to come?

He shook off the idea. So unlikely. Who didn't want to have an orgasm? Maybe he'd touched a too sensitive spot too quickly. Which meant he had to go even more slowly. Which frankly surprised him. It wasn't as if she were some skittish virgin—hell, the way she kissed was so damn hot and welcoming. But when he'd really begun to push for the ultimate? Boom. Was it simply a total withdrawal from a total tease?

Actually he didn't think so. Because her refusal hadn't been total. He didn't think she was playing games— the fact she'd tried to go down on him proved that. But it seemed she didn't want to receive the pleasure herself. Was it some weird control thing? Did she like the power of bringing a man to his knees and begging for her to swallow him whole? Or was she truly that little bit scared?

Wow. She really was a mass of contradictions and complications. And he was beyond intrigued—he was bound to follow through on this with her, he just had to figure out how. His muscles twitched beneath his skin. Patience wasn't one of his virtues. But for Penny Fairburn, he might have to make an exception.

He stretched out his legs and drew in a deep breath to ease the tension still wiring his body. The question now was how to fill in the time. How to tempt her back, how to find out what secrets he needed to unlock her totally. He couldn't make more moves, not in this place, not without warmth, comfort and contraceptive protection. Which left only one thing.

Talk.

'You've always swum?' Lame, but it was a beginning. He couldn't dive straight into all the intense, personal questions that were simmering within him.

'Since I started travelling,' she replied distantly. 'Most places have nice pools somewhere.'

Penny answered his light chat completely uselessly, her brain still barely processing that she was trapped in the pool room all night. With Carter. It was the 'with Carter' bit that really had her reeling. That and the extreme throbbing still going on in some sensitive parts of her body. Staying in control of the next eight hours was going to take serious concentration and she needed to stay in control. The avalanche of sensation he'd triggered in her had taken her by surprise—despite the warning signals she'd had from his earlier kisses.

Too much emotion—even just lust—led to fallout, not fun. She couldn't deal with fallout. Mind you, she might not have to, because he wasn't exactly busting his moves now. In fact he was quite carefully keeping a distance while she grew colder by the second.

He wasn't even looking at her any more. And now the last of the light let in by the high windows was fading so she couldn't hope to read his expression. But he did seem inclined to talk. And she was definitely inclined to ask.

'So your family's in Melbourne.' She'd picked up that nugget at dinner last night.

'Dad is. My mum died when I was fourteen.'

'Oh, I'm sorry.'

'It's okay. Dad's on his third marriage now.'

She clamped her lips to stop her 'oh'.

'He remarried within a year,' Carter continued bluntly.

'Twenty years younger than him, gold-digger. The whole cliché you can imagine, only worse.'

'Oh.' Couldn't stop it that time.

'Eventually he got out of it but went straight into the next marriage. Another much younger woman—Lucinda. They had a baby last year.'

'Really?' That was big.

'Yeah, Nick.'

'You have a baby half-brother,' she processed. 'And you're okay with it?'

'Actually, he's quite a little dude. Why, you don't like kids?'

'It's not that I don't like them…'

He twisted to face her. 'You don't want them?'

'Definitely not,' she answered immediately.

'Not now, or not ever?'

'Ever.'

'Really?' He sounded surprised. 'Me either.' He started to laugh. 'That's what's so great about Nick. He's the new generation Dodds boy to take over from me. No pressure on me to procreate now, Dad's done it.'

'Do you think they'll have more?' Penny couldn't imagine having a sibling she was old enough to be the mother of.

'I don't know. Lucinda probably doesn't want to risk her figure again. She has the new heir now—she has Dad round her little finger as tight as she can.'

'Maybe she loves him.' Penny just had to throw in that possibility because she suspected Carter might have his bitter eyes on.

'She loves his money and status.'

Yeah, bitter. 'Gee, not down on her at all, are you?'

'I've met her type before. The first stepmother—remember?'

'So you're not close to your dad.' She figured his scathing attitude might get in the way of that.

'Actually we are pretty close. He retired from the companies completely a few years ago—mainly to be with her. And part of me hopes their marriage will last because, I think it'd kill him to lose the kid, but it won't. Then he'll undoubtedly find someone else. I try to treat Lucinda with respect. But he knows I don't trust her. He tells me time will take care of that and I guess it will. They'll either break up or last the distance.'

'You don't think it's kind of romantic?'

'I don't believe anything is romantic.'

Ah. Penny sat up and repositioned her towel, her interest totally piqued. 'Who taught you not to?'

Even in the gloom she could see the devilish spark light up his eyes. 'My stepmother's yoga instructor.'

'You're kidding.' She couldn't help but smile. He was so naughty. 'A yoga instructor.' Giggles bubbled then. 'No wonder you won't settle for one woman—she gave you unrealistic expectations.'

'You think she set the bar too high?' he asked, all wickedness.

'A cougar who taught you hot yoga sex? Way too high.' And no wonder he'd shot her through the roof with a mere touch, probably some Tantric trick.

'My stepmother was only eight years older than me,' he pointed out sarcastically. 'And Renee was only six.'

Her name was Renee? Penny maintained her grin, but her teeth gritted. 'But you were how old?'

'Sixteen. What?' His grin broadened. 'Too young?'

'Too young to have your heart broken.'

He laughed. 'That wasn't what happened. It was just sex.'

'Your first time is never just sex,' she said with feeling. 'So what happened?'

'She had a fiancé I didn't know about. She wanted to play around on her man for the power trip. And she wanted to break me in.'

Penny had the distinct impression no woman had ever broken Carter, and none ever would. But he'd definitely been bruised. 'What happens with your first can really leave a mark.' She knew that for a fact.

'You think?' He laughed. 'Renee was just about fun. It was the next one who really tried to do me over.'

'Oh? How old was *she*?'

He chuckled. 'Three months younger than me, honey. She was Head Girl of the school, I was Head Boy. The perfect match—on paper.'

'You were Head Boy?'

He shrugged, looked a bit sheepish. 'Good all-rounder.'

She knew what it took to be appointed the head of one of those elite schools—excellent grades, good sporting or musical achievement, community spirit. The golden boy going with the golden girl. Yeah, she knew all about that. 'So you were King and Queen of the prom. Then what happened?'

'We went to university. She switched to be at the same as me.'

'Oh.' Penny smiled wryly. 'Her first mistake.'

'We were only eighteen, you know? I wasn't looking to settle down.'

She understood that too. And a decade or so later,

Carter still wasn't looking to settle. 'So it turned to custard?'

'She started getting serious about us getting married. Lots of pressure and angst. Eventually she used another guy to try to push me into it.'

'She tried to make you jealous?'

'Yeah, but I don't get jealous. Frankly, I didn't care that much—as bad as that sounds. So it didn't work. I just realised I couldn't trust any of your fair sex.'

He didn't trust women at all. But then who could blame him? His mother had left—okay, she'd died, but it was being left in a sense. His first lover had used him, his first serious girlfriend had tried to manipulate him into something he didn't want...and he'd got ever so slightly bitter.

Well, he didn't need to trust her. He just wanted some fun. In theory he was perfect. Because in theory he posed no threat—he wouldn't ask for anything she didn't want to give.

Except he already had. When he kissed her, his body demanded hers to surrender. Still that step too far for her, but she was so tempted by him she knew she was going to have to figure out a way of working it in a way she could handle.

He was looking at her slyly. 'So what's the deal with your family?'

'What do you mean?' She pulled her legs up tighter and wrapped her arms around her knees. The temperature was really dropping now.

'You haven't been home in years and you take me, a near stranger, to ride shotgun on a dinner with your brother. There's some kind of deal going on.'

'There's no deal,' she said innocently. 'I have a nice family.'

'So what, you're a runaway without a cause?' He looked sceptical. 'There has to be something. Some reason why you don't want to marry or have kids. Not many women don't want that. Most spend half their lives trying to manipulate their way into that situation.'

'You have such a nice impression of women.'

'I call it as I see it. And I like women a lot.'

'You mean you like a lot of women.'

His grin didn't deny it. 'Why limit yourself? And you're the same in that you don't want to settle. Why not? Your parents have an ugly divorce or something?'

'No, they've been married almost thirty years and they're still happy.' Her heart thudded.

'Oh.' Carter looked surprised. 'That's nice.'

'Yeah, they're good together. They're not like you, they fully believe in for-ever happy.'

'So why don't you?'

She fell back on her stock avoidance answer. 'I like my freedom. I like to travel. That's what I do.'

'And you really don't want kids?'

Oh. He'd gone back to that. 'No. I don't want children. Most men who want to marry do. I don't want to disappoint someone. It's easier to be with men who don't want either of those things.'

He looked serious. 'Can you not have kids, Penny?' he asked softly.

'Oh, no,' she said quickly. 'No, it's not that. As far as I'm aware, that's all...fine.' Even in the dim light, she figured her blush was visible. 'I just don't want to bring a kid into this world. It's too cruel.'

He said nothing and eventually she settled back

against the wall, tiredness beginning to pull her down. Age-old tiredness.

'Who's Isabelle?'

'Sorry?' Her tension snapped back.

'You clammed up when Matt mentioned her last night,' Carter said. 'You're clamming up now.'

Penny blew out a strangled breath. 'She's just someone from our home town.' Then she let enough silence pass to point out the obvious—that she wasn't talking any more. She suppressed a shiver and clamped her jaw to stop her teeth chattering. Curled her limbs into an even tighter bunch.

'You're cold.' Carter shuffled closer to where she sat. 'Come on, we have to keep warm.'

That was going to be impossible in this damp fridge. She went more rigid as he came close enough to touch. He sighed and put his arm around her, ignoring her resistance and pulling her down so they were half lying, half propped with their backs against the cold wall.

'Go to sleep,' he said softly, his body gently pressing alongside hers. 'Nothing's going to happen.'

Penny didn't want to wake up, didn't want to move. She was so deliciously warm, even her feet—which were like blocks of ice year round. And a soft wave of even greater warmth was brushing down her arm with gentle regularity.

She wriggled and the warm comfort tightened. The warmth was alive—male arms, bare arms, encircled her. So did bare legs. And against her back? Bare chest.

She jerked up into a sitting position. 'Where are your clothes?'

'You were freezing,' he answered with a lazy stretch.

'So you had to get naked to keep me company?'

'Skin on skin, Penny. It was the best way I could think to warm you up. You wouldn't wake up and I started to think you were getting hypothermic.'

Yeah, right. 'It's the middle of summer.'

'And you're in a basement that's as cold as an icebox,' he pointed out with a total lack of concern. 'You're warmer now, right?'

'Yes.' She was *sizzling*.

'And you're conscious, so it worked.' He pulled her back down to lie against him. 'And you liked it. You burrowed right up against me. You couldn't have got closer.' His arms tightened again. 'No, don't try to wriggle away. I'm feeling cold now. Your turn as caretaker.'

A tremor racked his body, but she could hear his smile. Faker.

She buried her smile in her arm so he couldn't see it. But she didn't try to move away again. Just another five minutes—what harm could that possibly do? He made a fantastic human hot-water bottle.

Then her stomach rumbled.

'You're hungry.'

Then his stomach rumbled too.

'You are too.' She giggled at how loud they gurgled.

'Mmm. We didn't have dinner.' His breath warmed her ear. 'What do you have for breakfast?'

'Fruit, yoghurt and a sprinkle of cinnamon.' Her mouth watered at the thought of it.

'Cinnamon smells good,' he drawled.

'Yeah, so much better than chlorine.' She could feel every inch of him. There were a lot of inches. 'You're in a bad way.' The hard length pressed against the top of her thighs.

'I can live with it.'

'You're sure?'

'Why?' He moved suddenly. 'You offering?'

He rolled above her. She shifted her legs that bit apart to welcome him. Yes, she was offering. Because she knew she couldn't deny herself any more. Desire finally outweighed fear. Some sleep had restored perspective. Besides, given how hard he felt now, she felt confident in her ability to bring him home quickly.

He looked at her closely. She felt his body tense up even more and he smiled, bending forward to close the last inches between them. She closed her eyes, anticipating a full passion blast of a kiss.

Except he merely brushed his lips on her forehead, her cheeks, her nose. So gently, too softly. 'We have the most insane chemistry, Penny.'

She opened her mouth to downplay it.

'No.' He put his fingers across her lips. 'Don't play games. Just be honest. Always be honest with me.'

'Okay.' She could let him have that. 'We have chemistry.' Actually they had more than chemistry. They had some experiences and likes in common. And they also shared no desire for any kind of a relationship.

'And we're going to experiment with it.'

Except there was still that niggling suspicion it might blow up in her face. 'What, like a science project?'

'Pretty much.'

'You weren't kidding about not being romantic.'

'You don't like flowers. You don't like chocolates. You hate romance too,' he teased, pressing even more intimately against her.

'I don't hate diamonds.' She shifted sassily.

He snorted. 'And what would you do if some guy

produced a diamond ring?' He ground his pelvis against hers in a slow circular motion. 'You'd run so fast you'd break the sound barrier.'

She bit her lip to stop her groan of defeat.

'We're going to have an affair,' he told her.

They'd been on this trajectory from the moment they'd laid eyes on each other. All she could do now was try to manage how it went. 'Yes.'

To her surprise the relief hit as she agreed. It was closely followed by excitement. Now she'd admitted it, she wanted it immediately. The sooner she could have, the sooner she could control.

'Tonight.' He levered up and away from her.

She sat up—unconsciously keeping a short distance between them. 'Tonight?'

He grinned at her obvious disappointment. 'No condoms in here.'

Oh. She hadn't thought of that. Thank goodness he had.

'Won't you let me help you out now?' She longed to feel him shaking in her arms. She could stroke him to glory in seconds.

'Will you let me do the same for you?'

She blinked rapidly and ducked his fixed gaze.

'Tonight,' he reiterated, amusement warming his authoritative tone.

She nodded. 'Just a little fun.'

'Can you handle that?' All hint of humour had gone.

Hopefully. If she could stay on top. She looked back into his eyes and waved her independence flag. 'Sure. Can you?'

CHAPTER SEVEN

TWENTY minutes later they heard the door lock click. They hid in the dark corner for another moment and dashed when the coast was clear.

'Get changed quickly,' he whispered.

Giggling in the women's, Penny tossed her skirt and top on straight over her togs, scooped up her bag and was out again in less than a minute. Carter was standing in the little foyer, his shirt water-stained and creased, his jaw dark with stubble. He looked sexier and more dangerous than ever.

He held out his hand. 'Let me take your bag.'

Penny walked quickly. 'I've got it.'

Already people were arriving to use the gym and swim facility and she wanted to get out of there before anyone saw the state she was in.

'No, let me take it,' he insisted, blocking her path.

She frowned but he came even closer, speaking through gritted teeth.

'Look, if you want everyone to see the size of my hard-on, sure, you take it. Otherwise let me just hold it while we get out of here, okay?'

Penny's jaw dropped.

He put a finger under her chin and nudged it closed

again. 'Don't act the innocent. You know exactly what you can do to me. Just like I know what I can do to you.' His gaze imprisoned hers and pierced deep. 'If you'll let me.'

Penny felt as if an adrenalin injection had just been stabbed straight into her heart. The feeling flickered along her veins, molten gold—sweeter than honey yet tart at the same time. Tantalising.

He smiled.

Excitement rippled low in her belly, blocking everything—nerves, memories, fears. All were swallowed in the rising heat. She shook her head but smiled back. Him wanting her felt good. He grabbed her hand and stormed them up the stairs and through Reception.

'Hell, you're not here already, Penny?' Bleary-eyed, Jed looked up from behind his desk.

She shook her head. 'You never saw me.'

'You and I are having a little chat later.' Carter scowled at Jed and held the door for Penny.

He flagged two taxis.

'We can't share?' she asked.

'We get in one of those together now and you know we wouldn't come back. I've got work I have to do.'

Eleven hours later, resentment-filled, she figured he'd done a lot of work. By the time she'd got home, showered, changed and returned to the office, he was already back there and concentrating. He hadn't moved from his chair for hours. She knew because she'd gone into his office a few times—delivering more of the massive numbers of faxes and courier parcels, more wretched files—and he'd ignored her. Hadn't even looked up, lost in a world of figures and transactions and tiny details.

And she hadn't been able to concentrate on a thing—

all jumpy and excited and impatient. Until the tiredness from the little amount of sleep had eaten her nerves and now she was grumpy and ready to stomp home alone because he hadn't even said hello to her all day.

Worst of all, it was only just five o'clock. Theoretically she had another couple of hours to put in first. She glared at her computer screen and banged the buttons on the keyboard.

'So.' He suddenly leant across her desk. 'Your place or mine?'

'So smooth, Carter.' She stabbed through another couple of keystrokes.

'Just answer,' he said roughly, putting his hand over hers. 'I'm barely able to pull together two syllables I'm that strung out.'

She looked at his face and was grateful she was sitting down. No muscles could stay firm against the heat in his eyes. And the grip he had on her now was thrillingly tight. It made her feel a lot better about his distance all day and she dropped any idea of holding out for some grovelling.

'Yours.' She was glad he'd asked. If she went to his it meant she could leave when she needed to, not have to wait for him to decide to go from hers.

'Then let's go.'

'Now?'

The taxi was already waiting and, even better, the trip was short. Her heart drummed faster than a dance-floor anthem and she concentrated on keeping her breathing quiet and even. He still had hold of her hand and as they rode the elevator up to his short-let serviced apartment he finally broke the silence.

'You're tired?'

Actually she was plotting how to handle him. She needed to take charge from the get-go—set the pattern for the evening—and she wanted him on fire as fast as possible.

He must have read her mind because he turned to her the moment he'd closed the door behind them. She melted against him and offered it all, pleased he was so hungry. She wanted him to be uncontrolled, to be in thrall. Passion was powerful and she wanted to succeed in hitting his pleasure high. She moved against him, dancing the way she knew best, her mouth open to his, her fingers working on his buttons—wanting him raw and hot.

But he laughed, low and pure. 'Why are you in such a hurry?'

Because that way she could control it. She shrugged her shoulders and simply smiled, pressing close again.

But he, damn him, suddenly slowed right down. He swept his lips gently across her skin as his fingers so carefully freed buttons. Why was he taking so long to undress her? Hell, they didn't even need to get undressed, he could just push her skirt up and pull her panties to the side—she was ready for him, she would ride hard for him—she badly wanted to feel him come.

Instead his hands drifted south and so did his mouth, gently caressing the skin he'd exposed. Until he was on his knees before her and sliding down the zip of her skirt. She twisted, her discomfort suddenly building, wanting to bring him back up, wanting her hands to be the ones taking the lead. But then his fingers slid higher and she flinched, the pleasure so sharp it was too much, and she couldn't let the sudden rushing feeling swamp her.

Carter had gone completely still. Then he leaned back

and looked up so he could see her face clearly as his hand gently brushed down the front of her thigh. 'I want you to enjoy it.'

'I will enjoy it,' she answered softly. But she knew what he meant. He wanted to hear her scream his name.

He stood, his keen eyes catching the way she wriggled back the tiniest bit from him. He swallowed. 'You don't want me to go down on you?'

She nodded, glad she didn't have to spell it out herself. 'I don't really like that…I…don't feel comfortable.'

He looked thoughtful. 'But you'll go down on me?'

'Oh, yeah, I like that.'

'Well, that's nice.' His devil grin flickered. 'But what turns you on most, Penny?' He watched her steadily.

The heat intensified in her cheeks and she tried to shrug his question off. 'Lots of things…' she mumbled. 'I like…lots of things…'

His head tilted a fraction to the left as he studied her. 'Oh, my…' His arms tightened, his body tensing too as he lanced right through her defences. 'You *fake* it.'

Her mouth opened in horror but the gasp never eventuated. Instead the blush burned all the way down to her toes. She blinked rapidly but she couldn't break away from his all-seeing stare. 'I do enjoy sex,' she said when she got her voice back. 'I like it a lot. It feels good. But… it's…it's just the way I am.'

'You always fake it?' His eyes widened.

'Sometimes it's easier that way.' She licked her lips— not as invitation, but because her mouth had gone Death Valley dry. 'Guys like to feel like they're…'

Carter rubbed his fingers across his forehead.

'It's not going to damage your ego or anything, is it?'

she asked, cringing at his obvious surprise. 'You'd rather I faked it?'

Blunt as she'd been with him before, this was his kind of sledgehammer stuff and she was shaking inside. She was never this honest. But then no one else had ever called her on it either and she was shocked he'd twigged at all, let alone so quickly. The fact was, she did fake it. She had an amazing array of squeals to let the guy think she was there. The Sally chick who met Harry in that movie had nothing on her.

But that didn't mean she didn't enjoy it. She did. She wanted it and she *wanted* Carter. The closeness was enough for her, feeling desired and making someone happy even for a few moments made her feel good too.

His gaze hadn't left hers and surprisingly his smile had gone less devilish, more sweet. 'My ego can handle you,' he said. 'So no faking. Total honesty. Deal?'

'I want to be with you,' she couldn't help reassuring. 'You turn me on, you know you do. But I just don't…'

'Get across the finish line.'

'But I still enjoy the race.'

He actually laughed. 'Don't feel any pressure to per-form for me, darling.' He rested his hands lightly on her shoulders. 'We can enjoy each other in our own ways. Let's just see what happens, okay?'

She released the breath that she'd been holding for ever. 'You're sure?' Even for a guy as confident as him she was surprised at his easy understanding.

'Yep.' He nodded. 'I'm sure.'

Carter was trying to stop his head spinning but every thought had just been blown from his brain cells. Wow. He just hadn't seen that coming and honestly he'd just blurted the thought that had occurred so randomly.

For him enjoying sex was so inextricably linked with orgasm it was as if she were talking in a foreign language. He tried to figure it out—was she not physically capable of coming?

Actually he didn't believe that. By the pool he'd felt her shaking in his arms, he'd felt the hunger in her mouth, felt the flood of desire between her legs when he'd touched her there. Physically she'd been all systems go.

But at that point she'd literally leapt out of his arms.

So it was her head that couldn't let go.

Of course, she was a complete control freak. It made sense. That was her job all over—keeping everything in its place and perfect. But at the same time it didn't make sense. The night he'd met her she'd appeared the absolute image of a hedonist. A beautiful young woman out for fun and frolics and seemingly assured of success should she want it. But it seemed she didn't want it—at least not on a level that she couldn't control. Did she pleasure her lovers rather than let them pleasure her? Because that wasn't right. For him sex was all about mutual delight and exploration. Pleasure for both—give *and* take.

Women didn't have total ownership rights on curiosity. Right now it was eating Carter alive. And so was the challenge. How could it not be a challenge? Because this woman could feel it. He could feel *her*—trembling, all hot and aching. He knew how much she wanted him. So how did he help her let go?

He swallowed again. Like anything it came down to the details. She was so sensitive and maybe it scared her. So he was going to have to take it easy.

She was watching him with a worried look. 'I've probably put you off now.'

And the sweetheart looked as if she utterly regretted that.

He grinned. She didn't need to worry—she would get every ounce of what he had to give. 'Not at all.' Oh, hell, no, now he was all the more desperate to strip her and, oh, so slowly warm her up.

But first what they both needed was a little more time. Just a very little. 'You know we haven't eaten,' he said, tucking his shirt back in. 'Come on, I'll make something.'

She looked surprised.

'You hadn't missed dinner?' Now he thought about it, he was starving.

She shook her head. 'Haven't had a chance to think about it.'

Carter smiled inside again. That was because she'd been thinking about him. The key was to get her to *stop* thinking.

He led the way to the kitchen. 'You don't mind a cold dinner?'

Penny was feeling so hot—from embarrassment—that cold sounded wonderful. In fact she'd dive deep into a pool right now if she could. By the time she'd straightened her clothes Carter was pouring the wine—crisp and cool enough to make condensation form on the glass.

He pointed to the stool on the far side of the bench. 'Sit there and talk to me.'

About what? She'd so killed the moment and she was gutted because she did want to have him. Ugh. She should run away, go dancing and forget everything. 'Are you making any progress with figuring out Mason's problem?'

She was reduced to talking work.

All he did was shrug as he pulled a bowl from the fridge. An assortment of salad greens. He deftly sliced tomato, cucumber, feta and tossed the chunks in, adding a few olives from a tin after. Her mouth watered; she loved a summer salad.

He got a pack from the fridge and forked smoked salmon from it onto plates. Then he got a wooden board and from a brown paper bag slid a loaf of round, artisan bread. Her stomach actually rumbled as he sliced into the loaf. He sent her a wicked look.

'Don't tell me you baked the bread,' she teased to cover it.

'Italian bakery down the road.' He winked. 'Looks good, huh?'

It looked divine. In five minutes he'd fixed the most delicious dinner and she was seriously impressed. 'You always eat this healthily?'

'I work long hours, I'm responsible for a lot of people's jobs. I need to keep fit so I can perform one hundred per cent.'

He picked up both plates. 'Come on, we'll go out onto the balcony. You bring the salad.'

He pushed the bifolding doors wide open. The sun was still high and hot but an aerial sail shaded the table and the view of the harbour was incredible. Pity she was too on edge to be able to enjoy it properly.

'How come it's you helping Mason? Not one of your employees?' From all the conference calls and faxes he'd been getting she knew he didn't usually spend his days on a detailed case analysis like this. He was the boss of more than one entity.

'He trusts me.' Carter lifted his shoulders. 'And he's an old friend. And I wanted a break anyway.'

'So this is a holiday for you?'

'It's a nice little change.'

'But you're still in contact with the Melbourne office all the time.'

He shrugged again. 'I'm responsible for a lot.'

'And you love it.'

'Sure. I like my career. I work hard to succeed.'

Yeah, she'd noticed that about him.

The cool wine refreshed and soothed and now she'd begun to eat she realised just how hungry she was. It was only another five minutes and she'd finished.

He looked at her plate and looked pleased. 'Better?'

'Much.'

He went inside and pushed buttons on the iPod dock in the lounge and then came back to the doorway, offering his hand to her. 'Come on, don't you like dancing?'

'To a much faster beat than this.' But she stood anyway.

He smiled as he drew her closer. 'You've got to learn to relax, Penny.'

The slow jazzy music made the mood sultry and they were barely swaying. His shirt was unbuttoned, so was part of hers, so skin touched. This kind of dancing wasn't freeing, it was torture. She was uncomfortably hot again, her breathing jagged. A half-glass of wine couldn't be blamed for her light-headedness, and she'd just eaten so it wasn't low blood-sugar levels either.

It was him. All him.

And she wanted to feel him wild inside her.

She reached up on tiptoe, deliberately brushing her breasts against his chest. His hand moved instantly to hold her hips tight against his.

She sighed deeply. 'Can we just get on with it?'

'So impatient, Penny.' Laughter warmed his voice. 'Come on.'

He danced her down the little hall to the master bedroom. She liked the anonymity of the room—only one step away from a hotel suite. There was nothing personal of him around to make her wonder beyond what she knew already. Burning out the chemistry was all this was. One week and he'd be gone. Another month and she would too.

He pressed a button and thick, heavy curtains closed, giving the room an even more intimate mood. 'You want the lights out?'

'No.' She smiled. 'I like them on.'

He kicked off his shoes and trousers, shrugging off his shirt. She was spellbound by his body. He caught her looking, sent her an equally hot look back. 'You like to be on top, Penny? You'd like to take the lead?'

She did but she hadn't expected him to let her so easily.

He smiled and kissed her, but then moved onto the bed. He lay, his shoulders propped up against the bed head, his legs long in front of him, and looked back at her in challenge. 'Come and get me, then.'

Oh, she would.

She stripped, her eyes not leaving his as she deliberately, slowly shimmied her way out of every single piece of fabric. His expression was unashamedly hot and he openly hungered as she revealed her breasts.

'You on top works for me,' he muttered hoarsely.

She'd been worried he'd get all serious—forgo his pleasure in the pursuit of hers and then they'd both end up unsatisfied. But it seemed he was happy to stretch back and enjoy everything easily. Thank goodness.

As she walked to the bed he reached out to the bedside table and swiped up a condom, quickly rolling it on. So he was ready. Well, so was she.

She knelt onto the bed, meeting his unwavering gaze, and began to crawl up his body. His smile was so naughty, so challenging, so satisfied.

But she'd see him *really* satisfied. She trailed light fingers up his legs as she moved, bent forward and pressed little kisses, little licks. Nothing but tiny touches designed to torment—his thighs, his hips, his abs, his nipples. She'd get to his erection soon—when he begged.

His breath hissed. 'Are you afraid to kiss me?'

She knelt up and smiled. No. She wasn't afraid of that. She moved up the last few inches and pressed her mouth to his—and felt him smile.

His hands settled on her hips, pulling her to sit on him, his erection only inches from her wet heat. How the man could kiss. Slow and then firm, his lips nipping and then his tongue sliding. He turned it into an art form. He turned it intense.

She shifted, wanting to move right onto him, wanting to tease him some more. But he took her hands in his and imprisoned them beside her hips—so she couldn't touch or move. Then he went right back to kissing her. Just kissing. As if they were young teens on a marathon make-out session.

She was getting desperate now—to touch more, feel more—because his kisses were driving her crazy, building the need inside her. Every one seemed to go deeper. Every one increased her temperature another notch. Every one made her kiss back with the same increasing passion—until it was at an all-new level. She closed her eyes, breathless, yearning for the finish.

Finally he kissed down the side of her neck—just a little. She shivered at the first development of touch.

'Cold?' he murmured against her.

She shook her head a fraction. She was anything but cold.

She was completely naked, so was he, but he didn't move to take her or let her slide down on him. His erection rubbed against the front of her mound, teasing exquisitely.

She wanted to diffuse his power and have him in thrall to her—just for the moments that they'd cling together. That was how she always liked it—to be close, to be held. Intimacy beyond that was too much for her to bear. But Carter didn't seem inclined to settle for anything less than absolute intimacy. Her eyes smarted; she shouldn't have admitted anything to him. She shifted again, eager to move things on more.

'We've got all night, honey,' he muttered between more searing kisses. 'I'm not going to explode if I don't come in the next ten seconds.'

Yeah, but she was afraid she was going to go *insane*— this was too intense.

She rose above him, escaping his grip, demanding they move forward. She glanced down at the broad, flat expanse of his chest and the ridges of his washboard stomach. He was remarkably fit. And before he could stop her she gripped the base of his erection and slid down on him hard and fast.

His abs went even tighter and she felt his quick-drawn breath, but his expression remained calm.

She smiled because he felt so good. So damn good. And she could make him feel even better. She circled, clenching her muscles at the same time, and watched his reaction—the glistening sheen of sweat, the dilation of his eyes. Yes, now she was back in control.

Sort of.

She moved, increasingly faster, increasingly desperate. She searched for that look—the harsh mask of rigid control that tightened a man's expression just before he lost it completely. But Carter stayed relaxed, gazing up at her, his hands trailing up and down the sides of her body, letting her set the pace while still teasing her so lightly.

But the thing was, she was tiring, every time she slid up and down his shaft she felt more sensitised—every stroke hammered at her control. Just looking at him made her senses swim, so feeling him like this had her dizzy. Her breathing fractured. She was unable to keep the swamping sensations at bay, and her head tipped back, her eyes closing. Every inch of her skin felt raw, and at that vulnerable moment Carter slid his hand to her breast.

She gasped, bending forward in an involuntary movement. He caught the back of her head, fingers tangling in her hair, pulling her further forward to meet him. He kissed her again, deep and erotic, while with his other hand his fingers and thumb still circled her screamingly sensitive nipple.

She groaned into his mouth, mostly wanting him to stop—and yet not. And he didn't. Instead he lifted up closer so his body was in a crunch position, his abs pure steel. He wouldn't free her from his kiss, from his caresses, from the powerful thrusts up into her. Slow, regular, his fingers mirrored the rhythm as they moved to scrape right across the tip of her breast. And she wanted to run, she wanted a break—to slow for a second so she could recover some sense.

But the relentless friction of him against her, inside her and the kisses all combined to bring her to a level of sensation she couldn't escape. Devastating. She groaned again, desperate—alarms were ringing but nerves were singing at the same time.

He nibbled on her lips, upping the pressure from every angle, the hand at her breast sliding down hard against her belly to below—to that point just above where their bodies were joined.

She couldn't think any more now. She couldn't move. Too overwhelmed to be able to do anything but be guided by him and that was too much, too scary. But his hands clutched and controlled. He filled her body and all of her senses—all around her, inside her—holding her more tightly than she'd ever been held. And suddenly she realised—she couldn't fall because he'd caught her so close and sure. She was all safe—and free. In the prison of his embrace, she could be free.

And now the heat was delicious. Delirious with it, she danced in the flames—and had no desire to escape any more. For the escape was right here in this moment as she moved with him. Groaning, she sank deeper into the kiss, her body yielding, letting him in that last bit more—she could do nothing except absorb all of him as he relentlessly drove into her.

She was so hot, so incredibly hot and wild and free. It was as if a river had burst inside—a lava flow of sensation and heated bliss. On and on he pushed her along it—intensifying the heat and ride to a point where the waves of fire rushed upon her. Her eyes opened for a second and she broke the seal of the kiss as her breath, heart and mind stopped. There was no scream, no cry, just a catch of breath as her muscles clamped and then violently convulsed.

She shuddered, releasing hard on him with an incoherent moan, her hands clawing, so out of control. She was intensely vulnerable and yet utterly safe in the cocoon he made for her.

She went lax, totally his to mould. And he did, hauling her closer still, his grip even firmer, both hands across her back, pulling her so from top to toe she was flush against his hot damp skin. He frantically ground up for a few more beats and in her mouth their moans sounded like magic.

Reality was on some other planet and she was protected from the harshness of it because she was floating in a pool of paradise set at the perfect temperature.

She'd never been out of her mind before but all her reason had been totally submerged. Now she kept her eyes closed as she glided on that warm tide of completion. Every muscle in her body had gone on strike anyway. She couldn't talk, couldn't open her eyes, would never move again.

He lay a few inches away alongside her, having eased her onto the sheets a while ago. She didn't know how long—time was something she couldn't hope to figure out.

His fingers loosely clasped her wrist and that small connection was just enough. Anything more would be too much, but it seemed he understood that. It seemed he understood a lot.

But he wasn't gloating, wasn't lying on his back and beating his chest like a victorious he-man. And he had every right to do that if he wanted. She wouldn't even mind if he did, she couldn't, because she was so completely relaxed. Actually, she was absolutely exhausted.

But that was okay, because she didn't want to think, to talk, to see. In this moment, she just wanted to be.

Carter really wanted to pull her close, but he suspected she might be feeling super-sensitive right now and he didn't want to overload her system—or freak her out emotionally. Taking it easy was the only way to go. So he fought the instinct to cradle; instead he watched her quietly, waiting for some sign of life. For her conscious reaction.

He already knew her unconscious one. He had his fingers loose on her wrist. He could feel her pulse tripping every bit as fast as his own.

She couldn't fake that.

Sparks of satisfaction fired in his chest and her sudden smile blew them to full-on flames. Because that smile was full of warmth.

'Wow.' Her voice hardly sounded, but he read her lips.

'Yeah.' He couldn't resist—reached out with his spare hand to stroke her hair.

His arms ached even more to hold her. Usually he hated post-coital cuddles—because usually he was too hot and sweaty. And he was damn hot and sweaty now. But he wanted to hold her, to keep the connection open between them. Having her collapse in his arms like that had filled him with the most pure pleasure of his life. He didn't care about his own orgasm after that—only in that instant it had hit and wiped him out.

But now he watched her eyes as the thoughts trickled back into her brain and she was too tired to hide the vulnerability as they darkened.

'I should go.'

He rolled onto his side, towards her, his muscles complaining at the movement. 'I'm only in town for another week. Don't think you're spending a minute of it alone.'

'You didn't say that earlier.' Her dark eyes darkened even more. 'I don't sleep well in a strange bed.'

'You slept okay with me by the pool last night.'

She had nothing to say to that. So he pressed home a point designed to lighten the scene.

'It'll make it easier to be near you at work knowing I'll have you with me all night.'

'Oh, you're back to that argument, are you?' She gave him the smile he'd been seeking.

'Yeah.' He chuckled. 'You'll just have to lie back and think of the company.'

'But I really should—'

'Have you honestly got the energy to get up, get dressed and get out of here right now?' he asked.

Silence for a second, then a very soft answer. 'No.'

'Then shut up and go to sleep.'

Her smile was drowsy and compliant and he switched off the light while he had the advantage. In the darkness he listened as her breathing regulated. He was shattered himself, but he couldn't stop thinking about the experience he'd just barely survived. Yeah, the most challenging moment of his life. He'd been holding back from firing from the moment he'd seen her naked, let alone finally been buried inside her.

She'd been out to claim him—she'd been all tease,

all sensual siren, twisting him hard to force his release, not hers. Now he knew why she liked the light on. She watched him as they moved—noting his reactions and adjusting her movements accordingly. Thinking too much—and all about him. On the one hand she was working out what he liked, and that was great. But not to the extent that she wasn't getting lost in the moment. She was too focused to be feeling it. Like her work, she was determined to be perfect at it. The best. Most guys would lie back and let her, loving it.

And, oh, he had loved it. She'd driven him insane with want for her. But he'd wanted more than that. He'd wanted her to surrender to the exceptional. He'd wanted her to realise and accept this *was* exceptional. And holding back long enough for her to become overwhelmed by their magic had almost broken him. Now he wanted an hour or so to pass quickly so he could recover even a bit of his energy. Because, although he was utterly drained, he couldn't wait to do it all again.

Asleep by the pool last night, she'd curled into his embrace so easily, as if it were the most natural thing in the world. As if it were home. And honestly, he'd enjoyed it. He'd thought that was because they'd both been cold. But he wasn't cold now and he wanted to sleep like that with her in this big, comfortable bed. So he flicked another switch—the air conditioner—cooling the room enough for them to need a light sheet for cover. And for her to want a warm body to curve into.

CHAPTER EIGHT

YAWNING, Penny opened the fridge, her eyes widening when she clocked the contents. 'I wouldn't have picked you to be so into yoghurt.'

'I'm not.' He reached past her for the milk. 'But you said you like it, only I didn't know which sort so I got one of everything.'

He wasn't kidding. There was an entire shelf crammed full of yoghurt cartons.

'I've got cinnamon and there's a ton of fruit in the bowl,' he added. 'Although I got tinned as well, just in case.'

When had he gotten all that exactly? She'd only told him her breakfast choices yesterday by the pool—he must have gotten them in before getting back to work after they'd finally escaped the place. That was efficient. And it deserved a reward.

She leaned closer to where he stood at the bench. 'What do you like for breakfast?'

He swept his arm around her waist and planted a kiss on her smiling mouth. 'You, sunny side up.'

Yeah, she liked that too. She'd woken swaddled in his arms again and the runny honey, so-relaxed-she-could-hardly-stand feeling was still with her. 'You need something more to sustain you.'

'Toast. Eggs. Fruit. Cereal. Breakfast's a big deal for me, especially on the weekend.' His brows pulled together. 'You know I have to work through.'

'I'd figured that already.' She smiled.

'But I have to have your assistance.' Both hands on her waist now, he hoisted her up to sit on the bench.

'Well, Mason did instruct me to do whatever you needed me to do,' she said, giving him a less than demure look from under her lashes.

'Excellent.' His hands wandered more freely. 'Then you're staying right here.'

It was two hours later that Carter sighed and slid out of the bed they'd tumbled back into. 'Come on, we have to go to the office for a few hours.'

Her cherry lips pouted irresistibly.

'I'll get you a coffee from the café on the way,' he said to sweeten the deal.

But it felt like hours later and Carter was sprawled back on the bed still waiting—fully dressed and ready to go. Penny could shower for all eternity, testing his patience even more than when he had sex with her. But then she made up for it by dressing in front of him. She was super quick then and he wouldn't have minded if she'd taken longer...so he avidly watched her every movement. He'd never have guessed that her perfect appearance would take only minutes to achieve. Her well-practised fingers twisted her hair into a plait. He reached across and undid it—earning a filthy look—but it was worth it to watch her weave it again. She had the most beautiful long neck and shoulders.

He drove the rental car he'd picked up at the airport

and ignored 'til now, detouring to her flat on the way so she could pick up some clothes. He insisted on enough for the week and to his immense satisfaction she didn't argue. He glanced round her shoebox while she expertly packed a small case. He looked at the few tiny knick-knacks she'd gathered on her travels. It seemed everything was small enough to fit into a couple of suitcases. Hell, the whole apartment could fit in a suitcase. It didn't surprise him that she lived alone, but he was disappointed not to discover anything much more about her from her few possessions. An ebook reader lay on the arm of the sofa. His fingers itched to flip it open so he could check out the titles she'd loaded.

After he'd stowed her bag in the boot, they stopped at the café just down from the office. He didn't want to take away, gave the excuse that he didn't want to face all those files again just yet, but really he just wanted to relax and hang with her some more. It was peaceful. They split the papers and he skimmed headlines, glancing at her as she concentrated on the articles that really caught her interest—in the international affairs section mostly. He asked and she talked through the list of places she'd lived in. He refused to believe her so she proved it by telling him who was prime minister or president in every one of those countries. Mind you, she could have made a couple of them up and he wouldn't have known. But she spoke bits of a billion languages and was totally animated when she talked about the highlights of each place.

It was almost another two hours and another coffee before they moved on. He picked up the little paper crane she'd made out of the receipt and pocketed it before she noticed.

In the office he had to force himself to pay attention.

But every few minutes his mind slipped to the sensual. He'd woken her through the night, warming her up again. He'd let her set the pace—initially—forcing his patience to extremes so she got so involved there was no pulling back, getting her used to letting go. She was starting to get a little faster already—turning easily into his arms, trusting him with her body. But not quite enough.

He wanted to please her all kinds of ways. He wanted her to trust him to do anything—and for her to enjoy it. She still tried to give more than she took, which was as wonderful as it was difficult. But he was determined to get her to the point of just lying back and letting him make love to her. Of becoming the pure hedonist he knew she could be.

As he had less than a week, he had to go for the intensive approach. Not that he had a problem with that either. He was having a ball thinking hard about ways to tease her into total submission. The trick was taking his time over the stimulation. Not too much, too soon. And maybe he needed to take her where she was at ease the most—on the dance floor or in the water. He liked the water idea. She spent hours in the shower. Uh-huh, he had some serious shower fantasies going.

Back at his apartment that night he cooked a stir-fry as fast as possible so he could focus on her. They hit a bar and club for a while but before long went home and continued their own dance party. She wouldn't let him put the jazz back on, instead she let him in on her favourite radio station—some Czech thing she listened to over the Internet. He'd never have imagined that having sex with Euro-techno blaring in the background would be such an amazing experience.

* * *

Early Sunday, Penny walked with him down to the craft and produce market that burst into being this time each week in the local primary school grounds.

Carter swung the bag. 'Free-range eggs and fresh strawberries—I'm happy.'

She was happy too, but not for those two reasons.

'There are some amazing markets in Melbourne,' he said. 'You ever been there?'

She shook her head.

'You've been to all these other capitals of culture and not Melbourne?' He looked disapproving.

She hadn't gotten there yet and she wouldn't ever live there now. When this week was over she didn't want to see him again. He would become the perfect memory. That was all this could ever be.

To stop suddenly melancholic thoughts sweeping in, she paid more attention to the products on display— organic honey, bespoke tailoring, spices, sausages, pottery, glass, jewellery... She lingered over them, tasting the samples, touching the smoothness of the craftsmanship.

'Perfect for Nick,' Carter called from a couple of stalls away. He waved a bright-coloured, hand-crafted wooden jigsaw puzzle at her. 'Help him learn his numbers.'

'But he's how old?' she teased, walking over to join him.

'Eight months,' Carter answered, unabashed. 'It's never too soon to start working on numbers. He's got to be groomed to take over the business.'

'Thus speaks the accountant.' Had he been groomed from birth too? 'Look.' She pointed out another puzzle that had six circles, the parts cut like pizzas. 'Get him that and he can get to grips with fractions before he's one.' She held it up as if it was the best invention ever.

'Oh, good idea.' Carter took it off her.

'You're not serious.'

Actually it appeared he was.

She shook her head. 'What about this one—this is much more cool.' Like a globe, a fanciful underwater scene with sharks and whales, seahorse, octopus, glitter and fake pearls.

He screwed up his nose. 'Bit girly, isn't it?' Then he shot her a look and winked. 'Okay, that's three.' He gathered them together and then glanced at her, a sheepish smile softening his face to irresistibly boyish. 'Am I going over the top?'

'No.'

'You're right.' Carter reached into his wallet and handed money to the stallholder. 'He's going to love them.'

Penny couldn't help but wonder what Nick looked like—was he a mini-Carter? Did he have his big brother's amazing multi-coloured eyes? She hoped so. She'd love a baby with big blue-green eyes and a cheeky smile. She'd sit her on her knee and pull faces to make her giggle.

Oh, hell, here she was so swamped by warm fuzzies from all the fabulous sex, she was having fantasies about what their babies would look like. She was pathetic.

She never wanted to have children. And Carter most certainly didn't want any.

What he wanted was a week's fling, nothing more. Nor did she. And that was all this was. Okay, so he'd made her feel everything she'd never before felt. But now she'd learned to let go, she would with other lovers, right?

She closed her eyes against the sudden sting of tears and her uncontrollable spasm of revulsion.

She didn't want another man ever to touch her. She only wanted Carter. And she wanted him again now—already addicted to the highs he gave. She felt so good with him. Except that was all this really was—he was the ultimate good-time guy, filled with fun and sun and laughter. He looked carefree in his casual clothes, his red tee shirt as cheerful as his demeanour.

She didn't want him to be so free and easy. It wasn't fair. She wanted him to want her with the same kind of underlying desperation she felt for him. The desperation she was trying to bury deep and deny.

But she had the compelling urge to push him into a glorious loss of control. Because even though she knew they shared the most amazing sex, it was she who lost it first. He always hung on until she was truly satisfied. And while he was the only lover ever to have been able to do that for her, part of her didn't like it. It made her feel like the weaker link. She knew that didn't really matter—this wasn't going past the one week. She wished she could shatter him just once.

But she was the one falling apart.

She tugged on his hand and turned to face him. 'Kiss me.'

Carter looked at her. He could feel the tremors running under her skin. What had happened in the last sixty seconds to make her so edgy?

'I thought you didn't like lust in public?' he teased to joke a smile out of her.

'Just kiss me,' she said.

And how could any man resist a sultry command like that? Carter pulled hard on her hair so her head tilted back. He kissed down the column of her exposed throat. With his other hand he pushed her pelvis, grinding it into his.

He stepped back pulling her into the shadows behind a row of stalls. Truthfully he didn't do public displays much—and certainly not of unbridled lust like this. But the moment he touched her he was lost. Uncaring about what anyone thought, he just had to hold her closer and let the glory wash through him.

'You are amazing.' Breathing hard and deep, she looked at him, her black eyes shining. Suddenly she smiled. 'You make me feel so good.'

His skin prickled. Okay, that was nice because he did aim to please, but it wasn't just the kissing that made him feel good. Fact was, he felt good every moment he spent with her.

After the market it was back to the office for a long afternoon that Penny struggled through every second of. Baby images kept popping in her head. Cute Carter-as-a-kid imaginings. So stupid.

When they finally returned to his apartment he went fussing in the kitchen, so Penny swam in the pool—needing twenty minutes alone to sort out her head. But a zillion lengths didn't really help so she went back upstairs. Something smelt good and Carter was busy on his computer. She didn't think he even noticed when she walked past on her way to shower. So much for the revitalising benefits of exercise—all she felt was even more tired and emotional. She wanted to fall into his arms again and let him take her to paradise. She wanted him to hold her and never let go.

It was the sex. Her weak woman's body wanted to

wrap around his and absorb his strength. But he was mentally miles away in an office in Melbourne controlling his companies. So she could control merely herself, couldn't she? She flicked on the lights in the big bathroom and twisted the shower on. She stood under the streaming jet and let the water pummel the tension in her shoulders.

'Is it okay if I join you?' His erection pointed to the sky, already condom sheathed.

Her bones dissolved, she leant against the wall, wanting to cling to him and just hang on for the ride. His face lit up, his low laugh rumbled and he flashed a victorious smile.

She closed her eyes because his all-male beauty was too much to witness. But when she opened them again, everything was still black. The room was totally dark.

'Carter?' she asked quickly. 'What happened?'

'Bulb must have blown.' He stepped into the wet space with her.

She slid her palms all over his chest, loving it as the water made him slick. It was like discovering him all over again only by touch this time, not sight. Somehow it seemed more intimate, more intense. He pulled her close and kissed her. Oh, she loved those kisses. She loved the way he twisted her hair into a rope and wound it against his wrist—pulling it back, exposing her throat to his hot mouth. And then he went lower.

She gasped and pressed back against the cool wet tiles as he licked down her torso. His hands cupped her breasts, lifting them first to the water, and then to his tongue. She shuddered, the sensations excruciatingly sublime.

In the velvety darkness all she could do was soak up

his caresses and listen to the falling water. As he gently, rhythmically tugged on each nipple with his lips, her knees gave out. He grasped her waist, easing her to the floor and following, kept doing those, oh, so wickedly delicious things with his tongue and hands.

Blind to everything but sensation, she groaned and his kisses went even lower. She reached, finding his broad shoulders with her hands and sweeping across them, loving the smooth hot skin and the hot water raining on them.

She arched up, unable to stop her response to the wide, wet touches, hardly aware of who she was any more. His hand splayed on her lower back, pushing her closer to his hungry mouth. The other he used to test her, torment her, tease her. Just one finger at first, smoothly entering her slick heat. She gasped, but his tongue kept stroking, and then she was blind to everything except how it felt. She moved uncontrollably, rocking to meet him. Panting, she shuddered as he plunged deeper, and withdrew only to return with more. She was so sensitive to the way he toyed with her, and in the dark, wet heat all she could do was *feel*. Her fingers, thighs, sex pulsed and gripped as all she felt was pure lightning-bright pleasure. The orgasm knifed through her—ripping her to exquisitely satisfied shreds. She totally lost her mind.

His muscles bunched and rippled beneath her clutching hands. Displaying a scary kind of strength, he scooped her up again and flattened her against the wet wall. His hands cupped her, spreading her so he could thrust straight in. She wound her legs around his waist and had no hope of controlling anything. Not her instinctive rhythm, her screams, her next orgasm. Not when he held her and kissed her and claimed her so completely.

The water ran down them as they leaned together, taking for ever for their breath to ease.

'Are you okay?' he finally spoke. 'That wasn't too uncomfortable?'

She mock-punched his arm. 'Carter.'

He started to laugh. And then she laughed too.

'You sure you didn't mind?' His laugh became a groan as he carefully curved his hands around her hips.

How could she mind that? 'Give me half an hour and then do it again, will you?'

'You don't need half an hour.' He swung her into his arms and carried her back to his bed. And made love to every inch of her all over again.

Monday morning she couldn't move. Wouldn't. Point blank refused to let the weekend be over. She screwed her eyes shut when he appeared by the bed dressed in one of his killer suits. 'Don't ask me to get up yet. Please.'

She just wanted to snuggle in the sheets and enjoy absolute physical abandonment. He was perfect. He was playful. He wasn't ever going to ask anything more of her. And now he was fresh from the shower.

All she could let herself think about was this. She buried herself in his sensuality, blinding herself to everything else that was so attractive about him. Ignoring the ways in which they were so compatible.

But the humour she couldn't avoid—not when he brought it into bed with them.

He tugged the sheet from her body; she stretched and squealed with the pleasure-pain of well-worn muscles. She really didn't want to get up yet. But then he unzipped his trousers. Delighted, she scrunched a little deeper into the mattress.

'Oh, my,' she murmured as he straddled her. 'You want me to set a personal record or something?'

'Well, it's like anything—the more practice you have, the better you get.'

'Then hurry up and practise with me.' Oh, she was so into it now—utterly free in the physical play with him.

His brows lifted.

'Come on,' she begged. 'You'll have me hit orgasm just from thinking about it soon.' Just from thinking about *him*.

'You're complaining?'

'No,' she giggled as he nuzzled down her stomach like a playful lion.

Suddenly he stopped and looked up her body into her eyes. 'Seriously, though, you're not too sore?'

She arched, brazenly lifting her hips to him. 'Don't you dare stop!'

Monday sucked. Monday meant other people were in the office—meaning he couldn't go and kiss her freely. So Carter locked himself in his office and ploughed on with the tedious task of hunting for tiny financial irregularities. He didn't move from his desk for hours—just to prove to himself that he could concentrate for that long. Because all he really wanted to do was hang out by Penny's desk and talk to her. He wanted to spend every minute with her, resenting the job he had to do, even though it was because of the job that he'd met her in the first place.

Tuesday sucked just as much—another night had gone and the ones remaining felt too few. Stupid. Because he'd achieved his aim—she was wholly his and he had the rest of the week to indulge and that should totally be enough.

And now he'd just found the needle in the haystack. He carefully pulled it out to inspect it—drawing with it the thread that could unravel the whole company. Once he'd followed the poison all the way to the source, and gathered the documentation, his job was done.

Success all round.

He could go back to his own business, in another city, and get on with it. So he didn't need to feel this rubbish.

Wednesday he was even more grumpy, the evidence was almost complete, but Penny was out and he wanted her to hurry up and get back so they could go to lunch. He went up to her office to see if she was back. There was someone there, but it wasn't Penny. It was her brother.

'Hi, Matt.' Carter held out his hand. 'Penny's not here. She's taken some stuff to Mason. She shouldn't be more than another half-hour.'

'Oh.' The younger man shifted on his feet. 'I can't wait. I have to get to the airport.'

'She'll be sorry she missed you.' Man, her family was awful at communication. This past fortnight he'd been away, Carter and his dad had Skyped a couple of times, and he'd been sent the latest picture of Nick looking cute. There were no excuses in the technology age. But Matt looked so disappointed, Carter felt bad for him. 'I'll walk out with you.' He led him back to the lift. 'Conference was good?'

'Yeah.' Matt smiled but looked distracted.

'You want a taxi called?' Carter blinked as they got out in the broad sunshine.

Matt didn't answer, still looked both disappointed

and distracted. 'You'll take care of her, won't you?' he suddenly said. 'She needs lots of support. She's been cut off for so long.'

Yeah, that was pretty obvious. Carter waited. Because Matt looked as if he had something on his mind he wanted to share. And it didn't look like happy thoughts.

'She hasn't been back home since she went away. Not once. That's seven years.' Matt stared across the street. 'Mum and Dad are desperate for her to. Maybe she'd come with you.'

'I'll talk to her about it.' That and a few other things. Carter wanted to know so much more. Like everything.

'I know I shouldn't have mentioned Isabelle. But I wanted to see what would happen.'

Carter knew he was in murky waters without any floatation device, so he just nodded and waited. Fortunately Matt soon filled the gap.

'I saw you taking care of that.'

Carter faked a small smile. He supposed kissing her was one way of taking care. Pretty basic but it had been effective at the time.

'I didn't think she was ever going to get over Dan and get that close to another guy,' Matt continued. 'When she started mentioning you in emails I couldn't believe it. For a while I thought she might have been making you up. But you're real. And I can see how it is between you.'

Carter's brain processed even faster than its usual warp-factor speed. Dan? Who the hell was Dan? Hadn't they been talking about someone called Isabelle?

'She looks better. She looks fitter than she did when I saw her in Tokyo last year,' Matt added. 'You're obviously good for her.'

Anger flared in Carter's chest. What did it matter if she looked fit? Maybe this was why she didn't want to see her family—were they too obsessed with a perfect image? Who cared if she put on a few extra pounds or didn't swim her lengths so religiously? He sure as hell didn't. He just liked her laughing. So he answered roughly. 'She likes my cooking.'

'After he died she never used to eat with us.' Matt shook his head. 'Those last months it was like she wasn't there. She didn't want to be. She got so skinny you could see every vertebra in her spine. Every rib. Every bloody bone.'

The bottom fell out of Carter's world completely. He couldn't speak at all now. He stared at Matt, replaying the words, reading the tension etched on the younger guy's face.

'But she seems really happy now.' Matt cleared his throat and kept staring hard at some building over the road. 'I want her to stay that way.'

Was that why Matt had looked so pleased to see her eating that chocolate mousse? Because Penny had once been so sad she'd starved herself sick? Tension tightened every muscle. Carter folded his arms across his chest to hide his fists.

'She's not going to move again, is she? She's settled, with you, right?'

Carter's brain was still rushing and he didn't know how he could possibly reply to that.

'Because it's coming up to moving time for her but she's not going to now, right?' Matt turned sharply to look at him.

Carter put his hand on Matt's shoulder—to shut him

up as much as anything. 'Don't worry.' He avoided answering the question directly. 'I'll take care of her.'

'Yeah,' Matt croaked. 'Thanks for caring about her.'

Matt was avoiding his eyes again now and Carter was glad because he wouldn't have been able to hide his total confusion.

'I better get going.'

Carter fumbled in his pocket and pulled out a business card. 'Stay in touch.'

Matt handed him his too. Carter pocketed it and got back into the building as fast as he could. Then he took the stairs—slowly.

Dan. Who the hell was Dan?

Some guy who had died. And Matt hadn't thought Penny would get close to another guy again. Penny, who hadn't been home since...

Seven years ago she'd have been seventeen or eighteen. It didn't take much to work it out. While he'd yet to figure Isabelle's place in the picture, the essentials were obvious.

Dan must have been Penny's first love—and hadn't she once said the first left a real mark? That it was never just sex? Carter felt sick, hated thinking that Penny had suffered something bad.

He'd never felt that kind of heartbreak. He'd been betrayed—but that had meant more burnt pride than a seriously minced-up heart. And since then he hadn't let another woman close enough to inflict any serious damage. But to love someone so deeply and lose them, especially at such a young age? Yeah, that changed people. That really hurt people.

And weirdly, right now, Carter felt hurt she'd held back

that information from him. Which was dumb, because it wasn't as if they'd set out for anything more meaningful than some fun.

But he knew how bereavement could affect people. Hadn't he seen it in his dad? His parents had been soul mates, so happy until the cancer stole his mum away decades too soon. And his father hadn't coped—couldn't bear to be alone—walking from one wrong relationship to the next. Searching, searching, searching for the same bliss. And every time failing because nothing could live up to that ideal.

For the first time he felt a modicum of sympathy for his father's subsequent wives. Imagine always knowing they came in second. They could never compete with that golden memory. But Lucinda was trying, wasn't she? Giving Carter's dad the one thing he'd wanted so badly— more family. And sticking with him now for years longer than Carter had ever thought she would—providing the sense of home and security that had been gone so long. Carter's respect for her proliferated just like that.

Then his attention lurched back to Penny. Questions just kept coming faster and faster, falling over themselves and piling into a heap of confusion in his head. He wanted to know everything. He wanted to understand it all.

But he didn't want to have to ask her—to hear her prevaricate, or dismiss, or, worse, lie. He wanted her to tell him the truth. He wanted her to trust him enough to do that. The hurt feeling in his chest deepened. Somehow he didn't think that was going to happen in a hurry.

He knew it was wrong. But he was a details man and he'd get as many as he could, however he could, because he was low on advantage points. In the office he opened the filing cabinet and pulled her personnel file. Her being a temp, there wasn't much—just a copy of her CV, security clearance and the references from the agency. Brilliant ones. But it was the CV that he focused on. The list of jobs was almost a mile long. And so were the towns. She'd been serious about her travelling. She'd moved at almost exactly the same time each year. Britain, Spain, Czech Republic, Greece, Japan, Australia.

The regularity with which she'd moved made his blood run cold. Never more than a year in the one town. He looked on the front of the file that recorded the date she'd started at Nicholls—seven months already. But she'd worked at another temp job in the city for four months before that. So her year in Sydney was almost up. When that time ticked over would she move to another place? If so, where? There seemed to be no pattern to the destinations. She just moved, running away—from something big.

Had her heart been that broken? His own thudded painfully because there was someone in her past whose death had cut her up so badly. Who'd put her off relationships—so far for life. She acted as if she wanted fun but she could hardly let herself have it—not really. She wasn't the brazen huntress he'd first thought. Not selfish or self-centred. Certainly not any kind of free spirit. She worked conscientiously—and she cared. She was a generous giver who struggled to accept the same when it was offered in return. And hadn't he seen it those few times—the vulnerability and loneliness in her eyes?

She was hiding from something even she couldn't admit to.

He flicked through the CV again and another little fact caught him. She'd been Head Girl at her school? He half laughed. No wonder she'd been interested when he'd mentioned he was Head Boy. And she'd said nothing, secretive wench. He looked closer. Her grades were stellar. Really stellar. He frowned—why hadn't she gone to university? She would have had her pick of colleges and courses with grades like those. But she'd gone overseas as soon as school had finished and she hadn't been back. She must have been devastated. And for all the party-girl, clubbing life she lived now, she obviously still was.

His upset deepened. He hated that she covered up so much. He liked her. He wanted to know she was okay. He wanted to be her friend. He actually wanted *more*.

Well. That was new.

He'd never met a woman who held back her emotions the way she did. Okay, he'd freed her from one aspect of that control. Maybe he could cut her loose from another? Even if he suspected it was going to hurt him to try. Could he bear to know the extent to which she'd loved that guy?

Pathetic as it was, he was jealous. She'd cared so much for Dan she'd been devastated. Carter wanted her to care about him instead.

But how could he ever compete with the perfect first love? He winced even as he thought that thought. He didn't have to. He didn't want her so totally like that— did he? Did he really want to be the one and only, the number one man in her life?

No. Surely not.

But in a scarily short amount of time she'd become important to him. Her happiness had become important to him. And he wanted her to trust him enough to talk. Sure she'd opened up sexually—but it was the only way she'd opened up. And in some ways it was another shield

in itself. Just a fling—it was the defence he'd used for
years himself, even with Penny to begin with. And hadn't
it turned around to bite him now? He'd never been in a
situation so confusing, so complicated. An adulterous
older woman and a manipulative girlfriend seeking an
engagement ring had nothing on Penny and her inability
to share. Hell, she must have such fear.

His anger deepened because he wanted her to be
over it and feel free to fall in love again. Preferably with
him.

In the evening at his apartment she was the same
smiling flirt, teasing him, talking it up—the banter that,
while fun, didn't go deep. He had to bite the inside of
his lips, bursting inside to ask her what had happened.
Desperate to know where her heart was at now. But he
wanted her to offer it, not to have to force it.

She let him lie between her legs, all warm and imp-
ishly malleable, smiling at him delightfully. It wasn't
enough.

He kissed her tenderly. As if she were one of the fragile flowers she said she didn't like.

'Don't.' She frowned and swept her hands across his
back. He knew she was trying to hurry him.

'Don't what?'

'Be so nice.'

He carefully studied her. 'You think you don't deserve
someone being nice to you?'

She just closed her eyes.

And then he didn't even pretend to let her take the
lead. He dominated. Intensely focused on making love
to her. It was about more than just giving her pleasure,
but about bringing her closer to him any way he could.

Afterwards he lay holding her sealed to him, refusing

to let her wriggle even an inch away, telling her more about his work in Melbourne. Stupid stories about his youth. Trying to grow the connection between them. To build trust. Blindly hoping she might talk back.

But all she did was listen.

CHAPTER NINE

CARTER took a taxi to Mason. He had the files; the job was done. In theory, after this meeting, he was free to fly out. But he couldn't bring himself to book a ticket.

The old man had aged more in the last week than he had in the last ten years. Guilt squeezed Carter—he should have been to see him sooner. But Penny had been making daily visits with paperwork and sundry items. Even so.

'I've got the information you need.' He dragged out a smile and put the small packet of printouts on the dining table. 'It's all there. Once spotted, the pattern is pretty obvious.'

'I knew I could rely on you.' Mason sank heavily into his favourite chair.

'Get in your auditors. It won't take much to sort it out.'

'He'll have to be prosecuted.'

'Yes.' Carter nodded. 'But I think the impact will be minimal because we caught him.' He tried to put the best spin on it. 'And quickly too. If anything the investors should be impressed at the efficiency of your system checks.'

'It was instinct, Carter.' Mason shook his head. 'Just a feeling.'

'Well, you've always had good instincts, Mason.'

'And now my instinct is telling me I've failed.'

'In what way?' Surprised, Carter nearly spilt the coffee he was pouring.

'That company is my life.' Mason stared past him to the big painting on the wall. 'And in the current climate it could have been swept away so quickly if this had got out of hand. It makes me wonder what's going to be left after I'm gone. It'll probably be bought out, the name will go. It'll be finished.'

Carter inhaled deeply. Mason had long been his mentor. He'd admired the dedication, the drive, the single-minded chase for success. And there had been huge success. 'You've already built an amazing legacy, Mason.'

Mason lifted his arms. 'What is there? A house? A few paintings that will be auctioned off? Where are the memories? Where's the warmth?'

The unease in Carter's chest grew. Mason's wife had died early on in their marriage—before they'd had time to have kids. And Mason had buried his heart alongside her. As far as Carter was aware there hadn't been another woman—totally unlike his father. Until now Carter had always respected Mason more for that. But now he wasn't so sure—not when he was confronted with Mason's obvious regrets. And loneliness. Another lonely person. 'You've given so much to charity, Mason. You've helped so many people.'

'Who have their own lives and families.' Mason sighed. 'I shouldn't have been such a coward. I should have tried to meet someone else. But I just worked instead.'

'And you've done great work. You've employed lots of people, you helped lots of people.' That was a massive achievement.

But personally fulfilling? Yes and no.

'How's Nick?' Mason asked.

Carter's grin flashed before he even thought. 'He's a little dude.'

'Your father is a braver man than me. I regret not having a family. I regret devoting all my life to accumulating paper.'

'Hey.' Carter leaned forward and put his hand on Mason's arm. 'You have me.'

Mason said nothing for a bit, just stirred the milk in his coffee. Then he set the teaspoon to the side. 'Is everything else at the office okay?'

'Penny has it all under control.'

'Told you she was an angel.'

Carter winced through a deep sip of the burning-hot coffee. 'Yeah.'

A broken angel.

He sat back in his chair and settled in for the afternoon. He'd hang with Mason. He needed the time out to think.

Penny had been desperate for Carter to return from Mason's—he'd gone to hand over what tricks he'd found but he'd been gone for hours and, being a complete Carter addict, she was antsy with unfulfilled need. Resenting the waste of the precious few minutes she had left. Finally he showed up, just as she was about to pack up and go to her own flat and cry.

So she went to his apartment instead. She had no shame, no thought of saying no. They only had a night or two left, and she wanted every possible moment with him. Because she wasn't thinking of anything beyond the present moment. She couldn't let herself.

He was unusually quiet as they walked into the apartment building. Maybe it hadn't gone well.

'Was Mason okay?' She finally broke the silence.

His shoulders jerked dismissively. 'Pleased with getting the result.'

Okay. He didn't just look moody, he sounded it too. Once inside, he tossed the key on the table and turned to look at her.

Wow. She walked over to him—obeying the summons. She tiptoed up and kissed his jaw. Did he want her to take the lead this time?

It seemed so. She kissed him full on the mouth—teasing his lips with her teeth and tongue. His eyes closed and she heard his tortured groan. It thrilled her—maybe this was her chance to make him shatter. Was he tired and needy and impatient? The thought excited her completely because she ached for him to want her so badly he lost all his finesse. Quickly she fought to free him from his clothes. Oh, yes, he wanted her—she could feel the heat burning through him. But his hands lifted and caught hers, stopping her from stroking him.

'Matt called by the office yesterday.' He all but shouted in her ear.

She pulled back to look at him. 'He did?'

'Passing by on his way to the airport.'

'Oh.' She was sorry she'd missed him. She had to do better at staying in touch. She'd text him later.

'We had a little chat.'

'Did you?' Little goose bumps rose on her skin—because Carter's expression had gone scarily stony.

'He said you're looking better than when he saw you in Tokyo. And way better than you did years ago.'

She blanched at the bitter tone in his voice.

'You've put weight on, Penny. Not taken it off.'

'Oh, don't, Carter.' She turned away from him.

'What, speak the truth?' He laughed roughly. 'Penny, what on earth is going on?'

'Nothing.'

'You lied to me. You said you were overweight as a teenager. But you weren't, you were a walking skeleton.'

'Does this really matter?'

'Yes, it does.'

'Why?'

'You've been using me this whole time to get off. To hide from whatever nightmares it is that you have.'

And what was so wrong with that? It wasn't as if he'd been offering anything more. 'I thought the whole point of this was for us to get off.'

'Yeah, well, if it's only orgasms you want, Penny, get yourself a vibrator.'

Oh, that made her mad. She turned back, found him less than an inch away—so ran her hand down his chest.

He jerked back. 'I'm not interested in being your sex toy.'

'Really?' She reached forward and cupped his erection. 'Maybe you'd better tell your penis that.'

'I can control it.' He stepped away. 'If you want to get off, why not go find someone else? Any of those analysts in the office will stand for you. Hell, you could have all of them at once if you want.'

She flinched. She didn't want another lover. None. Ever.

'I'm not interested in being your man whore,' he snarled. 'I actually have more self-respect than that.'

'What are you interested in, then?' she said, stung to anger by his sudden rejection. 'You were the one looking at me like that.'

'Like what?'

'You know what,' she snapped. 'All simmering sex.'

He just laughed—bitterly.

That pissed her off even more. She pushed back into his space. 'You were stripping me with your eyes and you know it.'

'And you were loving it.'

'So what the hell do you want?' Why was he going septic on her when they wanted the same thing?

'I want the *real* thing—if you even know what that is. Because maybe you've been faking all along? You said yourself you usually do. How would I know? You're so damn good at lying and holding back.'

She gaped for a stunned second. 'You think I was faking?' Now she was furious. And really hurt. She'd never felt like that with anyone, never let anyone...not like that.

He filled the room, his arms crossed, watching her with that wide bright gaze that revealed nothing but seemed to be searching through all her internal baggage.

'I *wasn't* faking.' Jerk. As if that kind of reaction happened every other day? She wouldn't have practically moved in with him and be making an idiot of herself lying back and letting him do anything, if she didn't feel as if it were something out of this world. And she wouldn't be so completely miserable about it being the end of the week if she hadn't been more than moved by him—in so many more ways than sexual. And she really didn't want to be getting upset about it this instant. But her eyes were stinging. Angrily she tried to push past him.

But his arms became iron bars that caught and brought her close against his body. 'I know you weren't.' He sighed. 'I'm sorry.'

'What is your problem?' she mumbled, completely confused now.

His hands smoothed down her back. His hardness softened her.

'I want to know where I stand with you,' he said. The gentle words stirred her hair.

'What do you mean?' She tilted her head back to read his expression and swallowed to settle her tense nerves. 'There's nowhere to stand. We're having a fling.'

'Not enough.'

Her heart thudded—beating caution now, rather than anger.

His gaze unwavering, he told her. 'I want more.'

How more? What more? Anything more was impossible. Tomorrow was Friday. They were almost at farewell point.

As his gaze locked hers the safe feeling she'd had all week started to slip. Why was he messing with the boundaries?

'You're leaving here…' Her breathing shortened. 'Like on Saturday. This was just for—'

'Fun,' he finished for her. 'Yeah, roger that. But we can still be friends, can't we?'

Friends? She didn't have that many of those. Plenty of acquaintances. But not very many friends. And what did friends mean—did he want this to go beyond the week? Because she couldn't do that—she had to keep this sealed in its short space of time. She *had* to keep those emotions sealed. She tried to step back but his hands tightened. She broke eye contact. 'I don't think we need to complicate this, Carter.'

'Talking won't make it complicated.'

He wanted to talk? About what?

'Can't you let me into your life just a little bit, Penny?'

'Will you put some clothes back on?' She couldn't think with him like this.

'Why?' he answered coolly. 'I'm not afraid to get naked with you, Penny. I'm willing to bare all.'

'Don't be ridiculous, Carter. This is a one-week fling.' She pushed away from him—and he let her. 'You don't want to talk any more than I do. Why waste that precious time?'

'When we could be rooting like rabbits?'

'You like it that way. It's what you've wanted from me from the moment we met.' She turned on him, hiding her fear with aggression. 'You're not interested in me opening up to you in any way other than physical.'

'Not true.'

'Totally true. As far are you're concerned all women are manipulative, conniving cows who're trying to trap men into marriage.'

'Many of the women I've met are.'

'Well, I'm not like them.'

'And that's one thing we will agree on.'

She blinked. Then shook her head. This conversation was going surreal. Why was her ultimate playboy going serious? 'Trust me, you don't want to get to know anything more about me, Carter.'

'Yes I do.'

Why? What had happened to turn him into Mr Sensitive? She wanted him back as Mr Sophisticated—and never-let-a-woman-stick smooth. 'You know, from the moment we met you thought the worst of me,' she provoked. 'I was a thief, I was "pulling favours" to get a good job...'

He actually coloured. 'I didn't really mean—'

'It must be so hard for you to swallow the fact that your thief is the most conservative *man* in the damn building.'

'Yeah, we both know I was wrong. I leapt to a couple of conclusions. You're nothing like what I first thought.'

She turned away from him. 'What if the truth was worse?'

'How worse?' He sounded surprised.

Way, way worse. But she shook her head and dodged it. 'You're as much of a commitment-phobe as I am. Can't we just have some fun, Carter? We've only got a night or two left.'

So many of the women in Carter's life had been total drama queens—living their lives from one big scene to the next, which they maximised as if they were the stars of their own reality TV shows.

Penny wasn't into big scenes at all, even though it appeared her life had had its share of real drama. She'd pared it down, trying to live as simply as possible—at least in terms of her relationships. Getting by on the bare minimum.

But she couldn't deny all of her needs all the time. She needed to be needed—hence her determination to be indispensable in any job she took on. She needed to care for someone—that came out in the way she tended to Mason. She needed physical contact—that came out in the way she sought Carter's body. But he wanted her to want more from him. More than just sex—even though that had been all he'd offered initially, now he wanted her to want it all. He'd always walked from any woman who wanted too much, so wasn't it ironic that, now he wanted to give it all, the woman in question was determined *not* to want it?

Perfectly happy in the past to provide nothing but pleasure, now he wanted to keep her fridge stocked, to make her salmon and salad, to watch her swim every night. He wanted her company, her quiet smiles, her interesting conversation, her compassion. He wanted his kitchen tinged with the scent of cinnamon. He wanted to travel the world with her, explore it the way she did— immersing in a different culture for a while, exploring the arts and politics and being interested. And damn it, there was even that newfound soft secret part of him that wanted to hold her, and to see her holding a tiny, sweet body. The thought of a baby with black-brown eyes and full cream skin made his arms ache.

He wanted everything with her. And he wanted her to have everything. She needed it and he yearned to give it to her—to make her smiles shadow free. To give her some kind of home. He, who'd been happy for so long in his inner-city apartment, was now thinking about a place with a private tennis court and swimming pool and space to play with her.

But he was in trouble. Because although she'd opened her body to him, he had a lot of work ahead of him to get anywhere near her heart.

Carter wasn't used to wanting things he might not be able to achieve. Carter wasn't used to failure. And the threat of failure made Carter angry.

He'd wanted her to tell him about Dan herself but she wasn't going to. The resulting frustration flared out of control. In desperation he wielded a sword, hoping to pierce through her armour to let whatever it was that festered deep inside her free, so she could heal.

He kissed her—hard, passionate and at great length. She wanted it. He could feel her shaking for it. And she thought she'd won—that she'd shut him up. At that moment he pulled back and hit her with it fast. So she'd be unprepared and unable to hide an honest response.

'I know about Dan.'

Her eyes went huge. Shimmering pits of inky blackness. 'What?'

'I know about Dan,' he repeated and then followed up fast. His need to communicate almost making him stumble. 'I know you loved him. I know how much you loved him. I know your grief literally ate you up.'

'What?' Penny couldn't feel her body, and her thoughts were spinning. What had Carter just said?

'I know how hurt you are.'

'You don't know anything.' She walked out of his arms as a ghost walked through walls. No resistance, not feeling anything. She didn't know who he'd been talking to but it was obvious he hadn't got even half the story.

'You can't let losing him stop you from ever loving

anyone again,' Carter said passionately. 'You can't be lonely like this.'

'I'm not lonely.'

'You're crippled with loneliness. You're screaming for affection but you're too scared to admit it.'

She stared at him, utter horror rising in every cell. This couldn't be happening, he just couldn't be going there. He couldn't be asking her about that.

'Please tell me about it,' he asked. 'Let me help you.'

She couldn't bear to see the concern in his eyes. The compassion. The sincerity. He really didn't know anything.

Sick to her stomach, she turned away, pulling the halves of her blouse back together.

'Damn it, don't hide from me.' His volume upped. 'You promised to be honest with me, remember?'

'You really want honesty?' She swung back, stabbing the question.

He paused, his eyes widening in surprise.

She puffed out angrily. He had no idea he'd just taken the scab off the pus-filled hole in her soul. And spilling the poison would spoil their last days together. But there was no avoiding it, he'd pushed over a line she never let anyone past and one look at him told her he wasn't going to let it go.

'It wasn't grief killing my appetite, it was guilt.' The raw, ugly truth choked and burned her throat. 'I didn't love him. That's the whole point.'

Carter froze. Her breathing sped up even more. She hated him for what he was asking her to do. Thinking on this, remembering, speaking of it… It had been so long but it still crucified her heart. She tried to say it simply, quickly. So then she could go. Because then Carter would want her to.

'Dan was my best friend's twin.'

She could see him processing—quickly.

'Isabelle.'

She nodded and pushed on. 'We were neighbours. Born the same year, grew up together. Like triplets, you know? But when we were sixteen, Dan and I...grew close.' She ran her tongue across dry lips. 'It just happened. It was so easy. We were just kids...'

But there was no excusing what she'd done. She closed her eyes; she didn't want to see Carter's reaction. Her breathing quickened more; she couldn't seem to get enough air into her lungs to stop the spinning.

'Everything changed that last year at school. I changed. Isabelle changed.' Penny shook her head, trying to clear it. 'Dan didn't change—at least, not in the same direction.' She sighed. 'We were together a year or so, but I was bored. I had plans and they were different from his.'

Icy sweat slithered across her skin, her blood beat just as cold.

'He didn't want us to break up. He cried. I hadn't seen him cry in years. And do you know what I did?'

Beneath her closed lids, the tears stung. 'I giggled. I actually laughed at him.'

Looking back, it had been the reaction of a silly young girl taken by surprise by his extreme reaction. She hadn't realised he hadn't seen the end of them coming—that she'd shocked him. But she was the one who hadn't seen the most important signs of all—his distance, his depression, his desperation.

She flashed her eyes open and stared hard at Carter,

pushing through the last bit. 'Our orchard ran between our houses and was lined with these big tall trees.'

Her heart thundered as the memory took over her mind completely. 'He was more upset than I realised. The next morning when I got up I looked out the window. And he…and he…'

She couldn't finish. Couldn't express the horror of the shadow in the half-light that she'd seen from her bedroom. She felt the fear as she'd run down the stairs, the damp of the dew on her bare feet as she'd run, slipping, seeing the ladder lying on the grass.

Carter muttered something. She didn't hear what but all of a sudden his arms were around her as her lungs heaved. And this time she heard his horrible realisation.

'You found him.'

Hanging.

Penny raised her hands, trying to hide from the memory. The scream ripped out from the depths of her pain. She twisted, to run, but his arms tightened even more. His whole body pinned her back and pulled her down to the ground.

Her scream became a wail—a long cry of agony that she'd held for so long. The expression of a pain that never seemed to lessen—that just lay buried for days, weeks, months, years until something lifted the veil and let it out.

And now it reverberated around the room—the anguish piercing through walls, smashing through bones. Until Carter absorbed it, pulling her closer still, pressing her face into his chest. His hands smoothing down her hair and over her back as she sobbed.

She hated it. Hated him for making her say it. Hated remembering. Hated the guilt. Hated Dan for doing it.

Hated herself for not stopping him.

And for not being able to stop her meltdown now. She cried and cried and cried while Carter steadily rocked her. She hadn't been held like this in so, so long. Hadn't let anyone—but she couldn't pull away from him now.

She'd broken.

He bent his head, resting it on hers as he kept swaying them both gently even as her shudders began to ease. He said nothing—something she appreciated because there really was nothing to say. It had happened. It was a part of her. Nothing could make it better.

Nothing could make it go away. It would never be okay.

Finally she stilled. She closed her eyes and drew on the last drops of strength that she knew she had—for she was a survivor.

But in order to survive, she had to be alone.

She pushed out of his arms. She didn't want to look at him, her eyes hurt enough already.

'Talk to me,' he said softly.

'Why?' What was the point? She wiped her cheeks with the back of her hand, shaking her head as she did. 'You didn't sign up for this, Carter. You're going away. You don't want baggage and I come with a tonne. A million tonnes.'

Finally she glanced at him. He looked pale. She wasn't surprised. It was a hell of a lot to dump on anyone. And the last thing Carter wanted was complication—he'd made that more than clear right from the start.

And, yeah, he wasn't looking at her any more. All the pretence had gone. All the play had gone. He'd wanted her naked? Well, now she was stripped bare and what was left wasn't pretty.

Anger filled the void that the agony had drained. Why had he forced it? Why pry where he had no right to pry? This was a one-week fling, supposed to be fun, and he'd wrenched open her most private hell.

And for what? Where was the 'fun' to come from this?

'Penny...'

'Don't.' She didn't want his pity. She didn't want him thinking he had to be super-nice to her now because she had problems in her past.

'I want you to talk to me. I want to help you.'

She wasn't a cot-case who needed kid gloves and sympathy. That was second best to what she really wanted.

'No, you don't,' she struck out. 'You think you're so grown-up and mature with your sophisticated little flings. All so charming and satisfying. But you don't want to handle anything really grown up. You don't want emotional responsibility.'

'Penny—'

'And I don't want anything more from you either.' Her fury mounted, and she lied to cover the gaping hole inside. Her biggest lie ever. Desperately she wanted forgiveness and understanding and someone to love her despite all her mistakes.

For Carter to love her.

But he wanted to be her *friend*. And she couldn't accept that because there was that stupid, desperate part of her that wanted to crawl back in his arms and beg him to hold her, to want her, to love her. She couldn't do that to herself. The end hurt enough already and he'd feel awkward enough about easing away from her now. She had to escape to save him from her humiliation. Tears streamed again so she moved fast. Scrabbling to her feet, she literally sprinted.

'Penny!'

She heard a thud and a curse. But she kept running. Running was the only right answer.

For hours she walked the streets, trying to pull herself together.

Putting the memories back into the box was something she was used to. But putting away her feelings for Carter was harder. They were new and fragile and painful. Yeah, she strode out faster, she was as selfish as she'd been as a teen—wanting only what she wanted. Wanting everything for herself.

But she wasn't going to get it.

Determinedly she thought back over what she'd eaten that day. Not enough. She made herself buy a sandwich from a twenty-four-hour garage. Chewed every bite and swallowed even though it clogged her throat. She grabbed a bottle of juice and washed the lumps of bread down. She wasn't going to get sick again. She wasn't going to let heartbreak destroy her body or her mind. She'd get through this—after all, she'd gotten through worse.

She'd stay strong. She'd rebuild her life. She'd done it before and she'd do it again. Only the thought made her aches deepen. Always alone. She was tired of doing it alone. But she always would be alone—because she didn't deserve anything more.

She didn't deserve someone like Carter. Funny, intelligent, gorgeous Carter who could have any woman on a plate and who frankly liked the smorgasbord approach. Her eyes watered and it hurt because they were still sore from her earlier howling. Pathetic. What she needed was to pull herself together and move on. For there was no way she'd stay any longer in Sydney now. Her skin had been burnt from her body—leaving her raw and bloody and too hurt to bear any salt. And, with the memory of a few days of happiness it would hold for ever, Sydney was all salt.

CHAPTER TEN

CARTER was furious. And desperate. Penny had jumped up so fast, and he'd followed only to trip, having totally forgotten that his damn trousers were still round his ankles. In the three seconds it had taken to yank them back up, she'd vanished.

He went to her flat. She wasn't there.

He went to her work. She wasn't there.

He went to her favourite club. She wasn't there.

He went to every open-late café in the neighbourhood, and the neighbourhoods beyond. And then back to the beginning again.

She still wasn't anywhere.

He searched all damn night. But he couldn't find her. Nor could he think of what to say or do when he did. He was beside himself. So upset for her and mad with his stupidity. Hadn't he always said it—the details, it was always in the details.

He hadn't realised the absolute horror of the detail.

Poor Dan. Poor Penny. Poor everyone in their families.

How did anyone get over that? What could he say that could possibly make it better for her? There was nothing. He felt so useless. Right now he *was* useless.

No wonder she'd been worried about how he'd spoken to Aaron-the-flowers-man. No wonder she skated through life with only the occasional fling with a confident player. She was terrified of intimacy. And he didn't blame her.

And she was right, he hadn't signed up for this. He hated this kind of complication, hadn't ever wanted such soul-eating turmoil. He liked fun, uncomplicated. Not needy.

But it was too late. Way, way too late.

He had too much invested already. Like his whole heart.

And despite the way she constantly uprooted her life, she couldn't stop her real nature and needs emerging. She was the one who knew all about the security guard's family, she was the one running round mothering Mason. She couldn't stop herself caring about people. She couldn't stop forming relationships to some degree. But she couldn't accept anywhere near as well as she could give.

Yet surely, surely in her heart she wanted to. That perfect boyfriend she'd described in her emails wasn't the ideal she thought her family would want, it was her own secret ideal.

Yeah, it was there—all in the details. That was her projecting the innermost fantasy that she was too scared to ever try to make real. Well, he could make her laugh. He'd dine and dance with her and take her away on little trips every weekend. He'd be there for her. Always there. Companionship. Commitment. For ever and happy.

Yeah, maybe there wasn't anything he could *say* to make it better. But there was something he could do. He could offer her security. The emotional security and commitment he'd sworn never to offer anyone. For her possible happiness he'd cross all his boundaries. She needed security more than he needed freedom.

Anyway, he wasn't free any more. He was all hers.

He just had to get her to accept it. As he'd got her to accept taking physical pleasure from him, he'd help her accept the love she deserved.

Somehow. He just didn't know the hell how.

As he drove round and round the streets he rifled through his pockets to find Matt's number. He didn't care about calling New Zealand at such an insane hour. He needed all the details he could get to win this one.

Penny rang Mason's doorbell, so glad he was having another day at home and she didn't have to go into the office. He opened the door and greeted her with a big smile. She tried so hard to return it but knew she failed. Nervously she followed him through to the lounge. But her fast-thumping heart seized when she saw someone was already sitting in there. Someone dishevelled in black jeans and tee with shaggy hair, stubble and hollow, burning eyes.

'Don't mind Carter.' Mason grinned, apparently oblivious to the tortured undercurrents. 'Is that for me?' He nodded at the envelope in her hand.

Penny couldn't take her eyes off Carter, but he had his eyes on the envelope.

She handed it to Mason, amazed she hadn't dropped it. It took only a moment for him to read it. Miserably, guiltily, she waited.

The stark disappointment in Mason's expression was nothing on the barren look of Carter's.

'I'm really sorry, Mason,' she choked out the inadequate apology.

'That's okay, Penny. I'm sure you have your reasons.'

He left the sentence open—not quite a question, but the hint of inquiry was there. She couldn't answer him. She didn't even blush—her blood was frozen.

'Well, you'll stay and have some tea?' Mason asked, now looking concerned.

'I'm sorry,' she said mechanically. 'I really have to go.'

'Right now?' Mason frowned.

'That's okay.' Carter stood, lightly touching Mason's shoulder as he walked past him. 'I'll walk you out, Penny.'

'You don't have to do this, you know,' he launched in as soon as the front door closed behind them. 'I'm leaving later. You can stay and carry on like normal.'

'It's got nothing to do with you,' she lied, devastated to hear he'd made his plans out of there. Even though she knew he would have.

His lips compressed. 'You're happy here, Penny.'

No, she'd been deluding herself. Pretending everything was fine. But he'd come along and ripped away the mirage and shown her just how unfulfilled she really was. It was all a sham.

So she'd go somewhere new and start over. Maybe try to stay there longer, work a little harder on settling. Because now she knew her current way of doing things wasn't really working. It was just a façade.

She knew she'd never forget what had happened between them, but she couldn't stay in Sydney and be faced with a daily reminder of how close she'd been to bliss. 'It's time for me to move on anyway.'

'So you're quitting? You're just going to run away?' Carter's composure started to crack. 'What about Mason? What about the company? You're just going to up and leave him in the lurch?'

'I'm just a temp, Carter.'

'You're not and you know you're not,' he said sharply. 'That old guy in there thinks the world of you. Jed thinks the world of you. All the guys think the world of you. I—' He broke off. 'Damn it, Penny. These people want you in their lives.'

'Give them a week and they'll have moved on.'

'While you'll be stuck in the same hell you've been in the last seven years.' He shook his head. 'You can't let what Dan did ruin the rest of your life.'

She wasn't going to. But she knew what she could and couldn't handle and she couldn't handle the responsibility of close relationships. It scared her too much. And it wasn't just what Dan had done—it was what she'd done.

'It was just as much me, Carter,' she said with painful, angry honesty. 'I was a spoilt, immature bitch who shredded his world. I was horrible to him.'

'He was high, Penny. You know they found drugs in his system. He was struggling with school, with sporting pressure, feeling left behind by your success. He had depression. You didn't know that at the time.'

Oh, he'd got the whole story now. He must have talked to Matt. And even though she knew those things were true, she still felt responsible—certain her actions had been the last straw for Dan's fragile state. 'But I should have known, shouldn't I? If I'd cared. Instead I lost patience. I told him he needed to man up. I was insensitive and selfish.' She admitted it all. 'It was my fault.'

'No.' Carter put heavy hands on her shoulders. 'You didn't kill him. That was a decision he made when he was out of his mind on pot and booze. He was sick.'

'And I should have helped him. Or found someone to help him. I should have told someone about the break-up.'

'There were many factors at play. What happened with you was only one of them.'

If only she'd told someone how badly Dan had reacted. If only she'd told Isabelle that he was really upset and to watch him. But she'd been too selfish to even think of it. She'd gone home feeling free—because he'd become a drain on her. But he'd gone home and decided which way to kill himself.

Even now, her self-centredness horrified her.

'Don't shut everybody out, Penny. Don't let two lives be ruined by one tragic teenage mistake.'

'I'm not shutting everybody out.' She tried to shrug him off. 'I like traveling, Carter. I'm happy.'

'Like hell you are.' His hands tightened.

'I want to go someplace new.' Doggedly she stuck to her line. It was her only option.

He drew breath, seeming to size her up. 'Okay, then I've got an option for you. Move to Melbourne. Move in with me.'

It was good he still had his hands on her—if it weren't for those digging fingertips, she might have fallen over. 'What?'

'Move to Melbourne with me.'

He couldn't possibly be serious. What on earth was he thinking?

'Penny, I've spent the last twelve hours out of my mind with worry for you. I don't want more of that.'

And there was her answer. He wasn't thinking. It was pity and responsibility he was feeling—and exhaustion. Not a real desire to be with her. He didn't love her. She couldn't possibly believe he did.

'I didn't mean to make you worry,' she said quietly. It was the last thing she'd wanted to do to him. That was the problem with her family too. She'd made them worry so much. That was why she tried to email home the breezy-life-is-easy vibe.

Only clearly she'd failed at that because Carter had been talking to Matt. And they'd conspired together to sort her out somehow. But she wasn't going to let compassion trick Carter into thinking he wanted to be with her. That was worse than anything his ex had deliberately tried to manipulate.

'I don't need you to rescue me, Carter,' she said softly.

'That's not what I'm trying to do.'

'Isn't it?'

'I want us to be together.'

'Well—' she took a deep breath '—I don't.'

'I know you're lying.' He leaned close. 'You want me to prove it to you?'

She stepped back. No, she did not want that. She couldn't bear it if he kissed her right now. She'd be ripped apart.

His smile flattened. 'What are you going to do, put us all on your occasional email list and send details of your fictional life?' His anger suddenly blew. 'The minute you feel yourself putting down roots, you wrench yourself away again. It's emotional suicide.'

She struck out—shoving him hard.

How dared he? How *dared* he say that to her?

'It *is*, Penny.' He squared up to her again. 'You're too scared to live a whole life.'

Her only defence was offence. 'And you're living a whole one?'

'I want to. I want you.'

'No, you don't.' He felt some stupid honourable responsibility.

'So you just quit? Is that the lesson you learned from Dan—to give up?'

'Don't.' She took another step back from him. 'Just don't. You can't ever understand what it was like.'

'Maybe not, but I can try—I would if you'd let me. Damn it, Penny, I don't want to just have fun any more. I want to be happy. I want you to be happy. I want everything. And I want it with you.' His words tumbled. 'We could do so much together. We could do great things.'

The urge to ask was irresistible. 'Like what?'

'Like have a family.'

She caught her breath in a quick gasp, blinking rapidly as she shook her head. But he knew, didn't he? He'd seen her flash of longing.

His fleeting smile twisted. 'You just told me you were selfish back then. But don't you think you're being selfish now? Denying not just yourself, but me too?'

'The last thing I need is more guilt, Carter.'

'No, I'm strong, Penny,' he answered roughly. 'You can throw your worst at me and I'll survive. You'll survive too. I know you've found yourself a way to survive. But you're too afraid to live.'

Her eyes burned, her throat burned, her heart burned.

'Are you brave enough to fight for what you really want?' Somehow he'd got right back in front of her, whispering, tempting. So beautiful that she couldn't do anything but stare.

And then her heart tore.

For there was no point to this—what she wanted she didn't deserve. And the person she wanted deserved so much more than what she could give him.

'I don't want to hurt anyone the way I hurt him,' she breathed.

'No, *you* don't want to be hurt. And that's okay. I won't hurt you.' His eyes shone that brilliant green-blue—clearer than a mountain stream. 'I'm offering everything I have. Everything I never wanted to give is yours—you just have to take it.'

'I can't.'

'Why not?'

Because she'd never believe that he really meant this. And he was wrong about how strong she was. She wouldn't survive it when he realised the huge mistake he'd made.

'I just can't.'

Carter stood on the path and watched her walk further and further away. Slowly ripping his heart out with every step. He hadn't meant to lay it all out like that—not when he was angry and she was angry. He knew she'd need time. But she'd blindsided him with the speed of her resignation and intention to run. And her rejection. It hurt. So he'd thrown all his chips down, gambled everything—too much, too soon. And he'd blown it.

CHAPTER ELEVEN

PICK a destination. Any destination. Anywhere had to be better than here.

Penny stared at the departures board but the only place her eyes seemed willing to see was Melbourne.

Melbourne, Melbourne, Melbourne.

She could go to Perth—lots of sun in Perth. But there was art and champion sport in Melbourne. How about Darwin or Alice Springs—maybe a punishing climate was what she deserved. But Melbourne had a superb café culture and fabulous shopping.

She slumped into the nearest seat.

Carter would be flying out there soon. If he hadn't already.

Yeah, that was the draw. Melbourne had Carter.

She really ought to go to the international terminal and go halfway round the globe. Instead she sat in the chair, tears falling. Not sobbing, just steady tears that leaked from her eyes and dribbled down her cheeks and onto her top. People were looking sideways but she didn't care. It was normal for people to cry at airports. Okay, so maybe it wasn't quite so normal to sit for over an hour staring at the destination board with only a small suitcase and not having bought a ticket yet. Not having even chosen where to go, let alone what to do once she got there.

She regretted the decision. But it was the only decision she'd been able to make and it had hurt. So much. There was no going back. She could never go back. She could never have what her heart wanted the most.

But it whispered. It constantly whispered—beating hope.

He'd said she was strong. She wasn't at all. He'd been more right when he'd said she was afraid. That was totally true. She hadn't laid herself on the line. And he had. What if he'd really meant it? Could she honestly live the rest of her life always wondering what if? And even if he hadn't meant it, even if he might change his mind, wasn't it time for her to be honest about her own emotions anyway?

He deserved her honesty. It was the one thing he'd asked from her but she'd lied to him at the most crucial moment and that was so unfair. Even to the last she'd held back. He'd been right. She did torpedo her relationships when people got too close. She was a huge coward.

No more. Even if nothing else happened, she needed to prove to herself that she could be more than that. She needed to express her feelings openly. It was beyond time she faced up to them. To her family. To everything.

Carter had shown her how beautifully her body could work if she let go, maybe his other gift was to help her grow true courage.

She went up to the counter. It took less than three minutes to purchase a ticket. The departure lounge wasn't far. She sat and waited for the boarding call. Beyond that she couldn't think.

Finally the call was made. She reached down to pick

up her pack, about to stand to join the queuing passengers. But right by her pack was a pair of big black boots, topped by black jeans. Someone was standing in front of her.

She looked up at the tall figure with the hair so tousled it stood on end, the creased tee and jeans, the unnaturally bright blue-green eyes.

'I've been sitting in that café over there,' he said. 'Watching, waiting, wanting to know what you were going to do. Where you were going to go. I've had four long blacks. It's been almost two hours.' He sat in the seat next to hers. 'So, where are you going?'

Surely he knew already—they'd just announced the flight. Emotion swelled inside her, becoming so huge she had to let it out. It was bigger than her, and she was only hurting herself more by trying to deny or control it or hide it. She held up the boarding pass for him to read: *Melbourne*.

As he stared at the card the colour washed out of his face, leaving him as pale as he'd been the night before. Then he looked at her again, she stared back. Her eyes filled with tears but she couldn't blink, couldn't break the contact with him. Wordlessly wanting him to know, to believe beyond any doubt just how much he meant to her.

Abruptly he turned, facing the window. The plane waited out on the runway, the luggage carts were driven warp speed by the baggage handlers. And with her fingers she squeezed her ragged tissue into a tighter and tighter ball.

She heard him clear his throat but still he said nothing. Her doubts returned—had she just freaked him out? Was he regretting what he'd said earlier already?

But then he held out his hand. The simple gesture seemed to offer so much. She drew a sharp, shuddering breath and put her hand on his.

He guided her to stand beside him. With his other hand he scooped up the handle of her case, wheeling it behind them—away from the flight queue.

She couldn't really see where they were going, the tears still fell too fast. And she kept her head down, unsure if she could believe this was actually happening or if she'd gone delusional.

'The great thing about airports is that they have hotels very close by.' He sounded raspy. He matched his pace to hers—slow—but kept them moving steadily. 'You need a shower and a rest, Penny. You look beat. And I need...' He stopped and closed his eyes for a moment. Then he took a deep breath and began walking again. 'We'll fly tomorrow.'

They went out of the doors and straight into a taxi.

'How did you find me?' she asked once Carter had instructed the driver.

'Been stalking you all day.' His hand tightened.

'Why did you wait so long?'

His expression twisted. 'I thought you were going to go somewhere else. I sat there and waited. It was torture. Every minute I expected you to just get up and go to the counter and buy a ticket who knew where. But then you did and you went to that departure lounge and I had to see if you were really going to do it.'

'It was the only place I could go.'

He was silent a long moment. 'Why did it take you so long to realise?'

'Because I was scared.'

'Of what?'

'My feelings for you.' Her whisper could hardly be heard. 'Your feelings for me.'

He turned his head sharply, but the taxi stopped, interrupting them. But it took only a few minutes to book into the hotel, another couple to ride the lift and then be in privacy.

She walked into the middle of the room—needing to say her piece before passion overtook her mind. 'I don't want you to feel like you have to rescue me, Carter. I don't want your pity.'

'I have no intention of rescuing you. I want to rescue myself.'

That startled her. 'From what?'

'From a life of meaningless flings.' He shrugged and looked sheepish. 'In fact there wouldn't be any more flings anyway. I don't want to sleep with another woman ever. Only you. So, you see, you have to rescue me from a life of celibacy and terminal boredom.'

'Carter—'

'I'm not the person I was a couple of weeks ago,' he said quickly. 'I believe in you like I've never believed in another woman. I trust you like I've never trusted another woman. You make me want to love and be with just one woman.'

She swallowed. Yeah, she still couldn't quite believe that. 'I'm hardly exciting. I'm not flashy or amazingly talented or anything. I'm just a temp PA.'

He walked nearer. 'You want to know what you are, Penny?' He reached up to tuck her hair behind her ear. 'You're warm, you're funny. You're competitive, you definitely have your ball-breaker moments. Sometimes you're misguided but you're passionate in everything you do. You have such heart. You can't hide it. And I want it.'

But it was still a very scared heart.

'You'll like Melbourne,' he said. 'We can find a house. My apartment is nice but we need more space and our own private pool and a deck big enough to dance on so you can have raves at home.' He winked. 'It takes a couple of weeks to organise the licence but we'll get married as soon as it's possible.'

She shook her head, had to interrupt the fantasy at that point. 'Carter, that's crazy talk. We've only known each other a week.'

'Nearly two,' he corrected.

'Yeah, and I've been on my best behaviour.'

Laughter burst from him—just a brief shout. She gave his shoulder a little push, but inside the fear was resurging. This was happening too fast—he'd changed his mind too fast; he might change it back again just as quick.

'I'm serious. You can't go making a decision like this so quickly. I'm a cow. I get moody. I get itchy feet.'

'Okay.' He gripped her just above the elbows and pulled her close. 'Here's the deal. You move to Melbourne and move in with me. I'm making my claim public and I'm proud to. Give us six months to settle, and then I'm asking you again. I guarantee we'll be even happier by then. There'll be no answer but yes.'

'Six months is still too soon.' It was still lust-fuelled infatuation territory—for him anyway. For her, well, her heart had long been lost to him already.

'It isn't. You know it isn't. You can trust me. There's nothing about you that's going to put me off. I already know you're not perfect, Penny. No one is. But we can both be better people together.'

She couldn't move, too scared to blink in case she was dreaming this. Was she really this close to having everything? Still the shadows in her heart made her doubt.

'Six months to the day, sweetheart,' he said firmly. 'And I'll tell you what else.' His hands firmed up too. 'I'm taking you home. You take my hand and we go to your parents' anniversary party Matt told me about. And you show me that tree. We'll face it together, and maybe we'll plant something under it. A bulb or something so every spring a new flower will grow and then it'll die and then another will grow. You like to leave the flowers to grow, right? But we'll grow too—we'll get on with life together. And maybe in a year or two we'll grow a family together.'

Penny pressed her curled hands to her chest, unable to say anything, unable to blink the searing tears away.

'I know you're scared.' He gently cupped her face. 'But I'll be with you and I won't let you down.'

She pressed her cheek into his palm. 'I don't want to let you down either.'

'You won't. Give us the time. You know this is right. You know how happy we're going to be. We already are. You just have to let it happen.'

'You have the details all worked out.'

'I do.' His gaze dropped for a moment. 'You once promised me honesty. Will you give me it now?'

'Yes.' That was the least she could give him.

He paused, seeming to consider his words. 'Do you really…want me?'

Her eyeballs ached, her temples, her throat and all the way down her middle right to her toes—every cell in her system screamed its agony. 'Oh, yes,' she cried. 'It hurts so much.'

'It doesn't have to hurt, sweetheart.' His arms crushed her tight. 'It doesn't have to.'

He lifted his head so he held her gaze, seeing right into her. And she should have been afraid. For a second the panic swept up in a wave inside her because he saw it all. How deep her longing went. But then he kissed her.

And then, for the first time, his patience left him.

'I need to be with you,' he groaned. 'I need to feel you.'

Now she saw his vulnerability. Saw just how much her leaving would have hurt him. How much he'd been hiding from her—or more that she'd been too blinded by fear to be able to see. How much he wanted her, and wanted to care for her.

He whipped off his top, undid hers too. His hands shook and fumbled to unzip her skirt and slide it off. His breathing roughened, his hands roughened.

So she helped and soon she was naked and he was naked and warming her. He didn't kiss her all over, didn't tease or torment her with his fingers or tongue. He just held her close and kissed her as if there was nothing else on earth he'd ever want to do, as if he needed her more than anything.

She loved the weight of him on her. The way he held her hair hard so he could kiss her. The way he ground his body and soul into her. He moved—all power and passion and pure frantic force. He held—truly, tenderly, tightly held her as he poured his want and need and love as deeply into her as he could. And she clung, feeling the sublime beauty between them, so awed that they could make such magic together. And then there was no room for thought. She was reduced to absolute essence—pure emotion.

'I'm sorry,' he panted. 'I just couldn't hold back.'

She turned towards him and smiled.

He lifted his head slightly from the pillow, his eyebrows shooting up. 'No way.'

She nodded.

'You're not just saying that?'

'I'll never fake it with you. Never have. Never will.' She gazed at him. 'I loved it. I loved feeling how desperate you were to touch me.'

'I've been desperate to touch you since the minute we met.' It wasn't a teasing comment, but honest vulnerability.

She snuggled closer, so content she thought she might burst. And the fantasy he'd painted for her rose in her head.

'You really want children?' she wondered aloud—her heart still stuttered over that step too far into the realm of paradise.

'Can't have Nick acting all spoilt like he's an only child. He needs a nephew or niece to give him a run for it,' he joked. But the next second he went totally sober again. 'I never thought I wanted them. Or marriage. You know that. But it took meeting the one woman who's so right for me to make me realise just how much I do want those things. The problem before was that I hadn't met you. Now I have. So now I know.'

The most incredible feeling of peace descended on Penny—as if he'd soothed every inch of her, inside and out. With utter serenity and certainty, her faith blossomed in the strong man beside her. In herself. In what they already shared and could yet share if she let them.

She shifted position, curling even closer and resting her head on his chest.

'Your heart is beating so fast.' She swept her hand across his skin, feeling the strong thudding beneath. 'Must be all that coffee.'

Carter let out a helpless grunt of laughter. 'No. It's you. All you.'

He slid his hand down her arm, down the slim wrist, until his palm pressed over hers. He bent his fingers and felt her mirror the action, locking their hands together.

'I love you,' she finally whispered. 'I love you so much. I want to live with you at my side.'

'Then that's where I'll be.' Carter trembled. Having never before in his life trembled, he trembled now as he felt her absolute acceptance of him. And of every ounce of love he had to offer.

Their future had just been born.

CHAPTER TWELVE

Five and a half months later.

PENNY sat glued to her laptop, trying to fritter away the last hour before Carter got home. Thank heavens that in New Zealand Matt was still at work and she could instant message him.

Have you asked that cute bookstore girl out for a date yet?

Working up the courage. Concentrate on your own love life.

Working up the courage here too.

Why are you scared? He'll love it. He loves you. He put up with Mum and Dad fawning for an entire week for you. Case proven.

Still scared. OK, excited too. Very excited.

Bordering on TMI.

Ha-ha. Wish it was over already.

'Where are you?'

Penny jumped as Carter called out downstairs. She hadn't even heard the door. A stupidly happy giggle bubbled out, even though her heart started thudding so fast it threatened to dance right out of her chest.

Have to go. He's here.

She slammed her laptop shut and raced down the stairs to meet her so very real man. Nervous as she was, she couldn't stop her smiles, lifting her face to kiss him. He was earlier than she'd asked him to be. But then he always gave her more than she asked for. And she loved him for that.

'So why do you need me home from work so early?'

'An adventure,' she said, her mouth cabin-bread dry. 'I'm driving,' she said. 'You just sit back and enjoy the ride.'

He followed her out to his car. 'A mystery tour?'

'Yes.' She bit her lip but still couldn't stop smiling. It was that or cry with the nerves.

He'd been right, of course, that day in the airport hotel. Everything had got better. They'd visited her parents, she'd gotten to know his dad and his wife and little Nick. They saw Mason regularly and his company had weathered the skimming scandal no problem. Even the sex between them continued to blossom—she'd never have thought that could possibly improve. But it had. She'd fallen in love with Melbourne too. She temped—short-term contracts—refusing to work for Carter, claiming she needed to maintain an element of independence. Something she knew he wasn't entirely happy about. But he had absolutely no cause to worry.

She, on the other hand, was still nervous.

She drove the route she'd been along a million times already. The last fifty times she'd rehearsed this moment in her head. But the reality wasn't anything like she'd imagined. Every cell was so aware and on edge it was as if she had acute vision and hearing and a heart still beating way too fast.

But in a good way. She wanted it to be so good.

It was the very end of winter, so the garden was at its most dormant phase. But still so very beautiful—private, tranquil and spacious. She walked slightly ahead of him, hoping he didn't mind the dropping temperature of the late afternoon. She showed him the lawn, pointed out the pathways and the water features of the by-appointment-only private grounds that had been built by an older couple—wonderfully mad visionaries whom Penny had gotten to know and adore.

'In six months it'll be summer and there'll be so much colour.' She gestured wide around her. 'Flowers every-where.' She turned back to face him. 'I won't need a bouquet because we'll be in the midst of one.'

'A bouquet?' A half-step behind, he didn't take his eyes off her.

'Yes…' She swallowed. 'I wanted to know if…' She took a breath. 'Will you marry me? Here? Then?'

He didn't move.

Nor did she.

It was one of those moments that took for ever but where the anticipation was a painful, heart-stopping pleasure. A moment she'd treasure the rest of her life. Because as she watched, the smile stole into his blue and green and gold eyes. It spread to his mouth. And his whole face filled with that rakish, irresistible charm.

'Yes.'

She simply fell into his wide open arms, struggled to get her own around him so she could hold on tighter than ever, kissing him with every particle of passion she had.

Eons later, she managed another breathless question. 'You don't mind I beat you to it?'

'I like it most when you beat me to it.'

She giggled and pressed her hot face into his neck as she whispered, 'I wanted to ask you. I wanted to offer you everything I have.'

Because he'd already given his all to her and she knew it and she wanted to be an equal match for him.

He tugged her hair so she looked back up at him.

'I'm honoured you asked,' he said, intensely sincere. 'I know what you're saying.'

That she truly believed in him, in them and finally in herself.

'I want you to understand how happy I am.' She smiled softly through a trickling tear.

'I do.' He smiled back. 'And nothing would make me happier than to be your husband. We're a really good team, Penny.'

Her smile spread. 'You do realise this means more time with my parents.'

'More time with my step-mother,' he countered.

'You know she's lovely.'

'Just as you know your parents are lovely. And so is Matt.'

She nodded vigorously and they both laughed.

The difference in her life was so dramatic—full of family, full of fun—real, every day and every night joy. It was because of her anchor—the strongest, most loving man. And the most shameless.

Because now he swept her back into his arms and took control of the situation. 'I'm so glad we've got you over your dislike of public displays.'

But there was no one around to watch him pick her up and carry her out of the chill wind, into the glass building that housed the exotic plants in the cold season. And there, under the bowers of some giant green monstrosity of a plant, they made sweet, perfect, sizzling love.

HER SECRET FLING

BY
SARAH MAYBERRY

Sarah Mayberry is an Australian by birth and a Gypsy by career. At present she's living in Auckland, New Zealand, but that's set to change soon. Next stop, who knows? She loves a good department-store sale, French champagne, shoes and a racy romance novel. And chocolate, naturally.

This one is for all my female friends—the passers of tissues, the sharers of chocolate, the givers of hugs. Having a laugh with my mates is one of the small, perfect pleasures in life.

And, as always, no words would be written if it was not for Chris cheering me on from the sidelines and Wanda coaching me from the finish line. You both rock—thank you for your endless patience.

1

WHATEVER YOU DO, don't throw up.

Poppy Birmingham pressed a hand to her stomach. The truth was, if her breakfast was destined to make a reappearance, that hand was hardly going to make a difference. She let her arm drop. She took a deep breath, then another.

A couple of people frowned at her as they pushed through the double doors leading into the *Melbourne Herald*'s busy newsroom. She was acutely aware that they probably recognized her and were, no doubt, wondering what one of Australia's favorite sporting daughters was doing hovering outside a newspaper office, looking as though she was going to either wet her pants or hurl.

Time to go, Birmingham, the coach in her head said. *You signed up for this. Too late to back out now.*

She squared her shoulders and sucked in one last, deep breath. Then she pushed through the double doors. Immediately she was surrounded by noise and low-level excitement. Phones rang, people tapped away at keyboards or talked into phones or across partitions. Printers whirred and photocopiers flashed. In the background, huge windows showcased the city of Melbourne, shiny and new in the morning sunshine after being washed clean by rain overnight.

A few heads raised as she walked the main aisle, following the directions she'd been given for the sports department. She tried to look as though she belonged, as though she'd been mixing it up with journalists all her life. As though the new pants suit she was wearing didn't feel alien when she was used to Lycra, and the smell of stale air and coffee and hot plastic wasn't strange after years of chlorine and sweat.

The rows of desks seemed to stretch on and on but finally she spotted Leonard Jenkins's bald head bent over a keyboard in a coveted corner office. As editor of the sports section on Melbourne's highest circulating daily newspaper, Leonard was the guy who assigned stories and had final say on edits and headlines. He was also the man who'd approached her six weeks ago and offered her a job as a columnist.

At the time she'd been thrown by the offer. Since she'd been forced into retirement by a shoulder injury four months ago she'd been approached to coach other swimmers, to work with women's groups, to sponsor a charity. A chain of gyms wanted her to be their spokesperson, someone else wanted her to endorse their breakfast cereal. Only Leonard's offer opened the door to new possibilities. For years she'd known nothing but the black line of the swimming pool and the burn of her muscles and her lungs. This was a new beginning.

Hence the urge to toss her cookies. She hadn't felt this nervous since the last time world championships were in Sydney—when she *had* thrown up spectacularly before her first heat.

She stopped in front of Leonard's office and was about to rap on the open door when he lifted his head. In his late fifties, he was paunchy with heavy bags under his eyes and fingers stained yellow from nicotine.

"Ah, Poppy. You found us okay. Great to see you," he said with a smile.

"It's good to be here."

"Why don't I introduce you to the team first up and show you your desk and all that crap," Leonard said. "We've got a department meeting in an hour, so you'll have time to get settled."

"Sounds good," she said, even though her palms were suddenly sweaty. She was hopeless with names. No matter what she did, no matter how hard she tried to concentrate on linking names to faces, they seemed to slip through her mental fingers like soap in the shower.

She wiped her right hand furtively down her trouser leg as Leonard led her to the row of desks immediately outside his office.

"Righteo. This is Johnno, Davo and Hilary," he said. "Racing, golf and basketball."

Which she took to mean were their respective areas of expertise. Johnno was old and pock-faced, Davo was mid-thirties and very tanned, and Hilary was red-haired and in her early thirties, Poppy's age. They all murmured greetings and shook her hand, but she could tell they were keen to get back to their work.

"This mob around here," Leonard said, leading her around the partition, "keep an eye on motor sport. Meet our resident gear heads, Macca and Jonesy."

"All right. Our very own golden girl," Jonesy said. He was in his late twenties and already developing a paunch.

"Bet you get that all the time, huh?" Macca asked. He smiled a little shyly and ran a hand over his thinning blond hair. "Price of winning gold."

"There are worse things to be called," she said with a smile.

Leonard's hand landed in the middle of her back to steer her toward the far corner.

"And last, but not least, our very own Jack Kerouac," he said.

Poppy's palms got sweaty all over again as she saw who he was leading her toward.

Jake Stevens.

Oh, boy.

Her breath got stuck somewhere between her lungs and her mouth as she stared at the back of his dark head.

She didn't need Leonard to tell her that Jake Stevens wrote about football, as well as covering every major sporting event in the world. She'd read his column for years. She'd watched him interview her colleagues but had somehow never crossed paths with him herself. She knew he'd won almost every Australian journalism award at least once. And she'd read his debut novel so many times the spine had cracked on her first copy and she was now onto her second.

He was wonderful—the kind of writer who made it look effortless. The kind of journalist other journalists aspired to be.

Including her, now that she'd joined their ranks.

"Heads up, Jake," Leonard said as they stopped beside the other man's desk.

Not Jakey or some other diminutive, Poppy noted. His desk was bigger, too, taking up twice as much space as those of the other journalists.

Jake Stevens kept them waiting while he finished typing the sentence he was working on. Not long enough to be rude, but enough to make her feel even more self-conscious as she hovered beside Leonard. Finally he swiveled his chair to face them.

"Right. Our new *celebrity columnist*," he said, stressing the last two words. He looked at her with lazy, deep blue eyes and offered her his hand. "Welcome on board."

She slid her hand into his. She'd only ever seen photographs of him before; he was much better looking in real life. The realization only increased her nervousness.

"It's great to meet you, Mr. Stevens," she said. "I'm a big admirer of your work—I've read your book so many times I can practically recite it."

Jake's dark eyebrows rose. "*Mr. Stevens?* Wow, you must *really* admire me."

The back of her neck prickled with embarrassment. She hadn't meant to sound so stiff and formal. Her embarrassment only increased when his gaze dropped to take in her business-like brown suit and sensibly heeled shoes, finally stopping on her leather satchel. She felt like a schoolgirl having her uniform inspected. She had a sudden sense that he knew exactly how uncomfortable she was in her new clothes and her new shoes and how out of place she felt in her new environment.

"I suppose you must have interviewed Poppy at some time, eh, Jake?" Leonard asked.

"No. Never had the pleasure," Jake said.

He didn't sound very disappointed.

Leonard settled his shoulder against the wall. "Big weekend. Great game between Port and the Swans."

"Yeah. Almost makes you look forward to the finals, doesn't it?" Jake said.

The two men forgot about her for a moment as they talked football. Poppy took the opportunity to study the man who'd written one of her favorite novels.

Every time she read *The Coolabah Tree* she looked at the photograph inside the back cover and wondered about the man behind the cool, slightly cocky smile. He'd been younger when the photo had been taken—twenty-eight or so—but his strong, straight nose, intensely blue eyes and dark hair were essentially unchanged. The seven years that had passed were evident only in the fine lines around his mouth and eyes.

The photo had been a head shot yet for some reason she'd

always imagined he was a big, husky man. He wasn't. Tall, yes, with broad shoulders, but his body was lean and rangy— more a long-distance runner's physique than a footballer's. He was wearing jeans and a wrinkled white shirt, and she found herself staring at his thighs, the long, lean muscles outlined by faded denim.

There was a pause in the conversation and she lifted her gaze to find Jake watching her, a sardonic light in his eyes. For the second time that morning she felt embarrassed heat rush into her face.

"Well, Poppy, that's pretty much everyone," Leonard said, pushing off from the wall. "A few odds and bods on assignment, but you'll meet them later. Your desk is over here."

He headed off. She glanced at Jake one last time before following, ready to say something polite and friendly in parting, but he'd already returned to his work.

Well, okay.

She was frowning as Leonard showed her the desk she'd occupy, wedged into a corner between a potted plant and a pillar. It was obviously a make-do location, slightly separate from the rest of the sports team. Pretty basic—white laminate desk, multiline phone, a computer and a bulletin board fixed to the partition in front of her.

"Have a bit of a look-around in the computer, familiarize yourself with everything," Leonard said, checking his watch. "I'll get Mary, our admin assistant, to fill you in on how to file stories and all that hoopla later. Department meeting's in forty minutes—in the big room near the elevators. Any questions?"

Yes. Is it just my imagination, or is Jake Stevens an arrogant smart-ass?

"No, it all looks good," she said.

It was a relief to be left to her own devices for a few minutes. All those new faces and names, the new environment, the—

Who was she kidding? She was relieved to have a chance to pull herself together because Jake Stevens had rattled her with his mocking eyes and his sarcasm. He'd been one of the reasons she took the job in the first place—the chance to work with him, to learn from the best. Out of all her coworkers, he'd been the least friendly. In fact, he'd been a jerk.

Disappointing.

But not the end of the world. So what if he wasn't the intelligent, funny, insightful man she imagined when she read his book and his articles? She'd probably hardly ever see him. And it wasn't as though she could take his behavior personally. He barely knew her, after all. He was probably a jerk with everyone.

Except he wasn't.

Two hours and one department meeting later, Poppy was forced to face the fact that the charming, witty man she'd imagined Jake to be did exist—for everyone except her.

The first half of the meeting had been a work-in-progress update. Everyone had multiple stories to file after the weekend so there was a lot of discussion and banter amongst her new colleagues. She didn't say anything since she had nothing to contribute, just took notes and listened. Jake was a different person as he mixed it up with the other writers. He laughed, he teased, he good-naturedly accepted ribbing when it came his way. He offered great ideas for other people's stories, made astute comments about what their competitors would be covering. He was like the coolest kid in school—everyone wanted him to notice them, and everyone wanted to sit next to him at the back of the bus.

The second half of the meeting consisted of brainstorming future stories and features. With the Pan-Pacific Swimming

Championship trials coming up, there was a lot of discussion around who would qualify. Naturally, everyone turned to her for her opinion—everyone except Jake, that is.

He didn't so much as glance at her as she discussed the form of the current crop of Australian swimmers, many of whom had been her teammates and competitors until recently.

"Hey, this is like having our own secret weapon," Macca said. "I love that stuff about what happens in the change rooms before a race."

"Yeah. We should definitely do something on that when the finals are closer. Sort of a diary-of-a-swimmer kind of thing," Leonard said. "Really get inside their heads."

"There's plenty of stuff we could cover. Superstitions, lucky charms, that kind of thing," she said.

"Yeah, yeah, great," Leonard said.

Her confidence grew. Maybe this wasn't going to be as daunting as she'd first thought. Sure, she was a fish out of water—literally—but everyone seemed nice and she understood sport and the sporting world and the commitment top athletes had to have to get anywhere. She had something to contribute.

Then she glanced at Jake and saw he was sitting back in his chair, doodling on his pad, clearly bored out of his mind. A small smile curved his mouth, as though he was enjoying a private joke.

It was the same whenever she spoke during the meeting— the same smile, the same doodling as though nothing she had to say could possibly be of any interest.

By the time she returned to her desk, she knew she hadn't imagined his attitude during their introduction. Jake Stevens did not like her. For the life of her, she couldn't understand why. They'd never met before. How could he possibly not like her when he didn't even know her?

She'd barely settled in her chair when her cell phone beeped. She checked it and saw Uncle Charlie had sent her a message:

Good luck. Come out strong and you'll win the race.

She smiled, touched that he'd remembered this was her first day. Of course, Uncle Charlie always remembered the important things.

She composed a return message. She'd bought him a cell phone a year ago so they could stay in touch when she was competing internationally, but he'd never been one hundred percent comfortable with the technology. She could imagine how long it had taken him to key in his short message.

The sound of masculine laughter made her lift her head. Jake was talking with Jonesy at the other man's desk, a cup of coffee in hand. She watched as Jake dropped his head back and laughed loudly.

She returned her attention to the phone, but she could still see him out of the corner of her eye. He said something to Jonesy, slapped the other man on the shoulder, then headed to his own desk. Which meant he was about to walk past hers.

She kept her focus on her phone but was acutely conscious of his approach. When he stopped beside her, her belly tightened. Slowly she lifted her head.

He studied her desk, taking in the heavy reference books she'd brought in with her: a thesaurus, a book on grammar and the Macquarie Dictionary in two neat, chunky volumes. After a short silence, he met her eyes.

"You do know that *A* to *K* comes before *L* to *Z*, right?" he asked. He indicated the dictionaries and she saw she'd inadvertently set them next to each other in the wrong order. He leaned across and rearranged them, as though she might not be able to work it out for herself without his help.

"My hot tip for the day," he said, then he moved off, arrogance in every line of his body.

She was blushing ferociously. Her third Jake Stevens–inspired blush for the day. She stared at his back until he reached his desk, unable to believe he'd taken a swipe at her so openly. What an asshole.

He thought she was a stupid jock. That was why he'd been so dismissive when he met her and why he hadn't listened to a word she'd said in the meeting. He thought she was a dumb hunk of muscle with an instinct for swimming and nothing to offer on dry land. Certainly nothing to offer in a newsroom.

She knew his opinion shouldn't matter. It probably wouldn't, either, if it didn't speak to her deepest fears about this new direction she'd chosen.

She'd finished high school, but only just. She read a lot, but she wasn't exactly known for her e-mails and letters. For the bulk of her life, she'd measured her success in body lengths and split seconds, not in column inches and words. Even her parents had been astonished when she accepted this job. She could still remember the bemused looks her mother and father had exchanged when she'd told them. Her brother had laughed outright, thinking she was joking.

She picked up her phone again and stared at her uncle's text:

Come out strong and you'll win the race.

God, how she wished it was as easy as that.

She was filled with a sudden longing for the smell of chlorine and the humid warmth of the pool. She knew who she was there, what she was. On dry land, she was still very much a work in progress.

Who cares what he thinks? He doesn't know you, he knows nothing about you. Screw him.

Poppy straightened in her chair. She reached out and deliberately put the *L* to *Z* back where it had been before Jake Stevens gave her his *hot tip for the day.*

She'd beaten some of the toughest athletes in the world. She'd conquered her own nerves and squeezed the ultimate performance from her body. She'd stood on a podium in front of hundreds of thousands of people and held a gold medal high.

One man's opinion didn't mean dick. She was smart, she was resourceful. She could do this job.

JAKE PULLED THE CORK from a bottle of South Australian shiraz and poured himself a glass. He took the bottle with him as he moved from the kitchen into the living room of his South Yarra apartment.

Vintage R.E.M. blasted from his stereo as he dropped onto the couch. His thoughts drifted over the day as he stared out the bay window to the river below. He frowned.

Poppy Birmingham.

He still couldn't believe the stupid pride on Leonard's face as he'd introduced her. As if she was his own private dancing bear. As if he expected Jake to break into applause because a woman who had never put pen to paper in her life had scored the kind of job it took dedicated journalists years to achieve.

He made a rude noise as he thought about the brand-new reference books she'd lined up on her desk. Not a wrinkle on the spine of any of them. What a joke.

He took another mouthful of wine as his gaze drifted to his own desk, tucked into the corner near the window.

He should really fire up his computer and try to get some words down.

He smiled a little grimly. Who was he kidding? He wasn't going to do any writing tonight, just as he hadn't done any real writing for the past few years. It wasn't as though his publisher was breathing down his neck, after all. They'd stopped doing that about five years ago, two years after his first novel had made the bestseller lists, won literary prizes and turned him into a wunderkind of the Australian literary scene.

He'd missed so many deadlines since then, they'd stopped hassling him. Now the only time he was asked when his next book was due out was when he met people for the first time—mostly because they assumed he'd written second, third, fourth books that they simply hadn't heard about. After all, what writer with any ambition to be a novelist wrote only one book and never completed another?

Ladies and gentlemen, I give you Jake Stevens.

He offered a mock bow to his apartment and poured himself another glass of wine.

Like a needle in the groove of a record, his thoughts circled to Poppy Birmingham. He'd never interviewed her, but he'd interviewed plenty like her. He knew without asking that she'd discovered a love of swimming at an early age, been talent scouted by someone-or-other, then spent the next twenty years churning up various pools.

She'd sacrificed school, boyfriends, family, whatever, to be the best. She was disciplined. She was driven. Yada yada. She could probably crack walnuts with her superbly toned thighs and outrun, outswim and out-anything-else him that she chose to do.

She was a professional athlete—and she had no place on a newspaper. Call him old-fashioned, but that was how he felt.

He leaned back on the couch, legs straight in front of him,

feet crossed at the ankle. His stereo stacker switched from REM to U2—the good angry old stuff, not the new soft and happy pop they'd been serving up the last decade.

He swirled the wine around in his glass, shaking his head as he remembered Poppy's brown suit and how wrong she'd looked in it—like a kid playing dress up. No. Like a transvestite, a man shoehorning himself into women's clothing.

Honesty immediately forced him to retract the thought. He might not approve of her hiring, but there was nothing remotely masculine about Poppy. She was tall, true, with swimmer's shoulders. But she was a woman, no doubt about it. The breasts and hips curving her suit had been a dead giveaway there. And she had a woman's face—small nose, big gray eyes, cheekbones. Her mouth was a trifle on the large size for true beauty, but her full lips more than made up for that. And even though she kept her blond hair cropped short, she didn't look even remotely butch.

He took another mouthful of wine. Just because his new "colleague" was easy on the eyes didn't make what Leonard had done any more acceptable. A smile curved his mouth as a thought occurred—if Poppy was anywhere near as inexperienced a writer as he imagined, Leonard was going to have his hands full knocking her columns into shape. It felt like a fitting punishment for a bad decision.

JAKE WALKED TO WORK the next morning, following the bike path that ran alongside the Yarra River all the way into the city. A rowing team sculled past. He watched his breath mist in the air and kept his thoughts on the interview he wanted to score today and not the words he hadn't written last night.

He was the first one in, as usual. He shrugged out of his

coat, hung it and his scarf across the back of his chair then headed for the kitchen to fire up the coffee machine.

Someone had beaten him to it. Poppy Birmingham stood at the counter, spooning sugar into a mug. He counted four teaspoons before she began to stir. That was some sweet tooth.

She glanced over her shoulder as he reached for the coffee carafe, obviously having heard him approach.

"Good—" Her mouth pressed into a thin line when she saw it was him and the rest of her greeting went unsaid. Her dark gray eyes gave him a dismissive once-over. Then she turned back to her sickly sweet coffee.

She was pissed with him because of his gibe about the dictionary yesterday. Probably couldn't conceive of a world where athletic ability didn't open every door. Because he was a contrary bastard, he couldn't resist giving her another prod.

"Bad for you, you know," he said.

She glanced at him and he gestured toward her coffee.

"All that sugar. Bad for you."

"Maybe. But I'll take sweet over bitter any day," she said. She picked up her mug and exited.

He cocked his head to one side. Not a bad comeback—for a jock.

He picked up his own mug and followed her. He couldn't help noting the firm bounce of her ass as she walked. Probably she could crack walnuts with that, too. He wondered idly what she looked like naked. Most swimmers didn't have a lot happening up top, but she clearly had a great ass and great legs.

She sat at her desk. He glanced over her shoulder as he passed. She'd started writing her debut article already. He read the opening line and mentally corrected two grammatical errors. As he'd suspected last night, Leonard was going to have his work cut out for him editing her work into something publishable. Thank God it wasn't Jake's problem.

Then Leonard stopped by his desk midmorning and changed all that.

"No way," Jake said the moment he heard what his boss wanted. "I'm not babysitting the mermaid."

Leonard frowned. "It's not babysitting, it's mentoring. She needs a guiding hand on the tiller for a few weeks while she finds her feet, and you're our best writer."

Jake rubbed his forehead. "Thanks for the compliment. The answer is still no."

"Why not?" Leonard asked bluntly.

Jake looked at the other man assessingly. Then he shrugged. What the hell. What was the worst thing that could happen if he told his boss how he really felt?

"Because Poppy Birmingham doesn't deserve to be here," he said.

He wasn't sure what it was—his raising his voice, a freak flat spot in the background noise, some weird accident of office acoustics—but his words carried a long way. Davo and Macca looked over from where they were talking near the photocopier, Hilary smirked and Mary looked shocked.

At her desk, Poppy's head came up. She swiveled and looked him dead in the eye. For a long moment it felt as though the world held its breath. Then she stood and started walking toward him.

For the first time he understood why the press had once dubbed her the Aussie Amazon—she looked pretty damn impressive striding toward him with a martial light in her eye.

He crossed his arms over his chest and settled back in his chair.

Bring it on. He'd never been afraid of a bit of truth telling.

2

POPPY HAD PROMISED HERSELF she'd speak up if he did something provocative again. She figured broadcasting his antipathy to all and sundry more than qualified.

Leonard looked as though he'd swallowed a frog. Jake simply watched her, his arms crossed over his chest, his expression unreadable.

She offered Leonard a tight smile. "Would you mind if I had a private word with Mr. Stevens?"

Her new boss eyed her uncertainly. His gaze slid to Jake then to her. She widened her smile.

"I promise not to leave any bruises," she said.

Leonard shrugged. "What the hey? Tear him a new one. Save me doing it."

He headed to his office and Poppy turned to face Jake. His mouth was quirked into the irritating almost smile that he'd worn every time she spoke during their meeting yesterday. She wanted to slap it off his face. She couldn't believe that she'd once thought he was good-looking.

"What's your problem?" she asked.

"I don't have a problem."

"Bullshit. You've been taking shots at me since I arrived. I want to know why."

He looked bored. "Sure you do."

"What's that supposed to mean?"

"You don't want to hear what I really think. You want me to be awed by your career and treat you like the department mascot like everyone else," he said.

She sucked in a breath, stung. "That's the last thing I want."

"Well, baby, you sure took the wrong job." He turned away from her, his hands returning to his keyboard. Clearly he thought their conversation was over.

"I'm still waiting to hear what you really think," she said. She crossed her arms over her chest. She figured that way he might not notice how much she was shaking. She didn't think she'd ever been more angry in her life.

He swiveled to face her. "Let me put it this way—how would you feel if your ex-coach suddenly announced I'd be leading the swim team into the next world championships because he liked a couple of articles I'd written?"

"You think I got this job under false pretenses."

"Got a journalism degree?" he asked.

"No."

"Done an internship?"

"You know I haven't."

"Then, yes, I think you didn't earn this job."

She blinked. He spread his hands wide.

"You asked," he said.

"Actually, you offered—to the whole office."

"If you think some of them haven't thought the same thing…" He shrugged.

She glanced at the other journalists who were all eavesdropping shamelessly. Was it possible some of them shared Jake's opinion?

"Leonard came knocking on my door, not the other way around." She sounded defensive, but she couldn't help it.

"You accepted the offer," he said. "You could have said no."

"So I'm not allowed to have a career outside of swimming?" she asked.

"Sure you are. You're even allowed to have this career, since we all know the Australian public is so in love with its sporting heroes they'll probably eat up anything you write with a spoon, even if you can't string two words together. Just don't expect me to like it," he said. "I worked long hours on tin-pot newspapers across the country to get where I am. So has everyone else on this team. I'm not going to give Leonard a standing ovation for valuing my skills so lightly he's slotted a high school graduate into a leading commentator's role just because she looks good in Lycra and happens to swim a mean hundred-meter freestyle. Never going to happen."

Poppy stared at him. He stared back, no longer bored or cool.

"You might have come to this job by working your way through the ranks, but I've earned my chance, too." She hated that her voice quavered, but she wasn't about to retreat. "I'm not going to apologize for the fact that I have a public profile. I've represented this country. I've swum knowing that I'm holding other people's dreams in my hands, not just my own. You don't know what that's like, the kind of pressure that comes with it. And while you're on your high horse judging me, you might want to think about the fact that you wouldn't even have a job if it wasn't for people like me sweating it out every day, daring to dream and daring to try to make those dreams a reality. You'd just be a commentator with nothing to say."

She turned her back on him and walked away.

The other journalists were suddenly very busy, tapping away at their keyboards or shuffling through their papers. She sat at her desk and stared hard at her computer screen, hoping it looked as though she was reading, when in fact, she was trying very, very hard not to cry.

Not because she was upset but because she was *furious*. Her tear ducts always wanted to get involved when she got angry, but she would rather staple something to her forehead than give Jake the Snake the satisfaction of seeing her cry.

Ten minutes later, Macca approached.

"I was just in, speaking to Leonard. I'm going to work with you on your first few articles, until you find your feet," he said.

She stared at him, chin high. "What did he bribe you with?"

"Actually, I volunteered."

She blinked.

"What can I say? I've always had a thing for water sports."

She gave him a doubtful look.

"And I think Jake was out of line," he added. "So what if you haven't earned your stripes in the trenches? Welcome to the real world, pal. People get lucky breaks all the time for a bunch of different reasons. And even if he disagrees with Leonard's decision, being an asshole to you is not the way to deal with it."

"Hear, hear," she said under her breath.

He smiled at her. "So, we cool? You want to show me what you've got so far?"

"Thank you." She was more grateful for his offer—and support—than she cared to admit.

He pulled up a chair beside her. She shifted the computer screen so he could read her article more easily and sat in tense, twitchy silence while he did so. She'd spent a lot of time working on it—all of last night and most of this morning. She knew it wasn't great, but she hoped it was passable.

"Hey, this is pretty good," he said.

She tried not to show how much his opinion meant to her.

She'd already been nervous enough before The Snake had aired his feelings. Now she knew all eyes would be on her maiden effort.

"You can be honest. I'd rather know what's wrong so I can fix it than have you worry about my feelings," she said.

"Relax. Ask anyone, I'm a hard bastard. Open beer bottles with my teeth and everything," Macca said. "If this was utter crap, I'd tell you. I think we can work on a few things, make some of the language less formal and stiff, but otherwise there's not much that needs doing."

Poppy sank back in her seat and let her breath out slowly.

"And if you're free for lunch, I'll give you the lowdown on the office politics," Macca said.

She smiled. Maybe there was an upside to being savaged by an arrogant, know-it-all smart-ass after all—she'd just made her first new friend at the *Herald*.

THAT NIGHT POPPY HAD her second Factual Writing for the Media class at night school. She'd enrolled when Leonard had offered her the job. So far, she'd learned enough to know she had a lot to learn. But that was why she was there, after all.

There was a message from Uncle Charlie when she finally got home. She phoned him on his cell, knowing he'd be up till all hours since he was a notorious insomniac.

"Hey there, Poppy darlin'," he said when he picked up the phone. "I've been waiting for you to call and fill me in on your first day at work."

"Sorry. To be honest, it was a little sucky, and day two was both worse and better. I was kind of holding off on calling until I had something nice to report."

She filled him in on Jake and their argument and the way Macca had come to her aid.

"Bet this Jake idiot didn't know who he was taking on when he took on you," Uncle Charlie said.

She laughed ruefully. "I don't know. I don't think he was exactly cowed by my eloquence. It makes swimming look pretty tame, doesn't it, even with all the egos and rivalries?" she said a little wistfully.

"Missing it, Poppy girl?"

She swung her feet up onto the arm of her couch.

"I miss knowing what I'm good at," she said quietly, thinking over her day at work and how lost she'd felt in class tonight.

"You're good at lots of things."

"Oh, I know—eating, sleeping…"

"You forgot showering and breathing."

They both laughed.

"Just remember you're a champion." He was suddenly very serious. "The best of the best. Don't let some jumped-up pen pusher bring you down. You can do anything you put your mind to."

Uncle Charlie was her biggest fan, her greatest supporter, the only member of her family who'd watched every one of her races, cheered her wins and commiserated her losses.

"You still haven't told me what you want for your birthday," she said.

He turned seventy in a few weeks' time. She already had his present, but asking him what he wanted had become a bit of a ritual for the two of them.

"A pocketful of stardust," he said. "And one of them fancy new left-handed hammers."

She smiled. He had a different answer every time, the old bugger.

"Careful what you wish for."

"Just seeing you will make my day."

She couldn't wait to see his face when she gave him her present. She'd had her first gold medal mounted in a frame alongside a photograph of the two of them at the pool when she was six years old. It was her favorite shot of the two of them. He was in the water beside her, his face attentive and gentle as he guided her arms. She was looking up at him, laughing, trusting him to show her how to get it right.

He always had, too. He'd never let her down, not once.

"Love you, Uncle Charlie," she said.

"Poppy girl, don't go getting all sentimental on me. Nothing more pitiful than an old man sooking into the phone," he said gruffly.

They talked a little longer before she ended the call. She lay on the couch for a few minutes afterward, reviewing the day again.

She was proud of herself for standing her ground against Jake Stevens, but she wished she hadn't had to. The only place she'd ever been aggressive was in the pool. She couldn't remember the last time she'd had a stand-up argument with someone.

Just goes to show, you've led a sheltered life.

She stood and walked to her bedroom. She was pulling her shirt off when she caught sight of a familiar orange book cover on the bookcase beside her bed. The name Jake Stevens spanned the spine in thick black print.

"Uh-uh, not in my bedroom, buddy," she said. She picked up *The Coolabah Tree* with her thumb and forefinger and marched to the kitchen. She dumped the book in the trash can and brushed her hands together theatrically.

"Ha!"

She'd barely gone three paces before her conscience made her swing around. Before she'd met Jake, *The Coolabah Tree* had been one of her favorite books. His being a jerk didn't change any of that.

She fished out the book and walked into her living room. She looked around. Where to put it so it wouldn't bug the hell out of her?

She laughed loudly as an idea hit her. She crossed to the bathroom and put the book amongst the spare toilet-paper rolls she stored in a basket in the corner near her loo.

She was still smiling when she climbed into bed.

"ANYONE WANT A COFFEE?" Poppy asked.

Jake didn't bother looking up from his laptop. There was no way she would bring him a coffee, even if he was stupid enough to ask for one. The three weeks she'd been at the *Herald* hadn't changed a thing between them.

"I'm cool," Davo said.

"White for me," Hilary said.

Jake glanced over his shoulder as Poppy moved to the back of the press box. The room was buzzing with conversation and suppressed excitement. In ten minutes, the Brisbane Lions and the Hawthorn Hawks would duke it out for the Australian Football League Premiership.

Jake still couldn't believe that Leonard had assigned the newest, greenest writer on the staff to cover the AFL Grand Final. It was the biggest event in the Australian sporting calendar, bar none. Even The Melbourne Cup didn't come close. The *Herald* would dedicate over six pages to the game tomorrow—and Poppy hadn't even clocked a month with the paper and had only a handful of columns under her belt.

Granted, her articles had been a pleasant surprise. Warm, funny, smart. She needed to loosen up a little, relax into the role. Stop trying so hard. But in general the stories hadn't been the disaster he'd been anticipating. Which still didn't make her qualified to be here.

They'd flown into Brisbane two days ago to cover the teams' last training sessions and interview players before the big event, and he'd been keeping an eye on her. What he'd seen confirmed she was a rookie in every sense of the word. She interviewed players from a list of questions she'd prepared earlier, reading them off the page. She studiously wrote down every word they said. She was earnest, eager, diligent— and way out of her depth. Yesterday, Coach Dickens had brushed her off when she tried to ask him about an injured player. She'd been unable to hide her surprise and hurt at the man's rude rebuff.

Better toughen up, baby, Jake thought as he watched her wait patiently in the catering line for her chance at the coffee urn. Most journalists would eat their own young for a good story. As for common courtesies such as waiting in line…

As if to demonstrate his point, Michael Hague from the *Age* sauntered up to the line and slipped in ahead of her, chatting to a colleague already there as though the guy had been saving him a place. Poppy frowned but didn't say anything.

Jake shook his head. She was too nice. Too squeaky clean from all that swimming and wholesome food and exercise. Even if she developed the goods writingwise, she simply didn't have the killer instinct a journalist required to get the job done.

He was turning to his computer when she stepped out of line. Hague had just finished filling a cup with coffee and Poppy reached out and calmly took it from his hand. She flashed him a big smile and said something. Jake couldn't hear what it was, but he guessed she was thanking him for helping her out. Then she calmly filled a second cup for Hilary.

Jake laughed. He couldn't help it. The look on Hague's

face was priceless. Poppy made her way to their corner, her hard-won coffees in hand. Her gaze found his across the crowded box and he grinned at her and she smiled. Then the light in her eyes died and her mouth thinned into a straight, tight line.

Right. For a second there he'd almost forgotten.

He faced his computer.

He was on her shit list. Which was only fair, since she'd been on his ever since he'd learned about her appointment.

He shook the moment off and focused his attention on the field. The Lions and the Hawks had run through their banners and were lined up at the center of the ground. The Australian anthem began to play, the forty-thousand-strong crowd taking up the tune. The buzz of conversation in the press box didn't falter, journalists in general being a pack of unpatriotic heathens. On a hunch Jake glanced over his shoulder. As he'd suspected, Poppy's gaze was fixed on the field and her lips were moving subtly as she mouthed the words to the anthem.

It struck him that of all the journalists here, she was the only one who could even come close to understanding how the thirty-six players below were feeling right now. He had a sudden urge to lean across and ask her, to try and capture the immediate honesty of the moment.

He didn't. Even if she deigned to answer him, just asking the question indicated that he was softening his stance regarding her appointment. Which he wasn't.

The song finished and the crowd roared its excited approval as the two teams began to spread out across the field. Jake tensed, adrenaline quickening his blood. He loved the tribalism of football, the feats of reckless courage, the passion in the stands. It was impossible to watch and not be affected by it. Even after hundreds of kickoffs over many years, he still got excited at each and every game. The day he didn't was the day he would retire, absolutely.

The starting siren echoed and the umpire held the ball high and then bounced it hard into the center of the field. The ruckmen from both teams soared into the air, striving for possession of the ball.

Jake leaned forward, all his attention on the game. Behind him he heard the tap-tap of fingers on a keyboard. He didn't need to look to know it was Poppy. What in hell she had to write about after just ten seconds of play, he had no idea. Forcing his awareness of her out of his mind, he concentrated on the game.

POPPY CHECKED HER WATCH as she stepped into the hotel elevator and punched the button for her floor. By now, most of the players would be drunk or well on their way to it, and probably half of the press corps, too. She'd been too tired to take Macca up on his invitation to join him, Hilary and Jake for a postcoverage drink. Even if she hadn't been hours away from being ready to file her story by the time the others were packing up to go, she'd had enough of The Snake over the past few days to last a lifetime. She wasn't about to subject herself to his irritating presence over a meal. Not for love or money.

She scrubbed her face with her hands as the floor indicator climbed higher. She was officially exhausted. The lead-up to the game, the game itself, the challenging atmosphere of the press box, the awareness that she was part of a team and she needed to deliver—all of it had taken its toll on her over the past couple of days and she felt as though she'd staggered over the finish line of a marathon.

She was painfully aware that she'd been the last of the team to file her stories every day so far. She'd sweated over her introductions, agonized over what quotes to use, fretted over her sign-offs. Writing didn't come naturally to her, and she was beginning to suspect it was something she would always have to work at. No wonder her shoulders felt as though they were carved from marble at the end of each day.

She toed off her shoes as she entered her hotel room. She'd given up on high heels after the first week in her new job. Not only did they make her taller than most men, she couldn't walk in them worth a damn and they made her feet ache. She shed her navy tailored trousers and matching jacket, then her white shirt. Her underwear followed and she made her way to the bathroom and started the shower up. She felt ten different kinds of greasy after a day of being jostled by pushy journalists and fervent football fans and hovering over her laptop, sweating over every word and punctuation mark. She tested the water with her hand and rolled her eyes when it was still cold. Stupid hotel. No one had warned her that the *Herald* were a pack of tightwads when it came to travel expenses. It was like being on the national swim team again.

She glanced at her reflection while she waited for the water to warm. As always, the sight of her new, improved bustline made her frown. She'd never had boobs. Years of training had keep her lean and flat. But now that she'd stopped the weights and the strenuous training sessions and relaxed her strict diet, nature had reasserted itself with a vengeance over the past few months.

She slid her hands onto her breasts, feeling their smooth roundness, lifting them a little, studying the effect in the mirror. She shook her head and let her hands drop to her sides. It was too weird. She wasn't used to them. Kept brushing against things and people. And she'd had to throw out half her

wardrobe. Then there was the attention from men. She didn't
think she'd ever get used to that. Never in her life had she had
so many conversations without eye contact. She'd quickly
learned not to take her jacket off if she wanted to be taken seriously. Which meant she wore it pretty much all the time.

The water was warm at last and she stepped beneath the
spray. Ten minutes later, she toweled herself off and went in
search of food. The room service menu was uninspired. What
she really felt like eating was chocolate chip ice cream and a
packet of salty, crunchy potato chips. She eyed the minibar
for a few seconds, but couldn't bring herself to pay five times
the price for something that was readily available in the con-
venience store two doors down from the hotel.

She pulled on sweatpants and a tank top, decided against
a bra since she was making just a quick pig-out run, then
zipped up her old swim team sweat top. Her feet in flip-flops,
she headed downstairs.

The latest James Bond movie was showing on the hotel's
in-house movie service. She smiled to herself as she thought
about Daniel Craig in his swim trunks. Sugar, salt and a buff
man—not a bad night in.

She was still smiling contentedly when she returned to the
hotel five minutes later, loaded down with snack food. She
was in the elevator, the doors about to close, when Jake
Stevens thrust his arm between them. She stood a little
straighter as he stepped inside the car.

Damn it. Was it too much to ask for a few moments' reprieve from his knowing, sarcastic eyes and smug smile?

She moved closer to the corner so there wasn't even the
remote chance of brushing shoulders with him.

His gaze flicked over her briefly. Suddenly she was very
aware of her wet hair and the fact that she wasn't wearing a

bra. She shifted uncomfortably and his gaze dropped to her carrier bag of goodies.

"Having a big night, I see," he said.

"Something like that."

He leaned closer. She fought the need to pull away as he hooked a finger into the top of the bag and peered inside.

"Chocolate-chip ice cream and nacho-cheese corn chips. Interesting combo."

Up close, his eyes were so blue and clear she felt as though she could see all the way through to his soul.

If he had one.

"Do you mind?" she said, jerking the bag away from him.

He raised his eyebrows. She raised hers and gave him a challenging look.

"Just trying to be friendly," he said.

"No, you weren't. You were being a smart-ass, at my expense, as usual. So don't expect me to lie down and take it."

His gaze dropped to her chest, then flicked back to her face. She waited for him to say something suitably smart-assy in response, but he didn't. The lift chimed as they hit her floor.

Thank God.

She stepped out into the corridor. He followed. She frowned, thrown. Then she started walking toward her room, keeping a watch out of the corner of her eye. As she'd feared, he was following her.

She stopped abruptly and he almost walked into her as she swung to face him.

"I don't need an escort to my door, if that's what you're doing," she said. "I don't need anything from you, which I know probably sticks in your craw since your ego is so massive and so fragile you can't handle having a rookie on the team."

Jake cocked his head to one side. Then he smiled sweetly

and pulled a key from his pocket. The number 647 dangled from it. Two rooms up from hers.

Right.

She could feel embarrassed heat rising into her face. Why did this man always make her so self-conscious? It wasn't as though she cared what he thought of her.

She started walking again. She had her key in her hand well before her door was in sight. She shoved it into the lock and pushed her door open as quickly as she could. She caught a last glimpse of his smiling face as she shut the door.

Smug bastard.

She grabbed a spoon from the minibar and ripped the top off the ice cream. She needed to keep an eye on her temper around him. And she had to stop letting him get under her skin. That, or she had to somehow develop Zen-like mind-body control so she could stop herself from blushing in front of him.

Large quantities of chocolate-chip ice cream went a long way to calming her. She turned on the TV and opened the corn chips. An hour into the movie, she was blinking and yawning. When the movie cut to a love scene, she decided to call it quits for the night. She liked watching James run and jump and beat people up, but she wasn't so wild about the mandatory sex scenes. She knew other people liked them, even got disappointed when they didn't get enough of them, but she so didn't get it.

She contemplated the issue as she brushed her teeth.

Sex, in her opinion, was one of the most overrated activities under the sun. She figured she was experienced enough to know—she'd had three lovers in her thirty-one years, and none of them had come even close to being as satisfying as George, her battery-operated, intriguingly shaped friend. Disappointing, but true.

Of course, it was possible that she'd had three dud lovers in a row, but she thought it far more likely that sex, like most anti-aging products and lose-weight-now remedies, was not all it was cracked up to be.

But that was only her opinion.

She spat out toothpaste and rinsed her mouth. Then she climbed into bed. Just before she drifted off, she remembered that moment in the hallway again. Next time she came face-to-face with The Snake, she was going to make sure she was the one who came out on top. Definitely.

THE NEXT DAY SHE CAUGHT A CAB to the airport for her flight home and discovered that while she and the bulk of Australia had been focused on the ups and downs, ins and outs of a red leather ball, the baggage handlers union had decided to go on strike.

The mammoth lines of irate and desperate-looking people winding through the terminal were her first clue that something was up. She collared a passing airport official and he filled her in. The strike was expected to run for at least three days. Most flights had been canceled.

"Damn it," she said.

He held up his hands. "Not my fault, lady."

"I know. Sorry. It's just my uncle's birthday is on Wednesday."

She'd planned to drive to her parents' place in Ballarat, about an hour north of Melbourne, for the party. But at this rate it didn't look as though she was even going to be in the same state come Wednesday.

"Lots of weddings and funerals and births, too," the official said with a shrug. "Nobody likes an airline strike."

He moved off and Poppy stared glumly at his back. This

was not the first time she'd been left stranded by an airline. As a swimmer, she'd been at the mercy of more than her fair share of strikes, bad weather and mechanical failures. Once, the swim team had almost missed an important meet in Sydney thanks to an airline strike, but their coach had had the foresight to hire a minibus and had driven them the thousand kilometers overnight.

A lightbulb went on in Poppy's mind. If it was good enough for Coach Wellington, it was good enough for her. She turned in a circle, looking for the signs for the car rental agencies. She spotted the glowing yellow Hertz sign. Then she spotted the lineup in front of it. Well, she could only try.

Fingers crossed, she headed over to join the masses.

JAKE WOKE, FEELING LIKE CRAP. Headache, furry mouth, seedy stomach—standard hangover material. He groaned as he rolled out of bed and blessed his own foresight in ensuring he had an afternoon flight out of Brisbane and not a morning one. He'd played this game before, after all, and he'd known last night would be a big one. And it had been. He'd lost track of which bar he'd wound up in, and who he'd been drinking with. There had definitely been some disappointed Bears players in the mix, drowning their sorrows. And he could distinctly remember someone singing the Hawk's club song at one stage.

Whatever. A fine time was had by all.

Well, not *quite* all. Some people had chosen to forgo the festivities and hole up in their room with chocolate-chip ice cream and nacho-cheese corn chips.

He rinsed his mouth out as the memory of Poppy's uptight little "I don't need an escort" speech filtered into his mind.

He didn't know what it was about her, but he couldn't seem to resist poking her with a stick. Maybe it was the way her chin came up. Or the martial gleam that came into her eyes. Or maybe it was the pink flush that colored her cheeks when he bested her.

He stepped beneath the shower and lifted his face to the spray. Oh, man, but he needed some grease and some salt and some aspirin. Big-time.

Of course, Ms. Birmingham wouldn't be in search of saturated animal fats this morning. She'd had hers last night, in the quiet privacy of her room.

Someone needed to tell her that road trips were a good opportunity to bond with her colleagues. Especially when you were a newcomer to the team.

He shrugged. Not his problem. And she was unlikely to take advice from him, anyway.

He recalled the way she'd looked last night, hair wet, face devoid of makeup. Sans bra, too, if he made any guess. She had more up top than he'd expected. Definitely a generous handful.

He soaped his belly and wondered again what she'd look like naked. She wasn't his type, but he supposed he could understand why Macca followed her with his eyes whenever he thought no one was watching. She was striking. She could almost look Jake in the eye, she was so tall. He bet she liked to be on top, too.

He stared down at his hard-on.

Okay, maybe she *was* his type. But only because it had been a while since he'd gotten naked with anyone. Four…no, five months. That was when he'd decided that his fledgling relationship with Rachel-from-the-gym was too much of a distraction from the book he still hadn't written.

He turned the water to cold. Brutal, but effective—his erection sank without a trace.

He dressed and packed his luggage. Then he checked out.

"We hope you enjoyed your stay with us, Mr. Stevens," the woman on the reservation desk said. "And we hope the strike doesn't inconvenience you too much."

He lifted his head from signing his credit card slip. "Strike? What strike?"

"The baggage handlers' strike. It looks like it'll last three days minimum at this point. We've had a lot of people coming back from the airport to check in again."

Shit. He had ten days vacation starting tomorrow. He had plans to go fishing with an old college buddy. No way was he going to kick his heels in Brisbane when there were rainbow trout going begging.

He grabbed his bags and headed to the taxi stand. He'd been caught out like this before and he knew that even during a strike there were still planes in the air. He might be able to talk his way onto one of them. And there was always the bus, God forbid, or a rental.

The moment he hit the airport he nixed the idea of talking himself onto a flight. Lines spilled out the door and every person and his dog was on a cell, trying to hustle some other way home.

He turned for the rental desks. No lines there. Bonus. Maybe no one else had thought of driving home yet.

He dropped his bags in front of the counter and smiled at the pretty blonde behind the desk.

"Hey, there. I need to rent a car," he said.

She rolled her eyes. "You and the rest of the country. Sorry, sir, as we announced five minutes ago, we're all sold out."

He kept smiling.

"There must be something. A car due back later today? Something that didn't pass inspection?"

"Many of our cars didn't come in when our customers

heard about the strike. We've been pulling cars in from our other branches, but there's no stock left. I'm very sorry, sir."

She didn't sound very sorry. She sounded as though she'd had a long and stressful day and was privately wishing him to hell.

"There must be something," he said.

"Where are you traveling to?"

He waited for her to start tapping away at her keyboard to find him a car, but she didn't.

"Melbourne."

"The only thing I can suggest is that you hook up with someone else who is driving your way. I know that blond woman over there is going to Melbourne. She got our last car—maybe she'll take pity on you."

Jake turned his head to follow the woman's finger. He stared in disbelief at the back of Poppy Birmingham's head.

"Shit."

"Excuse me, sir?"

There was no way Poppy was going to take pity on him. She'd more than likely laugh in his face—if he gave her the opportunity.

"Is there a bus counter around here?" he asked. He hated bus travel with a passion, but desperate times called for desperate measures. There were trout swimming in the Cobungra River with his name on them, and he intended to be there to catch them.

"They're on the west side of the airport. Just follow the crowd."

"Thanks."

He hefted his bags and started walking. He could see Poppy up ahead, talking on her cell phone. If it were anyone else— a complete stranger—he'd throw himself on her mercy in a split second. But Poppy didn't like him. Admittedly, he'd given her plenty of reasons to feel that way, but the fact remained that she was far more likely to drive over him in her rental car than offer him a lift in it.

He walked past her, wondering how she'd react if he snatched the keys from her hand and made a bolt for it. But she was probably pretty fast on her feet. She had those long legs and hadn't been out all night swilling beer and red wine the way he had.

He kept walking. Then he started thinking about sitting on a bus with seventy-odd other angry travelers, sucking in diesel fumes and reliving horror flashbacks from half a dozen high school excursions.

Man.

He stopped in his tracks. He lowered his chin to his chest. He thought about the bus, then he thought about his pride. Then he turned around and walked to where Poppy was finishing her phone call.

He stopped in front of her. She stared at him blankly. Then her gaze dropped to his luggage. A slow smile curved her mouth. He waited for her to say something, but she didn't.

She was going to make him ask.

Shit.

He took a deep breath. "Going my way?"

Her smile broadened. "I'm sorry, but you're going to have to do much better than that."

She crossed her arms over her chest and waited. He stared at her for a long moment.

Then he braced himself for some heavy-duty sucking up.

3

POPPY STILL COULDN'T BELIEVE she'd let Jake into her car. Even if she drove nonstop like a bat out of hell, she'd sentenced herself to twenty-four hours in The Snake's company in a small enclosed space. Had she been on drugs twenty minutes ago?

She slid him a look. His eyes were hidden behind dark sunglasses but he appeared to be staring out the windshield, his expression unreadable. He hadn't shaved and his face was dark with stubble. He hadn't said a word since they argued over who was driving the first leg and which route out of the city to take.

He resented having to kiss her ass, but she didn't regret making him do it. It was nice to have a bit of power for a change, even if it was only temporary.

She focused on the road. If he wanted to play it strong and silent, that was fine with her. She'd had more than enough of his smart mouth over the past three weeks.

"Do you mind if I turn the air-conditioning on?" he asked ten minutes later.

It was an unseasonably warm day for September and she was starting to feel a little sticky herself.

"Sure."

He fiddled with the controls. "Hmph." He sat back in his seat. "It's broken."

"It can't be."

He turned his head toward her. She didn't need to see his eyes to know he was giving her a look.

"Feel free to check for yourself."

She did, flicking the switch on and off several times. He didn't say a word as the seconds ticked by and no cool air emerged from the air vents.

"Fine. It's broken," she said after a few minutes.

"No shit."

She cracked the window on her side to let some fresh air into the car. He did the same on his side. The road noise was loud, the equivalent of being inside a wind tunnel.

Great. Jake the Snake beside me, and a bloody hurricane roaring in my ear. This is going to be the road trip from hell.

After half an hour she couldn't stand the noise any longer. She shut her window. A short while later, so did Jake.

The temperature in the car rose steadily as the sun moved across the sky. Jake shrugged out of his jacket and so did she. By the time they'd been on the road for two hours, her shirt was sticking to her and sweat was running down her rib cage.

Poppy spotted a sign for a rest area and turned into it when it came up on their left.

Jake stirred and she realized he'd been dozing behind his glasses and not simply staring out the windshield ignoring her.

"You ready to swap?" he asked, pushing his sunglasses up onto his forehead and rubbing his eyes.

"Nope," she said. "I'm changing into something cooler."

She got out of the car and unlocked the trunk. Jake got out, too, stretching his arms high over his head and arching his back. His T-shirt rode up, treating her to a flash of flat belly, complete with a dark-haired happy trail that disappeared beneath the waistband of his jeans. She frowned and looked away, concen-

trating on digging through her bag in search of her sports tank.
When she found it, she gave him a pointed look.

"Do you mind?"

He stared at her.

"What?"

"A little privacy, please." She spun her finger in the air to
indicate she wanted him to turn his back.

He snorted. "Lady, we're on a state highway, in case you
hadn't noticed. Everyone who drives past is going to cop an
eyeful unless you hunker down in the backseat."

"I don't care about everyone else. I have to work with you."

She didn't care if he thought she was prudish or stupid—
she was not stripping down to her bra in front of him. She absolutely did not want him knowing what she looked like in
her underwear. It was way too personal a piece of information for him to have about her. She wasn't exactly sure how
he could turn it to his advantage, but that was beside the point.

He sighed heavily and turned his back.

"If I see anything, I promise to poke an eye out," he said.

She unbuttoned her shirt and shrugged out of it. She checked
he still had his back turned. He hadn't moved. Her tank top got
tangled in her haste to pull it over her head. She twisted it
around the right way and tugged it on. She glanced at him
again. This time his face was in quarter profile as he gazed over
the acres of grassland running alongside the freeway.

Had he sneaked a look? She stared at him suspiciously, but
he didn't so much as blink.

"I'm ready," she said.

He turned and his gaze flicked down her body briefly before returning to her face. She was acutely aware that her tank
top was small and tight and a far cry from the business shirts
and jackets she'd been wearing to work to date.

She slammed the trunk shut and moved to the driver's side door. He met her there, his hand held out expectantly.

"I'll drive," he said.

"No, you won't."

If he'd asked, maybe she would have considered it. But there was no way she was taking orders from him. They'd be serving ice cream in hell before that happened.

"There's no way you're driving all the way to Melbourne," he said.

"I'm not an idiot. When I'm tired, I'll let you know."

His stared at her, his blue eyes dark with frustration. Then he turned on his heel and returned to his side of the car.

She waited till he had his seat belt on before pulling back onto the highway. Immediately he leaned across and turned the radio on. Static hissed and he fooled around with the dials until he found some music.

Johnny Cash's deep voice filled the car. Poppy forced her shoulders to relax. Jake Stevens got on her nerves. She wished he didn't, but he did. As she'd already acknowledged, she needed to get a grip on her temper when he was around.

It would also be good if she wasn't quite so aware of him physically. Her gaze kept sliding across to where his long legs were stretched out into the footwell. And she kept remembering that flash of flat male belly. It was highly annoying and disconcerting. She didn't like him. She didn't want to be aware of him.

She slid another surreptitious glance his way and tensed when she caught him looking at her. More specifically, at her breasts.

She glared at him until he lifted his gaze and met hers. He had the gall to shrug a shoulder and give her a cocky little smile.

"Hey, what can I say? I'm only human."

"Subhuman, you mean."

"Staring at a woman's breasts is not a capital offense, last time I checked," he said.

"Maybe I don't want you looking at my breasts. Ever think about that?"

"Don't worry, I won't make a habit of it."

She stiffened. What was he saying? That he didn't like her breasts? That he didn't consider them ogleworthy? She glanced down at herself and frowned.

"What's wrong with them?" she asked.

She could have bitten her tongue off the moment the words were out of her mouth. She could feel the mother of all blushes working its way up her neck.

She kept her eyes front and center as he looked at her.

"Relax," he said. "I didn't mean anything by it. Men check out women all the time. It's basic biology."

"I *am* relaxed," she said through her teeth. "And I didn't think you were about to propose because you checked out my rack. I might not be used to having boobs, but I know that much."

She didn't think it was possible, but her blush intensified. She couldn't believe she'd made such a revealing confession to The Snake.

There was a short silence before he spoke.

"I wondered about that," he said. "All the photos I ever saw, you looked about an A cup."

"You made a note of my *cup size?*" she asked, her voice rising.

"Sure. I'm not blind. So, what, you stopped training and puberty kicked in, is that it?"

He spoke conversationally, as though they were talking about the weather. As though it was perfectly natural for him to go around guessing women's breast size. And maybe it was—but not *hers*. She didn't want him looking at her and thinking about her like that. It made her feel distinctly…edgy.

She clenched her hands on the wheel. "We are not talking about my breasts."

"You brought it up."

"I did not! You were staring at me!"

"Because you changed into that teeny, tiny tank. I could hardly pretend I didn't notice."

"The air-conditioning is broken and I was hot and you could have tried. A gentleman would have," she said.

He laughed. "A gentleman? Baby, I'm a journalist. I wouldn't have a job if I was a gentleman. Something you better learn pretty quick if you want to survive in this game."

She held up a hand. "Spare me your sage advice, Yoda. You're about three weeks too late to apply for the position of mentor."

He shrugged. "Suit yourself."

"I will, thank you."

"Always have to have the last word, don't you?"

"Look who's talking."

"Thank you for proving my point."

She pressed her lips together, even though she was aching to fire back at him.

He angled his seat back and stretched out, his arms crooked behind his head. "Do you miss it?"

"I beg your pardon?"

"Swimming. Training. Being on the team. Do you miss it?"

She made a rude noise in the back of her throat. "Just because we're stuck in a car for a few hours doesn't mean we have to talk."

"It's a long drive."

"I'm not here to entertain you."

He was silent for a moment. She flipped the visor to the side to block the sun as it began its descent into the west.

"Okay, what about this? I get a question, then you get one. Quid pro quo."

"Thank you, Dr. Lecter, but I don't want to play."

"Why? What are you scared of?"

She shifted in her seat. He was goading her, daring her. She knew it was childish, but she didn't want him thinking he could best her so easily.

"Fine," she said. "Yes, I miss swimming. It was my life for twenty-five years. Of course I miss it."

"What do you miss the most?"

"You think I can't count? It's my turn. Why haven't you published a follow-up to *The Coolabah Tree*?"

She could feel him bristle.

"I'm working on one now," he said stiffly.

"What's it called?"

"Nice try. Why do you want to be a journalist?"

"Because it's not swimming. And because I feel I have something to offer. How long did it take you to write your first book?"

"Two years, working weekends and nights."

"How many drafts did you do?"

"Three. And that was two questions."

"You answered them."

He shrugged. "Do you ever think about the four-hundred-meter final at Beijing? Wish you could go back again?"

She should have known he'd bring that up. The lowest point in her swimming career—of course he'd want to stick his finger in the sore spot and see if she squirmed.

She put the indicator on and pulled into the approaching rest stop.

"What's wrong?" he asked.

"I'm tired."

"Right."

She got out and stretched her back. She was aware of Jake doing the same thing on the other side of the car. Dusk was falling and the world around them was muted in the fading light. They crossed in front of the car as they swapped sides.

She waited until he was on the highway again before answering his question.

"I used to think about it all the time, but not so much now. I had my chance and I missed it and I came home with silver instead of gold. I had a bunch of excuses for myself at the time, but the fact is that I simply didn't bring my best game on the day. It happens. If you can't live with your own mistakes, competing for a living will kill you."

"You're very philosophical."

"Like I said, I used to think about it a lot. But you can't live in the past."

He reached up and adjusted the rearview mirror. "Your turn."

She studied his profile. He was a good-looking man. Charming and interesting—when he wanted to be. Not that she'd experienced any of that firsthand, but she had eyes in her head. He'd cut a swath through the female contingent in the press box with his boyish grin and quick wit.

"Why aren't you married?" she asked before she could censor herself.

He frowned at the road. "I was. We divorced five years ago."

"Oh." She hadn't expected that. Watching him at work, the way he came in early and left late, she'd figured him for a loner, one of those men who had dodged commitment so many times it had become a way of life. But he'd been married. And he sounded unhappy that he wasn't still married.

"What about you? Why aren't you married?"

She smiled ruefully. Quid pro quo, indeed. "No one's ever asked me."

He glanced at her, a half smile on his mouth. "That's a cop-out."

She shrugged. "Maybe, but that's all you're going to get."

They lapsed into silence, even though it was her turn to ask a question.

"We should stop for food soon. And start thinking about where we're going to stay the night," he said.

They wound up at McDonald's since it was the only thing on offer. They studied the road map as they ate, deciding on Tamworth as their destination for the evening.

"There'll be a decent motel there, and a few places to eat," Jake said.

She pushed the remains of her burger and fries away.

"You going to eat those?" Jake asked, eyeing her fries.

"Go nuts."

He polished them off then went back to the counter to order an apple pie for the road.

She waited outside in the cold night air, looking up at the dark sky, listening to the rush of cars on the highway and marveling that she and Jake Stevens had spent several hours in a car together and no blood had been spilled.

Yet.

"Okay, let's hit the road," he said as he joined her in the parking lot.

She glanced at him, straight into his blue eyes. They stared at each other a moment too long before she turned away. He walked ahead of her as they crossed to the car. She found herself staring at his butt. She'd always had a thing for backsides and he had a nice one. Okay—a *very* nice one.

Why am I noticing Jake the Snake's butt?

She frowned and looked away. Must be the car equivalent of Stockholm Syndrome. At least she hoped that was what it was.

POPPY WAS DRIVING AGAIN when they pulled into Tamworth just before eight o'clock. Apart from one small disagreement over radio stations, their unofficial cease-fire was still in effect. Jake craned his head to read the brightly illuminated signs of the various motels as they cruised Tamworth's busy main street.

"That place, over there," he said, pointing to a blue-and-white neon sign in front of a brown-brick, two-story motel. "They've got spa baths."

She rolled her eyes but pulled over, since she didn't have a better suggestion.

"Park the car and I'll get us some rooms," he said.

Before she could say anything, he was out of the car and striding toward reception.

"Yes, sir," she said to herself. "Three bags full, sir. Have you any wool, sir?"

Because it would rankle too much to obey him to the letter, she joined him in reception as he was handing over his credit card to the middle-aged clerk.

"Hang on a minute," she said. "I'll pay for my own room."

"You got the car. I'll get this."

It was a perfectly reasonable argument but she opened her mouth to dispute it anyway.

"We can argue after dinner," he said. "You can arm wrestle me to the floor and pound me into submission."

"What makes you think I'm having dinner with you?"

"Because you can't sit in your room and eat ice cream and chips two nights in a row. You'll get scurvy. You need vitamin C."

The desk clerk was watching their interplay curiously. Poppy took her room key.

"This doesn't mean I'm having dinner with you," she said.

But after she'd had a long shower and changed into fresh clothes, the sterile cleanliness of the room started to get to her. Plus she was hungry. When Jake knocked on her door ten minutes later, she pocketed her room key and stepped outside.

"There's a steak place up the road," he said.

He hadn't doubted her for a moment, the smug bastard.

"This is only because I'm hungry and they don't have room service," she said.

"It's all right. I didn't think you were about to propose because you agreed to have dinner with me."

He was deliberately echoing her words from during their ill-fated breast discussion. She couldn't help it—she cracked a smile.

"You are such a smart-ass," she said.

"You're no slouch yourself."

"No, I'm strictly amateur hour compared to you. You're world-class."

They started walking toward the glowing roadside sign for Lou's Steakhouse.

"Now you've made me nervous," he said.

"Sure I have."

"You have. World-class—that's a lot to live up to. You've given me performance anxiety."

"I bet you've never had performance anxiety in your life."

"That was before I met you."

She became aware that she was still smiling and slowing her steps, dawdling to prolong their short walk to the restaurant. She frowned, suddenly uneasy. She looked at him and saw that he was watching her, an arrested expression on his face. As though, like her, he'd just realized that they were enjoying each other's company.

Good Lord. Next thing you know, the moon will be blue and a pig will fly by.

She lengthened her stride and fixed her gaze on the steak house. The sooner this evening—this *drive*—was over, the better.

"YOU ARE SO WRONG. He meant to get busted. Why else would he volunteer to do a second drug test when he'd already been cleared?"

Poppy leaned across the table as she spoke, one elbow propped on the red-and-white tablecloth. Jake tried not to smile at the earnest determination in her expression. She was pretty cute when she got all passionate about something.

They were the only customers left in the restaurant, even though it was barely ten. They'd been talking sports throughout the meal, their current topic being the recent drug scandal involving a well-known British cyclist.

"There's no way anyone would throw away their career like that. He's banned from cycling for life. He's lost his sponsors. He's screwed," he said.

She nodded enthusiastically. "Exactly, and that's what he wanted. Why else would he take that second test?"

The neck of her shirt gaped. Not for the first time that evening he noticed the lacy edge of her bra and wondered if she knew her underwear was on display. He suspected not—Poppy didn't strike him as the kind of woman who seduced with glimpses of lace and skin. She probably had no idea one of her buttons had slipped free.

Maybe it made him an opportunist, but he wasn't about to tell her. Not when the view was so rewarding.

He returned his attention to her face, aware that his jeans were a little snug around the crotch all of a sudden.

"No way. I just don't buy that anyone would throw it all away like that."

"You don't know what it's like," she said darkly. "Everyone looking at you, pinning their hopes on you, channeling all their ambitions and dreams into your life, your career, your achievements. Maybe he self-destructed rather than risk failing on the track."

He studied her. She looked so sunny and uncomplicated, even after several glasses of wine and a long day on the road. He couldn't imagine her ever wanting to throw her career in.

"Is this a confession? Did you injure your shoulder on purpose so you'd miss the World Championships?" he asked lightly.

She reached for her wine and took a big swallow. "You're joking, I know, but there were definitely times when I thought it would be easier if I simply couldn't swim anymore. Not because I decided not to, you know, but because I just *couldn't* and the decision was taken out of my hands."

"And then you got injured."

"Yep, I did. And I discovered that the grass is always greener." She laughed, then shrugged self-deprecatingly. "It's not like I could keep swimming forever. There are girls coming up now who are so strong and fast.... I would have been a dinosaur wallowing around the pool in a few more years."

She picked up the dessert menu and studied it. He took the opportunity to study her. She looked like everybody's idea of a poster girl for Australian swimming, the kind of athlete you'd find smiling from the back of a cereal box: the blond hair, the clear skin, the frank way she had of meeting his eye whenever she spoke. But she was more complicated than that. She was funny. She was honest. She was smart. She questioned things, was curious about the world.

He liked her.

"How have things been going with Macca?" he asked. "He been helping you out with your columns okay?"

She'd been about to take another mouthful of wine but she froze with the glass halfway to her mouth. She stared at him for a long moment, then put her glass down.

"Dear Lord. Someone pinch me—Jake Stevens has got a conscience."

He shifted in his chair. "I might be a smart-ass, but I'm not an asshole."

She raised an eyebrow. For some reason it seemed very important to him that she not believe the worst of him.

"I owe you an apology." The words came out a little stiffly but he was determined to set things right. "I shouldn't have taken my frustration with Leonard out on you."

"No, you shouldn't have."

"It's not your fault he turned into a publicity whore. And you've done a good job."

She raised a hand to her forehead and blinked rapidly. "Wow. Is there a gas leak in the room or did you just pay me a compliment?"

He poured himself more wine. They were both a little tipsy, which was no bad thing given the turn the conversation had taken.

"Okay, maybe I have been an asshole," he admitted.

"It's okay. You gave me something to worry about other than my writing. And you were entitled to be pissed about the situation—just not at me."

She smiled. He smiled back.

"You're being very generous," he said.

"I think I'm a little drunk. No doubt I'll regret not making you grovel more in the morning."

"That wasn't groveling. That was an apology."

"You say tomato…"

She was laughing at him, her gray eyes alight with humor. He raised his glass.

"To starting again."

She clinked glasses with him.

"To learning from the best," she said.

He frowned, then shook his head ruefully as he took her meaning. "You don't want me mentoring you. I'm a smart-ass, remember?"

"You're right, I don't. But I want your advice sometimes. I want to know when I'm screwing up and haven't realized it yet. You're the best writer on the paper. I'd be an idiot not to learn from you if I can."

She held his eye as she said it. There was no denying he was flattered. And a little embarrassed by her unflinching assessment.

"Macca's pretty good. And Hilary's up for a Walkley Award this year."

"Modesty, Mr. Stevens? I'm surprised." She propped her elbow on the table again and leaned her chin on her hand. "Come on, hit me with your next hot tip for the day. What do I need to know? Where have I gone wrong so far?"

He winced at the reminder of his comment regarding her reference books. Not his kindest act. He owed her.

"You should have come out with us last night," he said. "Everyone's tired after a long haul like the Grand Final, but you missed out on a chance to be part of the team."

She frowned, processing what he'd said.

"Okay, fair enough. Next time, I'll come out to play. What else?"

He poured her more wine and topped up his own glass. The waitstaff were standing at the counter looking bored, but he figured if they wanted Poppy and him to leave they could say so.

"You need to be tougher. When Coach Dickens ignored you the other day when you asked for a comment, you backed off. You should have tried again, said something to get his attention, made him stop and engage with you."

"I didn't want to alienate him. I know what it's like when the press get in your face."

"That's our job. He gets paid a lot of money to do what he does. If he didn't want the fame and glory, he'd be at home watching it on TV like everyone else."

She nodded. "I'll try to be pushier. Even if it does make my toes curl."

He settled back in his chair and let his gaze dip below her face again. He'd been thinking about her breasts on and off ever since their conversation in the car. He wondered if they were as firm as they looked. And if her skin was as warm and smooth as he imagined.

"One thing you should think about," he said. "The players. Football, tennis, cricket, it doesn't matter—they're hound dogs, even a lot of the married ones. No matter what, don't go there. Shortest route to trashing your career."

She waved a hand dismissively. "Not a problem. Next."

"I'm serious. Remember Joanne Hendricks? She would have been in line for Leonard's job by now if she was still around."

He didn't need to say more. He could see from Poppy's expression that she remembered the furor that had erupted when the high-profile journalist's affair with a married rugby player had gone public. She'd subsequently been forced to resign from the *Herald*.

"I take your point, but it's not an issue."

"You say that now, but I've seen some of those guys go to

work on a woman. They can be bloody charming when they want something."

Poppy made a frustrated sound. "As if I'm going to jeopardize my career for a bunch of pointless fumbling and huffing and puffing. I'm not a *man*." She drained her wineglass.

"*Huffing and puffing?* And what does being a man have to do with it?"

"Sex is for men," she said simply. "You get off on it more, therefore you're more likely to be idiots about it."

She said it as though reporting proven medical fact. He raised his eyebrows and leaned toward her.

"Let me get this straight—women don't enjoy sex? Is that your contention?"

"I can't speak for all women. But I bet I'm not the only one who thinks it's overrated."

She was drunk. That was the only reason she would ever say something so personal and revealing to him. If he were a gentleman, he'd ignore it and move on.

"You think sex is overrated?"

"In a word, yes."

"Baby, you're *so* doing something wrong."

She shook her head. "No. I've done it enough to know. Sex is like an Easter egg—big and impressive on the outside, but empty on the inside. All promise, no delivery."

"You've never had an orgasm," he said with absolute certainty.

"On the contrary. I have had many, thanks to the marvels of modern technology. Which is more than I can say for sex."

Oh, man, was she going to regret this conversation in the morning.

"There's no way a piece of plastic and silicone can match the satisfaction of real sex," he said.

"Your opinion. I'd take twenty minutes with George over

twenty minutes with a man any day. He never talks back, he always does what I want and he always delivers at least once."

"George? Your vibrator is called George?"

"After George Clooney."

He shook his head.

"You can't handle it because male egos like to think that women get off as much as they do during sex. It's a prowess thing."

"I don't *think* anything. I *know* women have a good time in bed with me."

She shook her head slowly.

"Remember the diner scene from *When Harry Met Sally?*" She thumped her fists on the table a couple of times. "Oh, yes. *Yesss. Yesss!*" She slumped in her chair languorously, ran a hand through her hair and looked at him with heavy, smoky eyes.

He had to admit, it was a pretty damn convincing impersonation of a woman having an orgasm.

She sat up straight and smiled at him. "I rest my case."

He narrowed his eyes at her. "Why do women have sex then if they don't enjoy it as much?"

"Because they want to keep men happy. Because they want them to put the garbage out and catch spiders and change the oil in the car and they understand sex is the currency of choice when dealing with the male of the species."

Jake simply couldn't believe a woman could be so messed up about something so simple.

"Come on," he said, standing. He threw some money on the table to cover their bill.

"It's not your fault. It's biology. You scored the penis. Every time you put it inside something, it feels good. We scored the clitoris. If they'd really known what they were doing, whoever designed human beings would have put it *inside* the vagina."

She was talking loudly and the staff were exchanging looks. He grabbed her hand and towed her out of the restaurant.

"The clitoris works just fine where it is," he said, leading her back toward the motel.

"With George on the job it does."

She stumbled and he steadied her. She rambled some more about the differences between men's and women's bodies as they completed the short walk to the motel. He was too busy focusing on reaching his room ASAP to pay much attention. Finally he opened his door and led her inside.

She blinked as she looked around. "This isn't my room."

"Nope. It's mine."

He kicked off his shoes. She blinked at that, too.

"What are you doing?"

"Setting you straight." He glanced over his shoulder at the clock on the bedstand. "Does the twenty minutes start from now or when we get naked?"

She stared at him for a long moment.

"You're drunk."

"So are you."

"Not that drunk."

"Me, either. So what are you waiting for?"

She hesitated another beat. Then her gaze dropped to his crotch where he was already hard for her. Her mouth opened. He swore her pupils dilated. Then she started shrugging out of her jacket.

"I hope your ego can handle this," she said.

"I hope your body can handle this," he said.

She pulled her shirt off and he stared at her full, lush breasts, covered in white lace. He was already hard, but he got a whole lot harder.

"Your time starts now," she said.

4

POPPY REACHED BEHIND HERSELF to unclasp her bra. If she stopped to think about it, she knew she'd lose her nerve. This was nuts. Absolutely bonkers.

For starters, until a few hours ago she'd loathed Jake Stevens, and she was pretty sure the feeling had been mutual. Then there was the small fact that she worked with him.

So why was she sliding her straps off her shoulders and letting her bra fall to the carpet?

Jake made a small, satisfied sound as he saw her breasts. Heat swept through her.

That was why—the rush of hot, sticky sensation that had hit her every time she'd caught Jake staring at her breasts over dinner.

He was attracted to her. He wanted to get her naked, touch her breasts, slide inside her.

And even though she was almost certain the buildup would be more fun than the actual main event, she wanted to do all those things, too.

"For the record, in case you have any doubts at all, you have great breasts," Jake said, his gaze intent on her. "Really, really great."

He stripped off his T-shirt and she stared at his broad shoulders and lean belly. He was tall and rangy but still firm and lean with muscle. Dark hair covered his pectoral muscles before trailing south. Her gaze dropped to his thighs where his erection was clearly visible against the denim of his jeans.

She imagined what he would look like—long and thick and hard. Need throbbed between her thighs.

She undid her belt and unzipped her fly, then worked her jeans over her hips. She hesitated, unsure whether to take her panties off at the same time. She shrugged; they were on the clock, after all. Might as well give him a fighting chance. She slid her thumbs into the side elastic of her underwear and tugged them off with her jeans. She kicked the lot to one side and looked at him.

He was pushing his jeans and underwear down his legs and his erection bounced free. Her eyes widened as she saw how big he was, how hard.

Oh, boy.

He looked up from kicking his clothes to one side and grinned when he saw her face. Then his gaze dropped to study her legs, her hips, the neat curls between her thighs.

"Come here," he said, crooking his finger.

She took a small step forward, all her doubts clamoring for attention. This was a bad idea. Really, really bad.

Jake closed the remaining distance between them. She opened her mouth to tell him she'd made a mistake, that she was sober now and this was a crazy. He reached out and slid both hands onto her breasts. His hands were warm and firm, and he locked eyes with her as he cupped her in his palms, then swept a thumb over each nipple. She bit her lip. He squeezed her nipples between his fingers, rolling them gently.

"Nice?" he said, his breath warm on her face.

"Yes."

"Good."

He lowered his head. She closed her eyes as his mouth covered hers, soft yet firm, his tongue sweeping into her mouth. He brought his body against hers, her breasts pressing against his chest, his erection jutting into her belly. His skin felt incredibly hot where it touched hers, his body hard where hers was soft.

He tasted of wine. His tongue teased hers, wet and hot. She shivered as his hand slid across her lower belly.

"Normally, we'd fool around a little more than this before I made a play for third base," he murmured as he kissed his way across to her ear. "But my honor's at stake here. So if you don't mind, I'm going to go for it."

She let her head drop back as he slid his tongue into her ear.

"I think I can make an exception this once," she said.

The truth was, she didn't know if it was the wine or the situation or Jake himself, but she could feel how wet she was for him already. Tension had been building between them all night. His clear blue eyes watching her across the table. The way he'd teased her. The way he'd looked at her body. It had all been leading to this moment. Why else had she issued her challenge?

And it *had* been a challenge. Definitely.

She shivered as he slid a single finger into the folds of her sex. Her hands gripped his shoulders as his finger slicked over her clitoris and then slid farther still until he was at her entrance.

Slowly, he circled his finger. She widened her stance, clenching her muscles in anticipation of his penetration. And then he slid his finger inside her. She tightened around him and he gave an encouraging groan.

"You're very tight, Poppy," he said near her ear.

She gasped as his thumb slid onto her clitoris and began to work her while his single, long finger remained inside her.

His other hand toyed with her breasts, plucking at her nipples, squeezing them, teasing them.

She ran her hands across his back and slid her hands onto his ass. It was every bit as firm and hard as she'd imagined it would be. She squeezed it, imagining holding him just like this as he stroked himself inside her.

Her legs started to tremble. She realized she was panting.

Jake walked her backward a few steps, his thumb still circling her clitoris. She felt the mattress behind her knees and sat willingly, lying backward and spreading her legs as he followed her down.

"Yes," he said as began to work his finger inside her, sliding in and out. She lifted her hips, wanting more. He lowered his head and drew a nipple into his mouth.

Men had touched her breasts before. They'd sucked on her nipples, bitten them. But none of them had made her moan the way Jake did. He alternated between licking and sucking and rasping the flat of his tongue over her, and it drove her crazy. She spread her legs wider, wanting more than just his hand between her thighs.

That was new, too—the need to be full, to have his erection inside her.

"I want you," she panted. "I want you inside me."

"Not yet."

She reached between their bodies to find his cock. It was very hard and she found a single bead of moisture on the head of it as she wrapped her fingers around him.

"Now," she said, stroking her hand up and down his shaft.

"Not yet," he repeated.

He slid another finger inside her and his thumb began to pluck at her clitoris, as well as circle it.

"Ohhh," she moaned, letting her head drop back.

Tension built inside her. She realized with surprise that she was close to coming.

Unbelievable. She gripped his shoulders, her whole body tensing.

He slid his hand from between her thighs. Her eyes snapped open and she saw that he was smiling and looking very pleased with himself.

"Don't you dare stop," she said.

He glanced at the bedside unit.

"There's still seven minutes on the clock. Just wanted to check in. How am I faring compared to George?"

She frowned and reached for his hand, placing it back between her thighs.

"Badly. George never stops before I say so."

He laughed. "You're not nearly ready yet, baby."

Then he lowered his head and licked first one nipple, then the other. Then he began kissing his way down her belly.

"Oh," she said.

She couldn't see his face, but she knew he was smiling again as he settled himself between her widespread thighs. Her hands fisted in the sheets as he opened his mouth and pressed a wet, juicy kiss to her sex. He pulled her clitoris into his mouth and began to trill his tongue against it, the sensation so intense, so erotic she gasped.

"Oh!" she moaned.

He slid a finger inside her, then another. Her whole body was trembling. She held her breath as her climax rose inside her.

And again Jake pulled away.

She opened her eyes and stared at him in disbelief. "You have got to be kidding."

She was ready to kill him—but not before she'd jumped him and taken what he refused to give her.

"Two minutes left on the clock," he said. "I'm a man on a mission."

He reached for his jeans pocket and pulled out a condom. She propped herself up on her elbows and watched as he stroked the latex onto himself. For some reason, it turned her on even more, watching him touch himself so intimately.

He caught her eye as he moved over her. Her breasts flattened against his chest and her hips accepted his weight as she felt the tip of his erection probing her wet entrance.

She tilted her hips greedily, and he obliged her by sliding inside her with one powerful stroke.

She forgot to breathe. He was big. Almost too big. She could feel herself stretch to accommodate him. He flexed his hips and stroked out of her. She clutched at his ass and dragged him back inside.

"That. Feels. Amazing," she said.

"Damn straight." He sounded as surprised as she felt.

He began to pump into her, long, smooth strokes that made her gasp and cry out and circle her hips. And then suddenly, at last, her whole body was shaking and she let out a long, low moan as she came and came and came.

She'd barely floated down to earth before Jake kissed her, his mouth hard on hers. He tensed. His breath came out in a rush. Then he thrust into her one last time and stayed there, his cock buried to the hilt. His body shuddered for long moments, then softened. After a few seconds he opened his eyes and stared down into hers.

"Want me to go get George from your room?" he asked.

He was so smug, so sure of the answer. But she was too blown away to care.

"No." She felt dazed, overwhelmed.

He withdrew from her and rolled away, disappearing into

the bathroom. She pressed a hand between her legs. Every-thing felt hot down there, hot and throbbing and wet. And su-premely, hugely satisfied.

Jake's eyebrows rose when he stepped back into the room and saw where she had her hand, but he didn't say anything.

"Just making sure it's all still there," she said.

He smiled. "Want a bath?"

She registered the sound of running water. Right. He'd chosen the motel with the spa baths.

"Okay."

She moved to the edge of the bed and stood. Ridiculously, her legs faltered as she took her first step, as though her knees had forgotten how to do their thing. Jake's smile widened into a grin.

"Wow. I've never crippled a woman before."

"It could have been a fluke, you know. A one-off. A freak occurrence, never to be repeated."

He stepped close and slid a hand between her thighs where she was still tender and throbbing from his ministrations. He kept his fingers flat, exerting the faintest of pressures on her sensitized flesh.

"You should probably know that I do my best work over long distances," he said, his voice very low, his eyes holding hers. "So if you're issuing another challenge, you better make sure you're up to it."

Despite the fact that she'd just had an orgasm that rocked her world, a shiver of anticipation tightened her body.

"I'm going to take that as a yes," he said.

She reached for him, sliding her hands over his shoulders, his chest, his flat belly, until finally she found his cock, already growing thick and hard again.

"Bring it on," she said.

SHE WAS INCREDIBLE. Jake wanted to be inside Poppy again, wanted to feel the tight grip of her heat around him. But first he wanted to drive her crazy once more, watch her eyes grow cloudy with need, listen to her pant and gasp and beg for him.

He led her into the bathroom where the tub was already half full. Bubbles foamed on top of the water. She followed him into the tub and he experienced a small moment of regret as her breasts disappeared beneath the foam.

They were way too good to hide. Twin works of art. Silky smooth. So responsive he'd almost lost it just playing with her nipples.

Which begged the question, what the hell had the other guys she'd slept with been doing that she'd had to resort to a battery-operated substitute to get off? She wasn't remotely frigid or unresponsive or prudish. She'd been so wet and hot for it, he simply couldn't understand how she could have gone unsatisfied for so long.

She settled against the edge of the tub, her arms spread along the rim. He sat opposite her, letting his legs tangle with hers beneath the water. She was still flushed, her eyes smoky. His gaze found her nipples as they broke the surface of the water.

"So, these other guys you slept with—were they swimmers?" he asked.

She eyed him warily. "Why? You planning on writing an exposé?"

"Just working on a theory. Were they all swimmers?"

"Yes."

"Ah."

He sank deeper into the water.

"*Ah* what? You can't just say *ah* then not explain."

"I'm not surprised things were tepid in the sack. You

trained together, ate together, hung out together. Kind of like brothers and sisters."

"Nothing like brothers and sisters. Not even close."

"Then maybe it was all the training. Maybe they were so beat from all those laps they didn't have anything extra to give."

She thought for a minute. "Maybe."

"Plus, I'm pretty good in bed," he said, to get a rise out of her. "We should definitely not overlook my awesome technique."

She laughed. "You want a medal? A badge of honor?"

He eyed the rosy peaks of her breasts. "How about an encore? Come here."

She hesitated a moment, the way she had earlier when he'd invited her to step closer. He hooked his foot behind her hip and tried to pull her toward him. "I'll make it worth your while."

Her mouth quirked into a smile. "Yeah? How so?"

"Come here and I'll show you."

She pushed away from the edge of the tub and floated toward him. He slid his arms around her and pulled her close for a kiss.

She had a great mouth. He couldn't get enough of it. He shifted in the water until she was straddling him. He deepened their kiss, his hands roaming over her breasts. She tensed slightly every time he plucked her nipples, a shiver of need rippling through her. It drove him wild.

He slid a hand between her thighs to where she was spread wide for him. She was slick and silky beneath his hands. He took his time exploring her, playing with her clitoris, teasing her inner lips, sliding one finger, then two inside her.

"Jake," she whispered, reaching for his cock.

He wanted it, too, but they couldn't use a condom in the water. She seemed to understand as he continued to work her with his fingers. She stroked her hand up and down his length as he stroked his fingers between her thighs. Soon she was shuddering, close to coming again. He was too greedy to let her climax without him.

"Let's go," he said, his voice very low.

She stood and stepped from the spa. She didn't bother toweling herself dry, simply strode straight into the bedroom and reached for his jeans.

"You'd better have another condom," she said.

She smiled triumphantly as she pulled the foil square from his back pocket.

"That's it, though," he said.

"Then we'd better make it count."

She climbed onto the bed on all fours, offering him a heart-stopping view of her slick heat and her firm, toned ass. She looked over her shoulder at him, her skin still glistening from the bath.

"What are you waiting for?"

"Excellent question."

He sheathed himself and moved to the bed. She arched her back and pressed into his hips as he came up behind her. He steadied his cock with his hand and slid it along the slick seam of her sex. She sighed and pressed back some more.

"Stop teasing," she said.

"Stop being so impatient."

But he loved how much she wanted it. He especially loved how wet she was. He pressed forward, the head of his penis sliding just inside her entrance. She arched her spine and took all of him. He closed his eyes as she clenched her muscles around him.

So good. So damned good.

He began to move, withdrawing until just the tip of his cock remained inside her then resheathing himself. She rocked to his rhythm, her body very warm and tight around him. Slowly the tension increased. He slid a hand over her hip and between her thighs. Her clit was swollen and slick and he'd barely touched it before she started to shudder around him.

"Yes. Oh, yes!" she panted.

Man, but she was hot. Tight, wet, her body firm and strong. He closed his eyes as his climax hit him, his hands gripping her hips as he pumped into her once, twice, then one last time.

They were both breathing heavily afterward. He withdrew from her and stepped into the bathroom to dispose of the condom. When he returned, she was lying on her side, the same dazed, slightly lost expression on her face she'd had the first time.

"You okay?" he asked.

"I think so. I feel like I just found out the earth is round after years of thinking it was flat."

He dropped onto the bed beside her. She rolled onto her back and his gaze traveled over her body. She was all woman, incredibly sexy. He remembered how round and firm her ass had been as he pounded into her from behind.

"Give me a few minutes and I'll give you another geography lesson," he said.

She shifted her head to look at him.

"I thought we were out of condoms."

"We are. But we've still got this." He leaned across and licked one of her nipples.

Her eyelids dropped to half-mast.

"And there's always this." He pressed a kiss to her belly, then the plump rise of her mound.

She held her breath and he glanced up at her. She wanted him again. Just like he wanted her.

"George would have run out of batteries by now. You realize that, don't you?"

She laughed and fisted a hand in his hair, using her grip to draw him back up her body.

"You win. Hands down. Happy?"

"Satisfied, I think you mean."

"Okay, are you satisfied?"

He looked at her body, remembering the too-brief taste he'd had of her earlier.

"Not yet," he said. "But I'm working on it."

POPPY WOKE TO THE SOUND of running water. She opened her eyes and frowned at the unfamiliar ceiling. Then memories from last night washed over her like a tsunami.

Right. She'd come to Jake's room. She'd challenged him and he'd taken her up on it and they'd spent the next several hours going to town on each other.

"Oh, God," she whispered, pressing her fingers against her closed eyes.

The things she'd done last night. The things he'd done. The way her body had responded.

What had she been thinking?

But there had been precious little thinking going on. From the moment she'd met him she'd been too aware of him physically. Then she'd caught him looking at her yesterday and understood she could have him. If she wanted him. And she had.

He'd given her more pleasure in one night than all of her other lovers combined. Hell, he even made George look average. She shifted restlessly as she remembered the feel of his hard cock sliding inside her.

The shower shut off and she sat up in bed.

Shit. She didn't know what to say to him. And he was going to be showered and fresh and possibly dressed, and she was lying here, naked and drowsy and stupid.

She scrambled from the bed and grabbed her jeans. Her panties were tangled in one leg. She didn't bother trying to get them on, simply dragged her jeans on and stuffed her panties into her pocket. Her bra was on the floor. She'd just fastened the clasp when the bathroom door opened and Jake entered. His dark hair was wet and sticking up in spikes. A towel rode low on his hips.

The sight of him made her mouth water.

He stopped in his tracks and they stared at each other for a beat. Then she bent and picked up her shirt.

"Sorry. I didn't mean to oversleep. We should probably be on the road by now," she said.

There was a short pause before he answered.

"No worries. We can make up the time during the day. I took a look at the map. What do you say we aim for Gundagai today?" he said, naming a town roughly halfway between Sydney and Melbourne.

"Sure. That sounds good. I'll, um, I'll grab a shower and meet you at the car."

She buttoned her shirt enough for modesty, picked up her shoes and jacket and headed for the door. She didn't breathe easily until she was outside. Then she closed her eyes and groaned.

"You idiot."

She'd never had a one-night stand in her life. Not that she thought sex was a sacred act that could only occur between two people who loved each other or anything like that. It just hadn't ever come up. She'd been so busy training, concentrating on her swimming, that huge aspects of her life had gone unexplored. Like good sex, apparently. And casual sex. Consequently, she was woefully ill-informed on how she should handle herself the morning after. Her bare toes curled into the concrete as she remembered the awkward pause when Jake had emerged from the bathroom. Was she supposed to have been gone? Was that what the shower had been about—to signal to her that the night was over and it was time for her to skedaddle back to her own room?

Good Lord, maybe she shouldn't have even fallen asleep. Maybe she should have gotten dressed and returned to her room at two or three in the morning, whatever time it had been when they'd finally given in to fatigue and stopped having at each other.

She let herself into her room and stripped. Her body felt strange under the shower, oddly sensitive and tender.

She dressed quickly in a pair of black linen drawstring pants and a white T-shirt. She finger combed her hair, then took a moment to study her face in the mirror.

She didn't look any different, but she felt it. Last night had been a revelation, pure and simple. She felt as though she'd been granted membership to a secret club. For years she'd read books and watched movies where people did crazy, hurtful, risky things for love and lust. She'd never understood why. Until now.

She could understand why a woman would risk a lot for another night in Jake Stevens's arms. The pleasure he'd given her last night was like a drug. She'd never felt more alive, more sensual, more passionate, more beautiful.

And it's never going to happen again.

She knew the practical voice in her head was right. Not for a second did she believe that what had happened between her and Jake was the beginning of something and not the sum total of it. She only hoped she could remember that for the next however many hours she was stuck in the car with him because thinking about him, about what had happened between them last night, made her want him all over again.

He was leaning against the car when she exited her room

with her overnight bag in hand. His arms were crossed over his chest and he had his sunglasses on. Her gaze dropped to his thighs for a second and she remembered the power of him as he'd thrust into her last night.

Never going to happen.

She had to keep reminding herself. She pulled her own sunglasses from her coat pocket and slid them on.

"Ready to go?" he asked.

"Yeah. We can grab breakfast on the road."

"Good idea."

He took the first turn behind the wheel. She cranked the passenger seat back and pretended to be getting a little extra shut-eye. Anything to avoid looking at him and remembering.

He spoke after an hour. "There's a truck stop coming up. You hungry?"

"Sure," she said.

They parked between two huge rigs and made their way inside the Do Drop In Tasty Stop. Jake slid into one side of a booth, she the other. The table was so narrow their knees bumped beneath it.

"Sorry," they both said at the same time.

Poppy studied Jake from beneath her eyelashes. She didn't know how to deal with him now. Before last night, he'd been her enemy and it had been easy to keep her guard up. Yesterday, they'd brokered a peace deal during the long hours on the road. And last night…well, last night they'd crossed the line, and she had no idea how to uncross it.

Right now, for example, she couldn't seem to stop herself from eyeing his broad shoulders and the firm, curved muscles of his pecs as he sat opposite her. He'd felt so hot and hard pressed against her. His skin was smooth and golden and she'd licked and kissed and sucked him all over until he'd—

"What are you having?" Jake asked.

She tore her eyes from his chest and saw that a waitress was hovering beside their booth, pen poised over her pad.

"Um, scrambled eggs on toast. Bacon. Coffee," she said.

"Same." Jake handed his menu to the waitress.

His blue eyes settled on her once they were alone. She remembered the way he'd looked into her eyes, his nose just an inch from her own last night after he'd made her lose her mind the first time.

"Looks like it's going to be another hot day," he said.

"Yep."

"Should grab some water for the road."

"Good idea."

Silence fell. She ran her thumbnail along the edge of the Formica table. If she was more experienced in the ways of the world, she'd know how to handle this situation.

But she wasn't, and she didn't.

They ate in silence, both of them staring out the window at the unexciting panorama of freeway, gas station and dry scrubland.

"I'll get this. You got dinner," she said when the waitress presented their bill.

"If that's what you want," he said.

She stared at him for a moment, frustration twisting inside her. What she wanted was for things to not be so awkward. She frowned as she registered the dishonesty of her thoughts. Okay, that wasn't what she *really* wanted. What she really wanted was for Jake to kiss her again and slide his hand between her legs and make her feel as liquid and hot as she had last night. But she would settle for not feeling stiff and uncomfortable and self-conscious around him.

It was just sex, she reminded herself. *Two adults enjoying each other's bodies. No big deal. Nothing to get your knickers in a knot over.*

She settled the bill and joined Jake at the car.

He'd bought a couple of bottles of water from the gas station and he handed her one. She settled in her seat and closed her eyes once they were on the highway again. If she could doze, it would help pass the time. And maybe a miracle would occur while she slept and she'd wake up and the tension in the car would be gone.

Her thoughts were too chaotic to be restful, however. She could smell Jake's aftershave, could remember washing it from her skin this morning. From her neck and her breasts. From between her thighs.

She pushed the memory away, deliberately focusing instead on Uncle Charlie's upcoming birthday. She thought about her present, tried to work out what to say when she gave it to him. More than anyone else in her life, he'd shaped her to be the person she was today. She didn't have the words to tell him how important he was to her, but somehow she had to find them.

She woke to the sensation of the car slowing.

"Ready to swap?" she asked, sitting up and stretching.

"Pit stop," Jake said. He indicated the toilet block in the rest area they'd pulled into.

She got out of the car and shoved her sunglasses into her pocket. She cracked the seal on her bottle of water as he walked across the gravel to the facilities. She took a mouthful and shielded her eyes to look out across the plains. The land looked brown and dry, unwelcoming.

Gravel crunched as Jake returned. He stopped in front of her and she offered him the water.

"Thanks."

He pushed his sunglasses on top of his head and took a long pull. She let her eyes slide over his chest and belly and thighs. She was gripped with a sudden urge to put her hand on his chest so she could feel the warm, strong resilience of his muscles.

Stop it. She curled her hands into fists, but she couldn't make herself look away.

He took the bottle from his mouth and a single drop of water slid over his lower lip and down his chin. She stared at his mouth, remembering what he'd done to her with his lips and his tongue and his hands last night.

She could feel her nipples hardening. From a look, a single small moment. She met his eyes. For a long beat, neither of them moved. She held her breath.

"Better hit the road." His voice sounded rough.

She climbed into the car and fastened her seat belt. She took a deep breath, then another. She'd never had to fight lust before. She wasn't quite sure how to do it. She was so damned aware of him, couldn't stop remembering small, breathless moments from last night: his harsh breathing near her ear as he pumped into her; the feel of his firm, muscular butt beneath her hands; the skilled flick of his tongue between her legs.

Stop it, she told herself again. She was practically panting. She had to get a grip.

The car dipped as Jake got in beside her and slid his sunglasses onto his face. He started the car and stepped on the gas. Almost immediately he slammed on the brakes. She looked across at him, surprised. He was staring straight ahead, his forehead creased into a frown.

"What's wrong?" she asked.

He turned to look at her. She couldn't see his eyes behind his dark glasses, but something—some instinct—made her look down.

He had a hard-on. The ridge of it was unmistakable beneath his jeans.

"Oh." She let her breath out in a rush, hugely relieved that the need throbbing low in her belly was not one-sided.

"Why didn't you say so?" she said. "I've never done it in a car before."

A slow smile curved his mouth. "Another first. We're really clocking them up."

He leaned across the hand brake and she met him halfway. His lips, his tongue, his heat—just the taste of him sent her pulse through the roof. Within minutes they were pulling at each other's clothes and breathing heavily.

"You stay where you are," she said when they both tried to clamber across the center console at once. She wriggled out of her trousers and underwear while he cranked his seat back. She climbed across the hand brake and into his lap. His erection sat hard and proud beneath her. She shifted her hips, rubbing herself against his length.

"Damn it," she said suddenly. "No protection."

How could she have forgotten something so fundamental? Jake gave her a wicked smile and reached for the glove box. She shook her head when he pulled out a pack of twelve condoms.

"A little cocky, don't you think?" she said, arching an eyebrow.

"A lot cocky," he said. He grinned and she found herself laughing.

She pulled a condom from the pack and tilted her hips to access his erection. The latex went on smoothly, all the way to his thick base. She held him there and rubbed herself back and forth across the plump head of his cock.

"That feels so good," she said, eyes half shut.

He grabbed her hips and pulled her down impatiently, thrusting upward at the same time. She bit her lip as he filled her. And then she was riding him, his hands on her breasts, his eyes on hers as she drove them both wild.

They came together, bodies shuddering. Poppy braced her arms on the seat on either side of his body afterward, her breath coming in gasps as she stared down at him.

Every time was better than the last. She wasn't sure how that was possible, but it was.

A semitrailer drove past and gave a long blast on its air-horn. They both startled, then laughed.

"Guess we're lucky he wasn't a few minutes earlier," she said, even as she was wondering at her own audacity.

Last night she'd had her first one-night stand and today she'd graduated to sex in a public highway rest stop. She felt as though she'd taken a crash course in sexual desire. Lust 101.

She slid off him and back to her side of the car. Jake took care of the condom, exiting the car to walk back to the toilet block. She struggled into her clothes, bumping elbows and knees in the cramped quarters.

It occurred to her then that, technically, what had just happened between them meant last night had not been a one-night stand.

She tightened the drawstring on her linen pants, frowning. She wasn't sure how to feel about the realization. Clearly, she and Jake had some pretty serious sexual chemistry going on. And they were stuck with each other for at least another day. Her thoughts raced ahead to tonight, to what might happen when they stopped and checked in to yet another motel. Would they pay for one room, or two?

Movement caught the corner of her eye and she turned to watch Jake walk back to the car.

It might be foolish, but she wanted more of him, more of how she felt when she was with him. If he asked—and she hoped he did—she'd opt for one room.

Jake slid behind the wheel. She smiled. He looked at her for a moment, his expression unreadable, then he reached for the ignition key. He didn't turn it. Instead, he took a deep breath and twisted to face her.

"We should probably talk," he said.

"Okay." Suddenly she felt incredibly transparent, as though he knew exactly what she'd been thinking as she watched him walk to the car.

"I'm not really sure how to say this...so I'll just say it. I'm not looking for a relationship right now," he said.

She took a deep breath. Wow. Talk about straight to the point.

"Sure. I know that," she said.

And she did. Just because she'd been thinking about sharing a room with him tonight didn't mean she thought this thing had a future. It was just sex. Nothing more.

"I wanted to be clear. I like you, Poppy. I don't want things to get messy between us, given the way we started out."

"I'm not going to start stalking you and stewing small animals on your stove, if that's what you're worried about," she said. "I had fun last night. But I know exactly what it was."

He studied her face for a long moment, as though he was trying to gauge the truth of her words. She smiled, then punched him on the arm. "Relax. I didn't think you were about to propose because you gave me a bunch of orgasms."

Finally he smiled. "Okay. Good. Great."

He started the car. She put her sunglasses on and made a big deal about getting comfortable in her seat. She stared out the side window as he accelerated onto the highway.

She could punch him on the arm and play it cool however much she liked, but she couldn't lie to herself.

She was disappointed.

It's the sex. You're disappointed there won't be any more of the amazing sex when you stop tonight.

It was true, but it was also a lie. She liked him. She hadn't realized how much until thirty seconds ago.

She crossed her arms over her chest. The sooner they got to Melbourne, the better.

5

JAKE'S CONSCIENCE WAS CLEAR. He'd looked Poppy in the eye and been honest. Admittedly, that had happened *after* he'd had the best quickie of his life with her, but he'd never claimed to be perfect.

Jake reached for his bottle of water and took a mouthful.

He had no idea why he was feeling guilty. She'd wanted it, too. She'd been more than ready to meet him halfway. And she'd been fast to acknowledge that what had happened last night and five minutes ago didn't have a future. No matter how spectacular the sex was.

So why did he feel like a horny teenager desperately trying to justify bad behavior to himself?

There were many solid, rational reasons why nothing beyond sex was ever going to happen between them. They worked together, for starters. And he'd made himself a promise not to get involved with anyone until he'd finished his second novel. The last thing he needed right now was the distraction of a new relationship, especially one with a woman like Poppy.

She'd expect things from him. Commitment being at the top of the list. His thoughts turned to Marly and the mess of their marriage. No way did he want to go there again. Ever. Which didn't leave a man and a woman much room to maneuver, at the end of the day.

He rolled his shoulders and eased his grip on the steering wheel. How in the hell had he gotten from vague guilt about a rest-stop quickie to thoughts of marriage and monogamy?

He slid a glance Poppy's way. She was staring out the window, her face angled away from him.

He thought about the dazed look in her eyes after they'd had sex last night. He remembered her laughter in the bath, and the way he'd caught her scrambling into her clothes this morning.

He was a moron.

He should never have touched her. He should have taken a deep breath last night and walked away instead of letting his hard-on do the thinking for him.

He reached out and punched the radio on, frustrated with himself. Dolly Parton's voice filled the car, wailing about eyes of green and someone stealing her man.

He sighed. What was with rural Australia and country music? Hadn't anyone heard of good old-fashioned rock'n'roll out here in the back of beyond?

The electronic ring of a cell phone cut into Dolly's refrain. Poppy stirred and reached into the backseat to pull her phone from her coat pocket. He tried not to notice the fact that her breast brushed his shoulder or that she smelled good, like sunshine and fresh air.

"Hey, Mom, what's up?" she said into the phone.

He punched off the stereo to make it easier for her to hear.

"What? No!"

He glanced across at her. She'd gone pale and her hand clutched the cell. He eased off the gas.

Something was wrong.

"No! He was fine when I spoke to him on Saturday. He was fine!" she said. Her voice broke on the last word.

Something was definitely wrong. Her eyes were squeezed

tightly shut and she bowed her head forward, pressing a hand to her forehead.

"Did they say... Did they say if he was in any pain? Was it quick?"

Jesus. A death.

He glanced around, but there was no rest area in sight. He pulled off the highway anyway, as far over on the gravel shoulder as he could go.

She didn't seem to notice. All her attention was focused on the bad news coming down the line.

"I understand. Yes. I'll be there as soon as I can. No, I'll drive myself. No. Yes. Okay, I'll...I'll see you soon."

She ended the call and simply sat there, shoulders hunched forward, hands loose between her legs. For a long moment there was nothing but the sound of her breathing and the tick, tick of the engine cooling. A truck sped past and their rental car rocked in its wake.

"Poppy. Is there anything I can do?" he asked quietly.

She didn't say a word, just reached for the door handle and shot from the car. She struck out into the drought-browned pasture alongside the highway as though she could outrun the reality of what she'd learned. Then she stopped suddenly, doubling over. He didn't need to hear her or see her face to know she was crying. She sank to the ground, her shoulders shaking.

Damn.

He had no clue what to do or say. No idea who had died. Her mother had called. Had her father died? Or a brother?

He shook his head and climbed out of the car. He walked slowly toward her, his gut tensing as he saw how tightly she had folded into herself, her arms wrapped tightly around her pulled-up legs, her face pressed into her knees.

He crouched down beside her and placed a hand in the middle of her back.

"Poppy."

She didn't lift her head. He sat down properly, keeping his hand on her back. After a few minutes, she shifted a little and her head came up.

Her eyes were puffy and red, her face streaked with tears. She looked gutted, utterly stricken.

"Uncle Charlie," she said. "Uncle Charlie died."

"I'm sorry."

Talk about inadequate. But there were no words that could take away her pain.

"It was his seventieth on Wednesday. That was why I wanted to get home so badly. He had a heart attack, Mom said."

"Sounds like it was quick."

Her face crumpled. "I should have been there. He was always there for me."

She started crying again. He gave in to his instincts and slid his arm all the way around her shoulders, pulling her against his chest. She let her head flop onto his shoulder and one of her hands curled into his T-shirt and fisted into the fabric. He held her as her body shook.

She was heartbroken. He didn't know what to do for her.

A few minutes later, she loosened her grip on his T-shirt and pulled away from him. He let his arm fall from her shoulders. She used her hands to wipe the tears from her cheeks, not looking at him. She took a couple of long, shuddering breaths. Then she stood.

"I need to get home," she said, still not looking at him.

"Okay. We're nearly to Sydney. We can cut around the city, be in Melbourne in about eleven hours."

He'd already done the math in his head, worked out the best route.

She nodded and started toward the car. She got in and stared straight ahead as he walked to the driver's side. He could almost feel her sucking her emotions back in, building a wall around herself until she could find a safe place to give vent to her grief.

She didn't say a word as they drove around the outskirts of Sydney. She lay on the half-reclined seat facing the window, her back to him. He had no idea if she was crying or sleeping or simply grieving.

He stopped in Goulburn, two hours south of Sydney, for food. She didn't touch her cheeseburger and he wrapped it up and put it aside in case she wanted it later. He stopped again in Albury for gas and coffee. She left the car and walked slowly toward the restrooms, her head down. When she returned her hair was wet and he guessed she'd splashed her face with water.

"I'll drive if you're tired," she offered. Her eyes were bloodshot and blank.

"I'm fine. Three more hours and we'll be home."

She nodded. "Thanks. I appreciate it."

He shrugged off her gratitude. He only wished there was more he could do or say, but they hardly knew each other. Sad, but true.

IT WAS DARK WHEN Jake pulled into the rental car return lot at Melbourne airport. Poppy had been sitting upright and staring grimly out the windshield for the last hour. He could almost hear her making plans in her head.

"Where's home? Can I drop you anywhere?" he asked as they collected their things from the trunk.

"My car's in long-term parking, and my parents are in Ballarat. Uncle Charlie lives— His house is down the road from them."

"Okay. I'll take care of the car return. You get going."

"Thank you. I owe you."

"No, you don't."

Even though he figured she probably didn't want him to, he pulled her close for a quick hug. She was hurting. He felt for her. Surely even a one-night stand and a work colleague was allowed to care that much?

She didn't meet his eyes when the embrace ended, just nodded her head and turned away. He watched her walk toward the pickup point for the courtesy bus to long-term parking.

For the first time since he'd met her, she looked small and fragile.

He turned away. She'd be with her family soon. She'd be okay.

POPPY THREW HER OVERNIGHT bag into the back of her Honda. At least the airport was on the right side of the city; she'd be in Ballarat within an hour. Her eyes filled with tears as she climbed behind the wheel.

Uncle Charlie was dead. She still couldn't comprehend it. It was too big. Too hard. She didn't want it to be true. Didn't want to accept that she would never hear his voice or hold his hand or feel the rasp of his stubble on her cheek when she embraced him.

She blinked the tears away. She couldn't give in and cry yet. She needed to get home. Then she could curl up in a ball and howl the way she wanted to.

She slid her key into the ignition and turned it. Instead of the reassuring roar of the engine starting, she heard a faint click. She frowned and tried the ignition a second time. Again she heard nothing but a faint click.

She stared at her dash and saw that the battery indicator light was shining.

She sat back in her seat. Her battery was dead.

Shit.

Tears came again. She swiped them away with the back of her hand and pulled her cell phone from her pocket. The auto club people could jump-start her. Or if worse came to worst, she could rent another car.

She got out of the car while she was waiting for the phone to connect to the auto club. Might as well look under the hood in case one of the clamps had slipped off a battery terminal or something.

She knew it was a faint hope. She listened to cheery hold music as she peered at her engine. It was hard to tell in the dark, but everything looked the way it should.

"Thank you for calling the Royal Auto Club of Victoria. How can we help you?"

Poppy leaned against the side of her car and explained her situation to the woman. Her eyes were sore and she rubbed them wearily.

"We'll have someone out to take a look at your car as soon as possible," the woman said.

"How long will that be?"

She wanted to be home. She *needed* to be home.

"At this stage, the system is telling me there's a two-hour wait. Our nearest mechanic is on the other side of the city, I'm afraid."

Poppy closed her eyes. Two hours.

"Forget about it. I'll take care of it myself." She ended the call.

She'd go and rent a vehicle. She didn't care about anything else. Her car could sit here until the end of time for all she cared.

A low, dark sports car cruised past, its engine a muted rumble. She grabbed her bag from the backseat and walked around to the front of her car to close the hood.

"What's wrong?"

She slammed the hood down. Jake was standing in the open doorway of the sports car, a frown on his face.

"Dead battery."

"Right." He checked his watch. "What are you going to do?"

She shouldered her bag and used her remote to lock her car.

"The auto club wait is two hours. I'm going to rent a car."

He frowned. "They're pretty busy in there. The strike's still on."

She shrugged. She'd get a freaking taxi all the way if she had to.

"Get in," he said.

She stared at him. "What?"

"I'll take you. Get in."

"It's an hour's drive out of the city."

"So what? You need to get home, right?"

She stared at him.

He was offering only because he felt sorry for her. And things were awkward between them.

But she really needed to get home.

"Okay." Pride was a luxury she couldn't afford right now.

He took her bag and put it in the trunk. She slid into the passenger seat.

"You've been driving for hours," she said when he got in beside her.

"One more hour won't make a difference. If I look like I'm dozing off, feel free to slap me."

She studied his profile as he navigated his way out of the parking lot.

"You didn't have to do this," she said after a short silence.

"I know. I'm a saint."

"Well, I appreciate it. And the fact that you did all the driving today," she said.

"If you're about to thank me for sleeping with you, you can get out now."

It was so unexpected she laughed.

"What's the best route out of the city?" he asked.

She gave him directions. He hit a switch and the mellow sounds of Coldplay eased into the car.

He didn't talk for the next half hour. She was grateful, just as she'd been grateful for his silence earlier today. She wasn't up to polite chitchat, and she wasn't ready to talk about Uncle Charlie. Certainly not to Jake Stevens. He was a virtual stranger, despite how intimate they'd been. There was no way she could share her pain and grief with him.

The exit for Ballarat came up quickly and she gave Jake directions to her parents' house. They lived on the outskirts of the rural center of Ballarat in a big, rambling farmhouse at the end of a long gravel drive. Jake's car dipped and rocked over the uneven ground as they covered the last few yards to the house. The porch light came on as she climbed out of the car. Her parents stood silhouetted in the light.

"You made good time," her mom said.

"We weren't expecting you for a while yet," her father said.

Poppy stood at the bottom of the steps, staring up at them. All the grief she'd held on to for so many hours rose up the back of her throat. She started to cry.

"Oh, Poppy. I knew you'd take it hard," her mother said.

Her mother embraced her with the awkward stiffness that characterized all their physical contact. Vaguely, Poppy was aware of her father introducing himself to Jake and of her mother shuffling her into the house. Then she was sitting at the kitchen table, a cup of sweet tea in her hands, tears still coursing down her face.

"He went the way he always wanted to go—quickly, not hanging around," her father said. "You know he dreaded having a stroke and lingering."

Her parents stood at the end of the table, concern and confusion on their faces. They didn't know what to do. They never did when it came to the world of the emotions.

Never had Poppy needed Uncle Charlie more.

She ducked her head, the tears falling from her chin to plop onto the tabletop.

"She's exhausted. We've been driving for hours," someone said, and she realized Jake was standing behind her.

For some reason it made the tears flow faster and she hunched further into herself.

"Sweetheart. I hate to see you so upset. Uncle Charlie had a good life. We're all going to miss him, but we all have to die sometime. Human beings are mortal creatures, after all," her mother said.

Poppy lifted her head, trying to articulate the gaping sense of loss she felt. "He was my best f-friend."

"I know. And he was my brother and it's very sad but you'll make yourself sick getting so wound up like this," her father said.

Poppy pressed the heels of her hands into her eyes. They didn't understand. They never had.

"What about a shower?" her mother suggested. "What about a shower and some sleep?"

"That's a good idea. What do you say, Poppy?" her father said heartily.

"Sure." Poppy stood and made her way to the bathroom

at the rear of the house. Her mother pressed a fresh towel into her hands.

"I'll turn down your bed," she said, patting Poppy's arm.

Poppy nodded. Then she was alone, the towel clutched to her chest.

She undressed slowly and leaned against the shower wall as the water ran over her, lifting her face into the spray so that she had to gasp through her mouth to breathe. A hundred memories flashed across the movie screen of her mind as the water beat down on her.

Uncle Charlie hooting and hollering from the stands at her first Commonwealth Games. Uncle Charlie sitting patiently beside the pool during her early-morning practice sessions, day after day after day. Uncle Charlie holding her hand in the specialist's office when she was waiting to hear the verdict on her shoulder injury.

She didn't bother drying herself off when she stepped out of the shower. She simply pulled on her old terry-cloth bathrobe and wrapped the towel around her wet hair.

The light was on in her old bedroom and she walked slowly toward it. She pulled up short when she heard her mother talking to someone.

"Don't be ridiculous. It's late, you've been driving for hours. I won't have an accident on my conscience."

Poppy moved to the doorway. Jake stood beside her old bed, watching her mother fluff the pillows. He looked bemused, like a man who didn't quite know what had hit him.

"I'm insisting that Jake stay the night," her mother said when she saw Poppy.

Jake's expression was a masterpiece of tortured middle-class politeness.

"I've just been explaining to your mother that my fishing buddy is expecting me. And that the last thing you probably want is me in your bed after the day you've had." He widened his eyes meaningfully.

"And I've been telling Jake that Allan and I aren't old-fashioned about these kinds of things."

Poppy stared at her mother, not quite getting it. Then her slow brain caught up—her mother thought Jake was her boyfriend.

No wonder he was looking so hunted.

"Jake and I aren't together."

"Oh!" Her mother blushed, one hand pressed to her chest. "I'm so sorry! I just assumed…"

"Jake was helping me out," Poppy said. She turned to him. "She's right, though. You should stay. You must be exhausted after all that driving. There are plenty of other bedrooms."

"Yes! Of course there are! Adam's room is right next door, and the bed is already made up." Her mother nodded effusively, eager to make up for her gaffe.

"I'm fine. Really," Jake said.

Poppy's mother looked to her, clearly expecting her to intervene.

Poppy shrugged. "It's your decision," she said, turning away.

He was a grown-up. If he thought he was okay to drive, it was up to him. She sat on the side of the bed and stared at her feet. She was numb and exhausted and so empty it hurt.

There was a short silence.

"Maybe I should get a few hours' shut-eye before I hit the road again," Jake said.

Poppy pulled the quilt back and crawled beneath the covers. She didn't look at either of them, just rolled onto her side and closed her eyes.

She wanted to wipe the day out, strike it from the record as though it had never happened. She wanted to turn back the clock to a time when Uncle Charlie was still a part of her world.

"I'll show you Adam's room," she heard her mother say.

There was the scuff of shoes on floorboards, then Poppy was alone. She opened her eyes and stared blindly at the far wall.

"Uncle Charlie," she whispered.

JAKE LAY IN POPPY'S brother's bed and stared at the ceiling. By rights he should be halfway to Melbourne by now, Poppy and her grief left far behind. Instead he was lying here, listening to the sounds of a strange house settling for the night.

The truth was, he hadn't been able to leave her.

Which was nuts. Even if she was devastated by grief, the last person Poppy would turn to was him. They'd been thrown together by circumstances, nothing else. Even the sex had been about availability and proximity. At least initially, anyway. And yet here he was in her parents' house, unable to abandon her to her family's distant, entirely inadequate sympathy.

His chest got tight every time he remembered the empty, sad look on Poppy's face as she sat at her parent's kitchen table, shoulders hunched forward as though making herself smaller could diminish her grief, protect her from it somehow. And her parents had simply stood there and let her ache.

His own family were far from perfect. His father had a temper and his mother wasn't above playing the martyr to get her own way. His brothers and sisters all had their fair share of flaws and foibles. And yet if someone close to them had died, if one of them was hurting or needy or in trouble, the Stevens family would not hesitate to circle the wagons and pull up the drawbridge. Hugs would be the order of the day, along with kisses and tears and laughter. It would be messy and loud and warm and real.

By contrast, Yvonne Birmingham had looked so uncomfortable embracing her daughter that she might as well have been undergoing root canal, while Allan had offered his grief-stricken daughter rational words and philosophy and precious little else. Jake had waited in vain for someone to offer Poppy the simple comfort of another warm body to cling to. Hell, even a hand on the shoulder and a sympathetic handkerchief or tissue would have done the trick. But the Birminghams were not huggers, he'd quickly realized.

Allan had given Jake their bona fides while Poppy was in the shower—they were both academics, tenured professors at Ballarat University. Allan taught history, Yvonne English literature. Jake had detected a faint accent in both their speeches and he guessed from the photographs on the wall that they had emigrated to Australia from England some years ago.

He couldn't think of a more unlikely pair to have produced a larger-than-life, earthy woman like Poppy. In fact, the more he thought about it, the more impossible it seemed. They were so self-contained and cerebral, and Poppy was so physical and full of energy and honesty.

Staring into the dark, he pondered what it must have been like for Poppy, growing up with parents who lived in their minds when she was a person who lived in her belly and heart. He might not know all the ins and outs of Poppy's world, but he knew that much about her.

Lonely, he guessed. Hence her close relationship with Uncle Charlie.

The second cup of tea Yvonne had pressed on him before bed made its presence felt and he swung his legs over the side of the mattress and went in search of the bathroom. He made a deal with himself as he shuffled up the darkened hallway. He'd try to grab a few hours' sleep when he got back to bed, but if sleep didn't come he'd dress and slip out the back door and head for Melbourne.

It wasn't as though he was serving any purpose here, after all.

He was passing Poppy's bedroom door on the way back to Adam's room when a low sound made him pause. He gritted his teeth; she was crying. He hesitated for only a second. He could be a stubborn bastard and a self-confessed smart-ass, but it simply wasn't in him to walk away from someone in so much pain.

He pushed her door open. "Poppy."

She didn't respond but he could hear her breathing.

Again he hesitated. Then he entered the room and closed the door. His shin found her bed before his outstretched hands did and he swore under his breath.

"Don't freak out, I'm getting into the bed," he said.

She didn't say a word as he pulled back the covers. It was only a double bed, but she was curled up on the far side. He slid across the cool sheets until his chest was pressed against her back. He wrapped an arm around her waist and pulled her tightly against his body. She was rigid with tension and as unresponsive as a lump of wood.

"It's okay, Poppy," he said very quietly.

She started to shake. He pulled her closer, curling his legs behind hers so that they were tightly spooned. He could feel her grief, her pain, vibrating through her.

"It's okay," he said again.

"No, it isn't."

Her chest heaved as she sucked in a breath, then she was shuddering, sniffing back tears, gulping for air. He held her tightly, not saying a word. It wasn't as though there was anything to say, anyway. There wasn't a well-formed phrase in the world that made losing someone less sad.

Slowly the crying jag passed. Poppy sniffed noisily and moved restlessly in his arms. He eased away from her and released his grip.

"I'm sorry," she said.

"For what?"

"All of this. My mom forcing you to stay the night. Taking more time away from your fishing trip. This wasn't exactly what you signed on for when you offered me a lift home."

"Your mom didn't force me to stay. I wanted to make sure you were okay."

Her head turned toward him on the pillow. In the faint light from the window he could see the dampness on her cheeks.

"Noble of you."

"Don't worry, I'm sure it won't last."

She managed a faint smile, then she used the sleeve of her robe to wipe her eyes. It was a child's gesture and it made her seem even more vulnerable.

"You want to talk?" he asked. His ex-wife would keel over in shock at hearing those four words leave his mouth, but he didn't know what other comfort to offer.

She shrugged and dabbed at her face again with her sleeve.

"Not much to say. He was my best friend. He taught me how to swim. Came to every major meet and most of the minor ones. And now he's gone."

"He was your father's brother, yeah?"

"Yes. But Charlie was older by twelve years. There was less money when he was born, so he didn't get the same education as my father. He was a house painter. He was the one who decided to emigrate to Australia. Mom and Dad followed him a few years later."

"I wondered about the accent."

"Cambridge."

"Right."

He thought about what she'd said about her uncle coming to every meet and what it implied about her parents—they hadn't. And for the first time it occurred to him that while he'd seen plenty of books piled all over the place and black-and-white photographs of England on the walls of her parents' home, there hadn't been a single shot of Poppy. No photos on the winner's dais. No newspaper clippings. No framed medals or ribbons. No indication at all that the Birminghams had a world-record-holding, gold-medal-winning daughter.

"You know what the crazy thing is?" Poppy asked after a short silence. "All I could think about when we were on the road is getting home. And once I got here, I realized that the thing I'd been holding out for was Uncle Charlie. And he's not here anymore." She tried to keep her voice light, as though she was telling a joke on herself, but there was a telltale quaver in it.

"It was his birthday on Wednesday, too. I'd been teasing him for months about what I was going to get him. And now he'll never know…" She was crying again, tears sliding down her face and onto the pillow.

"What did you get him?"

"I had a frame made for my first gold medal. And there was this picture of the two of us when I was a kid… I wanted him to know that I couldn't have done any of it without him."

"It sounds great. I bet he would have loved it."

She shifted, sitting upright then leaning over the side of the bed. He heard the rustle of paper as she fumbled in the dark, then she lifted a large, flat box from beneath the bed. The weight of it landed heavily on his legs as she placed it in his lap.

"Open it," she said.

He stilled. "Are you sure?"

"Yes. I want someone to see it."

There was an undercurrent to her words. Then he remembered the lack of photos in the house and thought he understood.

She flicked on the bedside lamp. They both blinked in the sudden light, even though it wasn't terribly bright. He glanced at her. Her eyes were puffy, her cheeks damp. Her hair had dried into messy spikes. She looked about fifteen years old.

"Open it," she said.

He pulled himself into a sitting position. She'd wrapped the box in shiny black paper with a bright yellow ribbon. He felt as though he was trespassing as he tugged the bow loose and slid his thumb under the flap of the paper.

"Tear it. I don't care," she said when he tried to ease the tape off neatly.

When he continued to be careful, she reached across and ripped the paper for him, shoving it unceremoniously to one side. Then she found the tab that released the lid on the plain packing box beneath and pushed it open. Jake eased a double layer of tissue paper aside to stare at Poppy's gift to her late uncle.

The frame was dark wood—walnut, he guessed—and deep, creating a three-inch recess behind the glass. Poppy's first gold medal was fixed to a dark green mount. A black-and-white photograph sat alongside it. The middle-aged man in the photograph had big shoulders and a craggy face. His dark eyes were gentle as he looked at the little girl standing beside him in the shallow end of the pool. She had short blond hair and two teeth missing from the front of her smile. And she looked up at him with absolute trust and adoration as he guided her arms into position.

Poppy sniffed loudly.

"He was so patient with me. He never got angry with me, except when I doubted myself," she said. "He loved swimming, couldn't get enough of it. Knew all the coaches, all my competitors' stats."

She shook her head. "I can't explain it."

"You don't need to. You loved him. And he loved you."

"Yes. He did."

Her chin wobbled as she reached out to press her fingers to the glass over her uncle Charlie's face.

"I'm going to miss him so much."

Jake slid his arm around her shoulders and pulled her against his chest. She didn't resist, didn't try to be strong. Her hands curled into the muscles of his shoulders and she pressed her face into his chest. Her breath came in choppy bursts and her tears were warm on his skin.

He eased against the pillows, one hand smoothing circles on her back. With the light on he could see more of her room. The far wall was covered in ragged posters of past Australian swimming greats—Dawn Fraser, Shane Gould, Kieren Perkins. A fistful of old swimming carnival ribbons were pinned together in the corner. All blue for first place, naturally. To the side of the bed was a battered dressing table. He couldn't help smiling to himself as he saw the earplugs, goggles, swim caps and other swimming paraphernalia strewn across it. Any other teenager would have loaded it with makeup, perfume and pictures of the latest teen heartthrob, but not Poppy.

"You must be tired," Poppy said after a few minutes. "You've been driving all day. Now you've got me sooking all over you."

"I'm fine."

"Still. You should try to get some sleep. You're going to be on the road again tomorrow, aren't you, driving to hook up with your fishing buddy?"

"Yeah."

She pushed herself away from his chest and reached for the frame. He watched as she set it beside the bed, leaning it against her bedside table. He pushed back the covers and swung his legs over the side of the bed, preparing to return to her brother's room. She frowned.

"What's wrong?" he asked.

"Nothing."

"Poppy."

She lifted a shoulder in a self-conscious shrug. "Would you mind sleeping in here with me? It makes it easier, not being alone."

"Not a problem."

She gave him a watery smile. "Thanks. I appreciate it."

She sat on the edge of the bed and shrugged out of the bathrobe. Then she strode naked across to the dressing table and tugged a drawer open. He told himself to look away, but it was too late—he'd seen the full swing of her naked breasts and the mysterious shadow between her thighs as she bent to pull an old T-shirt from the drawer. He'd traced the firm curve of her ass and the strong lines of her back with his eyes as she tugged the T-shirt over her head.

Only when she was walking back to the bed did he manage to make himself look away. Too late. Way too late.

Despite the fact that he knew it made him a cad of the highest order, he couldn't help responding to what he'd just seen. She had a great body and he'd enjoyed many hours of pleasure with her last night. He told himself she was grieving, in shock, sad. His penis didn't care. It remembered only too well the feel of her skin against his, the slick tightness of her body, the rush of her heated breathing in his ear.

The bed dipped as she got in beside him and flicked off the light. He closed his eyes. There was no way he was going to get any sleep lying here with a hard-on. He resigned himself to a long night.

"Jake. I know this is beyond the call of duty, but would you mind…would you mind holding me?"

Right.

"Um, sure. Not a problem. How do you want me to…?"

"Like you did before was nice." He could hear the shyness in her voice, knew how much it was costing her to ask him for comfort.

"Cool."

She rolled onto her side, her back to him. He reached down and adjusted his hard-on in his boxer briefs in a futile attempt to minimize the obviousness of his arousal. Careful to keep his hips away from her rear, he slid his arm around her torso and pressed his chest against her back.

Funny how last time he'd done this it hadn't been even remotely erotic. But then she'd been wearing the robe and he'd been too focused on how upset she was to register the warmth of her skin and the brush of the lower curve of her breasts against the back of his hand. He hadn't noticed the clean, fresh smell of her or thought for a minute about any of the things they'd done to each other last night. The way she'd taken him in her mouth. The way her eyes had widened when he'd found her sweet spot and touched it just right. The greedy, hungry way she'd reached for his cock and guided him inside her.

He gritted his teeth and forced his mind to something else. The stats for the top five teams on the AFL ladder. The chances of Roger Federer winning both Wimbledon and the U.S. Open again this year. His agent's recent phone message requesting a meeting with him.

Poppy sighed. Jake felt some of the tension leave her body as she relaxed into the bed.

"I really appreciate this, Jake," she said again.

He tightened his grip around her waist in response and she wriggled her backside more closely into the cradle of his hips. She stilled.

So much for his playing the chivalrous knight.

"Is that what I think it is?" she asked.

"Yes. But I would like to point out that sometimes it has a mind of its own. And you have a great body."

She rolled away from him, and he waited for her to kick him out of bed and tell him what an insensitive jerk he was.

"Where are the condoms?" she asked instead.

In the dim light from the partially open curtain he could see her pulling her T-shirt over her head. Any blood that wasn't already there rushed south and his cock grew rock hard. It got even harder when she slid a hand over his belly and into his underwear to wrap her palm around him.

"In the car."

"Huh. We'll have to be careful, then," she said.

Her hand was working up and down his shaft. He closed his eyes. Then his conscience came calling, tap-tapping persistently in the back of his mind.

"Are you sure you want to do this? I mean, you're upset. I don't want you doing anything you might regret."

She pressed a wet, openmouthed kiss to his chest.

"I want to feel alive right now. Do you mind?"

"Do I feel like I mind?"

"No. You feel good." She practically purred the last word.

She slid a leg over both of his and shifted so that she was straddling his hips. She pushed his underwear down and he shoved it the rest of the way down his legs. Then she slid his cock into her wet heat and bore down on him.

"Oh, yeah." He sighed as her body enveloped him.

She started to rock her hips. He could see her breasts swaying in the dim light, pale and full. He slid his hands up her rib cage and took the weight of her in his hands, sliding his thumbs over her nipples. They hardened instantly. She let her head drop back.

She felt so good. Soft yet firm. Silky and smooth. He drew her down so he could pull a nipple into his mouth. She shuddered and began to circle her hips. He slid a hand between their bodies to where they were joined. Her curls were wet and warm and she was swollen with need. He teased her with his thumb, working her gently. She started to pant. He felt her tense around him.

He thrust up into her and wished he could see her face properly. He had to settle for the fierce throb of her muscles tightening around him as she came and the low moan she made in the back of her throat. He closed his eyes and thrust up into her rhythmically, chasing his own release. Then he remembered they didn't have a condom.

Damn.

He stilled, his hands finding her hips to stop her from moving on him.

"No condom," he reminded her. She stilled.

"Right."

She slid off him, one last torturous stroke of her body against his. Before he could feel true regret, she shifted down his body and lowered her head. The wet heat of her mouth encompassed him and he groaned his approval.

She used her hand and her mouth and soon had him bowed with tension. He drove his fingers into her hair and held her head as he came. Afterward, she pressed a kiss onto his belly and rested her cheek on his hip.

"Come back here," he said.

Her body slid along his as she joined him on the pillow. He peered into her face, trying to see her eyes.

"You okay?"

"If you keep asking questions like that, you're going to ruin my image of you as a gifted-yet-emotionally-shallow pants man."

"I'd hate to do that. Not when I've spent so many years perpetuating that image. It's not something that happens overnight, you know."

She smiled. He looked at her and wondered if that was really how she thought of him—a pants man, out for what he could get, when he could get it. Then he thought over the past few years of his life and wondered how inaccurate the description was, at the end of the day.

As a teenager, the idea of being a celebrated swordsman had held enormous appeal. Lots of women, lots of sex, lots of variety. The Errol Flynn myth, basically. But as an adult man, he knew there was more to life than sex.

For a moment he was filled with a bittersweet regret for the early years of his marriage. For moments like these when he and Marly had laughed and talked while their bodies cooled. For the comfort and joy and familiarity of coming home to find the lights on, cooking smells in the kitchen and off-key singing coming from somewhere in the house. For shared jokes and favorite movies and the sense of achievement that came from finding the right birthday or Christmas gift.

But it was impossible to remember the good times without the bad memories crowding in. The bitter fights, the recriminations. The tears, the misery. The fury. The helplessness. And, finally, the emptiness when it was all over.

So, yeah, maybe being described as a pants man wasn't the

highlight of his life, but it beat the hell out of his marriage and his divorce. Hands down.

Poppy's head was heavy on his shoulder and her breathing had deepened. He peered down at her. She was asleep. Exhausted, no doubt, after the trials of the day. Slowly, he eased her head off his shoulder and onto the pillow.

He'd done his bit. He'd offered her all that he had to give. She would wake tomorrow and remember all over again that her uncle Charlie was gone. But she'd gotten through the first night, and she'd get through the rest, too.

His boxer briefs were lost somewhere beneath the quilt. He didn't bother looking for them, just slipped out of bed and back to Poppy's brother's room. He dressed in the dark and let himself out the back door. His car engine sounded loud in the quiet of the country night. He rolled down the driveway, then hit the gas when he reached the road. Before long he was turning onto the freeway toward town.

He spared a thought for how Poppy would feel when she woke. Then he remembered her pants man comment. She'd understand.

6

HE WAS GONE. POPPY REGISTERED the cool sheets and the absence of warm male body and lifted her head to confirm that Jake had left her bed.

She rolled onto her back, her forearm draped over her eyes to block out the sunlight shining between the half-open curtains. After a long moment she lifted her arm and squinted at the clock on her bed stand. It was nearly eight. She'd slept all the way through the night, exhausted by grief and a heart-pounding climax courtesy of Jake's clever hands and hard body.

He must have gone back to his own bed. She wished he hadn't. His warmth, the low timbre of his voice, the simple sound of another human being breathing next to her—he'd helped her get through the night.

He'd been kind to her. Very kind. He'd stayed overnight when he hadn't wanted to, he'd sought her out when he'd heard her crying. And he'd held her, offering her the reassurance of his body. And, later, he'd offered her his desire and a few precious moments of forgetfulness and release, too.

She'd called him a pants man afterward. It wasn't true. Men who were just after sex didn't take the time to offer comfort to someone in need.

Jake Stevens was a nice man. It was a surprising discovery, given the way they'd started out.

She pushed her hair off her forehead. It was time to get up. Time to face the day ahead. Her parents. Her brother and sister, most likely. The funeral arrangements.

Her belly tightened at the thought and she took a steadying breath. It was tempting to hide away and grieve. But putting Charlie to rest was the last thing she could do for him.

She rolled out of bed. She kept some old clothes at her parents' place for the weekends when she stayed the night and she pulled on a pair of worn jeans and the T-shirt she'd worn for just a few minutes last night before she'd felt the unmistakable hardness of Jake's erection against the curve of her backside.

Even now, hours later, the memory sent a wash of heat through her. She eyed herself in the dressing table mirror as she finger combed her hair. That was the thing about death—life went on despite it. People ate and slept and fought and laughed and cried and lusted and had sex, same as they always had.

Life went on.

"Uncle Charlie," she said quietly.

The world had not stopped because he was dead, but it had changed for her, irrevocably.

She could hear low conversation as she walked toward the kitchen. She recognized the pitch and rhythms of her sister's speech and the low bass of her brother's. They'd come up from the city, then, as she'd guessed they would.

"I still can't believe I missed him. All this way and he's gone already." This from her sister, sounding aggrieved.

"I thought you came all this way for Uncle Charlie?" Adam said.

Poppy stopped in the doorway. Her mother was at the sink, filling the kettle. Her father hovered over the toaster, eyeing the glowing slots like a cat at a mouse hole. Adam and Gillian sat at the table, the morning papers spread wide before them.

"Poppy. You're up," her mother said too brightly. "I hope you had a good night's sleep."

"It was okay."

Poppy stepped forward to kiss her brother and sister hello.

Gillian patted her arm briefly as Poppy pressed a kiss to her cheek.

"How are you holding up?" Gillian asked.

"You know." Poppy shrugged. "Did you two come up together?"

"Yes. I'm due back in the afternoon, but I thought I could help out with the funeral arrangements this morning."

"And meet a certain much-lauded author," Adam said with a dry smile.

Poppy frowned. "Sorry?"

Adam nudged Gillian's chair with the toe of his shoe. They were both small and dark-haired like their parents, dressed expensively and conservatively in dark business suits.

"Mom told Gill that Jake Stevens was here when she called early this morning and she was in the car like a shot," Adam said.

Gillian flushed a little. "Thank you for making me sound like a juvenile delinquent with a crush. I happen to be a great admirer of his work. *The Coolabah Tree* is a modern Australian classic."

Poppy crossed to the cupboard to grab a coffee mug. She should have known her family would be excited about meeting Jake. Her mother had taught a seminar on him a few years ago and her sister worked for a small feminist publishing house in the city.

"I didn't put two and two together until this morning, Poppy," her mother said. "You should have told me who Jake was. I'm so embarrassed I didn't recognize him."

"It wasn't exactly at the top of my mind last night."

"I know, but still…"

Poppy spooned instant coffee into her mug.

"I should go wake him. He probably wants to hit the road."

"Oh, but he's gone already," her mother said. "His car was gone this morning when I let the cats out."

The teaspoon clanged loudly against the side of the mug.

Not just gone from her bed, but gone from the house? Gone in the early hours of the morning?

"It was good of him to drive you up here when your car broke down," her father said.

"Yes," Poppy said. She stared at the brown granules in the bottom of the cup. It was ridiculous, but she felt abandoned. As though Jake had offered her something in the dark of the night that he'd reneged on this morning.

"I still can't believe you made that gaffe over the rooms, Mom," Gillian said. She shook her head, a wry smile on her lips.

Adam made a joke at their mother's expense, then her mother asked something about Gillian's work and her father asked who wanted more toast.

A great wave of sadness and loneliness and grief washed over Poppy as she watched her family. She'd never felt like one of them, had always felt like an outsider in the face of their collective academic and professional achievements. It had always been her and Uncle Charlie against the rest of them.

Her vision blurred and her shoulders slumped. Without saying a word, she moved to the back door and pushed her way out into the sunlight.

"Poppy," her mother called after her.

"Let her go," she heard Adam say. "She obviously wants to be alone."

Head down, she walked out into the backyard. She didn't know where she was going. She just knew that it would be easier to be on her own than to be with her family right now. They had loved Charlie, but they had never understood him. Just as they had never understood her.

A WEEK LATER, ALL THE LITTLE hairs on the back of Poppy's neck stood on end as she sat at her desk, working on her latest article. She didn't need to look up to know that Jake had walked into the department.

He was back from holidays. She told herself she didn't care and clicked to a new screen on her computer. Then, without her permission, her gaze flicked across to where he was shrugging out of his jacket.

Fishing obviously agreed with him. He was golden-brown and dark stubble covered his cheeks. He looked lean and a little dangerous and wild.

She returned her attention to the computer screen. She didn't care how he looked or whether he was dangerous or not. Sleeping with him had been a big mistake. As for allowing him to comfort her in her grief… Words were inadequate to describe the wholehearted chagrin she felt for ever allowing herself to turn to him.

She was more angry with herself than him. She'd known exactly what he was before she slept with him—a cynical, smart-mouthed pants man. She'd even told him so straight to his face while they were still basking in the afterglow of yet another round of spectacular sex. And yet she'd still allowed herself to hope. Not for long—only for those few almost-conscious seconds between sleeping and waking—but for long enough. She'd reached out a hand to touch him, to make sure he was real, to reassure herself that he had actually held her in his arms and said all the right things and been so…*human* and generous. And all she'd found was cold, empty sheets.

Stupid. He'd told her up front, hadn't he? He wasn't interested in a relationship. And yet for those few foolish seconds she'd imagined that he would be there for her when she woke. That he liked her. That there was more than great sex between them.

More fool her.

A shadow fell over her desk. She kept her attention on the computer screen and her fingers moving on the keyboard.

"Hey. How did your uncle's funeral go?" Jake asked.

"Fine. Thank you."

"I guess you took a few days off?"

"That's right."

Still she didn't look at him. She had no idea what she was typing. She was too busy concentrating on keeping her face impassive.

"What about your car? Did you get that sorted out?"

"Yes, thank you."

For a long moment there was nothing but the sound of her fingers tapping on the keyboard. She could feel him watching her, but she refused to look at him. Finally he turned and walked away. Poppy let her breath out and her shoulders drop.

What on earth had possessed her to get naked and sweaty with a colleague? She must have been sniffing glue that night in Tamworth. And in the car after that. And at her parents' place.

She risked a glance at his retreating back. Her eyes gravitated to his perfect ass, then dropped down his long legs.

Right. That was why. He was sexy as all get out.

She dragged her gaze away. She had no business being attracted to a man who'd proven himself so unworthy.

Poppy girl, just because you can sometimes see the bus crash coming doesn't mean you can always avoid it.

Uncle Charlie's voice sounded in her head as clearly as

though he was sitting beside her. An increasingly familiar pang of loneliness and sadness pierced her.

His funeral had been exhausting, a day of shaking hands and accepting hugs and condolences, of trying not to cry too much or too loudly. She had been surprised by the turnout, particularly by the number of people from the swimming community who came to pay their respects. Her old coach. Some of her former competitors. Former swimmers from the high school squad Charlie had coached way back in the day. His warmth and wisdom had touched a lot of lives. He'd been valued. He would be missed. And he would be remembered. At the end of the day, that knowledge had given her some solace.

Getting on with the plod of everyday life was hard, however. He had been her mentor, counselor and friend, and she picked up the phone countless times a day to call him and tell him some joke or small story she knew he'd relish, only to remember all over again that he was gone, that there would be no more phone calls or shared laughter.

Her mouth grim, Poppy deleted the paragraph she'd written while Jake hovered over her shoulder. Not gibberish, thank God, but not something she wanted her boss to read, that was for sure. She pushed her hair off her forehead and rolled her shoulders. Then she put her fingers to the keyboard again. This article was due by midday and she still wasn't happy with the intro and the conclusion. She'd sweated over both until late last night, staying at her desk until the cleaners came and began emptying trash and vacuuming around her.

It worried her that the writing wasn't getting any easier. If anything, it felt harder. The more she learned in her night classes, the more she could see the failings in her own work. And the worse thing was, she didn't know how to fix them.

Even though she and Jake were the only people in the department this early, Poppy glanced up as she eased her desk drawer open. It wasn't as though she'd care too much if someone else saw what she was doing, but if Jake caught sight of the underlined, annotated article in her drawer she didn't think she would ever recover from the humiliation.

He was busy checking his e-mail, one hand idly clicking away at the mouse. The glow from his desk lamp gave his dark hair golden highlights. She switched her attention to the article in her hand.

It had been her class assignment this week—select a piece of journalism she admired and analyze its structure and content. She'd agonized over her choice and then forced herself to admit that the only reason she wasn't selecting one of Jake's articles was because of what had happened between them. Dumb. He was the best writer in the department, one of the most awarded on the paper. And she'd admired him for years. She might feel foolish and naive and exposed because she'd slept with him and allowed herself to hope for more, but it didn't change the fact that he was one of the best. And if she was going to learn, she wanted to learn from the best.

She read his opening paragraph again, admiring the deceptively easy flow of it. It was impossible to stop at those few sentences, though—inevitably she wanted to keep reading, even though she'd gone over and over the damned thing many times already. He was a master of the hook, superb at delivering information in fresh and interesting ways and drawing the reader in. His observations were insightful, his judgments crisp and unapologetic.

She turned to her own opening paragraph, frowning at the stiffness of her phrasing. No matter what she tried—chatty and informal, choppy and succinct or somewhere in between—

she wound up sounding like a high school student laboring over an end-of-term paper.

The tap-tap of Jake's keyboard had her lifting her head again. Words filled the screen as his fingers flew. For a moment she simply stared at him, envying him his easy gift. He was in his element, utterly confident. She knew what that felt like. At least, she used to know.

She shoved the annotated article into her drawer and pulled her keyboard toward herself. She might not have natural talent, but she was smart and she learned fast. She would conquer this if it killed her.

Just as she would live down making the rookie's mistake of sleeping with a coworker.

LATER THAT AFTERNOON during the department meeting, Jake leaned back in his chair and studied the woman sitting diagonally opposite him. Poppy sat ramrod straight, a pad and pen at the ready in front of her like a good little schoolgirl, just in case Leonard said anything she needed to jot down. Her gaze was resolutely focused on their boss as he droned on and on about circulation figures.

She'd made a point of being everywhere he wasn't since their nonconversation this morning. If he entered the kitchen, she left. If he was collecting something from the printer, she gave it a wide berth. So much for hoping there would be no repercussions from their road-trip fling.

She was pale, he noted, her eyes large in her face. A tuft of hair stuck up on her crown as though she'd been running her fingers through her hair. Her lipstick had worn off, but her lower lip was wet from where she'd just licked it.

She looked sad. And sexy. A disturbing combination at the best of times.

He frowned.

As if she could sense his regard, her gaze flicked up to lock with his. Her face remained expressionless, utterly still for a long five seconds. Then she coolly returned her attention to their boss.

Jake shifted in his seat. He told himself that there was no rational justification for her anger, that he had no reason to feel guilty. He didn't owe her anything, after all. He'd gone beyond the call of duty, driving her home when her car had broken down, hanging around at her parents' place to make sure she was okay.

Yeah, and then you crawled into her bed in the middle of the night when she was at her most vulnerable and threw the leg over.

He would swear on a stack of Bibles that sex had been the last thing on his mind when he'd heard her crying. Absolutely. And yet somehow he'd still ended up shagging her again.

Never screw the crew.

Don't dip your pen in the office ink.

Don't shit in your own nest.

There was a reason there were half a dozen colloquial warnings against sleeping with a coworker—the aftermath sucked.

I was honest with her. I told her I wasn't looking for a relationship.

Which gave him the perfect get-out-of-jail-free card—in theory. Things got a little muddy once he factored in her grief and the way he'd felt compelled to comfort her and the truths they'd shared in the small hours of the morning. Oh, and the sex. The postcomforting, postsharing sex.

He should have said no. Should have ignored his hard-on, rolled out of bed and gone back to her brother's room. Instead, he'd gotten lost in the warmth of her body then bailed without saying goodbye.

He waited until she was filing out of the meeting room with the others before approaching her.

"Poppy, can I have a word?"

Several sets of eyes turned their way and she had no choice but to agree. She hovered near the door as the last person exited.

"What?" she asked.

She crossed her arms over her chest and set her jaw stubbornly. Clearly, she wasn't about to make this easy.

"Look, I would have woken you but I thought you needed the sleep more," he said.

"No, you didn't. You didn't wake me because you were worried I would take what had happened the wrong way."

"Yeah, and I was right, wasn't I?" he said, gesturing to indicate the discussion they were having, their mutually closed-off body language, the tension in the room.

"You're so arrogant it blows my mind," she said, shaking her head. "For your information, you are not God's gift to women. A handful of decent orgasms doesn't even come close to making you irresistible."

He crossed his arms over his chest and leaned his hip against the table. For the first time all day she had some color in her cheeks and there was life in her eyes. He wasn't sure if he should be pleased or not. And whether he should be worried about noticing in the first place.

"Why are you so pissed with me, then?"

"I don't know. Maybe because you sneaked out of my parents' house like a thief in the night?"

"So? You knew I needed to get going, that I wanted to catch up with my buddy. What was the big deal if I left early or not?"

She opened her mouth then shut it without saying anything. Her gaze slid over his shoulder and her jaw tensed. Her eyes were angry when they met his again.

"Fine, I admit it. You're right. I was surprised when you weren't there in the morning. I thought at the very least that we were friends after everything that had happened. That you cared enough to say goodbye. I felt stupid when I realized you were gone."

He stared at her. Her confronting honesty left him nowhere to go. It was his turn to look away. "We both agreed that it was just sex."

"I know."

And they both knew it had become more than sex when he slid into her bed and wrapped his arms around her.

"I'm sorry," he said after a long silence. "I only wanted to help. I didn't mean to hurt you."

"I'm not crying myself to sleep over you, Stevens," she said drily. "Get over yourself."

He shrugged. "For what it's worth, I'm a shit prospect anyway. Workaholic. Messy. Hopeless with birthdays and anniversaries. Cranky in the mornings."

She simply looked at him, her big gray eyes depthless. "Are we done here?"

"Yeah, we're done."

She walked away, her spine very straight. He watched till she turned the corner, aware that he still felt dissatisfied, as though they had unfinished business.

What had he expected from their confrontation, anyway? What exactly had he been trying to achieve?

He remembered the way they'd sparred in the car, the push and pull of their conversation over dinner at the steak house. He remembered her laugh, the deep throaty pleasure of it.

And he remembered the utter vulnerability of her as she wept in his arms.

He liked Poppy Birmingham. Hell, he even admired her, especially after meeting her parents and gaining a small glimpse into the indifference she'd had to fight against to rise to the top of her sport. If he hadn't messed things up by sleeping with her, he'd like to think they could have been friends.

But he had. And, worse yet, he still wanted her, even though he knew he was never going to have her again.

JAKE LEFT THE DEPARTMENT earlier than usual that night. His agent had called to set up a meeting, and Jake had been unable to put him off any longer. Poppy was still at her desk, bent over her keyboard, one hand absently combing her hair into spikes. She worked long hours. He wondered if journalism was living up to her expectations.

His agent was waiting for him at the wine bar in the nearby restaurant precinct of Southgate when Jake arrived. Dean Mannix waved a hand when he spotted Jake but didn't bother standing. Nearly sixty years old, he had bad knees and walked with the aid of a cane. His improbably black hair gleamed with hair oil and Jake pretended not to notice the discreet touch of eyeliner around the other man's eyes.

"Where's Rambo?" he asked, glancing around for his agent's much-cosseted Chihuahua.

"Spa day," Dean said with the flick of a limp wrist.

"Ah. What are you drinking?" Jake asked, seeing Dean's glass was almost empty.

"Surprise me with something sweet and sticky."

Jake suppressed a smile and crossed to the bar. It had been nearly twelve months since he and Dean had spoken face-to-face. In the early days, his agent had practically lived on his doorstep. Marly had called him "that little man" and rolled her eyes every time he called. But there hadn't been much need for Dean to make contact recently.

Jake scanned the cocktail menu and ordered a Fluffy Duck and a glass of merlot. Dean's mouth quirked into a smile when he saw the umbrella poking out the side of his drink.

"Fabulous." He took a long pull from the straw. "And absolutely disgusting."

He said it with such relish Jake could only take it as high praise.

"So, what's up?" Jake asked.

He waited for Dean to ask him about his writing, when Jake might have something for him. That was usually why Dean requested a face-to-face.

"Did I mention I saw Bryce Courtney the other day?" Dean said instead. He went on to tell an anecdote about the other author. Jake listened and made the appropriate noises, growing more and more tense with every passing minute. Finally Dean drank the last of his cocktail and sat back in his chair.

"Isn't this the part where you ask me what I've been working on and I lie and tell you I've got a good start on something?" Jake joked.

Dean smiled but his eyes were sad.

"Jake, I'm going to let you off the hook," he said. "Make it official and tear up our agreement."

Jake let his breath out on a rush. This was the last thing he'd been expecting. "You're cutting me loose? You don't want to represent me anymore?"

"I'd love to represent you. I think you're a wonderful, talented writer and you've made me a lot of money. I've been proud to have your name on my books for the past seven years. But the truth is that you aren't writing anything for me to represent."

"So I'm a little blocked. I've got the second book outlined, the broad strokes are there. I just need a clean run at it."

"Jake, it's been seven years. And, yes, I know things with Marly were messy for the first two years, but you've had five years since the divorce and you haven't brought me anything."

Jake stared at him, unable to refute his words. "So I'm deadwood now? You're just going to cut me off?"

Dean sighed heavily. "No. Like I said, I'm letting you off the hook. No expectations. No guilt. No niggle in the back of your mind. You're free to write or not write as you choose. No pressure from anyone but yourself."

"Wow. I feel so free. What a gift you've given me."

Dean didn't flinch at his sarcasm and Jake immediately felt like an asshole. It wasn't as though Dean hadn't been patient. Seven years was a long leash by anyone's standards. Jake rubbed a hand over his face.

"Sorry. I just…I understand. You've been very patient."

"You start writing again, call me. Call me anyway, let me know how you're doing," Dean said.

Jake forced a smile. "Sure."

Dean leaned forward. "I know you've got another book in you, Jake, but you need to give yourself permission to write it."

Jake frowned. "What the hell is that supposed to mean?"

"Why do you think you haven't been able to get the words down?"

"I've been busy. I've let other things get in the way. No discipline."

"You know what I think? I think Marly spent so much time blaming you for being away on a book tour when she miscarried that you couldn't help but absorb some of it. And now you won't let yourself write again because giving up something you loved is your way of punishing yourself."

Jake flinched. "Didn't realize you'd hung up your shingle as a headshrinker since we last saw each other, mate. Or have you just been watching too much *Dr. Phil?*"

"Something has held you back all these years."

"I don't need counseling, for Christ's sake. I need an agent."

Dean braced his arms on the table and pushed himself to his feet.

"When you need an agent, you'll have one," he said. He grabbed his cane. "Look after yourself. Call me every now and then, let me know how you're doing."

Jake watched Dean walk away, anger and shame and regret burning in the pit of his belly. Then Jake downed the last of his wine and walked slowly to his apartment, squinting against the last rays of the setting sun.

He dumped his bag and coat by the front door and went straight into the kitchen to grab a bottle of wine and a glass.

So, it was official—he was no longer a writer. Just another journalist. He walked to the living room and stared at the half a dozen copies of *The Coolabah Tree* on his bookcase. First editions, foreign translations, international editions. Jesus, he'd been so proud when he'd held his book in his hands for the first time. He and Marly had danced around the apartment and spilled champagne and gotten in trouble with the neighbors for making too much noise. He'd imagined half a dozen books filling the bookcase alongside his debut work.

Swearing, he crossed to his desk and powered up his computer. He pulled up a chair in front of a blank screen. He placed his fingers on the keyboard, his mind going over the story he'd outlined all those years ago, the story that was supposed to be the spine of his second novel.

Words formed in his mind, sentences. He began to type. But after a few minutes, his hands fell into his lap.

It wasn't right. Maybe he'd been out of the habit of writing fiction for so long, he'd forgotten how. Maybe the story was stale. Or maybe it really was over.

He stared at the screen.

I know you've got another book in you, Jake, but you need to give yourself permission to write it.

"What a load of bollocks."

Angry, he pushed away from the desk and reached for the wine bottle again. Dean could get stuffed. As for his amateur-hour theories about Marly and the baby… It was probably as well the old man wasn't representing him anymore.

7

A WEEK LATER, JAKE WAS making notes on an article in the café in the foyer of the *Herald* building when Macca and Jonesy pulled up chairs at the adjacent table. Jake exchanged a few words of greeting then returned to his work. He must have been listening to the other men's conversation on some level, however, because his ears pricked up when he heard Poppy's name. His pen stilled on the page but he didn't look up as he waited to hear more.

Macca had been mentoring Poppy since her first week on the job. In Jake's opinion, the other man was way too smitten to be objective. The way he followed Poppy around with his eyes was becoming the office joke.

"You're never going to know if you don't sling your hook, mate," Jonesy was saying, taking a huge bite out of a chicken schnitzel sandwich.

"There's no way she's single." Macca spoke with the resigned hopefulness of the truly besotted.

"Won't know till you ask. She's never mentioned anyone. Give it a go, see what she says."

Macca made a noncommittal noise.

"Up to you, buddy, but you're not the only one who wouldn't mind going for a bit of gold." Jonesy laughed at his own joke. "Saw Patrick from advertising sales doing the old smoothie routine on her the other day."

Jake frowned. Patrick Larson was a slick dickhead in an expensive suit. The thought of him smarming all over Poppy made Jake's neck itch.

"Matter of fact, if you're not going to make your move, I might just ask her out myself," Jonesy said.

Jake's head came up at that. Jonesy was leaning back in his chair, his belly pouring over his belt, crumbs from his lunch scattered over his shirtfront.

In your dreams, pal. Poppy is way too fine for you.

The flash of territorialism was disturbing. Poppy was nothing to him. They were barely on speaking terms, despite having cleared the air last week.

He must have been glaring because Jonesy glanced at him, offering a just-between-the-boys grin. Jake frowned and the other man's smile faded.

"Anyway. Better get back to it," Jonesy said, standing and brushing debris from his shirt.

Jake sat staring at his notes after they'd left. Someone should say something to Poppy. Warn her. Because it was obvious what was going to happen—Macca would ask her out. Or Patrick. Or—God forbid—Jonesy. And before she knew it, guys would be nudging each other all over the building. It wasn't only male athletes a female reporter had to worry about in this profession. Like it or not, journalism was still a boys' club.

He grabbed his notes and crossed to the elevator. As he exited on the fifth floor, he saw Poppy shuffling papers together near the printer and diverted from his course to his desk to stop in front of her.

"Got a minute?" he asked.

She flicked a look at him. He'd never noticed before, but she had very long lashes. So long that they swept her cheekbones when she glanced down at the papers in her hands.

"It depends," she said.

"What on?"

"What it's about."

"Right." He'd walked into that one. "It's, uh, private."

One of her eyebrows rose. "Please don't tell me you've got a nasty rash."

It was so unexpected he laughed. He'd forgotten how dry she could be. How fast on her feet.

"No rash. Everything's in tip-top working order," he said.

"So did you just want to give me a status report or was there something else?" she asked.

"It's about Macca."

"Right."

"And Jonesy. And that Patrick dickhead from sales."

"He's not a dickhead. He was very helpful when I was looking for some information the other day."

Jake stabbed a finger at her. "Exactly. He wants to get you into bed. Along with Macca and Jonesy."

"You mean like a…a foursome?" she asked, incredulous.

She looked so appalled he had to laugh.

"No. Separately. Every man for himself."

"Right. Very funny." She shook her head and turned to walk away.

He grabbed her arm. "Don't you believe me?"

She gave him a withering look. "I'm not an idiot. Despite recent behavior that might indicate otherwise."

She glanced pointedly at his fingers circling her arm, but he didn't let go. Partly because he hadn't finished talking to her, and partly because she felt good and it had been too long since he'd touched her.

"Trust me. Macca has a crush on you. And Patrick collects scalps like baseball cards. As for Jonesy…well, he's not blind."

She shook her head again. She had no idea how attractive she was. Tall and strong and supple. Curvy in all the right places, with a pretty, open face that hinted at an enjoyment of the simple things in life. Like food and wine and sex.

"Why are we even having this conversation, Stevens?"

She'd started calling him by his last name since their road trip. He didn't like it. He'd been inside her. He'd pressed his face into the soft, silken skin of her inner thighs. He'd made her purr with pleasure. He figured at the very least that put them on a first-name basis.

"A while back you asked me to step in if I thought you were putting a foot wrong. One pro to another," he said.

"And?"

"I just wanted to warn you that sleeping with one of the guys from the department would definitely fall under that category."

She stared at him. She opened her mouth, closed it, then shook her head. "Are you *seriously* warning me against screwing one of my coworkers?"

"You asked me to give you a heads-up if you needed it."

She huffed out a laugh, but he didn't think she was amused. More incredulous, if he didn't miss his guess.

"Unbelievable," she muttered under her breath. Then she turned away from him.

"Hang on a minute." She had no idea how gossipy a bunch of guys could get over a few beers. He grabbed her arm again.

"Do you mind?" she said coolly.

"I don't think you're taking this very seriously," he said.

She stared at him. They were standing so close he could see her nostrils flare. He could smell her deodorant and whatever soap she washed her clothes in, could feel the warmth of her body.

"Do you honestly think I need another lesson on why screwing someone I work with is a sucky idea, Stevens? Really?"

For a moment he saw clear through to her soul, saw the regret and the embarrassment she felt over their few sweaty, hot encounters.

She wished it had never happened. It was there as plain as day in her eyes. If she could, she'd wind back the clock and reclaim the hours they'd lost in each other's arms. Even though it had been the best sex he'd ever had. Even though he couldn't stop thinking about it, about her, she wished it out of existence.

He let her go. She strode to her desk. He crossed to his own desk and dumped his jacket and notes. His wine club order had been delivered while he was at lunch and he shoved the carton to one side as he sat and called up his e-mail in-box. Then he stared at it unseeingly.

He didn't regret sleeping with her. Not for a second. Even though it had made things weird at work. It had been worth it—that was how good it had been.

But to Poppy, he was just some guy she worked with who she'd slipped up with on the road. She'd filed him under the same heading as Macca and Patrick and Jonesy. Despite the many moan-inducing orgasms he'd given her. Despite the fact that he'd left George, her battery-operated friend, for dead. Despite the laughter they'd shared and the challenge of their conversations.

It was a humbling realization. And an uncomfortable one.

You should be thanking your lucky stars. She could be crying all over the place, blabbing to the other women on the floor. You could be getting dirty looks from everyone with two X chromosomes within a one-mile radius.

He didn't feel grateful, however. He felt pissed. Dissatisfied. Frustrated.

A phone rang across the office and he came out of his daze. He reached for his mouse. What was it Poppy had said to him last week?

Get over yourself.

Maybe she had a point. He had no right demanding anything from her, including recognition that what had happened between them had been out of the ordinary. Not when he had nothing to offer in exchange. He wasn't looking to start something up with someone. Not now, not ever.

He concentrated on proofing his article with new resolve. So what if he was too aware of everything Poppy said or did, every move she made? So what if he only had to think of touching her breasts, sliding his hand between her legs and he had a hard-on that wouldn't quit? It didn't matter. It meant nothing. It was over.

THE NOTICING-POPPY'S-every-move thing came back to haunt Jake later that evening as he worked at his desk. Slowly the department emptied until only the hard-core workaholics were left. Which meant it was down to him and Poppy, essentially. He was aware of her crossing back and forth between the printer and her desk, then going in to talk to Leonard before hitting her computer again. Leonard left at seven, but Poppy remained at her desk. He glanced at her as he headed for the kitchen to forage for something to keep him going for a few more hours. She was kneading her forehead as she frowned at a page, red pen in hand. The page was covered in little notes to herself, lines and arrows, deletions and insertions. Tension radiated from her in palpable waves.

He poured himself a tall glass of water in the kitchen and unearthed a stash of muesli bars someone thought they'd hidden at the back of the cupboard. He grabbed one for himself, then went back for a second. He dropped it on her desk as he walked past.

"Can't think without food," he said over his shoulder.

She didn't say a word, but he heard the rustle as she tore open the package. She was still working away with the red pen when he shrugged into his jacket and picked up the carton of wine. He hovered for a beat, watching her. She looked tired, but he knew there was no way she was leaving her desk until she was satisfied.

She'd probably tell him to take a long walk off a short pier, but he couldn't help himself. Which was becoming a bit of a recurring theme where she was concerned. Couldn't stop himself from poking her with a stick. Couldn't stop himself from wanting her. Couldn't stop himself from having her. Couldn't stop himself from feeling for her.

She slid the printout she was working on under today's edition of the paper when he stopped beside her desk. She sat back in her chair and looked up at him, one eyebrow raised.

"What?" she asked as though he was a pesky kid annoying her in the playground.

"You want some help?"

Her expression immediately became guarded. "I'm fine."

"Yeah? How late were you planning on working? How many red pens you planning on running through?"

Her mouth tightened. "I'll work it out."

"Anyone ever told you you're stubborn?"

Before she could react, he snatched her article out from beneath the newspaper.

"Hey!" She was on her feet in a second, trying to grab the paper from his hands.

He held it out high from his side. If she wanted to get it, she was going to have to wrestle him for it. She seemed to be considering doing just that for a moment, then her shoulders slumped.

"Fine. I'm sure you could do with a good laugh after a long day."

He frowned at her defeated posture and lowered his hand so he could read what she'd written. The page was so crossed and marked with red it was almost impossible to decipher the original text.

"Move over," he said, nudging her to one side.

Without asking, he took her seat and used the mouse to take him back to the top of her article on the computer screen. He could feel her nervousness as she hovered behind him while he read. It took him thirty seconds to see where the problem lay.

"This isn't as bad as you think it is," he said.

"Thanks," she said drily.

He shot her a look. "Pull up a chair."

She eyed him for a long moment, then slowly pulled over the chair from a nearby desk.

He pointed to the screen.

"You're overthinking this too much, overwriting. It's an interview. People will read it because it's about David Hannam and he's the country's number one tennis star, not because you're being clever. You just need to feed them some of what they expect, then throw in a few little surprises. Make them feel they've found out something they didn't know before."

"Easy for you to say."

He could hear the tiredness in her voice. She was running on empty.

"What's the most interesting thing he said to you when you interviewed him?" he asked suddenly.

She blinked, then frowned.

"No, don't think about it—just say the first thing that comes into your head."

"Okay. When he was a kid, he wanted to be an astronaut. He didn't discover tennis until he was fifteen."

"Great. There's your opener."

He rolled his chair to one side and gestured for her to take his place at the keyboard. She did so slowly, warily.

He watched as she placed her fingers on the keys. Then she sighed and let them drop into her lap.

"I can't do this with you watching."

"Yeah, you can. They're just words, Poppy. Words and ideas."

"Not by the time I'm finished with them," she said ruefully.

"Pretend you're having a beer with some mates and telling them about the interview. You're not going to bother with any of the boring crap up front. Who cares what his stats are? Bury that stuff toward the end for the nerds. Tell a story."

She put her fingers to the keyboard again and started writing.

When David Hannam was a kid, he wanted to be an astronaut. He figured that flying through space and looking at the earth would be about the coolest thing ever. Of course, that was before he discovered the thrill of standing in a packed stadium with the winner's trophy in his hands…

She wrote for twenty minutes, stopping and starting. Every time she went to press the delete key he caught her hand.

"Just write what comes to you. You can edit later."

Finally she stopped typing.

"Good. Now cut and paste this paragraph. And this one. And those two," he said, pointing out the material from her previous draft.

He sat beside her for another hour as she finalized the interview. Finally she hit the key to send it to the subeditor for tomorrow's edition.

She let out a sigh, then scrubbed her face with her hands.

"Thank you," she said.

"It was no big deal."

"To you, maybe. This stuff is second nature to you."

"I've been doing it for fifteen years, Poppy."

She shrugged. She was a perfectionist, that was her problem. And she was used to being the best.

"If it makes you feel any better, I can't dive worth shit. And my backstroke is laughable."

She gave him a dry look.

"It's true." He stood and grabbed her elbow to encourage her to stand, also. He passed her her jacket.

"Go home. Eat. Sleep. Stop thinking."

"Easy for you to say," she said for the second time that night.

He laughed. "You think I don't think?"

"I have my doubts sometimes. Like this afternoon when you warned me not to screw the crew." She was smiling. He felt an absurd sense of achievement.

"I was protecting your honor."

"Is that what you call it? I thought you were pissing in the corners."

Startled, he looked at her face. She cocked an eyebrow at him and he realized she was right—he *had* been pissing in the corners, marking his territory. Making sure she didn't hook up with one of the other guys from work.

"Well, I never said *I* was honorable," he said.

They walked toward the elevator. The cleaners had come and gone and the lights were dim, only the glow from various computers and electrical devices and the occasional desk lamp illuminating the newsroom. He stood to one side to let Poppy enter the elevator before him. He didn't mean to, but somehow his eyes sought out the shadowy V at the neckline of her shirt as she moved past him. He could see a thin line of black lace and his mind filled with images of Poppy's full, creamy breasts spilling out of black satin.

He reined in his libido in time to note that she hit the button for the foyer rather than the basement parking garage. There was only one reason for her to be getting out at ground level— she planned to walk across to Flinders Street station and catch the train home.

"Car still in the shop?" he guessed.

She gave him a startled look. "How did you—"

"I'm a journalist. We notice things."

"Right."

"You want a lift?"

Given the black lace fantasy that he'd just beaten back with a stick, it wasn't such a smart idea. But he had a long track record of not being smart around Poppy.

"It's out of your way."

"You don't know that. Where do you live?"

"Malvern. Miles away from South Yarra."

She kept her eyes on the floor indicator but a small frown appeared between her eyebrows. He smiled. Poppy had looked up his home address. Interesting.

"I'll drive you. Might as well—I've got the car tonight, since I knew this was coming." He indicated the carton of wine in his arms.

"I'll be fine."

"It's past nine, Poppy. Don't be stupid."

"That's why I'm saying no—I'm not being stupid."

She met his eyes then and he knew that she'd noticed him

looking at her breasts. She was probably aware that he was half-hard, too, in the same way that he was aware that she was breathing a little too quickly and her pupils had dilated with desire.

"It's just a lift home."

He wasn't sure if that was a lie or not. All he knew was that he wanted to spend more time with her.

She looked at the floor. The lift pinged open at the foyer level. She didn't move. He reached out and hit the door closed button.

"Nothing is going to happen," she said.

"I know."

But he was fully hard now, every inch of him craving her. He wanted to duck his head and inhale the scent from the nape of her neck. He wanted to slide his hands beneath her shirt and cup her breasts. He wanted to watch her face as she moaned and pleaded and came.

He couldn't sleep with her again. Not after the conversation they'd had last week where she'd more or less confirmed that she wasn't the kind of woman who did casual sex.

It was a pity his body hadn't gotten the memo yet. Forcing his mind to thoughts of frolicking puppies and old ladies with canes, he led Poppy to his car.

POPPY SLID INTO THE SMOOTH embrace of butter-soft leather upholstery and reached for her seat belt.

Was she *nuts?* What on earth was she doing letting Jake Stevens drive her home?

And how had she not noticed last time she'd been in his car that he drove a Porsche? She'd been so numb she'd barely registered the color, let alone the make, but now she was fully aware that he drove the kind of sleek and sexy car that screamed sex and power and lots of other things that weren't doing anything to slow the pulse beating low in her belly.

You idiot.

Self-abuse wasn't going to help, either. She'd been a goner the moment Jake had stopped beside her desk and leaned close enough for her to smell the unique scent that was aftershave, soap, laundry detergent and hot male skin. Heady at the best of times, but absolutely deadly when her dreams had been haunted by long, liquid moments from her two nights with Jake.

She wasn't sure what it said for her psyche that even though she wasn't sure she liked him much, she still craved his body.

She winced and stared out the passenger side window. Who was she kidding? She liked him. She liked him plenty. She thought he was funny and clever. And he'd proven himself to be kind, in action if not in word. Just because he wasn't interested in having a relationship with her didn't negate any of that. Even if he had embarrassed her and made her feel gauche and foolish with his midnight flight. And even if he'd had the outrageous gall to point out to her that sleeping with a work colleague was a dumb idea—as though she hadn't worked that one out about five seconds after discovering the other side of the bed was empty.

At the end of the day, he'd never promised her anything. And she was aware that her grief and upset over Uncle Charlie probably didn't put her in the best position to judge this situation rationally. But she was also aware that only a very, very foolish and self-destructive person would put her head in the lion's mouth twice. Especially when said person had a weakness for said lion, and said lion was licking his chops and had a speculative gleam in his eye.

"Whereabouts in Malvern are you?" he asked. He held up a hand. "Wait, let me guess. Near the pool, right?"

She hated giving him the satisfaction of being right, but he was.

"Yes. How did you know?" she asked, irony heavy in her tone.

"I'm a journalist. We—"

"Notice things. Thank you, I got that the first time."

He was grinning, and the corners of her own mouth were curling upward.

"Do you still swim?"

"Every day." She felt a little stupid admitting it. She was retired, after all. She was supposed to be getting a life outside of the pool. But ever since losing Uncle Charlie, she'd craved the comfort of the familiar and she'd given in to the urge to swim every day, either before or after work.

"Not today, though, right?" he asked. "Surely even you aren't going to do laps after nine at night?"

"The pool is closed," she said. "Plus I swam this morning."

"Better be careful, Birmingham. You're gonna lose that spectacular rack if you keep training so hard."

She shot him a startled look. His attention was on the road but he was grinning hugely.

"I think the less attention you pay to my rack the better."

"Wise words. Would you consider wearing a burlap bag as your part of the bargain?"

She laughed. As always with him, she couldn't help it. He was just so damned cocky and incorrigible. If someone had asked her beforehand if such a combination would appeal to her, she would have laughed in their face. Which went to show how well she knew herself.

Another disturbing thought.

"Do you have these kinds of conversations with Hilary or Mary? Because it's not going to be long before you're up on sexual harassment charges if you do."

"I haven't slept with Hilary or Mary," he said.

"Very restrained of you."

"I've never slept with anyone from the paper before."

He was still watching the road. She eyed his profile for a long moment.

"Wow. I guess I should feel flattered."

He smiled faintly. "But you don't?"

"It was a stupid thing to do."

"Maybe."

She frowned, wondering what he meant by that. There was no doubt in her mind that she'd screwed up monumentally when she'd let him lay hands on her. Amazing orgasms aside.

The sustained gurgle of her hungry stomach cut through the silence in the car. She pressed a hand to her belly.

"Sorry."

"I'm starving, too. Maybe we should stop for a burger. There's a drive-through on High Street, isn't there?"

She made a face. "Plastic food. Disgusting."

"Says Ms. Chocolate Chip and Nacho Cheese."

She blinked. He remembered what she'd had in her shopping bag up in Queensland. Either he had an amazing memory, or... She didn't allow herself to complete the thought. No doubt, if she questioned him under bright lights, he'd tell her he was a journalist, and he noticed things.

"At least it's made from real cream and real sugar and real fat," she said. "Haven't you seen that documentary about fast food?"

"No. Why on earth would I voluntarily rule out one of the major food groups from my diet by learning a bunch of stuff that would make it impossible for me to ever eat it again?"

She shook her head. "So bad for you."

"Lots of things are. Doesn't stop most of us from indulging."

There was something about the way he said *indulging* that made her want to squirm in her seat. Damn him. Only Jake Stevens could make a single word sound so...provocative.

"There's an Indian takeout a little farther up. If you must eat crap."

"I must. And so must you. I have it on good authority that your body requires sustenance."

She was about to argue but her stomach growled again. "See?"

She rolled her eyes but still ordered chicken tikka masala, vegetable korma and a plain naan bread when they stopped at the Indian restaurant. Ten minutes later they were back in Jake's car, the heady smell of spicy food rising around them. She directed him to her street and he stopped outside her apartment block. She opened the car door before she turned to thank him.

"I appreciate the lift. I know it was out of your way."

"Not a problem," he said.

His face was cast in shadows, but she could see the gleam of his eyes in the soft light from the dash. She felt a ridiculous impulse to lean forward and press a kiss to the angle of his jaw. Just to see if he felt and tasted as good as she remembered.

Hunger was clearly making her light-headed. She swung her legs out of the car and stood.

"Anyway. See you tomorrow," she said. Then she remembered it was Friday. "I mean, Monday," she quickly amended.

"Have a good weekend, Poppy."

She pushed the car door closed and turned away, but she couldn't help thinking that he was a good fifteen minutes from home and by the time he got there his naan bread would be more soggy than light and fluffy and his samosas more spongy than crunchy. Before she could edit herself, she turned on her heel and rapped on the side window of his car.

The glass lowered with a discreet hum and Jake looked out at her, eyebrows raised questioningly. She studied his mouth before she spoke. If there was even a hint of that knowing, smug smile of his… But he wasn't smiling. He was watching her, his expression unreadable.

She swallowed a sudden lump of nervousness.

"If you want to come up and eat your food before it gets cold, that would be okay."

As invitations went, it wasn't the most gracious she'd ever issued. But maybe that was for the best. Maybe her awkwardness would make him say no and she could put this moment of madness behind her.

"That would be great. If you don't mind."

"Of course not."

They sounded like two scrupulously polite old ladies. She waited for him to exit his car and lock it. Then she led him upstairs to her second-floor apartment. Her gaze immediately went to the stack of newspapers piled on the dining room table, then to the tower of dirty cereal bowls on the kitchen counter, then to the basket full of laundry on her armchair. If she'd known she'd be entertaining guests, she'd have cleaned up a little this morning instead of gulping down her breakfast and racing for the bus.

"Um, sorry about the mess," she said. She dumped her bag of food on the counter and began clearing up.

"Relax. I'm not about to whip out my white gloves. My place is a pigsty."

"Really?"

"Hell, yeah. Who has time to clean? I thought about hiring someone to come in once a week, but it seems pretty shameful when I live in a two-bedroom apartment."

"Ditto." She forced herself to relax and dumped the cereal bowls in the sink instead of stacking them in the dishwasher. She pulled out two plates and some cutlery, then gestured for him to take a seat at the table. "Your food's getting cold."

He sat at the end of the table and she sat on one of the sides, facing the window. For a moment there was only the rustle of plastic bags and the snap of containers being opened as they loaded up their plates.

She stole a glance at him as she tore off a chunk of her naan bread. Jake Stevens, in her apartment. She couldn't quite believe it. After the way he'd treated her when she first started at the paper, then the way she'd felt when he'd pulled his midnight disappearing act... Well, she hadn't exactly anticipated this moment.

"You own this place or rent?" Jake asked as he dipped one of his samosas into yogurt sauce.

"Own. Uncle Charlie insisted I do something sensible when I started getting sponsorship money."

"Smart man."

"Yeah. What about you? Own or rent?"

Good grief. Could this conversation be any more stilted? Jake smiled at her as though he could hear her thoughts.

"Own. Same deal—I decided to do something a little more long-term than buy a hot car when *The Coolabah Tree* was a surprise success."

"Then you went ahead and bought the car anyway."

"I'm only human. I believe Tom Cruise said it best in *Risky Business*—'Porsche. There is no substitute.'"

"Wow. You sure know your Tom Cruise. I'm...disturbed. Which is your favorite scene in *Top Gun?* The topless volleyball game or the topless shower scene?"

He grinned and scooped up a spoonful of rice. "And you think I'm a smart-ass."

She smiled down at her plate. She liked sparring with

him. A little more than was healthy, if she was being honest with herself.

His gaze wandered to the pile of newspapers. He frowned slightly, then tugged the top paper toward himself. It was opened to the sports section and she realized too late what he was looking at—the notes she'd made in the margin when she read his article this morning. She'd gotten into the habit of analyzing his writing, trying to deconstruct it so she could pick up some clues for her own work.

She leaned across the table, ready to snatch it from his hands. Jake threw her a curious look and she retreated to her chair.

"It's nothing. Just some notes for school," she said.

"School?"

"I'm taking a journalism course at night school."

She waited for him to say something mocking but he didn't. He simply returned his attention to the newspaper and her penciled-in notes. She tried to remember what she'd written.

Please, nothing about how much I admire his writing. Anything but that.

"You enjoying it?" he asked after a long moment. He put the paper down and slid it away from himself.

"Um, school, you mean?" she asked, her attention on the newspaper. She desperately wanted to grab it and check that she hadn't written anything too revealing, but she knew that would only make her look even more foolish.

"School, the paper. The whole thing."

"Sure. It's a challenge, but that's only because it's new. And I feel like I'm slowly starting to find my feet."

Okay, that was a lie, but she wasn't about to admit the truth.

He nodded, using his bread to wipe sauce off his plate. "You were right—this is good stuff. Much better than a burger."

She watched as he licked a smudge of sauce off his bottom

lip. Between anxiety about what he might have read in the margins of the paper and her hyperawareness of him physically, her appetite had completely deserted her. She pushed her half-finished plate away and used a paper napkin to wipe her own mouth.

"You don't do anything by halves, do you?" Jake asked suddenly. Her startled gaze found his. They stared at each other for a long moment.

"No. Sometimes I wish I could. But I can't. It's just the way I'm built."

He reached across and caught her hand in his. His thumb stroked the back of hers as he cradled her palm.

"You have beautiful eyes, Poppy Birmingham, you know that? Someone should have written about them when they were mentioning all those gold medals you won."

She forgot to breathe for a moment. His hand slipped from hers and he pushed back his chair. He started shoving empty take-out containers into one of the bags.

She felt very uncertain all of a sudden. She didn't understand him. Every now and then she thought she had a reading on him, but he kept taking her by surprise.

"Leave it. I have to clean in the morning, anyway."

"Do you mind if I use your bathroom before I go?" he asked. She nodded. "Down the hall, to the right."

He'd have to pass her bedroom on the way. She resigned herself to the fact that he'd see her wildly messed bed, the clothes strewn everywhere, her underwear kicked into the corner, the books piled beside her bed. So much for keeping her distance from him. By the time he left her apartment there wouldn't be a single one of her shortcomings and foibles he wouldn't be aware of.

Which reminded her…

She grabbed the newspaper he'd abandoned and reviewed her notes. She'd underlined a couple of phrases, passages that had really appealed to her. Nothing too incriminating—except for the two words she'd scribbled in the margin: *talented bastard*.

Great. Now he knew she admired him professionally, as well as desired him personally.

She heard footsteps in the hallway and hastily dropped the newspaper onto the table. She tried to look casual and at ease, but her shoulders felt as though they were up around her earlobes.

Jake was holding something in his hand when he entered. It took her a moment to recognize the copy of his book that she'd exiled to the toilet-paper basket.

She closed her eyes. This evening was getting better and better.

"I'm curious. If I look through this, are there going to be any pages missing?"

"Oh. Um. No. Of course not. I'm not even sure what that was doing in the bathroom…."

Jake cocked his head to one side and the lie died in her throat.

They stared at each other, then his mouth stretched into a grin.

"Just how long have I been gracing the smallest room in the house, anyway?"

"Since my first day on the paper." He'd surprised her again. His writing was not something she'd expected him to have a sense of humor about.

"That long. Did it make you feel better, putting me in there?" he asked, weighing the book in his hand.

"Yes."

"Good."

He turned to leave the room and she realized he was going to put the book back where he'd found it.

"No. Don't," she said. "I don't think I want it in there anymore."

He stilled. "It's not a bad place for it."

"Maybe."

Jake turned to face her. Their eyes met across the space
that separated them, and suddenly they were at the point
they'd both been dancing around all night. Poppy could feel
her heart kicking in her chest, feel the flood of adrenaline
racing through her body. Deep inside, her body throbbed in
anticipation.

She wanted him. And she knew he wanted her. Could practically smell it in the air.

"Where do you want it, then?" he asked.

"I used to keep it in my bedroom."

His eyes darkened. "I don't think that's the best place for it."

"Why not?" She held her breath, waiting for his answer. They
both knew they weren't talking about his book or her apartment.

"Because it's your space. It's too personal," he said quietly.

So.

She nodded to let him know she understood his message.
She hoped her disappointment didn't show on her face. Maybe
this time she'd learn her lesson where he was concerned.

She held her hand out for the book.

"Okay. I guess I'll have to find a new home for it. Somewhere between the toilet and the bedroom."

He passed the book over. They both turned toward the hall.
She moved ahead of him to open the front door. She kept her
hand on the lock, gripping the cool metal tightly as he hesitated in the doorway.

"It's not you, Poppy. I really like you."

She shrugged. "I get it. We work with each other. Things
have already been awkward. I get it."

"It's not about work." He ran a hand through his hair, stared at the floor for a long beat. "I don't want to hurt you."

"Then don't," she said simply.

He lifted his head to meet her eyes. "It's not that simple."

"Yeah, it is. I'm not asking for a marriage proposal, Jake. I just want you to be there when I wake in the morning. Or to at least say goodbye before you go."

He searched her face. She could feel the tension in him. "I don't have anything to offer you."

Right now she was focused on only one thing—the rush of blood in her ears, the spread of warmth in the pit of her stomach.

"Can you be here in the morning?" she asked. "That's all I want from you right now."

He closed his eyes. "Do you have any idea how much I've thought about you over the past few weeks?" His voice was rough and low. It scraped along her senses and sent a shiver through her.

"It's not like I've been counting sheep at night, either."

His eyes opened. "What have you been counting, then?"

She smiled slowly. "What do you think?"

By slow degrees his smile grew to match hers. He took a step forward and she met him halfway. The press of her breasts against his chest was almost a relief.

His eyes glinted as he lowered his head toward hers. She opened her mouth to him and closed her eyes as his tongue swept into her mouth. He sipped at her lips, stroked her tongue with his, murmured something deep in his throat. She let go of the door and reached for his hips, pulling him closer. He was already hard, his erection straining the fine cord of his pants. She slid a hand onto his butt and held him against her, savoring the heat and hardness of him.

After a long moment he lifted his head. She stared into his face, drugged with need.

"Yes. The answer is yes. I can be here in the morning," he said.

Just as well, because she wasn't sure she had the willpower to push him away if his answer had been anything different.

"Then what are you waiting for?"

Taking his hand, she shut the door behind them and led him to her bedroom.

8

POPPY'S ROOM LOOKED AS THOUGH a bomb had hit it. Clothes and shoes everywhere, books stacked beside the bed, her chest of drawers strewn with papers and toiletries. About the only space that was clear was the bed. Which was good, since that was Jake's destination.

"Sorry about the mess," she said.

Jake grunted to let her know he didn't give a damn about the cleanliness or otherwise of her bedroom and pulled her down onto the mattress, eager to feel the warmth of her beneath him. Every night she'd slipped into his dreams, taunting him with remembered passion. He wasn't sure where he wanted to touch first, which part of her he needed to taste the most. He tugged at her clothes, yanking off her jacket then fumbling with her shirt.

"Slow down." She laughed.

"Can't."

And it was true, he couldn't. He'd been convinced he'd never slide his hands over her breasts again, and yet here they were, warm and full and soft in his hands, her nipples hard beneath the silk and lace of her bra. He'd been certain he'd never feel the greedy press of her hips against his again, or the firm strength of her long legs tangling with his. And yet she was even now rubbing herself against him, one leg wrapped around his waist as she sought satisfaction.

It was too much. She was too much. He sucked a nipple, lace and all, into his mouth, laving her with his tongue. She moaned and he slid a hand down her belly and into the waistband of her tailored pants. The button gave way easily, the zipper hissed down, then he was sliding his hand over the plumpness of her mound, his fingers gliding into damp curls then into hot, slick flesh. He slid a finger inside her, felt the instinctive tightening of her muscles as she clenched them around him. She was so hot, so tight. He wanted to be there, needed to be there. He pushed her trousers down, as clumsy and urgent as a schoolboy. She laughed, the sound low and sultry, as he freed himself from his pants. A moment to protect them both, then he was inside her, his pace already wild, his whole body taut with need.

No laughter from her then, just a dreamy, distant look in her eyes as she bit her lip and tilted her head back and thrust her hips in rhythm with his.

He ducked his head to her breasts again, using his teeth to pull the silk of her bra cup down so he could bite her dusky nipple before tugging it into his mouth. Her hips bucked beneath him as he flicked his tongue over and over her. He slid his hands beneath her hips and drove himself to the hilt again and again. She felt so good. Everything about her. Her skin. The softness of her breasts. The plumpness of her mound. The slick tightness between her thighs.

"Poppy," he whispered against her skin.

"I know," she whispered.

Then he was coming, his climax squeezing his chest, his belly, his thighs. He ground himself against her, feeling her own climax pulse around him. For long seconds he remained tautly above her and inside her. And then he collapsed on top of her, his breath coming in choppy gasps.

"Pinch me," she said after a short while.

"Is this a kinky thing or…?"

"I just want to make sure this is real."

He lifted his head to look into her face. Man, he loved the slightly bewildered look she got on her face after he'd made her come. As though she wasn't one hundred percent certain which way was up or down.

He withdrew from her and rolled to the edge of the bed.

"Come on," he said, reaching for her hand. "Let's have a shower. I couldn't help noticing you have this handy bench tiled into the wall in there."

"For when I was training, to help loosen me up. Back when we weren't on water restrictions because of the drought."

"Ah, the good old days," he said. His trousers and boxer briefs were still tangled around his ankles and he kicked them off. He tugged her pants the rest of the way off, too, then ran a hand from her knee up her thigh, over her hip, stopping on the flat plane of her belly. He felt her muscles contract beneath his hand, watched as her nipples hardened all over again. Her lips parted and she watched him through half-lowered lids.

"Come have a shower," he said.

"Okay."

She led the way up the short hallway. He watched the sway of her hips, the tight flex of her butt. He couldn't resist sliding his hands onto it, cupping it in his palms.

"Just out of curiosity, you ever tried to crack a walnut with these suckers?" he asked, squeezing the twin cheeks of her derriere firmly.

She gave him a look over her shoulder. He grinned and shrugged.

"Just curious."

"Hmm," she said. "I'm not sure I want to know what other questions you have floating in that brain of yours."

He stood back and watched some more as she reached to turn on the shower. Even in winter she had a light tan from her hours in the pool. He eyed the lines on her ass from her swimsuit and remembered how creamy and smooth her breasts were in comparison with her golden arms and legs.

He was hard again. More than anything he wanted to press her against the shower wall and slide inside her again, but there were other, more pressing issues to attend to. Like the fact that he'd been craving another taste of her for weeks now.

"You coming?" she asked as she stepped beneath the water.

He smiled and stepped in after her. "Definitely."

He reached for the soap and the washcloth hanging from her shower organizer. She watched as he worked up a good lather on the cloth.

"Now," he said, drawing her toward him. Slowly he washed her from head to toe. He traced the whorls of her ears, mapped the elegance of her long neck. Paid loving, intimate attention to her breasts and her armpits and the curve of her hip. Dipped between her thighs, washed behind her knees. Then he knelt and lifted her feet, one by one, and washed her toes and her soles and her heels, his fingers massaging the washcloth against her skin.

When he was finished, he looked up at her.

"Sit down," he said.

Poppy's eyes widened as she guessed his intention. Then her focus dropped to his erection where it pressed, hard and ready, against his belly.

"I want—"

"Later."

She sat on the tiled bench behind her. He moved between

her legs, pushing them apart. The air was thick with steam and moisture and warm water pounded down on both of them. He parted the pinkness of her folds. She sucked in an anticipatory breath. He glanced up at her, taking in the flush on her cheeks, the heaviness of her eyelids.

Then he lowered his head and tasted her.

Better than he'd remembered. Slick, silky flesh, the gentle musk of her sex, the freshness of her arousal. He used his hands to keep her open, circling his thumbs around and around her entrance as he teased her clitoris with his mouth. She was very turned on, the bud stiff against his tongue and he sucked her into his mouth again and again. Her hips bucked and one of her hands slid into his hair and fisted there. She lifted a leg to brace it on the seat beside her, offering him greater access. He slid a finger inside her and stroked her inner walls. He knew the moment he found the spot he was looking for—her whole body tensed as though she'd been shocked.

"Jake," she panted.

He smiled against her sex and renewed his assault, stroking her clitoris with his tongue, stroking her G-spot with his finger. It didn't take long. She sucked in a deep breath, her hips lifting. He clamped a hand onto her thigh to hold her in place. He stayed with her as her body convulsed with pleasure, her inner muscles vibrating around his finger.

He lifted his head at last and looked up at her, savoring the abandoned, provocative picture she made, her head dropped back against the shower wall, water streaming down her peaked breasts and her flat belly.

He'd meant to wait, to dry her and take her to bed, but he couldn't hold off a second longer. Standing, he took himself in hand and nudged her folds with his erection.

"Yes," she said, lifting her hips.

He was inside her, gritting his teeth at how wet she was, how good she felt. She shuddered, a whole body ripple of need.

He withdrew until just the tip of his cock remained inside her then watched as he pressed forward and his cock disappeared into her body once more. He repeated the move, reveling in the greedy clutch of her body, savoring the glide into tightness as he drove into her. He glanced at her face, saw she was watching the place where they were joined, too, and that her breasts were rising and falling rapidly. They locked gazes and suddenly he was on the verge, just like that, pleasure rushing through his body. Swiftly, he withdrew from her, stroking himself once, twice with his hand until he came on her belly, his body shuddering.

"I think maybe I just died," she said.

He laughed. He'd never met a woman so open about her own pleasure. With Poppy there had never been any games, no pretense that she didn't want him, that she didn't enjoy the sex, that it wasn't important to her.

She was equally honest about her feelings, too. Another thing he found attractive. He couldn't ever imagine Poppy sulking or punishing him with silence. If she wanted something, she either asked for it or dealt with her need in some other way.

They made love again when they returned to the bedroom. He honestly hadn't thought he was up to it—he wasn't a perpetually horny teenager anymore—but watching her crawl on all fours to the far side of the mattress had his cock flooding to life again. He slid into her from behind this time while they both lay on their sides, her backside cradled by his hips. They rocked together for long, lazy minutes until desire took over. Then Poppy moved onto her hands and knees and he slammed himself into her until they both came yet again.

Poppy dragged the quilt up over their bodies afterward,

shaking her head and laughing ruefully when he slid a hand onto her breast.

"Give me five minutes," she said.

They fell asleep, his hand on her breast, his body curved against hers. His thoughts drifted to the way they fit as he slipped into sleep. She was so tall, he felt all of her against all of him. A good feeling. Complete.

JAKE WOKE WITH SUNLIGHT warm against his face. He turned his head, and there Poppy was, golden light streaming in her bedroom window, gilding her breasts. She was awake, too, her hair was mussed, her eyes heavy.

She smiled faintly when she caught his eye. "You're here."

"Yep."

"A minor miracle."

He smoothed the sole of his foot down the side of her smooth calf. "Hardly." He held her gaze when he said it, wanting her to know that if it was only about her, her honesty and funniness and desirability, he would never have left her bed. Her gaze slid away, but her smile remained.

She didn't know where she stood with him. Which was fair enough—he had no idea where he stood, either.

"There's cereal and bread if you're hungry, but I usually have breakfast at the pool on the weekends. There's a cute little café, and they make great pancakes." She said the words carefully, not quite issuing an invitation.

"Does a person have to swim laps to qualify for breakfast? Or can a person just sit back like a fat bastard and watch other people exercise?"

Her eyebrows rose, then a smile spread across her face. She tried to get it under control, to tame it, but he could still see her pleasure in her eyes even after she'd reined in her mouth.

A moment of doubt bit him. She was so damned open, the way she broadcast everything via her big gray eyes and her expressive face.

He didn't want to hurt her. He remembered what she'd said last night—*then don't.* She'd been asking him to be honest with her. To commit to a night. To one moment at a time.

Could it really be that easy?

Poppy made him walk the two blocks to the pool, claiming it was a good warm-up. The sky was a pale blue, but the sun was shining. The Harold Holt Memorial Pool had two offerings for patrons to choose from: a smaller, heated indoor pool and a competition-length beast outside. The indoor pool was frothing with bodies, since it was September and the tail end of winter was still in the air outside. Only the serious swimmers were prepared to brave the elements for a more challenging swim. Predictably, Poppy led him outside.

She shucked her tracksuit pants immediately and started swinging her arms in broad circles. He frowned and eyed the swimmers churning up the lanes.

"Come on, scaredy cat," she said.

She'd talked him into borrowing a pair of board shorts a "friend" had left behind in her apartment, promising him that while he could still have his pancake breakfast without doing some laps, it would be that much more delicious once he'd earned it.

He'd always been skeptical of that argument—he'd enjoyed plenty of things in his lifetime that he hadn't strictly earned. But he could see she wanted him to swim with her. And it seemed like a small, simple sacrifice to make to bring that slow smile to her lips again.

"I wasn't joking when I said I can't dive for shit," he said.

She shrugged. "So use the steps or jump in."

"I'm not that hopeless."

"Come on, stop stalling and get undressed."

She moved to the diving block at the head of the fast lane while he undressed. He watched her tug her goggles into place and step onto the block. Despite the cold wind and the gooseflesh prickling his arms, he felt a thrill as he watched her bend into position. She looked magnificent, all muscle and long legs and coiled potential. For long seconds she hovered on the verge of exploding off the block, waiting for the lane to be clear. Then she dived, her body arching out over the water for what seemed an impossibly long time before she sliced cleanly into the blue of the pool. He watched her power her way up the lane, marveling at the precision and economy of her stroke.

A particularly chill gust of wind reminded him that he was freezing his proverbials off, and he crossed to the medium lane and dived into the water in his own messy, unaccomplished way.

He'd had enough after ten laps. Running kept him fit, but swimming made different demands on his body. He hauled himself out of the pool and dried off, searching for Poppy's blond head in the water. He found her at the far end of the pool, surrounded by half a dozen young swimmers. A middle-aged woman who he guessed was their coach squatted on the deck, her face intent as she listened to Poppy talk to the swimmers. Jake watched as Poppy lifted her arms, demonstrating a stroke technique. The children all imitated her, their small faces filled with reverent awe as they looked at her. Poppy reached out to correct the angle of one boy's arm, talking all the while. The boy laughed, but Jake saw he kept his elbow high as Poppy had shown him when he tried the stroke again.

Poppy looked up and caught Jake's eye. She signaled that she would be with him shortly, and he signaled back that she should take her time. He was almost fully dressed by the time she joined him on the wooden bleachers beside the pool.

"Sorry. I got caught up. Sally—that's the coach for the under-fourteens—keeps asking my advice when she sees me down here. It's becoming a bit of a habit."

"They like you."

She shrugged as she pulled on her sweatpants. "I've been on TV."

"You're a hero, Poppy. They probably have posters of you on their walls at home."

She looked startled at the thought, then she smiled the sweetest, shyest smile he'd ever seen. "Maybe. They're good kids. Some of them can really swim."

She led him to the café and they ate pancakes with berries, surrounded by the high-pitched squeals of children from the indoor pool and the warm, humid smell of chlorine.

They talked about work on the way back to her apartment block, their steps slowing as they approached his car.

"Well. Thanks for giving me the opportunity to freeze my ass off," he said.

"It wasn't that bad."

"You're only saying that because you didn't see my dive."

"I did, actually."

"And?"

She held her hand out palm down and seesawed it back and forth. "So-so. I've seen worse."

"Let me guess. In the five-year-old class?"

Her smile turned into a grin. "Seven-year-old, actually."

"Hmm."

They smiled at each other. Sunlight filtered through the bare branches overhead, brushing her cheek, setting her hair on fire. He didn't want to go home.

He pulled his car keys from his pocket. "Well. I guess I'd better get going."

He waited for her to say something, give him an excuse to come back upstairs with her.

"Yeah. Thanks for the lift home last night," she said. "And for the help with the Hannam article."

"Always so well mannered, Birmingham," he said, shaking his head.

"Always so rude, Stevens."

Even though he wasn't certain she'd welcome it, he ducked his head and kissed her. No tongue, just warm lips and a too-brief taste of her.

"I'll see you later, Poppy."

"Sure."

He got in his car, dumping his wet gear on the passenger side floor mat. Poppy waved once before turning to walk up the path to her apartment.

He pulled away from the curb, hands tight on the wheel.

This is already getting out of hand.

The thing was, after a night in her arms, he couldn't remember exactly why that was such a bad idea anymore.

9

POPPY SPENT SATURDAY tidying her apartment and catching up on her homework for school. Every time her phone rang her heart leaped, even though she told herself that there was no way she would hear from Jake again that weekend.

She was wrong. He called at six that night and they went out for dinner before going to his place. Sunday night they went to an Al Pacino double feature at an old Art Deco cinema near Jake's house and wound up necking in the back row and making love in Jake's car because they couldn't wait to make it home. She left his bed at two in the morning to get some sleep before starting the working week.

She had no idea what was going on between the two of them—great sex, definitely. But there was more to it than that, too.

She felt incredibly self-conscious when she entered the newsroom the next morning, late for the first time since she'd started at the *Herald*. She hadn't given much thought to work during the weekend, how things might play out, how she might feel. Perhaps she should have. She felt as though there was a flashing neon sign above her head announcing that she and Jake had spent the past two days skin to skin.

She kept her head down, but she couldn't resist shooting a quick glance toward Jake as she sat at her desk. He had his back to her as he wrote something in a notepad, one elbow braced on his desk. She studied the breadth of his shoulders, the subtle strength of his arms. His dark hair just brushed the collar of his shirt, the ends curling slightly. She knew exactly how soft that hair was, what it felt like in her hands, against her skin...

She was staring. She forced her gaze away and concentrated on unpacking her bag. The last thing she wanted or needed was people at work guessing what had happened between them. If this was a mistake—and despite how he made her feel, how drawn she was to him, she suspected it was—then she wanted it to be a private one, not a public debacle open to her colleagues' scrutiny and discussion.

She straightened her in-tray, untangled her phone cord. Dusted her computer monitor, culled the out-of-date sticky notes from her diary. Only then did she allow herself to look at Jake again.

He was still writing in his notebook. She wondered if he'd even noticed her arrival, if he was as acutely conscious of her as she was of him.

Stop staring and do some work. Because that's where you are: at work. Where people do stuff other than stare at their lovers.

This was new territory for her, all of it. The hot need he inspired in her. The nature of their relationship, if it could even be called that. The fact that they worked with each other. Her previous life of discipline and focus had left her woefully unprepared to deal with these kinds of situations. Which was probably why she felt so out of control.

She concentrated on calling up a new file and saving it. She had a profile on an up-and-coming runner to write, and she frowned over the notes she'd taken from the interview. Out of the corner of her eye, she registered movement. Her whole body tensed as Jake pushed back his chair and stood. He turned toward the kitchen, started walking. She held her breath, lifted her gaze as he passed her desk. Waited for him to make eye contact or smile, do something to acknowledge that the weekend had really happened.

He was almost past the point of no return when he turned his head toward her. He nodded once, briefly, his gaze glancing over her face.

"Hey," he said.

Then he was gone.

She stared after him.

Hey. That was it? That was all she got after half a dozen orgasms, two movies, dinner and some seriously funny pillow talk?

She turned to her article but all she did was frown at the screen.

What were you expecting? A declaration of love?

No. But she hadn't expected *Hey,* either.

It was a long day. She had to stop herself from staring at Jake in their department meeting. At lunchtime, she went down to the café and ate her lunch two tables away from him, pretending she didn't care that he was sitting and talking and laughing with Jonesy and Davo.

By the time Jake threw her a casual goodbye wave just after six and headed for the elevator, she understood why workplace romances were frowned upon. She'd been unfocused and distracted all day, had a headache that wouldn't quit and was so confused she didn't know where to put herself.

Then she stepped out of the elevator into the underground garage and saw the note folded under her windshield wiper and her stomach lurched with excitement.

Pathetic, Birmingham. Really, really sad.

She waited until she was in the relative privacy of her car before unfolding the note. She stared at the single line:

Dinner after your swim? J.

A more sophisticated woman would wait awhile before texting to accept such a last-minute invitation. Poppy dug her phone out of her bag and sent a quick confirmation.

It wasn't simply that he wanted to see her, despite his cool demeanor all day. He'd remembered that she swam every day. A small thing, perhaps, but it felt as though it meant something. At the very least, it meant he listened to what she said, remembered it.

Yes. That had to mean something.

THEY SAW EACH OTHER every night that week, even Tuesday night when Poppy had night school till nine. By Friday, she was growing used to Jake's cool friendliness at work. It still gave her pause when he treated her as casually as he did everyone else, but she knew it was smart to keep their private life private. After all, the odds were good this thing of theirs had only a finite lifespan. This way, she got to keep her dignity afterward.

Friday night, Jake took her to an out-of-the-way Malaysian restaurant he'd been hearing good things about. They both went into raptures over the pork in coffee sauce and tamarind prawns, and Jake insisted she try a Malaysian beer with their meal.

"It's what the locals drink. It makes the experience authentic," he said.

She obliged him by taking a mouthful from his glass.

"Okay, it's nice," she conceded. "Even though I am not a beer fan."

"And you call yourself an Australian."

"I know. It's my dirty little secret."

"What other dark truths lurk in your soul, Poppy Birmingham?" Jake asked, leaning toward her. "Hmm?"

His eyes were bright with laughter, his hair ruffled. He was smiling, one eyebrow quirked in expectation. She stared at him and knew that she'd never meet a more attractive man in her life.

"I don't think I have any dark truths."

"I refuse to accept that. There must be something."

"Sorry, my conscience is clean."

He grinned. "Well, maybe I should make it my mission to dirty it up a little."

"Yeah? How exactly do you plan on doing that?"

"Well, for starters—"

"Poppy! God, of all the places!"

Poppy's head came up at the sound of her sister's voice. Sure enough, Gillian stood beside the neighboring table, about to sit down with a large group of friends.

"Gill," Poppy said. For absolutely no reason, she felt acutely self-conscious. She never, ever ran into her sister or brother around town, mostly because they moved in very different circles. To run into Gillian while she was out with Jake felt…awkward. She wasn't quite sure why.

Gillian's gaze shifted to Jake, then back to Poppy again.

"I've been meaning to call you. How are you doing?" Gill asked. Her sister wiggled her eyebrows meaningfully. She wanted an introduction.

"I'm good. Work's been busy. Um, Gill, this is Jake. Jake, this is my sister, Gill," she said.

Gill turned the full force of her charm on Jake, smiling and offering her hand. "Jake, pleased to meet you. I'm going to be gauche and come right out and say I'm a big fan of your book. I work in publishing and I still think it's one of the best Australian novels of the last decade."

Jake sat back a little in his chair. "Nice of you to say so."

Even though his face was completely impassive, Poppy could feel his discomfort. He didn't like talking about his writing. She'd never really registered it before, but it was true.

"Well, I'm not the only one to say so. I was talking to Robert Hughes the other day and he was raving about you, wondering why we haven't seen a second novel yet," Gill said, shamelessly dropping the name of Australia's foremost art critic.

"You know how it is, life gets in the way," Jake said.

Gillian propped her hand on her hip and gave him an appraising look, a half smile on her lips. Poppy could see her sister was about to launch into a full interrogation, despite Jake's patent reluctance. She did the only thing she could think of— she reached across the table, took Jake's hand in hers and smiled at her sister.

"Have you been here before? The food is really great. Jake's friend recommended it to him, otherwise we never would have heard about it. Which I'm glad we did, because, honestly, the coffee pork is to die for." She was talking too fast, had said too much, but her sister took the hint.

Gill's gaze rested on their joined hands for a moment before lifting to Poppy's face.

"No, I haven't. But I've heard a lot of good things." She turned to Jake. "It was nice to meet you. We should do lunch or something soon, Poppy."

"Sure," Poppy said easily.

Gill rejoined her friends, and Poppy tried to ease her hand from Jake's. His fingers curled around hers, refusing to let go. She met his eyes and saw he was smiling at her.

"Slaying my dragons for me, Poppy?"

She shrugged, embarrassed. "She can be a bit scary sometimes. And I could tell you didn't want to talk about it."

He turned her hand over and lifted it to press a kiss into her palm. Her breath caught in her throat as he looked at her.

"Thank you."

Warmth expanded in her chest. When he looked at her like that...

Finally he let her hand go. She tucked it into her lap, still feeling the brush of his lips against her skin.

"So, where does the Amazonian gene come from? Is your brother blond like you?" he asked.

"Nope. He's small and dark, like the rest of them. Charlie said I was a throwback to our long-lost Viking heritage."

Jake smiled. "Poppy the Conqueror. Yeah, I can see you wearing a helmet with horns, waving a big sword around."

"Thank you. I think that's the nicest thing anyone's said to me all day," she said drily.

He laughed. She loved that he got her jokes. And she loved the way his gaze kept dropping to the neckline of her shirt, making her think of what would happen when they got home. She especially loved the way he'd looked at her just now, his gaze warm and intense.

"I'm going to go powder my nose," she said.

She wove her way through the crowded dining room to the restrooms. When she exited the cubicle to wash her hands, her sister was standing by the hand basin.

"Gill," Poppy said, not really surprised to see her. They weren't the closest of sisters, but she knew Gill was interested in Jake because of who he was.

"Poppy, you dark horse. I thought you and Jake were just friends."

"We were."

"But you're not anymore?"

"Um, no. I guess not." Poppy shuffled from one foot to the other. She'd never been the kind of woman who talked about her sex life with friends.

Gill eyed her speculatively as Poppy washed her hands. "He's much better looking in real life."

"Yes."

"Very sexy."

"Mmm."

"Well, Mom will be thrilled. She'll get to grill him properly now."

"Oh, no. It's not like that. We're just… It's very casual. Very," Poppy explained. The last thing she wanted was her mother on the phone, asking twenty questions about her literary boyfriend.

Gill frowned. "That doesn't sound like you."

"First time for everything." Poppy made a point of checking her watch. "Better get back to the table…"

Gill caught her arm before she could go. "Poppy, wait a minute." Gill searched Poppy's face, her eyes concerned. "Are you sure you know what you're doing?"

"Of course. I *have* had sex before, you know."

"In a relationship, though, right?"

"Honestly, Gill…"

"I'm only asking because I don't want you to get hurt."

"I won't. I know exactly what this is. Jake's not up for anything serious. He made that clear up front."

"And what about you? What are you up for?"

Poppy shrugged. "I'm going along for the ride."

Gill studied her face for a long moment. "Well, I hope that's true. Because if you're hanging in there, hoping your casual thing will turn into something less casual, you're setting yourself up to be hurt, Poppy. Believe me, I've been there, and if there's one piece of advice I can give you, it's to believe a man when he says he's not interested in having a relationship. Women always think they know better, or that once the guy gets to know them that rule won't apply to them, but it always does."

For a moment Poppy could see every one of her sister's thirty-five years in the lines around Gill's eyes and mouth. Then Gill patted her arm.

"Sorry—here endeth the lesson, I promise. Have fun with your sexy writer. And look after yourself, Poppy."

She kissed Poppy's cheek and gave her a brief hug, both enormously demonstrative gestures for her typically stand-offish sister.

"I will. You, too," Poppy said.

Jake was talking on his cell phone as she picked her way through the dining room to their table. She watched as he laughed at something his caller said, then started talking animatedly.

He was so damned *compelling,* it almost hurt her to look at him.

Her sister's words echoed in her mind: *you're setting yourself up to be hurt, Poppy.*

She lifted her chin. She wasn't stupid. She knew the score. As long as she kept reminding herself that what was happening between her and Jake was about sex and nothing else, she would be fine.

Absolutely. And in the meantime, she would have fun. After years of swimming drills and discipline, she figured she'd earned a little.

THE FOLLOWING SATURDAY, Jake poured himself a cup of strong black coffee and walked to the living room to sit at his desk. He'd just returned from Poppy's. She'd been headed for the pool as he left, a towel slung over her shoulder, long legs eating up the sidewalk.

He'd been tempted to join her, but he had to polish a feature on Australian cricketing greats that was due on Monday. For the first time in a long time, he resented the fact that his work often bled into his personal life. Maybe because for the first time in a long time he actually had a personal life. Today, for example, it would have been nice to swim with Poppy, then take her to the old Abbotsford Convent, where he'd heard there was an organic bakery and a vegetarian restaurant. Poppy would get off on the healthy food, and afterward they could walk around and look at the old buildings. Instead, he was writing about Donald Bradman and Dennis Lillee.

Jake frowned and took a mouthful of coffee. He was thinking about Poppy way too much. Making plans in his head, coming up with new places to take her, things she might enjoy. For a casual thing, their relationship had quickly taken on a life of its own.

He had no idea what he was doing. Every day he told himself to back off, take it easy with her. And every day he found an excuse to touch her, to be with her. He wasn't ready to give her up yet. He knew he would have to, eventually, but right now he didn't have it in him to walk away.

He forced himself to focus and two hours later he hit Save for the last time. According to his complaining belly, it was well past lunchtime. He stood and stretched, then walked into the kitchen in search of food. He hadn't been shopping all week, so it was probably going to have to be cereal or toast. He opened the freezer to make sure he had no frozen pizzas left and barked out a laugh when he saw what was in there—

a neat stack of frozen meals, a sticky note stuck to one of the boxes. He smiled as he read Poppy's sloping, messy scrawl:

In case of nutritional emergency, break box and heat contents. Then get your pitiful bachelor ass to the supermarket to buy some real food.

He wondered when she'd sneaked the meals into his freezer, then remembered he'd jumped into the shower to wash off the sweat from his run shortly after she arrived on Wednesday night.

"Sneaky," he said into the depths of his freezer.

He chose a stir-fry dish, pierced the top and popped it into the microwave. Then he reached for the phone and dialed her number.

She answered on the third ring.

"Hey," she said.

"Hey, yourself. Ask me what I'm having for lunch."

He leaned a hip against the door frame and slid his free hand into the front pocket of his jeans.

"Lunch? Oh, right. You found the meals."

"Pretty sneaky, getting them into my freezer without me noticing. Ever thought about a career in industrial espionage?"

"Every other day."

"Worried about me starving to death, Poppy?"

"Just making sure you keep your strength up. For entirely selfish purposes. Don't want you passing out at a vital moment or anything."

"Hmm. I guess I should probably return the favor. Keep your strength up, blah blah."

"Well, you know my great love of frozen food," she said with heavy irony.

He grinned. He could imagine the exact look she had in her eyes, the tilt to her head.

"You've been ruined by years of good nutrition, that's your problem."

"Yeah, it's a killer."

"Come to dinner," he said. "I'll cook you something nice."

There was a short pause. He frowned.

"If you have other plans, we can do it another night," he said, even though what he really wanted to ask was what she was doing and who she was doing it with.

"What time do you want me?"

His shoulders relaxed. "Seven. How does that sound?"

"Okay. I'd better get out of this wet swimsuit. Wash the chlorine off."

"Sure. I'll see you later."

He ended the call and stared at the receiver for a few minutes. He hadn't planned on seeing her tonight, but now he was. He shrugged. Poppy was a big girl, she could take care of herself. If she didn't want to see him, she'd say so.

HE SPENT THE REST OF THE afternoon doing some much-needed laundry. At four he went out for groceries. It was close to seven and the kitchen was rich with the smell of baking lasagna when the phone rang. He wiped his hands on a tea towel before taking the call.

"Jake Stevens."

"Jake."

One word was all it took for him to recognize his ex-wife's voice, even though it had been four years since they last spoke. Slowly, he put down the tea towel.

"Marly."

"How are you?"

"I'm good."

"I've been reading your columns. I liked that piece you did on retiring footballers."

"Thanks." He took a deep breath. "Listen, Marly, did you want something?"

There was a small silence on the other end of the line.

"Wow. That's certainly straight to the point."

"Sorry." He pinched the bridge of his nose. It had been five years since the divorce, and he still couldn't talk to her without feeling the old tension in his chest.

"It's all right. We haven't exactly been on talking terms, have we?"

"No."

"That's kind of why I'm calling, actually. I know you still see Marian and Paul sometimes, and I didn't want you hearing it from them." She paused. "I'm pregnant."

He should have expected it. What other reason would she have for calling, after all? She and Gavin had been married for two years now, they'd probably been trying for a while. It was only natural that having a baby together would be high on their list of priorities.

But still he felt winded.

"Jake? Hello?"

He took a deep breath and pulled himself together.

"Congratulations. When are you due?"

That was what he was supposed to ask, right? There was no way he could ask the other questions crowding his mind. Are you still going to call the baby Emma if it's a girl and Harry if it's a boy? Do you still want a natural birth?

Will it make you forget the baby we lost?

"I'm twenty weeks. Halfway."

Four weeks past the point when she'd miscarried last time.

"That's great. Everything good? Mother and baby both well?" he asked.

"Yes."

"Well. I'm happy for you."

"Gavin's taken some time off work and we're going to take it easy for the last few months. Just to make sure everything is okay this time," Marly said.

He closed his eyes, hearing the implied criticism in her tone. Even now, she couldn't let it go.

"Should give you plenty of time to prepare for the baby," he said neutrally.

She was silent for a beat. He could hear her breathing on the other end of the line.

"Do you ever think about her?" she finally asked.

"Yes. Of course I do."

"She'd be six years old. In grade one at school." She was crying, her voice breaking.

"Marly…"

"I'm sorry. It's just been on my mind a lot lately. For obvious reasons."

"Sure."

"Anyway, I'll let you go. Stay well, Jake."

"I'll keep an eye out in the paper for the announcement," he said.

He ended the call. For a long moment he simply stood there, trying to keep a lid on all the shit she'd stirred up.

It was amazing, but even after five years he still felt the tug of responsibility toward her. The tears in her voice, the thread of misery—like Pavlov's dogs, all the old instincts roared to life inside him. The need to make her happy, to heal her, to somehow find the one magic thing that would make it all okay.

The old anger was there, too. Anger at himself, for not being around when she needed him. Anger at her for not being stronger. Anger at life for throwing more misery at them than they'd been able to handle.

Memories he'd thought long buried rose: the emptiness in Marly's eyes when he'd finally arrived at the hospital after she'd lost their baby; the oppressive darkness of their bedroom for months afterward, Marly curled on the bed day after day. And finally Marly's body stretched on the bathroom floor, pale and lifeless.

He swore under his breath and strode to the living room. He didn't know where to put himself. He didn't want to relive this shit. He wanted it gone, forgotten. But all the old stuff was welling up inside him.

Why the hell had she called? He didn't need to know she was having another baby. It was none of his business. Nothing to do with him.

His movements jerky, he grabbed a bottle of wine and pulled the cork. He was taking his first mouthful when the doorbell rang.

It took him a moment to remember that he'd invited Poppy over.

Shit.

He passed a hand over his face and took a deep breath. Then he went to open the door.

"Hey," she said brightly. She held up a supermarket bag. "I brought ice cream for dessert."

He forced a smile.

"Great. Come on in. The lasagna's almost done."

She followed him into the kitchen and unloaded a tub of chocolate-chip ice cream onto the counter. He shoved it into the freezer and grabbed another wineglass. All the while he avoided her eyes. If he looked at her, he was afraid it would all come tumbling out—all the misery, all the grief, all the anger.

"Did you get your article finished?" she asked as he poured her a drink.

"Yes."

He slid her glass across the counter. The wine slopped dangerously close to the rim.

"Is there anything I can do to help?" She looked expectantly around the kitchen.

"You know what, why don't you go to the living room and find something to put on the stereo while I make the salad?"

He felt as though his skin was too tight, as though one wrong word or gesture would shred what little control he had.

She hesitated for a moment.

"Sure, no worries. I'll leave you to it."

Once she was gone, he braced his arms against the counter and hung his head.

It's the past. It's gone. It doesn't mean anything.

"Jake, is everything okay?" Poppy asked quietly from behind him.

He straightened. She was standing in the doorway, a wrinkle of concern on her forehead.

"Did you find something you want to listen to?"

He reached for his wine and took a good swallow. Poppy watched him, her eyes wary.

"If you need to talk… I mean, it's not as though I don't owe you on that front, after Uncle Charlie and everything."

"I'm fine," he said. It came out a little more curtly than he'd meant it to and she flinched.

"Okay." She gave him a small, uncertain smile and returned to the living room.

The timer sounded and he grabbed the oven mitts. He'

barely got a grip on the stoneware lasagna dish when his wrist contacted one of the hot wire shelves. He jerked away from the pain, and the dish slid from his hands and hit the tiled floor with a crack. Lasagna went everywhere.

"Shit. Bloody hell."

He threw the oven mitts to one side and sucked on the burn on his wrist. Couldn't he catch one freaking break tonight? Was that too much to ask?

"You've hurt yourself. Let me see."

Poppy was in the room, reaching for his arm. He pulled away, unable to tolerate her gentle sympathy.

For a moment they were both very quiet. Then she took a step backward.

"Listen, Jake. If this is a bad time for you, I can always go home."

He stared at the mess on the floor. His chest ached with guilt and anger and grief.

"Yeah. Maybe that's a good idea."

She blinked and he realized she hadn't expected him to take her up on her offer.

"Okay. I guess I'll see you at work, then."

He moved to walk her to the door. She held up a hand.

"It's fine. I know the way out," she said.

She was gone then, the front door closing behind her with a decisive click.

He swore again and closed his eyes.

He'd hurt her feelings. Again.

Grim, he squatted and used the tea towel to scoop the bulk of the ruined lasagna into the two halves of the dish. He dumped the lot in the sink then decided the rest could wait till morning. He needed to get out of the house.

He grabbed his car keys and his wallet and took the

stairs to the back of the building where his Porsche was parked.

He shot out into the street and wove through the traffic, working his way north and east until he was turning into the darkened road leading into Studley Park. Just four kilometers from the city center, the park sprawled over more than six hundred acres and featured one of Melbourne's most challenging roads. Jake put his foot down and took the first corner hard. The Porsche growled beneath him as he changed down a gear and punched the accelerator.

By the time he roared to a stop at the lookout point, he'd wrestled his way around enough corners to take the edge off. The engine quieted to a low rumble, then fell silent as he switched it off.

He walked to the lone picnic bench at the lookout, cold wind biting through his sweater. He sat on the table, feet on the bench seat, elbows braced on his knees. He stared out at the city spread below—the towering skyscrapers, the many twinkling lights of the sprawling suburbs, the constantly moving red-and-white dots of cars on the roads.

Marly had caught him off guard with her news, but it scared him how quickly the old shit had come up at him. He'd thought he'd put it all behind him. Wanted to, more than anything. He'd taken what lessons he could from the experience and moved on.

So why was he sitting up here alone, tears burning at the back of his eyes as he thought about the child he'd lost and his broken marriage?

He stood and walked to the very edge of the lookout, right to the safety barrier where the land fell away abruptly.

Shit happens, man. Deal with it.

It had been his motto for the long months of Marly's de

pression. Deal with her silence. Deal with her tears. Deal with her accusations and blame. Deal with her attempt to take her own life.

The truth was, he'd spent so much time looking after her, he'd barely had time to feel anything for himself. But someone had had to be the strong one.

Slowly the churning in his gut settled. He returned to the picnic table and sat, breathing in the cool night air. Inevitably, his thoughts turned to Poppy.

He'd hurt her, the way he'd pushed her away. He scrubbed his face with his hands. Maybe it was for the best. The past few weeks had been crazy, but maybe now was the time to start being smart. Before great sex turned into something more than it was ever meant to be.

He stared at the night sky and thought about cutting Poppy out of his life. About never touching her again. Never laughing with her, never teasing her.

Letting her go, before she got hurt.

He turned and went back to his car.

HE'D LET HER WALK OUT the door so easily. That was what killed her the most.

Poppy pushed away the untouched bowl of pasta she'd made for herself and stared at the worn spot on the arm of her couch.

He'd been upset, wounded in some way. She'd seen it in his eyes, his face, the moment he'd opened the door to her. And instead of seeking comfort from her, instead of sharing or taking solace, he'd blocked her out. Literally kicked her out of his kitchen, then let her walk away when she offered to give him space.

Shouldn't have offered to leave if you didn't mean it, her cynical self said.

She'd wanted him to talk to her—that was why she'd offered to leave. She hadn't expected him to let her go.

Which said a lot about the dynamics of their relationship.

Time to face the music, Poppy.

She took a deep breath and then let it out again.

She wanted more from Jake than he was willing to give. This wasn't casual for her. Maybe it never had been.

And she knew, absolutely, that Jake did not feel the same way. Even though things had been pretty damn intense between them the past few weeks, even though when they were together they laughed and had great sex and interesting discussions about everything under the sun, there was always a part of Jake that was constantly checking the exits, in case he had to leave in a hurry. He was drawn to her despite himself, a reluctant recruit to their mutual attraction.

What was it her sister had said?

If there's one piece of advice I can give you, it's to believe a man when he says he's not interested in having a relationship.

Good advice. Pity Poppy had already been too far gone by then to take it.

Poppy pulled her legs tight to her chest and rested her chin on her knees. This was new territory for her, this aching vulnerability, this tenderness. It scared her, because she knew there was a part of her that wanted Jake so much that she'd take whatever scraps of himself he was willing to throw her way. And she might not be an expert on relationships or love but she knew that that way lay great heartache.

The doorbell rang. She stared down the hallway. It was Jake. It had to be—it was nearly ten and she couldn't think of anyone else who'd come calling unannounced at this time of night.

Plus, her heart was racing. Usually a reliable sign he was somewhere in the vicinity.

All the same, she checked the peephole before opening the door, just in case. Jake stood in profile to her, his head down. He was holding flowers. His expression was unreadable, utterly neutral.

She rested her forehead against the cool surface of the door for a second, love for him washing over her. She wanted to open the door and cling to him, press her face into his neck and inhale his smell, wrap her body around his, get as close as it was humanly possible for two people to be.

She was such an idiot.

It had crept up on her when she wasn't looking, but it had probably been inevitable from the moment she asked him to stay the night. She wasn't the kind of woman who could be casual with her body or her feelings. Her sister had seen it— and deep in her heart, Poppy had known, too.

She took a deep breath. Then she opened the door. Jake swung to face her. Up close his eyes were watchful, wary. He offered her the flowers.

"I'm a dick. I was having a bad day. I shouldn't have taken it out on you," he said simply.

She stared at the flowers, then his face, wanting more. Some small sign that he trusted her. That this was about more than sex for him. That the ache in her chest was not about to become a permanent fixture.

His mouth quirked into a half smile. "If you're interested, there's a little café in Fitzroy that serves great lasagna. Even better than the stuff I scraped off my kitchen floor."

She waited, but there was nothing more.

So.

He wasn't going to give her a reason why.

He wasn't going to share his pain with her, the way she'd shared hers with him.

It's early days yet. He's wary. He's obviously had a bad divorce. Give him time.

Of course, it was also entirely possible that the only part of himself that Jake would ever willingly share with her was his penis, and that holding out for more would only make the inevitable that much more painful.

"Can I come in?" Jake asked.

She realized she'd been standing staring at him for a long time. Slowly, she stepped to one side.

She followed him to the living room and watched him take in the abandoned bowl of spaghetti on her coffee table.

"You've eaten already," he said.

"Yes."

End it. End it now. Save yourself a world of disappointment. End it while you can still look him in the eye and be his friend and work with him.

Her sensible self, speaking with her sister's voice.

She stared at the flowers in her hand. They were something, right? He'd gone to the trouble of finding a florist that was open at this time of night. He could have shown up empty-handed, or gotten some nasty, limp bouquet from the gas station.

She looked at him.

"There's some spaghetti left, if you want it. I could heat it in the microwave."

"Yeah? To be honest, I'm starving," he said. He looked tired. She wanted to cup his face in her hands and draw the pain out of him.

Instead, she went into the kitchen and took the bowl of leftover pasta from the fridge. She could feel him watching her as she put cling film over the bowl and set the microwave timer, but she deliberately didn't look at him. She needed a few seconds to get her game face on. The last thing she wanted was for him to look into her eyes and understand she'd fallen in love with him.

He was studying the dancing monkeys on her baggy old pajamas when she turned around.

"I'm not exactly dressed for company," she said.

His eyes were warm on her from across the small room. "Come here."

When she didn't move, he reached out and caught her elbow, tugging her toward him.

"The spaghetti…"

"I came here for you, not for food."

He kissed her then, his hands cradling her head, and she closed her eyes against the tide of longing and need that rose inside her. One kiss, one caress was all it ever took with Jake.

"I'm sorry, okay?" he said against her mouth. "I was an asshole. It won't happen again, I promise."

He held her eyes until she nodded.

"I'll hold you to it," she said.

"Good."

They kissed again and he slid his hands down her back and beneath the waistband of her pajamas. She shivered as his hands cupped her bare backside, his fingers curving beneath her cheeks.

"No underwear, Ms. Birmingham?"

"As I said, I wasn't expecting company."

"So this is what you get up to when you're on your own, swan around the apartment commando?"

"George likes it that way."

He grinned and backed her against the kitchen counter. "George. I was kind of hoping he was off the scene."

He was, but she wasn't about to tell Jake that he'd ruined her for all other forms of pleasure.

He slid his knee between her legs, nudging them apart. One of his hands found the buttons on her pajama top and he slid them free while he kissed the tender skin beneath her ear, his tongue sending prickles of desire racing through her body.

He murmured his appreciation as he bared her breasts, then he lowered his head and she let her head drop back as he pulled a nipple into his mouth.

He felt so good. She was so ready for him it hurt.

She fumbled with his belt, then his fly. He took care of protection while she kicked her pajama pants off, then she lifted her leg over his hip and he pushed inside her, big and thick and long.

She clutched his bare ass, holding him still inside her for a few precious seconds, savoring the moment. Then he started to move, his cock stroking her, the friction exquisite. His backside flexed and contracted beneath her hands. His breathing became ragged. She could hear the sounds of their bodies meeting and parting, could feel the hot wetness of her own desire.

She pressed her face close to his chest and inhaled, consciously absorbing his smell, the feel of his skin against hers, the power of his body as he pressed himself into her.

I love you, she told him in her mind as she pulled his hips closer, urging him inside her. *I love you, Jake Stevens.*

He kissed her, his tongue sweeping her mouth, his lips teasing hers. She held her breath. Tensed. Closed her eyes.

Then her body was pulsing with pleasure, wave after wave washing over her. She clutched him to her, calling his name over and over. She felt him tense. His body stroked into hers one last time. He shuddered, his body as hard as granite as he came.

For a moment there was only the sound of their harsh breathing. Then Jake drew back a little so he could look down into her face.

"I think the spaghetti is done," he said.

She hadn't even heard the timer sound. Amusement danced in his eyes, along with something else. Something warm and real. Something that made her fiercely glad that she'd let him in, despite the lack of explanation and her realization that she was far more invested in their relationship than he was.

He cares. He may not love me yet, but he cares.

He smoothed her hair from her forehead with his thumb. Then he kissed the corner of her mouth and withdrew from her. She listened to the heavy tread of his footsteps as he headed for the bathroom.

She closed her eyes for a moment, savoring the satisfied pulse of her body. Maybe she was stupid. Maybe she was going to get hurt, but so be it. Right now, right this minute, she'd take what she could get of Jake Stevens and hope like hell that the warmth she saw sometimes when he looked at her was not wishful thinking and self-delusion.

And maybe next time he was troubled or his demons came calling, he would turn *to* her instead of away.

10

THE NEXT MORNING, JAKE woke with words in his head. Poppy was breathing deeply beside him, still asleep, and he kept his eyes closed as images and ideas swirled in his mind. Slowly, the words became phrases, then sentences. He shuffled them in his head like a deck of cards. More words came to him. His fingers itched to pick up a pen and find some paper.

It had been so long since he'd woken like this, he was almost afraid. Once, it had been commonplace, a part of his world. But he hadn't wanted to write, needed to write, for a long time.

Finally the urge to put it down on paper became too much for him. He eased out of bed, tugged on his boxer briefs and went to the living room. Poppy kept scrap paper by the phone to take down messages and he helped himself to a few pages. He sat at her dining room table and started to write. After a few minutes, he stood and grabbed more paper. A few sheets wasn't going to be enough. He felt as though a floodgate had opened inside him. The words and images were flowing fast, and he needed to get them down.

His hand flew across the page. Twenty minutes in, his fingers began to cramp. He shook them out and kept writing.

"Hey. You're up early."

Poppy stood in the doorway, a T-shirt barely skimming the

tops of her thighs. Her hair was ruffled and there was a crease on her face from the pillow.

"Couldn't sleep," he said.

Her gaze dropped to the pages of closely written script in front of him. There was a question in her eyes when she raised them to his face. He shrugged self-consciously.

"An idea for work," he said.

"Ah. I was wondering what had you so fired up so early."

He felt bad for lying to her, but the truth was that he didn't know what this was yet. He started gathering the pages together.

"You want cereal or toast?" she asked as she moved toward the kitchen.

He shook his head, standing. "I'm all right, thanks." He went to the bedroom and began pulling on his clothes.

Poppy looked surprised when he stepped into the living room, fully dressed, pages folded into his back pocket.

"You're going?"

"I've got some things I need to do," he said. "But I'll call you this afternoon, okay?"

She nodded. "Sure."

He kissed her goodbye, savoring the cool softness of her cheek against his. Then he was heading down the stairs, his mind full of more words, more ideas.

He spent the day writing. A story was starting to emerge from the conversations and scenes he'd woken with. The man in his story took on flesh, found his voice. The woman, too. It wasn't until she became pregnant that Jake understood what he was doing. His fingers slowed on the keyboard then stopped. He stared at the screen.

He couldn't write this. Could he?

But already he knew where he wanted to go next, what he needed to put on the page. He wanted to tell it all, every ugly, sad, messy moment of it. He wanted to lay it all out on clean white paper and sweep it out of the dark corners of his mind.

No one need ever read it. Certainly he would never publish it—it was too raw, too personal. But maybe it was something he needed to do. And since it was the first time he'd felt the urge to write in years, it didn't feel as though he had a choice. Not if he ever wanted to reclaim his life.

He took a deep breath. Then he started to write.

TWO WEEKS LATER, POPPY LAY on her bed and watched the morning sun paint patterns on the far wall.

Her body was warm and languid from Jake's lovemaking, her blood still thrumming through her veins. She turned her head and stared at the hollow his head had left in the pillow. She could hear him in the bathroom down the hall, singing his version of Madonna's "Like a Virgin" while he showered. She smiled as he reached for a high note.

That was the thing about Jake. He could always make her laugh, be it with an arrogant comment, a smart-ass quip or boyish stupidity. It was one of the things she loved about him.

The list was growing longer by the day.

Don't start, Birmingham.

She pulled the sheet up to cover her breasts and grabbed his pillow, piling it behind herself before reaching for the book she was reading. It was a Saturday and she didn't have to be anywhere in a hurry. In the bathroom, Jake switched to Nina Simone.

Two weeks ago, she would have been in there with him, but staying in bed this morning and letting him shower alone was today's proof to herself that she could live without Jake Stevens in her life. She made a point of doing something every day to reassure herself that she could. She might love him, but she could live without him. And she would. If she had to.

Loving Jake was like riding a roller coaster. Sometimes when he looked at her, she was so sure she saw something more than lust in his eyes. She had no doubt that he liked her, that he enjoyed spending time with her. He cared about her feelings. And he wanted her. If all of that didn't add up to love, it came pretty damn close.

She could almost let herself believe the fantasy. Almost. But she still had no idea what had cut him so deeply the night of their disastrous dinner. And he still hadn't told her what he was working on. A new book, she guessed. But that was only a guess, because he hadn't shared it with her.

She ached to ask him. Just as she ached for him to confide his pain in her. She wanted to share his life, in every sense of the word. But Jake had to want to share it with her, he had to offer himself up—his trust wasn't something she could demand.

The water shut off and she opened her book and started reading. She was doing a credible impression of an engaged reader when Jake came into the room, a towel slung low on his waist. She tried to keep herself from following him with her eyes as he dressed, but she was powerless against her desire for him.

He had a beautiful body, long and strong and lean. Her gaze swept the width of his torso then ran down his spine. He had a great ass, round and firm from running. And his legs were corded with muscle and dusted with crisp, dark hair. He pulled on boxer-briefs and she watched as he adjusted himself.

Man, it got her hot when he touched himself like that.

She shifted in the bed and he glanced at her.

"Good book?" he asked.

She had to flick a look at the cover to remember what she was reading.

"Yeah. It's funny. He's a good writer," she said.

"When are you going to your parents' place?" he asked as he tugged on jeans.

"Early afternoon. Mom and Dad's party isn't till tonight, but I promised I'd help out."

Jake finished buckling his belt and crossed to sit on the side of the bed.

"Drive carefully, okay?" he said.

He took her hand, his thumb running across the top of her knuckles. Her heart swelled in her chest as she looked into his face. He cared. Definitely he cared.

"I've driven that road about a million times," she said.

"Still." He leaned forward and kissed her gently. Then he stood and grabbed his T-shirt from the top of her chest of drawers.

"When do you think you'll be back?"

"I'll probably leave after breakfast tomorrow, be back midmorning. Don't worry, I haven't forgotten your precious Martin Scorsese double feature."

Jake had been eyeing the Sunday matinee all week.

"This is for your edification, not mine. I can't believe you haven't seen *Goodfellas*. It's a classic."

"I'm prepared to be moved."

He grinned. "Oh, you will be."

He finished tying his shoes and straightened. She put down her book.

"Well. I guess I'll see you tomorrow," he said.

"Yep."

This would be the first Saturday night they'd spent apart in four weeks. She wondered if he'd even noticed.

He leaned down to kiss her. She slid her hand around his neck for just a second, holding him close, then she forced herself to let him go.

"See you," she said.

She made herself stay in bed, supremely casual, as he let himself out. Once she'd heard the door close behind him she fell back against the pillows and closed her eyes. She could still smell his deodorant hanging in the air.

"I love you," she told the empty room.

Before she could start thinking things to death, she threw the covers back and hit the shower. If she went to the pool now, she could get her laps done and spend some time helping Sally with the under-fourteens. At least that was one area where she felt on solid ground.

She spent an hour cutting through the water, losing herself in the rhythm of the pool. Sally was teaching her kids tumble turns, and Poppy showed them a few tricks of the trade before showering and hitting the road.

It was nearly midday when she pulled into her parents' driveway. She spent the afternoon helping prepare for their anniversary party. Gill arrived at four with her new boyfriend, Daniel, followed shortly by Adam with his long-term partner, Wendy. Poppy was acutely aware that Uncle Charlie was missing from the family circle as they all stood in the kitchen talking and laughing. For a moment she was overwhelmed with sadness. Then her mother asked for help stirring the gravy and she didn't have time to think until it was time to file into the dining room.

It wasn't until they were all seated that Poppy registered she was the only person without a partner. Normally, Uncle Charlie sat beside her, so she wasn't as aware of her single status. Certainly it had never bothered her before. But tonight she looked around the table and felt her aloneness acutely.

Her sister must have noticed the same thing because she cornered Poppy in the kitchen after dessert.

"I was kind of thinking Jake might be here," she said.

"No."

"Family dinner too dull for him, huh?" Gill asked. She was joking, her attention more than half-focused on cutting herself a second slice of cake.

"I didn't ask him. I figured mentioning a family gathering would be a surefire way to send him running for the hills."

Poppy closed her mouth with a click. Where the hell had that come from?

Gill's face was an advertisement for sisterly concern.

"Oh, Poppy," she said.

Suddenly Poppy was blinking away tears. "I'm fine. It's all good. We're having a good time, no strings."

"Except you want there to be strings."

It wasn't a question. Poppy nodded miserably. It was almost a relief to admit it to someone.

Gill shook her head. "Men are such assholes sometimes."

"I'm the one who broke the rules," Poppy said. "This was supposed to be a casual thing."

"Yeah, right. I told you, didn't I? It always gets messy. If you like a man enough to spend that much time with him, to share your body with him, what the hell is going to stop you from falling all the way in love with him?"

"Excellent question," Poppy said with a watery smile.

Gill grabbed her forearm, very earnest. "Tell him how you feel, Poppy. Don't do what I did. I hung on and hung on with Nathan, hoping and hoping he'd realize he cared. I wasted a year eating my heart out for him, going alone to parties because we weren't a couple despite the fact that we slept with each other all the time, turning away other men because I was always holding out hope that Nathan would get it. And he never did."

Poppy stared at her sister. She remembered Nathan. He was a senior executive at the publishing house where Gill worked.

Poppy had been introduced to him once when she'd dropped into the office to pick up her sister for a lunch date.

"I always thought Nathan was only a work colleague," Poppy said.

Gill's smile was tight. "You were right. It just took me a while to work that out."

"I'm sorry things didn't work out for you."

"Hey, it's old news. And Daniel is a sweetie, don't you think?"

"Yeah, he seems great."

Gill squeezed Poppy's arm. "Do yourself a favor—tell Jake how you feel, what you want. At least that way you'll know now, rather than waiting and waiting and finding out down the line that you'll never get what you want."

Poppy shook her head. Even the thought of telling Jake made her belly tense. "It's too soon. It's only been a few weeks."

"It was long enough for *you* to fall in love with *him*, wasn't it?" Gill asked.

Poppy stared at her sister, utterly arrested. She knew Gill was right. In her bones she knew.

Their mother entered, a stack of plates in her hands.

"Your dad's pulling out the liqueur glasses. I think it's going to be one of those nights."

Without giving herself time to stop and think, Poppy turned to her mother.

"Mom, I think I'm going to head back into town," she said.

Her mother frowned. "I thought you were staying the night? And haven't you been drinking?"

"I've had one glass. And there's something I need to do," Poppy said.

Gill met her eyes and gave her an encouraging nod.

Ten minutes later Poppy was on the freeway to Melbourne, her gut churning with nerves. She went over and over what she wanted to say in her head, imagining what Jake might say in response. By the time she hit the city she was half nervous, half terrified.

She had no idea how Jake would react. She was very, very afraid that he would reject her. But there was also a flicker of hope in her heart.

She found a parking spot right in front of his apartment building. She told herself it was a good omen. She figured she needed every scrap of luck she could get right now. Her boots rapped sharply against the marble stairs of his building as she climbed to the second floor. She paused outside his door, her hand fisted, ready to knock.

He wasn't expecting her. She probably should have called, warned him she was on the way.

She knocked. There was a short silence, then she heard the sound of footsteps on the other side of the door.

"Jake," she said.

But it wasn't Jake standing in front of her, it was a tall, elegantly dressed woman in a white silk blouse and tailored black pants. About thirty-five, maybe a little older, her hair long, dark and smooth, her makeup flawless.

Poppy stared. She didn't have it in her to do anything else.

Another woman. God, why hadn't she even considered it? It wasn't as though she and Jake had ever discussed being exclusive, after all. She had just assumed...

Which, clearly, had been a stupid, naive thing to do.

"Sorry, Jake's not here right now," the woman said. "But he shouldn't be long, if you want to come in and wait?"

Poppy took a step backward.

"No, no. Um, it's okay, I can talk to Jake later. At—at work. I didn't mean to barge in. I should have called."

Dinner burned the back of her throat. While she'd been falling in love with Jake, he'd been...what? Romancing this other woman on the side? Sleeping with her the few nights he hadn't been with Poppy?

"Seriously, he just ducked out. Gerome wouldn't quit whining about there being no beer."

"Hey! I made one comment. Hardly whining," a male voice said, then a dark-haired man in his early forties stepped into view and rested a hand on the woman's shoulder.

Poppy stared at him. Then she stared at his hand. Some of the panicked urgency left her body.

The woman stuck her hand out. "I just realized, I should have introduced myself. You probably think we're breaking into Jake's place or something. I'm Fiona, Jake's sister."

Somehow Poppy managed to clasp Fiona's hand and shake it.

"I'm Poppy. Um, I work with Jake," she said.

"When you're not whipping ass for Australia. I'm Gerome, Fiona's whining, beer-loving husband." He smiled. "I've got to say this, even though you probably hear it all the time, but that was an amazing final in the relay you guys pulled off in Beijing. I nearly wet my pants when you outtouched the Poms to come home with the gold."

Fiona rolled her eyes. "Can't take him anywhere." She waved Poppy forward. "Come in, please. Jake will be angry with us if we let you go before he gets back."

Before Poppy could protest, she was drawn into Jake's apartment. It was only when she followed Fiona into the living room that she saw his sister and husband weren't the only visitors. An older couple sat on the couch, wineglasses on the coffee table in front of them.

"Poppy, these are my parents, Harriet and Bernard Stevens. Guys, this is Poppy Birmingham."

"You don't need to tell us that," Jake's dad said. He stood and offered her his hand. "An honor to meet you. My wife and I are big fans."

Poppy smiled and said something appropriate. At least she hoped it was appropriate—she was too busy trying not to stare at the half-eaten birthday cake on the coffee table. She could just make out the words that had been iced on the cake before someone had cut into it: Happy Birthday, Jake. Her gaze shifted to the crumpled wrapping paper on the floor, then to the stack of obviously new books on one arm of the couch.

It was Jake's birthday. And he hadn't told her. He had his family over from Adelaide, and he hadn't told her.

Why would he? a cynical little voice said in the back of her mind. *You're just the warm body he screws. You're not part of his life. Why would he share his family with you?*

His mom was saying something. Poppy shook her head, tried to focus.

It was too much. She'd come here, ready to bare her soul to him, and he hadn't even bothered to let her know it was his birthday.

"I'm sorry. I—I have to go," she said suddenly, interrupting Jake's mother. The other woman looked startled, but Poppy didn't care. She had to get out of there before she burst into tears in front of a roomful of strangers.

"I'm sure Jake will be here any minute. He said the liquor shop was around the corner. I'll call him," Fiona said, pulling out her cell phone.

"No!" Poppy practically yelled it. They all stared at her. "I'll catch up with Jake another time. There's nothing I need to say that can't wait."

She headed for the door and took the stairs two at a time, desperate to avoid bumping into Jake. If she saw him right now, there was no way she'd be able to stop herself from breaking into big, blubbering, self-pitying tears. She hit the foyer at speed and barreled into the street. Relief hit her as she slid behind the wheel.

She'd made it.

Now she just had to do what needed to be done and learn to live with the consequences of her own foolishness.

THE SIX-PACK OF BEER SWUNG heavily in the bag as Jake climbed the stairs to his apartment. At least now his brother-in-law could stop looking so hangdog about the lack of malt-and-hops-based beverages in the house. He'd have to warn his family that if they planned to ambush him on his birthday again they needed to bring their own drinks or possibly end up disappointed.

He smiled to himself as he pulled his keys from his pocket. He still couldn't believe his sister and his parents had flown all the way from Adelaide to Melbourne to surprise him. Although the "casual" phone call he'd had from his sister during the week was now explained. Crafty bastards.

He let himself into the apartment and shrugged out of his coat.

"Okay, Gerome, you fussy bugger—it's beer o'clock," he said as he walked to the living room.

"See, I told you he'd walk in the door the moment she'd gone," Fiona said. She sounded frustrated. "Your timing has always sucked, Jake."

"Sorry?"

"You just missed your friend," his mother said.

Jake frowned.

"Poppy Birmingham," Gerome explained. "She of the long legs and many gold medals."

"Yeah? Poppy was here? She's supposed to be in Ballarat at her folks' place."

"We told her to wait for you, but she wouldn't stay," his mother said.

"Huh." He pulled his cell phone from his back pocket and dialed her cell. She wouldn't have had time to drive far; she could turn around and come back to meet his family.

He frowned as the call went to voice mail.

"Poppy, it's me," he said. "Give me a call when you get this." He thought for a second. She hadn't said anything, but he'd been very aware that this was her first family occasion without Uncle Charlie being around. Maybe it had been too tough and she'd bailed. "Hope everything went okay tonight."

"She said she'd speak to you tomorrow," Fiona said when he'd ended the call.

"And in the meantime, I believe there are six perfectly good beers calling my name," Gerome said.

Jake handed the bag over, still thinking about Poppy.

"She's very striking," his mother said. "I've only ever seen her on TV but she's got a real presence, hasn't she?"

"Yeah," Jake said. He'd wait until she was home then call her to check everything was okay.

"Why don't I make us some coffee?" his mother said, standing and starting to collect wineglasses.

"I'll get it. What does everyone want?" he asked.

He took orders and his mother followed him into the kitchen, clearly determined to help out. He pulled coffee mugs from the cupboard while she filled the kettle, and all the while his mind was on Poppy. Ten more minutes and he would go into his bedroom and call her, make sure she was all right.

"Jake, I know this makes me the worst sort of interfering mother, but I have to ask. Are you seeing Poppy? Is she your girlfriend?"

He pulled the coffee out of the freezer. "You're right, it does."

His mother gave him a dry look. "Well, tough. I'm your mother and I've been worried about you, so I get a free pass now and then."

"I'm fine," he said.

His mom crossed her arms over her chest and leaned against the sink. "Are you?"

"Yes."

"It seems to me that all you do these days is work. That's all you ever seem to talk about when I call."

"Well, you know, unless I win the lottery that's the way it's probably going to be until I retire."

"Jake, stop bullshitting me. I'm serious here."

He stared at her. His mom never swore.

"Ever since the divorce I feel as though you've forgotten how to really live."

"Mom, I'm fine. I swear. I go out, I do stuff. It's not like I'm some bitter divorcé holed up in my apartment, living off canned food."

His mother walked to the freezer and opened the door like a lawyer inviting the jury to examine exhibit A. Jake stared at the neat stack of frozen meals and pizzas filling the small space.

"Okay, maybe I could eat a little better," he conceded.

His mother looked at him sadly. "I wish I could show you how much you've changed. The look in your eyes, the way you carry yourself—it's as though you're always braced, ready to defend yourself in case someone gets too close."

He didn't know how to respond. What his mother was saying was probably true. His marriage had changed him. Made him wary. Worn him down.

"I'm doing okay, Mom," he said.

"I want you to be doing more than okay. I want you to find someone you can love again, someone who loves you.

I want you to have children and write more beautiful books and live a full life instead of this frozen-dinner existence you've been enduring."

"I'm not getting married again, Mom." He said it very seriously, so she'd know it wasn't open to debate. "I don't want to go through any of that crap ever again."

"But what about love? Companionship? What about having a warm body to wake up next to and someone to share jokes with and someone to rub your feet at night?"

His thoughts flew to Poppy, to the way they'd laughed and kissed and fooled around for an hour in her bed this morning before he'd finally got his ass into the shower.

"Never say never," he heard himself say.

His mother blinked. She didn't look any less surprised than he felt himself. When had his strict no involvement, no commitment policy gotten so ragged around the edges?

"Well. I guess I'm going to have to settle for that, aren't I?" his mother said. She was looking rather pleased with herself. And why not? He'd pretty much confirmed her guess about Poppy.

She left him to finish making the coffee alone. He set out sugar and milk on a tray, his thoughts circling.

So much for keeping Poppy at arm's length. She'd crept into his life a moment at a time, even though he'd been telling himself to back off, to be careful. And now it was too late. He cared. He didn't want their relationship to have an expiry date. He was hooked, well and truly.

He rolled his eyes.

Hell, might as well admit it, while he was being honest with himself: he was probably even in love. Wait until his mother worked that one out. She'd be skipping and singing.

He waited for the old tension to grip him as he faced his

feelings at last. Loving Marly had been a burden in the end, a weight that he carried with him every minute of every day. He'd been driven by the need to help her, heal her, protect her. And in the end he'd had to let her go. He'd never wanted to go there again.

And yet here he was. Poppy had sneaked under his guard and into his heart while he wasn't looking. He'd thought he was indulging in hot sex and a bit of fun, but all the while he'd been falling for her honesty and earthiness and warmth.

He touched a hand to his chest, but there was no band of tension there, no sense of heaviness in his body. He didn't feel burdened by his feelings for Poppy.

He felt…warm. Grateful. Relieved.

A smile spread across his face.

For the first time in years, he felt hope.

"Damn," he said softly.

He wanted to jump in his car and go find her, but he settled for calling her house. He wasn't about to blurt out his feelings over the phone, but he really needed to hear her voice.

The phone rang and rang before her answering machine picked up. Disappointed, he left another message asking her to call him when she got in.

She didn't. He was half tempted to call her after another hour had passed, but it was late. And there was always tomorrow. His feelings weren't going anywhere, right? They'd still be there when he woke. And so would Poppy, even if he felt a ridiculous, adolescent urge to stand beneath her window and serenade her and make absolutely certain that she was his.

HE TRIED PHONING POPPY again first thing the next morning and got her answering machine once more. He wanted to go straight over to her place, but his parents and Gerome and Fiona had flown all the way from Adelaide to see him. Swallowing his impatience, he took them for breakfast at the café in the nearby Royal Botanic Gardens. His gaze constantly strayed to his cell phone throughout, but still Poppy didn't call. To his great relief, his family decided to check out the galleries and shops after breakfast. Jake walked to his apartment alone, planning to try Poppy one last time before heading over to her place.

He spotted her car in front of his apartment block when he turned the corner. A smile curved his mouth. It had never occurred to him before, but he was always smiling when she was around. She was sunshine in human form—strong and proud and beautiful, and he couldn't believe it had taken him so long to see what was right under his nose.

She got out of her car as he approached. By the time he'd reached her side, she'd removed a bag from the trunk.

"Hey," he said. "I was worried about you."

He leaned in to kiss her, but she turned her cheek so that his lips landed on the side of her jaw. He pulled back to look at her. She met his eyes, her expression utterly impassive.

Something was wrong.

"I came over to return the things you left at my place," she said. "Some underwear and a book or two."

She offered him the bag. He looked at it but didn't take it.

"What's going on?"

"I don't want to do this anymore. Sleep with you, I mean."

He felt as though she'd sucker punched him. For a long moment he just stared at her.

"Where is this coming from?" he finally asked. His voice sounded rough, as though he'd forgotten how to use it all of a sudden. "I thought we were having a good time together."

Her gaze slid over his shoulder. "It was always a casual thing, right? I figure it's run its course."

He shook his head. "No. Something happened." He reached for her arm. "Let's go upstairs, grab some coffee, talk properly."

She shrugged away from him. "There's nothing much to say, is there? We were always only about the sex. Once that got old, this was pretty much inevitable. I'm calling it before it gets messy."

She was so damned matter-of-fact. Utterly unmoved, unemotional.

"I wasn't aware that the sex *had* gotten old," he said. He'd meant to provoke her into something, some sign that she felt something as she stood there, kissing goodbye to the most intense four weeks of his life.

She simply lifted a shoulder. "I wanted to tell you to your face."

She offered the bag again. When he still didn't take it, she placed it by his feet.

"It's been a lot of fun. I hope we can still be friends," she said.

Then she offered him her hand. He stared at it. A handshake. She wanted to shake his hand after all the things they'd done together. After he'd made her sob with pleasure. After he'd kissed and caressed and tasted her all over. After he'd fallen in love with her.

"This is bullshit, Poppy. Tell me what's really going on."

"I'm being smart." She turned toward her car.

"Hang on. You can't just drop your little bombshell and drive off."

She kept walking. "You made the rules, Jake." She sounded resigned and sad.

"Poppy."

"I'll see you tomorrow at work."

She got into her car. He swore and reached for the passenger side door, but it was locked. She pulled out into the street. He started after her, then realized what he was doing. He couldn't chase her car down. And even if he could, it wasn't going to get him anywhere. Poppy had made up her mind. She'd cut him loose.

"Shit."

He stood staring after her, his body tight with frustration. There had been no sign that this was coming, not a hint. Yesterday morning, she'd clawed at his back as he made love to her. She'd laughed with him and promised to call the moment she was back from Ballarat. She'd teased him about the Scorsese double feature.

"Shit."

He walked to the sidewalk and picked up his belongings, staring at his neatly folded boxer-briefs and T-shirts in the bottom of the bag. She'd even cleaned him out of her apartment.

By the time he'd climbed the stairs to his apartment his temper was firing on all cylinders. He kept remembering the distance in her voice, the way she'd offered him her hand as if she was some goddamned business associate or something.

"Bullshit, Poppy. This is bullshit," he said as he threw the shopping bag onto the couch.

She'd said that they'd always been only about the sex, but that wasn't true—that hadn't been true from the first time they slept with each other. They were friends. At the very damned least they were friends, and friends owed each other a little more explanation than a handshake and a casual "so long and thanks for all the orgasms."

He was pretty sure that if he didn't feel like hitting something, he'd almost be able to laugh at the irony of the situation. For over a month she'd been his and he hadn't appreciated her, hadn't understood exactly how freaking lucky he'd gotten when those baggage handlers had gone on strike and he'd been trapped in a car with her. And now he knew, and it was over. She was walking away.

Images flashed across his mind: Poppy smiling at him sleepily when she opened her eyes first thing in the morning; Poppy giving herself a shampoo Mohawk in the shower and insisting that he have one, too; Poppy standing in his kitchen, folding pizza boxes for recycling and reprimanding him for his crappy eating habits.

For five years he'd been sandbagged inside his own life, too exhausted, too goddamned weary and wary to risk feeling anything for anyone. Then he'd met Poppy, and she'd burned her way into his heart with her warmth and her spirit.

He stood.

"No way is this over. No freaking way."

He grabbed his car keys and headed for the door.

POPPY MADE IT AROUND the corner from Jake's apartment before she had to pull over. The ache in her chest was so painful she rubbed the heel of her hand over her sternum, over and over. Tears slid down her face.

She'd done it. And she'd done it without crying or breaking down and asking him if he loved her or felt anything for her beyond desire. A small victory, but an important one.

She stared out the windshield of her car. Who was she kidding? There was no upside to this situation. She'd fallen in love with a man who wasn't interested in anything other than sex. She'd done it with her eyes wide-open, telling herself every step of the way that she could handle it, that she was in control.

Hah.

She was so tired. She'd had a terrible night tossing and turning then finally pacing as she came to the inevitable, painful conclusion that she needed to end things with Jake.

She kept thinking of the previous day, the moment when she'd understood that he'd celebrated his birthday without her. She'd let him into her heart and her life, confided her fears, cried out her grief, shared her secrets. And he hadn't even been able to let her know it was his *birthday,* or that his family were in town to celebrate it. That was how little she meant to him. How compartmentalized she was in his life—Poppy Birmingham, slotted neatly away in the pigeonhole marked "sex, when you like it, how you like it, no strings attached."

Well, not anymore.

Poppy took a deep, shuddering breath and started the car again. She knew that on one level it was unfair of her to be angry with Jake. He hadn't promised her anything, after all. Not a single word regarding the future, his feelings, their relationship had ever passed his lips. In fact, he'd warned her that he was a poor prospect, that he didn't want to settle down or commit. Yet their relationship had quickly gone beyond the bounds of what anyone would define as casual. It had become intense and all-consuming and both of them had been a party to that. Except she was pretty sure she'd have to hold a gun to Jake's head before he admitted as much. God forbid he ever trust someone enough to talk about his feelings. God forbid he ever let his guard down for one second.

She made an impatient noise as she signaled and turned onto her street. She was hurt, and she was angry with him for being so damn stubborn and obtuse and disinterested that he'd let that happen, but she also knew that Jake couldn't help being the way he was. He was damaged. Someone—his ex-wife, probably, but how would Poppy know since he hadn't seen fit to confide in her?—had hurt him and he was determined not to let the same thing happen again. It was a pity she hadn't understood all of that before she'd lost her heart to him.

She thought she was going home until she found herself turning into the parking lot at the pool. She smiled a little grimly as she grabbed her swim bag from the backseat. It wasn't as though she had anywhere else to go to seek comfort. Uncle Charlie was gone, and her parents had never been her confidantes.

She changed into her swimsuit with brisk economy. The fast lane was empty when she made her way to the outdoor pool. She performed a racing start even though she hadn't taken the time to warm up, exploding out of the block with everything she had. The water rose up to meet her and she closed her eyes for a second as she felt its familiar, all-encompassing embrace. She started to swim, powering up the pool with a length-eating freestyle stroke. The end of the lane arrived quickly and she did a tumble turn, surging away from the wall. Her shoulders were tense, her stroke choppy. If Uncle Charlie or her coach were watching, they'd tell her she needed to pace herself, that she'd burn out well before the race was done.

She didn't care. She wanted to not feel and not hurt and the only way she knew how was to push herself to the limit. She swam faster and faster, her muscles screaming, her lungs on fire. And then somehow she was swimming and crying at the same time and she was swallowing water and choking. She stopped midstroke, reaching blindly for the line-marker. The plastic dug into her armpits as she threw her arms over it and tried to breathe.

It hurt. It physically hurt to love Jake Stevens and know he didn't love her back.

For the first time in her life, the pool failed to offer the sanctuary she craved. Go figure. Just when she needed it the most, the comfort of the familiar deserted her.

Her arms and legs heavy, she swam slowly to the end of the pool. It wasn't until she'd pulled herself up the ladder that she saw Jake waiting for her where she'd left her towel on the bleachers. She stiffened, wondering how much he'd seen. Her thrashing up and down the pool? Her crying and holding the lane marker?

She squared her shoulders. It didn't matter. She felt the way she felt. There wasn't anything she could do about it, and it suddenly seemed supremely foolish to pretend she didn't care. Besides, telling Jake she loved him was probably the one surefire way to get him to keep his distance.

Face set, she walked toward him.

SHE'D BEEN CRYING. Jake fought the urge to haul Poppy into his arms and instead offered her her towel.

"Can we talk?" he asked as she patted her face dry.

"Why?"

"Because I want to know what happened. Why one minute we were okay, and then the next you were gone."

"There is no *we*. There never has been." She pushed past him and walked toward the change rooms.

"That's bullshit, Poppy. We've practically lived in each other's pockets for the past month. What the hell was that about?"

"Sex, apparently."

He grabbed her elbow before she could disappear inside the women's change room.

"You can't bail on me like this. At the very least I deserve an explanation," he said, fear and confusion getting the better of him. She was so adamant, so damned determined.

What on earth had happened?

She stiffened then jerked her arm away from him. "Why should I tell you anything about how I'm feeling or what I'm thinking? Why should I bare my freaking soul to you when you can't even bother to let me know it's your *birthday?*"

He stared at her, the pieces falling into place. Damn. It hadn't even occurred to him.

He almost laughed with relief as he understood why she was upset. This he could fix. Definitely.

"My family surprised me, Poppy. They turned up on my doorstep Saturday afternoon. I had no idea they were coming over from Adelaide. I swear, if I'd known, you would have been there," he said.

He reached for her, needing to touch her, but she took a step away from him.

"So you had no idea it was your birthday? Is that what you're telling me?"

He frowned. "It wasn't exactly a red-letter celebration, Poppy. I'm thirty-six. It's no big deal."

"You don't get it, do you? You know everything about me. You've met my sister and my parents, you know about Uncle Charlie. You know how hard it's been for me to adjust to working at the paper. You know I'm messy and that before I met you I had no idea about sex. I've cried on your goddamned shoulder, Jake. And you can't even tell me it's your birthday."

"Poppy…"

"No. No more. I'm sick of being on the outside of your life. I'm sick of being someone you sleep with but don't share with. I deserve more."

"You're not on the outside of my life. Not by a long shot. There's no one else but you, Poppy."

"If that's true, then what happened the night you sent me home, Jake? What made you so upset that you couldn't stand being near me?"

He stared at her. His past with Marly had nothing to do with this. Poppy was a clean slate, a fresh start. He didn't want any of the past clinging to his future.

"It was nothing to do with you, I swear it," he said.

"See? You don't trust me. You can't even tell me that you've started writing your next book. You think I don't notice when you shut me out, Jake? You think it doesn't mean anything?" Her face crumpled for a moment. She pressed her fingers against her closed eyes, took a deep breath as she tried to regain control.

He couldn't stand seeing her like this. He pulled her into his arms. Her body felt cold against his chest.

"Poppy. Please," he said. He wasn't sure what he was asking for.

She rested her forehead against his chest for a few seconds, then she pushed away from him, shaking her head.

"No. I can't live like this. I can't give you all of me and accept a part of you. I can't love you and take the crumbs from your table."

He stilled. Poppy loved him? He closed his eyes. Of course Poppy loved him. He was the biggest freaking idiot under the sun.

When he opened his eyes again, she was about to disappear into the change rooms.

"Wait!"

"There's nothing more to say, Jake," she said sadly.

She turned the corner. He lunged after her, only to pull up short when a middle-aged woman and her grandchildren emerged from the change rooms. The woman gave him an outraged look.

"This is women only!" she said.

"Sorry," Jake said, grinding his teeth with impatience.

He needed to go after Poppy, to explain to her that he loved her, too. He needed to convince her that he did trust her, that the only reason he hadn't told her about Marly and the baby and all that mess was because it didn't matter. It wasn't a part of his life anymore. As for his writing… Surely once he'd explained that it wasn't a book he was working on, that he didn't really know what it was himself, she'd understand why he hadn't mentioned it, why he'd kept it so close to his chest?

Jake closed his eyes as he realized what he was doing: making excuses, coming up with ways to convince her to give him another chance on his terms.

She was right. He'd shut her out.

He'd been so busy fooling himself he wasn't falling in love with her. He'd given ground by slow degrees—first admitting he found her desirable, then giving in to the need to spend more time with her, get to know her. And all the while he'd been quarantining the parts of himself that held his saddest, ugliest truths.

He remembered something his mother said last night: *the look in your eyes, the way you carry yourself—it's as though you're always braced, ready to defend yourself in case someone gets too close.*

Loving Marly had just about finished him. She'd needed so much from him, been so vulnerable. By the time it was over, he'd been empty. Exhausted. Loving someone who was in so much pain and being unable to help her had been the hardest, saddest thing he'd ever done. He'd been determined to never, ever put himself in a position of caring that much again. Of being that vulnerable.

But Poppy was not Marly. She was her own person. Strong, determined, disciplined. Funny, wise, honest. He loved her. Irrevocably. Even though he'd resisted his feelings every step of the way.

And he'd hurt her, time after time.

He ran his hand over his face, thinking of all the times he'd kept her at arm's length. She was right—she deserved more. She deserved everything he had to give.

He started walking.

Suddenly he knew exactly what he needed to do to make things right.

IT WAS NEARLY DARK by the time Poppy returned to her apartment. She'd been reluctant to go home after her swim, afraid that Jake would be there waiting for her, so she'd driven into the city and drifted through the shops. She didn't want to face him again, not today. It would be bad enough tomorrow and for all the days after tomorrow when she'd have to work with him and try not to blubber every time she saw him.

Her steps slowed when she approached her front door. Jake was sitting there, his head leaning against the door. His eyes opened when he heard her and he stood.

"I wanted to give you this," he said.

For the first time she saw that he had a sheaf of papers in his hand.

"This is what I've been working on," he said. "It's not a new book, it's something else. A record, maybe. Of my marriage. Of what went wrong."

She stared at him.

"Will you read it?" he asked.

"If that's what you want."

"It is." He frowned, looked away for a moment. "It's pretty sad and small, but it's what happened. It's part of me. And I want you to know." His voice was thick with emotion.

"Jake—"

"There's more, but it can wait," he said. "I know I've hurt you, Poppy. I'm more sorry than you'll ever know. But I want to try and make it up to you."

He handed her the papers then turned away. Poppy opened

her mouth to call him back, but then she glanced down at the top page of his story.

> He wasn't sure when it ended. It wasn't as though a light switched on or off inside him, or he woke one day and the world had changed. It just…happened. She was still his wife. He still loved her. But it hurt him to look at her sometimes. So much pain. Leaking out of her, all the time. And he'd run out of fingers to plug the holes….

When she looked up again, Jake was gone. She stood frozen for a moment, half-afraid of what she held in her hands. Then she unlocked her front door and entered her apartment. She shed her coat and sat at the dining room table, Jake's story in front of her. She smoothed her hands over the crisp white pages with their neat lines of print.

A record, he'd called it. He wanted her to know.

It felt like a huge step forward. It felt like everything.

Lowering her head, she started to read.

It took her nearly three hours to reach the final page. She felt drained. She pushed the manuscript away from herself and used the sleeve of her sweatshirt to wipe the tears from her face.

As Jake had said, it was small and sad, the kind of everyday tragedy that happened to many, many people. The loss of a much-anticipated baby. Marly's subsequent depression. Jake's guilt for being on a book tour when it happened. The counseling. The terrible day when he came home from work to find Marly unconscious in the bathroom, an empty bottle of sleeping tablets beside her. Her first words on waking: *I hate you.* Jake's pain and rage and guilt and love and hate.

It was all there, captured as only Jake could capture it—

honestly, vividly, emotionally. It made her want to howl for him. And it helped her understand.

Why he'd locked himself away. Why he'd denied what was happening between them. And how much it must have cost him to hand over his intensely personal, revealing story to her.

She reached for a tissue and blew her nose. Then she grabbed her car keys and headed for the door. Her feet were a blur on the stairs and she broke into a run as she exited her building. She needed to see him, right now. She needed to tell him—

"Poppy."

She stopped in her tracks. Jake was leaning against her car, his arms crossed over his chest. He straightened, arms dropping to his sides. She frowned, then she understood: he'd waited for her. He'd hand-delivered his story and waited out front of her apartment in the dark for three hours while she read it.

She walked toward him. He met her halfway.

"I'm sorry," she said.

He shook his head. "You don't need to apologize to me."

"I'm not. I'm just sorry." She reached out and cupped his face. "I know it must have been incredibly hard for you to let me read this."

"I trust you, Poppy. I never didn't trust you. I think it was myself I didn't trust."

"It doesn't matter."

"It does. I pushed you away so many times. You're the best thing that has ever happened to me and I almost lost you."

"It doesn't matter."

To prove it to him, she pressed a kiss to his mouth. She broke the kiss and rested her cheek against his, her hand still cupping the side of his jaw.

"I love you, Jake."

His hand came up to hold her face and they stood cheek to cheek, holding one another close for long moments.

"I love you, too, Poppy. More than I can say."

She closed her eyes. It was nice to hear the words at last, but she didn't need them. Not now.

Jake's hand slid from her cheek, and he wrapped both arms around her and held her so tightly it almost hurt. He pressed his face into her neck and she could hear him breathing, struggling for control.

"Thank you," he said, his voice muffled. "Thank you for giving me another chance."

He was crying. She held him tightly, fiercely. She'd wanted to share his pain, and here it was. She closed her eyes, pulled him closer.

"I'm not going anywhere," she said quietly. "I love you and I'm not going anywhere and no matter what happens we'll always work it out."

He pulled back so he could look into her face. Her heart squeezed in her chest as she looked into his eyes. There was so much raw vulnerability there, and so much determination. And, finally, at last, so much love.

"Poppy Birmingham, you are the most amazing person I've ever met. Freaking courageous. So bloody determined you put me to shame. Sexy as all get out." He shook his head, made a frustrated noise. "There are no words. I adore you. I don't know what I did to deserve you, but I've got you and I'm not letting you go."

"No words, my ass."

He smiled. Then he looked into her eyes and the smile slowly faded.

"Forgive me for being the stupidest man on the planet?"

"Careful. You're talking about the man I love."

"Poppy."

She kissed him. "We both made mistakes. Ever heard the saying it takes two to tango?"

"You're always letting me off the hook."

"I know. Kind of makes you wonder what's in it for me, doesn't it?"

As she'd hoped, he laughed. Then he slid his hand into hers and began to lead her up the path toward her apartment.

"Where are we going?" she asked, even though she knew. It had been a whole twenty-four hours since they'd been naked, after all.

"I'm going to show you what's in it for you. It may take a while. How does fifty or sixty years sound?"

He glanced at her over his shoulder. Warmth unfolded in her chest at the look in his eyes.

"Wow. That's a lot of showing. You sure you're up to it?"

"The question is, are you?"

She was grinning. She couldn't help herself. Jake loved her. He'd let her in, finally.

He smiled back at her and used their joined hands to tug her close.

"Answer the question, Birmingham," he said, his mouth just inches from her own.

"Yes," she said. "Yes. Yes to the moon. Yes to infinity. Yes."

He smiled into her face.

"Correct answer."

THE ULTIMATE RISK

BY
CHANTELLE SHAW

Chantelle Shaw lives on the Kent coast, five minutes from the sea, and does much of her thinking about the characters in her books while walking on the beach. She's been an avid reader from an early age. Her schoolfriends used to hide their books when she visited—but Chantelle would retreat into her own world, and still writes stories in her head all the time. Chantelle has been blissfully married to her own tall, dark and very patient hero for over twenty years, and has six children. She began to read Mills & Boon® novels as a teenager, and throughout the years of being a stay-at-home mum to her brood found romantic fiction helped her to stay sane! She enjoys reading and writing about strong-willed, feisty women, and even stronger-willed sexy heroes. Chantelle is at her happiest when writing. She is particularly inspired while cooking dinner, which unfortunately results in a lot of culinary disasters! She also loves gardening, walking, and eating chocolate (followed by more walking!).

CHAPTER ONE

Did every woman remember her first lover? Gina wondered.

Surely she was not the only woman to have felt her heart slam against her ribs when she had glanced across a crowded room and caught sight of the man she had once been madly in love with?

It was definitely Lanzo. Their brief affair had taken place ten years ago, but he was regarded as one of Europe's most sought-after bachelors. Photographs of him regularly featured in celebrity gossip magazines and he was instantly recognisable. She couldn't help staring at him, conscious of that same swooping sensation in the pit of her stomach that she had felt when she had been eighteen and utterly in awe of him.

Perhaps he felt her scrutiny? Her breath caught in her throat when he turned his head in her direction. For a few seconds their eyes met and held, before Gina quickly looked away and pretended to idly scan the other guests at the party.

The tranquillity of Poole Harbour, on England's south coast, had been shattered over the weekend by the staging of the international offshore powerboat racing championships. Generally regarded as the most extreme and dangerous of all watersports, powerboat racing had been going on all day far out in the bay. But this evening the engines were silent, and dozens of sleek, futuristic-looking powerboats were moored in the harbour, bobbing gently on the swell.

It was certainly a sport that attracted the beautiful people, Gina noted, as she glanced around the restaurant where the after-race party was being held. Glamorous promotional models—uniformly tanned, blonde, and sporting unnaturally large breasts and very short skirts—flocked around bronzed, over-loud male boat crews, the drivers and throttle-men, who between them sent their boats skimming over the waves at death-defying speeds.

She had never understood why anyone would choose to risk their life for fun, and she had taken no interest in the racing. The party was definitely not her scene, and she had only come because her old schoolfriend Alex had recently taken over as manager of the exclusive Di Cosimo restaurant, and had requested her moral support on his first big event.

Instead, it was she who was in need of support, Gina reflected ruefully. Her legs felt like jelly and her head was spinning—but she could not blame either on the one glass of champagne she had drunk.

She was so shocked to see Lanzo again. She hadn't realised he was still involved in powerboat racing, and it had not crossed her mind that he might attend the party. True, he owned the restaurant, but it was one of many around the world belonging to the Di Cosimo chain, and she had not expected Lanzo to be in Poole. She was unprepared for her reaction to him, for the way her stomach muscles clenched and the tiny hairs on her arms prickled when she studied his achingly familiar profile.

With his striking looks—olive-gold skin, classically sculpted features, and silky jet-black hair that showed no signs of grey, even though he must be in his mid-thirties by now—Lanzo di Cosimo looked like one of those impossibly handsome male models who featured in fashion magazines. Tall and powerfully built, his tailored black trousers emphasised his height, and his white shirt was of such fine silk that the hard ridges of his abdominal muscles and the shadow of his dark chest hairs were visible beneath the material.

But it was more than just looks, Gina thought, as she stared down at her empty glass and dragged oxygen into her lungs. Lanzo possessed a simmering sensual magnetism that demanded attention. Supremely self-assured and devastatingly sexy, he was impossible to ignore, and the women who thronged around him made no attempt to hide their fascination with him.

He was a billionaire playboy whose passion for dangerous sports matched his passion for leggy blondes—none of whom remained in his life for long before he exchanged them for another model. Ten years ago, Gina had never really understood what he had seen in her—an averagely attractive brunette. But at eighteen she had been too overwhelmed by his interest to question it, and only later had realised that her attraction had probably been her embarrassingly puppy-like eagerness. Lanzo had not had to try very hard to persuade her into his bed, she acknowledged ruefully. For him she had been a convenient bedmate that summer he had spent in Poole, and no doubt he hadn't meant to break her heart—she only had herself to blame for that.

But time and maturity had healed the wounds of first love, she reminded herself. She was no longer the rather naïve girl with a massive crush on him she had been a decade ago. Resisting the urge to glance over at Lanzo again, she turned her back on him and strolled over to the huge wall of windows that ran the length of the restaurant and offered wonderful views over the harbour.

* * *

Lanzo shifted his position slightly so that he could continue to watch the woman in the blue dress who had caught his attention. He recognised her, but to his frustration could not place her. Now that she had her back to him he saw that her gleaming brown hair fell almost to her waist, and he imagined threading his fingers through the silky mass. Perhaps he had noticed her because she was so different from the blonde groupies who always attended the after-race parties, he mused, feeling a flicker of irritation when the young woman at his side, sensing that he was distracted, moved closer and deliberately pressed her nubile body up against him.

The girl *was* young, he thought with a frown as he glanced at her face, which would be far prettier without the thick layer of make-up. In her thigh-high skirt and ridiculous heels she reminded him of a baby giraffe—all gangly legs and long eyelashes. He doubted she was much over eighteen, but the invitation in her eyes told him he could bed her if he chose to. Once he would have been tempted, he acknowledged. But he was no longer a testosterone-fuelled twenty-year-old; his tastes had become more selective over the years, and he had no interest in girls barely out of high school.

'Congratulations on winning the race,' the blonde said breathlessly. 'I think powerboat racing is so exciting. How fast do you go?'

Lanzo stifled his impatience. 'The boat can reach a top speed of one hundred miles an hour.'

'Wow!' She smiled at him guilelessly. 'I'd love to go for a ride some time.'

He winced at the idea of giving 'rides' in his pride and joy. *The Falcon* was a million pounds' worth of superlative marine engineering. 'Racing boats are not ideal for sightseeing trips because they are built for speed rather than passenger comfort,' he explained. 'You would have more fun on a cruiser. I'll speak to a friend of mine and see if he'll take you on a trip along the coast,' he murmured, as he gently but firmly prised the girl's hand from his arm and moved away from her.

Gina watched the setting sun cast golden rays across the sea and gild the tops of the trees over on Brownsea Island. It was good to be home, she mused. She had spent most of the last ten years living and working in London, and she had forgotten how peaceful it was here on the coast.

But thinking about home, and more specifically her new, ultra-modern flat with its sea views, a little way along the quay, filled her with anxiety rather than pleasure. Since she had lost her job with a local company she had been unable to keep up with the mortgage repayments. The situation was horribly similar to the time when she had struggled to pay the mortgage and bills on the house she and Simon had owned in London, after he had lost his job and she had become the only wage earner.

After she had left him the house had been sold, but because it had been in negative equity she had come away with nothing. She had no savings—hence the reason why she had taken out such a large mortgage to buy the flat. But now it looked increasingly as though her only option was to sell her new home before the bank repossessed it.

Her life wasn't turning out the way she had planned it, she thought dismally. She had always assumed that a few years spent building her career would be followed by marriage and two children—a boy and a girl called Matthew and Charlotte. Well, she'd had the career, and she'd had the marriage, but she had learned that babies didn't arrive to order, however much you wanted them, and that marriages didn't always last, however hard you tried to make them work.

Her hand strayed unconsciously to the long, thin scar that ran down her cheek close to her ear, and continued down her neck, and she gave a little shiver. She had never expected that at twenty-eight she would be divorced, unemployed and seemingly infertile—the last evoked a familiar hollow ache inside her. Her grand life-plan had fallen apart, and now the prospect of losing the flat that she had bought when she had moved back to Poole, in the hope of starting a new life away from the bitter memories of her failed marriage, was the final straw.

Lost in her thoughts, she jumped when a voice sounded close to her ear.

'How do you think it's going?' Alex asked tensely. 'Do you think there's enough choice of canapés? I asked the chef to prepare twelve different types, including three vegetarian options.'

'It's a great party,' Gina assured him, pushing her concerns to the back of her mind and smiling at Alex. 'Stop looking so worried. You're too young for grey hairs.'

Alex gave a rueful laugh. 'I reckon I've gained a few since I took over as manager here. Lanzo di Cosimo demands the highest standards at all his restaurants, and it's important that I impress him tonight.'

'Well, I think you've done a brilliant job. Everything is great and the guests seem perfectly happy.' Gina paused, and then said in a carefully casual tone, 'I didn't realise that the head of Di Cosimo Holdings would be here.'

'Oh, yeah. Lanzo visits Poole two or three times a year. If you had come home more often instead of living it up in London, you would probably have seen him around,' Alex teased. 'He comes mainly for the powerboat racing, and a year or so ago he bought a fabulous house on Sandbanks.' He grinned. 'It's amazing to think that a little strip of sand in Dorset is one of the most expensive places in the world to live.' He suddenly stiffened. 'Speaking of the devil—here he comes now,' he muttered below his breath.

Glancing over Alex's shoulder, Gina felt her stomach lurch when she saw Lanzo striding in their direction. It didn't matter how firmly she reminded herself that she was a mature adult now, and well and truly over him. Her heart was pounding and she felt as awkward and self-conscious as she had been when she'd had a summer job as a waitress in this very restaurant ten years ago.

His eyes were hypnotic—perhaps because their colour was so unexpected, she thought shakily, her gaze drawn against her will to his face. With his swarthy complexion and jet-black hair, brown eyes would have seemed more likely, but his irises were a startling vivid green, fringed with thick black lashes and set beneath heavy brows.

Time had done the impossible and improved on perfection, Gina decided. At twenty-five, Lanzo had been a sleek, incredibly handsome man who had still retained a boyish air. A decade later he was rugged, sexy, and utterly gorgeous—his face all angles and planes, his slashing cheekbones and square jaw softened by a mouth that was full-lipped and blatantly sensual.

Something stirred inside her—something that went deeper than sexual attraction. Although her physical reaction to him *was* shockingly intense, she acknowledged, flushing when she saw Lanzo lower his gaze to the outline of her nipples, clearly visible beneath her dress.

A long time ago he had held her in his arms and she had felt certain that he was the only man in the world for her. So many things had happened since then. She had escaped from a violent marriage and knew that she was strong and could look after herself. But for a crazy moment she wished Lanzo would draw her close against his broad chest and make her feel safe and *cherished*, as he had made her feel all those years ago.

But of course Lanzo had never really cherished her, she reminded herself sharply. It had just been an illusion—part of a silly daydream that he would fall in love with her as she had fallen in love with him. And, like most daydreams, it had turned to dust.

'The party is superb, Alex.' Lanzo greeted his restaurant manager, his eyes still focused on the woman at Alex's side. 'The food is excellent—as people expect from a Di Cosimo restaurant, of course.'

Alex visibly relaxed. 'Thank you. I'm glad you approve.' He suddenly realised that he did not have Lanzo's full attention, and gestured to Gina. 'Allow me to introduce a good friend of mine—Ginevra Bailey.'

'Ginevra—an Italian name,' Lanzo observed softly. He was intrigued by her obvious reluctance to shake his hand, and the slight tremble of her fingers when she placed them in his palm. Her skin was soft and pale, in stark contrast to his deep tan, and he had a sudden erotic image of her naked—of milky-white limbs entwined with his darker ones. He lifted her hand to his mouth and grazed his lips across her knuckles, feeling an unexpectedly sharp tug of desire in his gut when her eyes widened and darkened.

Gina snatched her hand from Lanzo's grasp, feeling as though an electrical current had shot along her arm. She swallowed and struggled for composure. 'My grandmother was Italian, and I was given her name,' she murmured coolly, thankful that the years she had spent working for the very demanding chairman of a world-renowned department store chain meant that she was an expert at hiding her private thoughts. Hopefully no one would guess that

Lanzo's close proximity was making her heart race so fast that she felt breathless and churned up inside.

His green eyes glittered and she quickly looked away from him, assuring herself that he could not possibly read her mind. He gave a small frown as he studied her intently. She sensed that he was intrigued by her, but she had no intention of reminding him that they had once, very briefly, been lovers. Ten years was a long time, and undoubtedly countless other women had shared his bed since her. It was far better, and less embarrassing, that he did not recognise her. And, to be fair, it was not his fault that, while she had not forgotten him, he had presumably never given her a second thought after he had casually announced at the end of that summer a decade ago that he was returning to his home in Italy.

Lanzo's eyes narrowed as he studied Ginevra Bailey. Something about her tugged on his mind, but the faint memory was elusive. And as he skimmed his gaze over her hourglass figure, displayed to perfection by a navy blue silk-jersey dress that clung to her curves, he was certain that if they *had* met on a previous occasion he would not have forgotten her.

Her beauty was understated: a perfect oval-shaped face, skin as smooth as porcelain, and deep blue eyes that were almost the exact shade of her dress. Once again something stirred in his subconscious—a distant recollection of eyes as intensely blue as the deep ocean—but the memory remained frustratingly intangible, and perhaps it was nothing. He had known many women, he acknowledged wryly. It was possible that Ginevra Bailey simply reminded him of a past mistress whose identity eluded him.

Beside him, Alex made a slight movement, and Lanzo realised with a jolt that he was staring at the beautiful brunette. He resisted the temptation to reach out and run his fingers through the long chestnut-brown hair that rippled down her back and inhaled sharply, his body taut with sexual anticipation. He had not been so instantly turned on for a long time, and his reaction was all the more surprising because he was usually attracted to tall, willowy blondes. The woman in front of him was a delectable package of voluptuous curves who was having a profound affect on his libido, and Lanzo was in no doubt that he intended to bed her at the first opportunity.

'I hope you are enjoying the party, Ginevra,' he murmured. 'Are you a fan of powerboat racing?'

'No. I've never seen the attraction of dangerous sports,' Gina replied shortly.

She was struggling to disguise her overwhelming awareness of Lanzo, and must have sounded more abrupt than she had intended because Alex interspersed quickly, 'Gina was responsible for the floral displays tonight. The table centrepieces are beautiful, don't you think?'

'Indeed.' Lanzo glanced at the arrangement of red and white roses and trailing variegated ivy on a nearby table. 'You are a florist then…Gina?' He frowned, wondering why the shortened version of her name seemed familiar.

'Not professionally. It's simply a hobby,' she replied. During her marriage to Simon he had encouraged her to take an expensive flower-arranging course, as well as an even more expensive course of lessons in French cuisine, so that she could be the perfect hostess at his business dinner parties. The cookery lessons were not of much use now that she was only preparing meals for herself—often a ready-meal heated up in the microwave, Gina thought ruefully—but she had enjoyed making the floral displays for the party.

'The floristry firm I'd originally booked were forced to pull out because of staff illness,' Alex explained. 'Luckily

Gina offered to step in and decorate the tables.' He paused as he caught sight of one of the waiters frantically signalling to him from across the room. 'There seems to be some sort of crisis in the kitchen,' he muttered. 'Would you excuse me?'

Gina watched Alex thread his way through the throng of guests, feeling a flutter of tension now that she was alone with Lanzo. Of course they were not really alone, she reminded herself impatiently. The restaurant was packed with party guests, but as she slowly turned back to him she felt the strangest sensation that they were in a bubble, distanced somehow from the hum of voices around them.

Surely every woman remembered her first lover? she told herself again. Her response to Lanzo was a natural reaction to seeing a face from the past. But deep down she knew it was more than that. She'd had a couple of relationships before she had married, but no other man—not even Simon in the happier times of their marriage—had evoked this helpless, out-of-control longing; this violent, almost primitive desire that shocked her with its intensity.

Lanzo had been incredibly special to her, she acknowledged. Although their affair had not lasted long, the discovery that a man like him—an international jet-set playboy who could have any woman he wanted—had desired her, had boosted her confidence. Because of him she had changed from a shy teenager into a self-assured woman who had built a successful career and later caught the eye of an equally successful City banker.

But if Lanzo had given her confidence Simon had stripped it from her, she thought ruefully. Thanks to her disastrous marriage she no longer had faith in her judgement of others. She felt stupid that she had not realised what Simon was really like beneath his charming exterior, and right now she was wary of Lanzo's potent masculinity and felt painfully vulnerable.

To her relief a waiter approached and offered to refill her glass. Usually she only had one drink at social events—a throwback to all the times Simon had drunk too much at parties and become embarrassingly loud and unpleasant. But tonight she was grateful for any distraction from Lanzo's overwhelming presence, and when the waiter had gone and she was alone with him once more she took a hurried sip of her champagne and felt the bubbles explode on her tongue.

'So you don't like powerboat racing?' he drawled, in his gravelly, sexy accent. 'Are there any forms of watersports you *do* like?'

'I enjoyed learning to sail in the bay when I was a child. Sailing is rather more peaceful than tearing through the water at a ridiculous speed,' she said pointedly.

'But not as adrenalin-pumping,' Lanzo murmured, his eyes glinting with amusement when she blushed.

Gina had a horrible feeling that he knew her adrenalin levels were sky-high as her instincts sensed the threat he posed to her peace of mind and she prepared to fight him or flee.

'Do you live locally, Gina?' The way he curled his tongue around her name caused needle-darts of pleasure to shiver across her skin.

'Yes, I was born here. Actually, I'm the fourth generation of Baileys to be born in Poole—but the last, I'm afraid, because I don't have any brothers to carry on the family name.' She knew she was babbling but it was preferable to an awkward silence, when Lanzo might hear the loud thudding of her heart. She took a deep breath and prayed that her usual calm nature would reassert itself. 'Are you staying in Poole for long, Signor di Cosimo?'

'Lanzo,' he corrected her. 'Regrettably, this is only a short trip as I have other business commitments, but I hope to return soon.' He studied her flushed face and smiled. 'Perhaps sooner than I had planned,' he drawled.

Gina felt trapped by a powerful force that would not allow her to tear her eyes from Lanzo's face. They were alone in a room full of people, bound together by a powerful chemistry that held them both in its thrall.

Lanzo watched her pupils widen until her eyes were deep, dark pools, and his body tautened as heat surged through his veins. She had intrigued him from the moment he had glanced across the room and discovered her watching him. It happened to him all the time. Women had stared at him since he was a teenager. But never before had he felt such a strong urge to respond to the desire that darkened her eyes to the colour of midnight.

The loud smash of glass shattering on the tiled floor hurtled Gina back to reality, and she looked around to see that one of the waitresses had dropped a tray of glasses. She was shocked to realise how close she was standing to Lanzo and she jerked back from him, her face burning when she caught the hard gleam in his eyes. How long had she been staring at him like an over-awed teenager? she wondered, feeling hot with embarrassment. She had no recollection of either of them moving, but their bodies had been so close that her pelvis had almost brushed against his.

Tearing her gaze from him, she saw that the waitress was trying to gather up the shards of glass with her hands. 'I'll get a broom,' she muttered, and hurried across the restaurant, grateful for the chance to escape Lanzo's intent stare.

He watched her walk away from him, feeling himself harden as he studied the gentle sway of her bottom beneath its covering of tight navy silk.

Oh, Gina! What a transformation time had wrought, he mused, for he had suddenly solved the puzzle of why she seemed familiar. He remembered her now—although she looked very different from the shy waitress who had followed him around with puppy-dog devotion and been so sweetly anxious to please him that summer he had spent in England.

He had not known that her proper name was Ginevra. It suited the sophisticated woman she had become. And really it was not surprising that he had initially failed to recognise her, he assured himself, because this elegant woman, with her toned figure and her mane of glossy chestnut hair, bore scant resemblance to the slightly plump, awkward girl who had delighted him with her unexpectedly passionate nature when she had been his lover for a few weeks one summer, a long time ago.

Was the grown-up Gina still the sensual, uniquely generous lover who had appeared in his dreams for several months after he had returned to Italy? Lanzo brooded. Events in his life had taught him to live for the present and never revisit the past. But he was prepared to make an exception in this instance, he mused, watching her until she disappeared into the kitchens with a determined gleam in his eyes that would have worried her had she seen it.

CHAPTER TWO

IT STILL wasn't completely dark, even though it was almost eleven o'clock, Gina noted when she emerged from the restaurant and glanced up at the indigo sky which was studded with a few faint stars. The water in the harbour was flat and calm, and the salt tang carried on the breeze was a welcome contrast to the stifling atmosphere of the restaurant.

She loved the long days and balmy evenings of June, and she paused for a moment, enjoying the fresh air which was cool but did not require her to slip on her jacket, before she turned and began to stroll along the quay.

'I did not realise that you still lived in Poole.' A tall figure stepped out of the shadows, and Gina's heart skittered when Lanzo fell in step beside her. 'I visit several times a year and I'm surprised I haven't seen you around.'

Gina gave him a startled glance, her heart thudding with the realisation that he had finally recognised her. The expression in his eyes made her pulse quicken. It was the intense, predatory look of a panther stalking its prey, she thought, and then gave herself a mental shake. He was just a man, she reminded herself irritably. But the soft night air carried the spicy drift of his aftershave, and as her senses quivered she ruefully acknowledged that Lanzo would never be 'just' anything.

'Perhaps you did see me on one of your previous visits, but you didn't remember me,' she said tartly, still feeling faintly chagrined that he had not realised her identity back at the restaurant.

'Oh, I remember you, Gina,' he said softly. 'Although I admit I did not immediately recognise you tonight. You've changed a lot since I knew you.'

He wanted to run his fingers through her long silky hair, but he had noticed how she had tensed the moment she had seen him outside the restaurant. The flash of awareness in her deep blue eyes when she had first spotted him had told him that she was as conscious of the fierce sexual chemistry between them as he, but for some reason she seemed determined to ignore it.

'Your hair especially is different from the style you wore ten years ago,' he commented.

'Don't remind me,' Gina groaned, utterly mortified by the memory of the curly perm she had believed would make her look older and more sophisticated than the ponytail she'd had since she was six. The perm had been a disaster, which had transformed her hair into an untameable bush with the texture of wire wool, and rather than looking sexy and sophisticated she had resembled a chubby poodle. As if the perm hadn't been bad enough, she had been a few pounds overweight, she remembered grimly. 'I can't imagine why you ever noticed me,' she muttered.

In all honesty he had *not* taken much notice of her when he had first arrived in Poole to oversee the launch of the Di Cosimo restaurant here all those years ago, Lanzo remembered. Gina had simply been one of the staff—a part-time waitress who helped out with the washing up on nights when the restaurant was especially busy.

She had been a shy, mousy girl, with an annoying habit of looking at the floor whenever he spoke to her—until on one occasion he had been so irritated by her studious inspection of the carpet that he had cupped her chin in his hand and tilted her face upwards and had found himself staring into the bluest eyes he had ever seen.

The unremarkable waitress was not so ordinary after all, he had been amazed to discover, as he had studied her flawless peaches-and-cream complexion and her wide, surprisingly kissable mouth. He could not remember their conversation—it had probably been something inconsequential, like asking her to fill the salt-cellars—but after that he had noticed her more often, and had invariably found her watching him. Although she had blushed scarlet and hastily looked away whenever he had met her gaze.

That summer ten years ago had been a dark period in his life, Lanzo reflected grimly. Alfredo had died in the spring, and he had been struggling to come to terms with the loss of the man he had regarded as a second father—the man who would have been his father-in-law had it not been for the devastating fire that had swept through the di Cosimo family home and taken the lives of Lanzo's parents and his fiancée five years before that.

Cristina's face was a distant memory now—like a slightly out of focus photograph—and the pain of her loss no longer felt like a knife being thrust through his heart. But he remembered her; he would always remember the gentle girl he had fallen in love with all those years ago.

Widower Alfredo and Lanzo's parents had been delighted when he had announced that Cristina had agreed to be his wife. But a week before the wedding tragedy had struck.

The familiar feeling of guilt made Lanzo's gut clench, and he stared out across the harbour to where the darkening sky met the sea, lost in black memories. He should not have gone on that business trip to Sweden. Cristina had begged him not to, saying that they needed to talk. But he had been shocked by her revelation that she was pregnant—so unprepared for the prospect of having a child when they had both decided that they would wait at least five years before they started a family.

He had been so young—only twenty—and determined to make his father proud of him as he took on more responsibilities at Di Cosimo Holdings. But that was no excuse, he thought grimly. He'd known Cristina had been hurt by his lack of enthusiasm for the baby. He hadn't wanted to talk about it, and instead had insisted on going on the business trip when he had known full well that he could have sent one of his staff in his place. But he had wanted time alone, to get his head around the idea of being a father, and so he had ignored Cristina's tears and flown to Sweden.

Within twenty-four hours he had realised that he had behaved like an idiot. He loved Cristina, and of course he would love their child. He had been impatient to get home and convince her that he was delighted about the baby, but his meeting had overrun, meaning that he had missed his flight, and he'd had to spend another night away. The following morning he had arrived in Italy and been met by Alfredo, who had broken the devastating news that his parents and Cristina had all died in the fire that had destroyed the di Cosimo villa.

Lanzo's jaw tightened as he remembered the agony of that moment—the feeling that his heart had been ripped from his chest. He had not told Alfredo that Cristina had been a few weeks pregnant. The older man had been utterly distraught at the loss of his only daughter and there had seemed little point in making his grief worse. But the bitter truth was that he could not bear anyone to know how he had failed his fiancée and his unborn child, Lanzo acknowledged. He should never have gone away. Cristina had died believing that he did not want their child, and he had never been able to forgive himself for not being with her when she had needed him most.

Alfredo had never got over losing his daughter, but the older man had become an invaluable father figure and advisor, for with his own father gone Lanzo had become the head of Di Cosimo Holdings at the age of twenty. Five years later Alfredo's death had hit him hard, but he had dealt with it as he had dealt with the loss of Cristina and his parents—by burying his grief deep in his heart.

The opening of a new restaurant in England had given him an excuse to spend some time away from Italy and his memories. He had thrown himself into work, and into offshore powerboat racing, which was a popular sport along the south coast. It had satisfied a need in him to push himself to his limits and beyond. He'd loved the speed, the danger and the adrenalin rush, the idea that death was one flip of the boat away—for deep down he had not really cared what happened to him. Subconsciously he had hoped that one day he would push himself too far and death would take him, as it had Cristina. But for fifteen years he had cheated death and been left alone to bear his grief. Sometimes he wondered if it was his punishment for those first doubts he'd had about being a father.

'I noticed you,' he told Gina abruptly. She had been a calming influence on his crazy mood that summer—a nondescript girl with a gentle smile that had soothed his troubled soul.

For the first two years after Cristina's death he had not looked at another woman, and when he had finally started dating again his relationships had been meaningless sexual encounters. He had closed the door on his emotions and deliberately chosen mistresses who accepted his terms. But Gina had been different. Something about her youthful enthusiasm had reminded him of the carefree days of his own youth—a time that seemed bathed in perpetual sunshine before the black cloak of grief had settled on his shoulders. When he'd been with Gina his mood had lightened, and he had enjoyed spending time with her. It had only been when he had found himself thinking about asking her to return to Italy with him that he had realised there was a danger she was starting to mean something to him—and he had immediately ended their affair. For he associated love with pain, and he never wanted to experience either emotion ever again.

'You were sweet and shy, and you used to stare at me when you thought I didn't notice,' he said gruffly. She had seemed painfully innocent, although she had assured him that she'd had several boyfriends, Lanzo recalled.

Sweet was such an unflattering description. It conjured an image of a silly lovesick teenager—which of course was exactly what she had been ten years ago, Gina thought ruefully. She remembered how her heart had thudded with excitement whenever Lanzo had been around—rather like it was doing now, a little voice in her head taunted. But the difference now was that she was a confident career woman—albeit one without a career at the moment—and she was perfectly in control of her emotions.

'I admit I had an outsize crush on you,' she said lightly. 'But it was hardly surprising when I'd attended an all-girls school and had little contact with the male species—especially the exotic Italian variety.'

'Why didn't you remind me tonight that we knew each other?' Lanzo asked her curiously.

She shrugged. 'Because it was a long time ago, and I barely remembered you.'

His mocking smile told her he knew she was lying, and she was thankful that it was probably too dark now for him to notice her blush. They had reached the attractive block of six flats on the quayside where she lived, and as she slowed her steps he halted in front of her.

'But you did not forget me completely during the past ten years,' he stated arrogantly, his deep, velvety voice sending a little quiver down Gina's spine. 'Are you cold?' he asked, noticing the tremor that ran through her.

'Yes,' she lied again, 'but I live here. Well,' she said briskly, desperate to get away from him before she made a complete idiot of herself, 'it's been nice to meet you again.'

She stepped back from him, but instead of bidding her goodnight he smiled and moved closer, so that they were enclosed in the shadowed porch area in front of the flats.

'You can't have lived here long. These flats were still under construction when I was here last year,' he commented.

'I moved here from London four months ago.'

'That must have been a big change,' Lanzo murmured, glancing over his shoulder at the fishing boats moored in the harbour.

Gina nodded. 'I worked in the City and I'd forgotten how quiet it is here.'

'What job do you do? I assume you have moved on from waiting tables?' he said, his eyes glinting as he allowed them to roam over her navy silk dress and matching stiletto-heeled sandals. It was impossible to equate this elegant woman with the curly-haired young waitress from ten year ago.

'Until recently I was PA to the chairman of the Meyers chain of department stores.'

He looked impressed. 'That's certainly a long way from waitressing. Meyers have outlets in virtually every major city around the world. But surely you don't commute to the City from here every day?'

'No, I decided to leave the company when my boss retired. There were a number of reasons why I wanted to move out of London.' Not least the late-night abusive phone calls from her ex-husband, Gina thought grimly. 'My father suffered a heart attack at Christmas. He's recovered well, thankfully, but I decided to move closer to my family. Dad's illness brought it home to me that you never know what the future holds.'

'Very true,' Lanzo said in a curiously flat tone. Gina gave him a curious glance, but his expression was unfathomable. 'Too often we take the people we care about for granted.'

She nodded. 'I came back to Poole to work as the PA for the head of a construction company. Unfortunately the market for new houses has been hit by the recession, and Hartman Homes went into liquidation last month. I've been looking for a new job, but there's not a lot around. The way things are going I might need to take up waitressing again,' she quipped, trying to quell the familiar flare of panic that thoughts of her precarious finances induced.

'Come and see me at the restaurant in the morning. I may be able to help you,' Lanzo murmured.

She gave him a startled glance. 'I was joking about being a waitress,' she told him, privately thinking that she would consider almost any job in order to keep up with her mortgage repayments.

'I'm serious. I urgently need a personal assistant to fill in for my usual PA while she is on maternity leave. Luisa had planned to work up until her baby was born, but she has high blood pressure and has been advised to give up work early. Her absence is causing me all sorts of problems,'

Lanzo added, sounding distinctly unsympathetic for his secretary.

'High blood pressure can be dangerous for an expectant mother and her unborn child,' Gina told him. 'I'm not surprised your PA has been told to take things easy. She couldn't have travelled with you in the later stages of her pregnancy anyway. Pregnant women shouldn't fly after about thirty-six weeks.'

'Shouldn't they?' Lanzo shrugged. 'I admit I know little about pregnancy—it is not something that interests me.' He had never come to terms with his belief that he had failed his unborn baby, and he had vowed never to have another child. 'But you seem very knowledgeable on the subject.' He frowned as a thought struck him. 'Do you have a child?'

'No,' she said shortly. Since she had moved back to Poole she had met several of her old schoolfriends, pushing prams around the town, and invariably the question of whether she had children had cropped up. The answer always hurt, Gina acknowledged, however much she laughed and made the excuse that she had been too busy with her career, and there was plenty of time for babies.

'Some of my friends and both my stepsisters have children, so obviously I've picked up a few facts about pregnancy. I hope your PA keeps well in the final weeks before her baby is born,' she murmured, feeling a sharp pang of sadness that every woman but her, it seemed, had no problem conceiving a child.

That wasn't true, she reminded herself. Endometriosis was a well-known cause of female infertility, although for years she hadn't realised that her heavy and painful periods were an indication of a medical condition that could affect her chances of having a baby.

Her gynaecologist had explained that there were various

treatments available that might help her conceive, but he had emphasised that to maximise her chances she should try to fall pregnant before she reached her thirties. As a recently divorced twenty-eight-year-old, she had been forced to face the heartbreaking fact that she might never be a mother, Gina acknowledged bleakly.

'Where have you gone?'

Lanzo's voice tugged her from her thoughts and she stared at him helplessly. Seeing him tonight had taken her back in time. Life had been so optimistic and so full of exciting possibilities when she had been eighteen, but the last few years especially had been chequered with disappointments, she thought sadly.

That summer she had spent with Lanzo was a golden memory she had treasured, and even the misery she had felt after he had returned to Italy had served a purpose. Desperate to put him out of her mind, she had decided to move away from Poole, where it had seemed that every street and quaint country pub held memories of the few weeks they had spent together, and instead of accepting a place at nearby Bournemouth University she had taken a secretarial course, moved to London, and forged a highly successful career.

But Lanzo had been right when he had guessed that she had never forgotten him. Oh, she'd got over him—after a while. She had grown up and moved on, and he had faded to the background of her new, busy life. But occasionally she had found herself thinking about him, and curiously it had been Lanzo, not Simon, she had dreamed about on the night before her wedding. Now, unbelievably, he was here, watching her with an intense expression in his mesmeric green eyes that made her heart-rate quicken.

'I...I really must go in,' she said faintly.

His slow smile stole her breath. 'Why?'

'Well…' She searched her blank mind for a good reason. 'It's getting late. I should get to bed…' She cringed. Why had she used *that* word? She had been fighting her memories of his toned, tanned, naked body—of his hands gently pushing her thighs apart so that he could sink between them. She felt the hot throb of desire low in her pelvis and closed her eyes, as if blotting him from her vision would free her from his sorcery.

'Stay and talk to me for a while,' he said softly. 'It's good to see you again, Gina.'

His words were beguiling. Her eyes flew open. It was good to see him too, she acknowledged silently. During the last grim months of her marriage and her subsequent divorce she had felt as though she were trapped in a long dark tunnel. But the unexpectedness of seeing Lanzo again made her feel as though the sun had emerged from behind a storm cloud and was warming her with its golden rays.

Her blue eyes clashed with his glinting gaze. She did not want to talk, she admitted shakily. She was so aware of him that her skin prickled, and her nipples felt as hard as pebbles, straining against the constriction of her bra. Perhaps he really was a magician and could read her mind. Because his eyes had narrowed, and to her shock and undeniable excitement he slowly lowered his head.

'Lanzo…?' Her heart was thudding so hard she was sure he must hear it.

'*Cara,*' he murmured silkily. He had wanted to kiss her all evening. Even though she had carefully avoided him for the rest of the party after she had gone to report the broken glass to the restaurant manager, his eyes had followed her around the room and he had found himself recalling with vivid clarity how soft her mouth had felt beneath his ten years ago. Now the sexual tension between them was so intense that the air seemed to quiver. Desire flared, white-hot, inside him, and his instincts told him that she felt the same burning awareness. Anticipation made his hand a little unsteady as he lifted it to smooth her hair back from her face.

Gina stiffened at Lanzo's touch and instinctively jerked her head back. She had concealed her scar with make-up, but she was mortified to think that he might feel the distinct ridge that ran down her cheek and neck.

'Don't.' The plea left her lips before she could stop it. She flushed when his brows rose quizzically. He had every right to look surprised, she thought miserably. Seconds ago she had been leaning close to him, waiting to feel the first brush of his mouth over hers. But when he had touched her face she had been catapulted from her dream-like state back to reality.

She could not bear to see the desire in his eyes turn to revulsion—as would surely happen if he saw her scar. Even worse would be his curiosity. What if he asked her how she had been injured? Nothing would induce her to make the humiliating admission that her ex-husband was responsible for the unsightly scar that now served as a physical reminder of her gullibility.

It sickened her to think that once she had believed she loved Simon, and that he loved her. Only after their wedding had she realised that she had not known the true nature of the man, who had hidden his unpredictable temper beneath a charming façade. She felt ashamed that she had been taken in by Simon, and had sworn that she would never be so trusting again. What did she really know of Lanzo? her brain questioned. Her heart had leapt in recognition when she had first seen him tonight, and all evening she had been swamped with memories of their affair, but in truth her relationship with him ten years ago had lasted for a matter of weeks and he was virtually a stranger.

Lanzo's eyes narrowed as he watched Gina physically and mentally withdraw from him, and for a few seconds a mixture of anger and frustration flared inside him. She had wanted him to kiss her. He knew he had not imagined the desire that had darkened her eyes to sapphire pools. So why had she pulled back?

The young Gina of his memories had been open and honest, and she had responded to him with an eagerness that he had found curiously touching. It appeared that the more mature, sophisticated Gina had learned to play the games that so many women played, he thought grimly. He had had mistresses in the past who had calculated his wealth and made it clear that their sexual favours came at a price: jewellery, designer clothes, perhaps being set up in a luxury apartment. He presumed that Gina was no different, but he was surprised by the strength of his disappointment.

He stepped back from her and gave her a cool smile. 'I was wondering if you would like to have dinner with me at my house on Sandbanks?'

The address was a sure-fire winner—reputed to be the fourth most expensive place in the world to live. He had never met a woman yet who had not known that properties on that exclusive part of the Dorset coast were mostly worth in excess of ten million pounds. No doubt Gina would be rather more willing to kiss him now that she realised quite how loaded he was, he thought sardonically.

Lanzo had issued his invitation in a perfectly polite tone, but something in his voice made Gina glad that she had not allowed him to kiss her. The warmth had faded from his eyes, and as she met his hard, glinting green gaze a little shiver ran though her. He was a stranger, her brain reiterated, and there was no reason why she should trust him.

She forced her own polite smile. 'That's very kind of you, but I'm afraid I'm busy every day next week—and as you told me you are only in Poole for a short visit I doubt we will be able to fit dinner into our respective schedules.'

Lanzo stared at Gina in astonishment, hardly able to believe that she had turned him down. It had never happened to him before, and for a moment he was lost for words. He was used to the fact that his looks and wealth were a potent combination which guaranteed him female attention wherever he went. He only had to click his fingers to have any woman who caught his eye. Ten years ago he had recognised that Gina had had a crush on him. She had fallen into his bed with little effort on his part, and if he was honest he had confidently assumed that she would do so again.

But it was not only her appearance that had changed, he mused. At eighteen she had been shy at first with him, but when he had got to know her and she had relaxed with him he had been charmed by her love of life and her cheerful, carefree nature. At that black period of his life she had seemed like a breath of fresh air, and a welcome distraction from the grim memories of his past.

What had happened in the ten years since he had last seen Gina that had robbed her of her youthful exuberance? he wondered. The woman standing before him had appeared sophisticated and self-assured at the party, but now that they were alone she was tense and on edge, watching him warily—as if she expected him to do what...? he wondered with a frown. *Dio,* she was afraid of him, he suddenly realised. She had not pulled away from him because she was playing the coquette, but because she did not trust him.

Outrage caused him to stiffen. What in heaven's name had he done to make her think he might harm her in some way? Following swiftly on the heels of that thought came the realisation that something, or *someone*, from her past must have caused her to change from a fun-loving girl to a woman who was desperately trying to disguise the fact that she was nervous of him. He wanted to ask her *who*? *What* had happened to her that made her flinch from him?

He looked at her tense face and acknowledged that she was not likely to confide in him. More surprising was the feeling of protectiveness that swept through him—together with anger that someone had turned her from the trusting, happy girl he had once known to a woman who was wary and mistrustful, with an air of sadness about her that tugged on his insides.

'What a busy life you must lead if you do not have one free night,' he murmured. 'Perhaps we can postpone my invitation to dinner until my next visit to Poole?' he added softly when she blushed. He held out his hand. 'Give me your key.'

'Why?' Gina could not hide the suspicion in her voice. What did he want? Was he hoping she would invite him in for coffee, and then expect the invitation to lead to something more? Panic churned inside her. Since her divorce she had been on a couple of dinner dates, but she had never been alone with a man. Simon had caused untold damage to her self-confidence, she acknowledged heavily. She wanted to move on, have other relationships and maybe even fall in love, but sometimes she despaired that she would ever be able to trust a man again.

'I was merely going to see you safely inside,' Lanzo explained steadily, taking the key that Gina was clutching in her fingers.

He stood staring down at her for a few moments, and her breath caught in her throat when something flared in his eyes. She wondered if he was going to ignore her earlier plea and kiss her after all, and she realised that part of her wished he would pull her into his arms and slant his sensual mouth over hers. She wanted to forget Simon's cruelty and lose herself in Lanzo's potent magnetism. Unconsciously she moistened her lower lip with the tip of her tongue, and heard his swiftly indrawn breath.

'*Buona notte*, Gina,' he said quietly, and then, to her shock, he turned and walked away, striding along the quay without a single glance over his shoulder. His tall, broad-shouldered figure was gradually swallowed up by the darkness, and the ring of his footsteps faded into the night, leaving her feeling strangely bereft.

For a few moments she stared after him, and then stepped into her flat and shut the door, realising as she did so that she had been holding her breath. Why on earth, she asked herself angrily, did she feel an overwhelming urge to burst into tears? Was it the thought that she would probably never see Lanzo again after she had refused his invitation to dinner? He was a billionaire playboy who could have any woman he wanted and he was not likely to bother with her again.

She was too wound up to go to bed, and after flicking through the TV channels and finding nothing that captured her attention she headed for the bathroom and ran a bath. Lanzo's darkly handsome face filled her consciousness, and with a sigh she sank into the fragrant bubbles and allowed her mind to drift back ten years.

She had been so excited to be offered a job as a waitress at the swanky new Italian restaurant on the quay, Gina recalled. She'd just finished her A-levels and been desperate to earn some money to spend on new summer clothes. While she had been at school she had received a small allowance from her father, but the family farm barely made a profit and money had always been tight.

Lanzo had arrived in Poole for the opening night of the

Di Cosimo restaurant and stayed for the summer. Golden-skinned, exotic, and heart-stoppingly sexy, he had been so far removed from the few boys of her own age Gina had dated that she had been blown away by his stunning looks and lazy charm.

He had a reputation as a playboy, and he'd always had a gorgeous woman clinging to his arm. How she had envied those women, Gina remembered ruefully. How she had longed to be beautiful and blonde and thin. But Lanzo had never seemed to notice her—until one day he had spoken to her and she had been so tongue-tied that she had stared at the floor, praying he would not notice her scarlet face.

'Don't slouch,' he had instructed her. 'You should hold your head up and be confident—not scurry around like a little mouse. When you look down no one can see your eyes, which is a pity because you have beautiful eyes,' he had added slowly, and he had tilted her chin and stared down at her.

She had hardly been able to breathe, and when he had smiled she had practically melted at his feet and smiled shyly back at him. And that had been the start, she thought. From that day Lanzo had made a point of saying hello to her, or bidding her goodnight at the end of her shift. When he had learned that she had to race out of the restaurant when it closed so that she could catch the last bus home he had insisted on driving her back to the farm, and those journeys in his sports car had become the highlight of her days.

Lanzo drove at a hair-raising speed, and that first night Gina had gripped her seat as they had hurtled down the narrow country lanes, the hedgerows flashing past in a blur.

'Relax—I'm a good driver,' he had said in an amused voice. 'Tell me about yourself.'

That had certainly made her forget her fear that he would misjudge the next sharp bend and they would crash. What on earth was there to tell? She'd been sure the mundane details of her life would be of no interest to a playboy billionaire, but she had obediently chatted to him about growing up on the farm with her father and stepmother, and her two stepsisters.

'My parents divorced when I was eight, and when Dad married Linda a few years later she brought her daughters, Hazel and Sarah, to live at the farm.'

'What about your mother?' Lanzo asked. 'Why didn't you live with her after the divorce?'

'Dad thought it would be better for me to stay with him. My mother had been having an affair behind my father's back, and one day I came home from school to find a note saying she had left us for one of the labourers Dad had employed on the farm. Mum never stayed in one place for long, or with one man,' Gina admitted. 'I visited her occasionally, but I was happier living with Dad and Linda.'

Witnessing her mother's chaotic lifestyle and her numerous volatile relationships had made Gina realise that she wanted her future to be very different. Marriage, a happy home and children might not be fashionable goals, but she wasn't ashamed to admit that they were more important to her than a high-flying career.

Lanzo drove her home several times a week, and she slowly grew more relaxed with him—although her intense awareness of him never lessened. He was always charming, but sometimes she sensed a dark mood beneath his smile. There was a restless tension about him, and an air of deep sadness that puzzled and disturbed her, but he never spoke of his personal life and she was too shy to pry.

'I find you peaceful company, Gina,' he told her one night when he stopped the car outside the farm gates.

'Is that a polite way of saying I'm boring?' she blurted out, wishing with all her heart that he thought she was gorgeous and sexy. *Peaceful* made her sound like a nun.

'Of course not. I don't find you at all boring,' he assured her quietly. He turned his head towards her, and the brilliant gleam in his green eyes made Gina's heart lurch. 'You are very lovely,' he murmured deeply, before he brushed his mouth over hers in a kiss that was as soft as thistledown and left her yearning for more.

'I checked the rota and saw that it's your day off tomorrow. Would you like to come out with me on my boat?'

Would she?

She barely slept that night, and the next day when she heard Lanzo's car pull up on the drive she dashed out to meet him, her face pink with an excitement that at eighteen she was too young and naïve to try and disguise.

It had been a glorious day, Gina remembered, sliding deeper beneath the bathwater. The sun had shone from a cloudless blue sky as Lanzo had steered the luxurious motor cruiser he had chartered out of the harbour. His dark mood seemed to have disappeared, and he'd been charismatic and mouth-wateringly sexy, his faded jeans sitting low on his hips and his chest bared to reveal an impressive six-pack. Gina had watched him with a hungry yearning in her eyes, and her heart had raced when he had pulled her into his arms and kissed her.

They had cruised along the coast, picnicked in a secluded bay, and later he had made love to her in the cabin below deck. The sound of the waves lapping against the boat and the mewing cry of the gulls had mingled with his low murmurs of pleasure when he had stroked his hands over her trembling, eager body.

There had been one moment when her hesitancy had

made him pause. 'It's not your first time, is it?' he had asked with a frown.

'No,' she'd lied, terrified that he would stop if she admitted the truth.

But he hadn't stopped. He had kissed her with a feverish passion that had thrilled her, and caressed her with gentle, probing fingers until she had been so aroused that when he had finally entered her there had been no discomfort, just a wonderful sense of completeness—as if she had been waiting all her life for this moment and this man.

The bathwater had cooled, and Gina shivered as she sat up abruptly and reached for a towel. She had not only give Lanzo her virginity that day, she had given him her heart—naïvely not realising that for him sex was simply a pleasurable experience that meant nothing to him. Now she was older and wiser, and she understood that desire and love were not inextricably entwined.

She would not be so careless with her heart again, she thought as she stared at her smudged reflection in the steamed-up mirror. In fact, since her marriage to Simon had proved to be such a mistake, she had lost all confidence in her judgement and wondered if she would ever fall in love again.

But she was not an over-awed eighteen-year-old with a head full of unrealistic expectations, she reminded herself. She knew Lanzo had desired her tonight, and she could not deny her fierce attraction to him. She could not allow her experiences with Simon to ruin the rest of her life, and perhaps a passionate fling with a drop-dead sexy playboy was just what she needed to restore her self-confidence after her divorce? she mused.

But much later that night, when sleep still eluded her, she acknowledged that only a fool played with fire and did not expect to get burned.

CHAPTER THREE

THE *Queen of the East* was a sixty-metre-long luxury yacht owned by a wealthy Arab sheikh, and was currently moored in St Peter Port off the island of Guernsey. The yacht was certainly impressive, Lanzo thought as he steered his powerboat alongside, shrugged out of his waterproof jacket and prepared to climb aboard.

'I'm glad you could make it, my friend,' Sheikh Rashid bin Zayad Hussain greeted him. 'Your business call was successful, I hope?'

'Yes, thank you. But I apologise once again for my lateness,' Lanzo murmured, accepting a glass of champagne from a waiter and glancing around at the other guests who were milling about the yacht's breathtakingly opulent salon. 'The refit is superb, Rashid.'

'I admit I am impressed with the quality of workmanship and attention to detail by Nautica World. The company is small, but Richard Melton has certainly delivered. That is him over there.' The Sheikh dipped his head slightly. 'A pleasant fellow—married with two small children, I believe. He has built his company up from nothing, which is no mean feat in these economic times.'

Lanzo followed the Sheikh's gaze and stiffened with shock. He had been unable to dismiss Gina from his mind for the past twenty-four hours, which had made a mockery of his decision not to contact her again. He desired her, but it was more than that. He was intrigued by her, and curious to discover why she was so different from the girl he had once known.

'Is the woman with Melton his wife?' he demanded tersely.

'The beautiful brunette in the white dress?' Sheikh Hussain looked over at the Englishman, whose hand was resting lightly on his female companion's slender waist. 'No. He simply introduced her as a friend when they came on board. I have met Mrs Melton once, and I understand that she is expecting another child.' To the Sheikh's mind there was only one explanation as to the identity of the mystery woman. 'It would seem that Richard Melton's good taste extends to his choice of mistress,' he murmured.

Lanzo's jaw hardened as he stared at Gina and her male companion. Last night he had puzzled over why she had seemed so wary of him, and had felt concerned that she had been hurt by an event or a person in her past. But now, as he noted her designer dress and the exquisite pearl necklace around her throat, he was sure he had imagined the air of mystery about her, and cynically wondered if she rejected him in favour of a married lover.

'So, what do you think of the yacht?'

Gina glanced at her brother-in-law and grimaced. 'It's stunning, but a bit over the top for my liking,' she replied honestly. 'There's a lot of gold. Do you know that even the taps in the bathroom are gold-plated? Well, of course you know—your company was responsible for the refit. I suppose the important thing is that Sheikh Hussain likes it.'

Richard grinned. 'He loves it—which is why he's throwing a party to show it off. Even better, several of his friends here tonight also own yachts and are interested in having them refitted, which is good news for Nautica World.' He paused. 'Thanks for accompanying me tonight, Gina. The party is a fantastic opportunity to drum up new business. Usually Sarah comes with me, but she's finding the last few weeks of this pregnancy exhausting, and I know she was grateful you agreed to take her place.'

'I'm happy to help,' Gina said easily. Her smile faded as she thought of her stepsister. 'Sarah does seem a bit fed up—but I suppose three pregnancies in four years is a lot to cope with.'

'To be perfectly honest, this last baby was a bit of a mistake,' Richard admitted ruefully. 'I only have to look at Sarah and she falls pregnant,' he joked.

Lucky Sarah, Gina thought wistfully. Her stepsister had no idea what it was like to be unable to conceive, to have your hopes dashed every month, and to feel a pang of longing every time you saw a newborn baby.

She knew her family would have been surprised to learn that she and Simon had tried for over a year to have a child. 'Oh, Gina is a career woman,' they'd explained, whenever the question of babies was mentioned by other relatives. She had never spoken about her infertility; she felt enough of a failure as it was, without her family's well meaning sympathy. And so now she smiled at her brother-in-law and bit back the comment that she would give anything to be happily married with two adorable children and a third on the way.

Richard glanced across the salon. 'You see that man over there?' he murmured. 'He's one of Sheikh Hussain's cousins, and he owns a forty-foot motor cruiser. I think I'll go and have a chat with him.'

Gina laughed. 'I hope you can convince him that he needs Nautica World's services.' She was very fond of her brother-in-law. Richard worked hard, and certainly deserved to be successful.

'You look stunning tonight, *cara.*'

The familiar, sexy drawl caused Gina to spin round, and her heart missed a beat when her eyes clashed with Lanzo's glinting green gaze. Once again his appearance had taken her by surprise, and she had no time to disguise her reaction to him, colour flaring in her cheeks as she acknowledged how incredibly handsome he looked in a black dinner jacket and a snowy white shirt that contrasted with his darkly tanned skin.

'If I'm not mistaken, your dress is a couture creation. Business must be booming if your boyfriend can afford to buy you pearls and designer clothes, as well as supporting his children and a pregnant wife,' he drawled.

Gina stared at him, puzzled by his words and the flare of contempt in his eyes. 'I don't have a boyfriend—married or otherwise,' she told him shortly.

'You're saying that you are not Richard Melton's mistress?'

Shock rendered her speechless for twenty seconds. '*No!* I mean, *yes.* That's exactly what I'm saying.' Twin spots of angry colour flared on Gina's cheeks. 'Of course I'm not Richard's *mistress.*' Her fingers strayed unwittingly to the rope of perfect white pearls around her neck. 'Why on earth would you think that?'

Lanzo's eyes narrowed. 'Sheikh Hussain has met Melton's wife. Why else would he parade you on his arm if you are not lovers?'

'He's my brother-in-law,' she explained angrily. 'Richard is married to my stepsister. Sarah is expecting a baby in a few weeks, and she was too tired to attend the party tonight, so I came with Richard instead.'

She thought of all the newspaper stories she had read

over the years about Lanzo's numerous affairs with glamorous mistresses. The Sheikh was no better. Richard had told her he had a wife in Dubai, but he was obviously having an affair with the voluptuous redhead who was hanging on his arm tonight.

She gave a harsh laugh. 'You and your Sheikh friend might be notorious womanisers, but don't judge everyone by your low standards. Richard is devoted to Sarah and the boys, and I would *never*—' She broke off, suddenly aware that her raised voice was drawing attention from other guests. 'I would never have a relationship with a married man. My necklace was left to me by my grandmother, if you must know,' she said coldly, dismayed to feel her heart-rate quicken when Lanzo ran his fingertip lightly over the pearls and then, by accident or design, traced the line of her collarbone.

'The pearls were a wedding present to Nonna Ginevra from my grandfather, and I'll always treasure them.' Her grandparents had been happily married for sixty years before they had died within a few months of each other. Gina regarded the necklace as a symbol of hope that marriages could last, even though hers had ended after two years. She glared at Lanzo. 'Excuse me, I need some fresh air,' she snapped, and spun round to walk away from him.

She had only taken two steps when a voice called her name.

'Gina—just the person I wanted to see. You'll be pleased to know that I've found tenants who want to rent your flat.'

Gina smiled faintly at Geoffrey Robins, who owned an estate agency in Poole. 'That *is* good news,' she agreed.

'They want to move in at the end of the month, if that suits you. And the rent they are prepared to pay will cover your mortgage repayments. Did you say you were going to move back to your father's place until you find another job?' Geoffrey asked her. 'Only I heard on the grapevine that Peter is putting the farm on the market following his heart attack.'

She nodded. 'Yes, Dad *is* selling the farm. But Sarah and Hazel have both said that I can stay with them, and hopefully I'll find a job soon.' Both her stepsisters had growing families and small houses. Moving in with one or other of them was not going to be ideal, but Gina knew that her only hope of keeping her flat was to rent it out for a few months.

'Well, I'll catch up with you next week and let you know a few more details,' Geoffrey said. His eyes lit up when he saw a waiter approach them. 'Ah, I think I'll have another glass of that excellent Burgundy.' He reached out his hand to take a glass of wine, but as he did so the waiter stumbled, the glasses on the tray shot forward, and Gina gave a cry as red wine cascaded down the front of her dress.

'*Scusi! Mi dispiace tanto, signora!*' The horrified waiter apologised profusely in his native Italian. The yacht's crew were of a variety of nationalities, and this waiter was young and very good-looking—another heartbreaker in the making, Gina thought wryly.

'*E'bene. Non si preoccupy.*' It's fine. Don't worry, she assured him calmly.

'Apparently the best way to remove a red wine stain is to cover it in white wine,' Geoffrey advised, handing her a small white handkerchief which was of no use at all.

'I'm quite wet enough, thanks,' Gina said dryly, supremely conscious of the interested glances she was receiving from the other guests.

She *was* annoyed that her dress was probably ruined. Her days of being able to afford expensive clothes, which had been a requirement of her job at Meyers, were over, and she would not be able to replace the dress. But far worse was the knowledge that she was the centre of attention. She frantically scanned the salon for Richard, her heart sinking when she saw that he was still deep in conversation with a potential client.

'Come with me,' a deep, gravelly voice commanded, and before she could think of arguing Lanzo had slipped his hand beneath her elbow and steered her swiftly through the throng of guests out onto the deck.

'I don't believe it,' she muttered as she dabbed ineffectively at the spreading wine stain with the handkerchief. 'Dinner is going to be served in a few minutes. I wonder if the Sheikh has anything I could change into?'

'I doubt it. Rashid probably keeps a selection of skimpy negligees for his mistresses, but you might not feel comfortable wearing one to dinner.'

'You're right. I wouldn't,' Gina muttered, infuriated by the amused gleam in Lanzo's eyes.

'There's only one thing to do. I'll take you home.'

She glanced pointedly at the sea stretching far into the distance. The English coastline was not even visible. 'What a brilliant suggestion,' she said sarcastically. 'The only snag is that I can't swim that far.'

'You don't have to, *cara*. My boat is moored alongside the yacht.'

Frowning, Gina followed Lanzo to the stern of the yacht and stared down at his powerboat. 'I'm not sure...' she said doubtfully.

'Come on.' He was already climbing down the ladder which hung over the side of the yacht, and glanced up at her impatiently. 'Climb down. Don't worry. I'll catch you if you fall.'

Gina hesitated, deeply reluctant to go with Lanzo. Her

heart had leapt the instant she had seen him tonight, and she was irritated that she seemed incapable of controlling her reaction to him. But the red wine had soaked through her dress, and she felt sticky and urgently in need of a shower.

'All right,' she said slowly. 'But you won't go too fast, will you?'

'Of course not,' he assured her smoothly.

It was no easy feat to climb down the ladder in heels and a long skirt, and she gasped when strong hands settled around her waist and Lanzo lowered her into his boat.

'There's not a lot of room.' He stated the obvious as he helped her slide into one of the two front seats, before easing himself behind the wheel. 'Powerboats are designed for speed rather than comfort. Here—slip this around your shoulders,' he told her as he shrugged out of his dinner jacket and handed it to her. 'It might help shield you from the spray.'

His voice was drowned out by the throaty throb of the engine, and as the boat shot forward Gina gripped the edge of her seat and closed her eyes. 'Remember you promised not to go too fast,' she yelled, but her words were whipped away on the wind.

'Didn't you find that exhilarating?' Lanzo demanded, a hair-raising half-hour later, as he cut the throttle and steered the boat alongside a private jetty in Poole Harbour.

Gina unclenched her fingers from the edge of her seat and put a shaky hand up to push the hair out of her eyes. They had sped across the sea so fast that the wind had whipped the clip from her chignon, and now her hair fell in a tangled mass down her back. 'That's not quite how I would describe it,' she said curtly. 'I was terrified.'

'You had no reason to be.' He frowned when he saw how

pale she was. 'I know what I'm doing. You were perfectly safe with me.'

She did not doubt his ability to handle the powerboat, but she did not feel safe with Lanzo even on dry land, Gina admitted to herself. She did not fear that he would hurt her, as Simon had done. Her wariness stemmed from the feelings he evoked in her—the hot, flustered feeling of sexual desire that she had not felt for a very long time.

She looked up at the row of huge houses set back from the jetty and stiffened. 'Why have we come to Sandbanks?' she asked sharply. 'I thought you were going to take me home.'

'I have brought you to my home. My housekeeper will know how to clean that wine stain.' Lanzo had jumped onto the jetty and, ignoring her mutinous expression, swung her into his arms and set her down beside him. 'I want to talk to you.'

'About what?' she demanded suspiciously.

'I have a proposition that I am confident will suit both of us. Come up to the house and we can discuss it,' he ordered, and strode along the jetty, leaving Gina with no option but to trail after him.

Twenty minutes later she emerged from the marble-tiled bathroom Lanzo had shown her to after he had ushered her into his house, feeling considerably cleaner after a shower. She had blasted her hair with a hairdryer and donned a white towelling robe, and now she stepped hesitantly into the main hall, wondering what to do.

'Feeling better?' Lanzo strolled through one of the doors leading off the hall. 'Daphne has prepared us something to eat. Come on through.'

He had discarded his bow tie and unfastened the top few buttons of his shirt to reveal several inches of bronzed skin overlaid with whorls of dark chest hair. Gina's stomach lurched and she took a steadying breath. 'Who is Daphne?'

'My housekeeper, cook and general all-round saint. Daphne travels with me to my various houses around the world, and is the only woman I can't live without,' he told her, his smile revealing his perfect white teeth.

It transpired that Daphne was a tiny, dark-haired woman with a lined brown face and brilliant black eyes. Why on earth did she feel so pleased that Lanzo's housekeeper was not a gorgeous, leggy blonde? Gina asked herself irritably as she followed him into a huge open-plan lounge, with floor-to-ceiling windows that looked out over the sea.

'What an incredible view,' she murmured, distracted from her acute awareness of him for a few moments. 'My flat overlooks the harbour, but the view is nothing as spectacular as this.'

Sliding glass doors opened onto a decked area where a table was laid with a selection of colourful salad dishes and crusty rolls. Of course—they had missed dinner aboard the yacht, Gina remembered, discovering suddenly that she was hungry.

'I didn't know that you speak Italian,' Lanzo commented when they had sat down and he'd indicated that she should help herself to food.

'My grandmother taught me. She moved to England when she married my grandfather, but she missed Italy and loved to speak her own language.'

'Whereabouts in Italy did she come from?'

'Rome.' Gina heaped crispy lettuce leaves onto her plate, and topped them with a slice of round, creamy white mozzarella cheese. 'I've been there several times for work, but never had time to explore the city. One day I plan to go back and look for the house where Nonna used to live.'

'Di Cosimo Holdings' head offices are in Rome.' Lanzo

filled two glasses with wine and handed her one. 'To old friendships and new beginnings,' he murmured, touching his glass to hers.

'Oh…yes…' Gina hesitated fractionally. 'To old friendships.' She wasn't convinced about new beginnings, and to avoid his speculative gaze she took a sip of deliciously cool Chardonnay.

'Come and work for me and I promise I'll give you a guided tour of the city. I know Rome well, and I'm sure I'll be able to find your grandmother's house.'

Her eyes flew to his face. She had been so absorbed in her intense awareness of him last night that she had forgotten his offer for her to work for him as a temporary PA. Now she hurriedly shook her head. 'No—I don't think so.'

'Why are you so quick to dismiss the idea?' Lanzo sat back and studied her broodingly. 'And why do you need to rent out your flat?'

'Were you eavesdropping on my conversation with Geoffrey?' Gina began hotly.

'I was standing close by and couldn't help but overhear.'

She was tempted to tell him to mind his own business, but after a moment she shrugged and put down her fork, her appetite fading as it always did when she remembered her financial worries.

'When I moved back to Poole I took out a big mortgage to buy my flat,' she admitted. 'It wasn't a problem at the time, because I was earning a good salary at Hartman Homes, but since I lost my job I've fallen behind with the repayments.'

'I'm prepared to offer you a six-month contract and pay you a generous salary—higher than you were earning at Meyers.'

Gina's brows lifted. 'That's a rather rash statement when you don't *know* what I earned at Meyers.'

'I have a fair idea. A good PA is like gold-dust, and I expect to pay good money to ensure the best staff.'

'How do you know I'm good at my job?'

He shrugged. 'I checked your references. Did you think I would offer you the vital role of my personal assistant without first making sure you could handle the responsibility?' he queried coolly when she opened her mouth to tell him he had a nerve. 'I am a businessman, *cara*, and I never allow emotions to dictate my decisions.

'I spoke to your previous boss, Frank Wallis, and he assured me that you were the most dedicated and efficient PA he'd ever had—with an almost obsessive attention to detail,' Lanzo added, looking amused. 'Apparently you had a complicated system of colour-coded notes.'

Gina flushed. 'I like to be organised,' she defended herself. Maybe she *was* a bit obsessive, but she wasn't a control freak as Simon had accused her of being. She simply liked things to run like clockwork.

'I have no problem with you being organised,' Lanzo assured her. 'In fact it is a necessity. I work long hours and travel extensively. I will expect you to accompany me on business trips and also to act as my hostess occasionally when I hold social functions.'

He was going way too fast, Gina thought frantically, panic flaring inside her that he seemed to think her agreement was a given. '*If* I accept the job,' she muttered.

'Why wouldn't you?' he demanded.

There were so many reasons, but the main one was her strong attraction to Lanzo—an attraction that she had decided during a sleepless night that she dared not take any further. He had broken her heart once, and she was not prepared to risk her peace of mind by becoming involved with him again.

But it would only be for six months, a voice in her head pointed out. His job offer was a fantastic opportunity for her to sort out her finances and ensure that she kept her flat that she loved. If she went to Italy to work for Lanzo she would not have to impose herself on her stepsisters while she rented the flat out, and the six months' rent paid by the tenants would cover the mortgage repayments. On top of that she would have six months of earning a high salary that she could put away to cover the mortgage when she returned to Poole and looked for another job.

But move to Rome, work closely with Lanzo every day, and travel to business meetings around the world with him? She chewed on her bottom lip, torn between the temptation of solving her financial problems that were growing worse with every day that she failed to find a job in Poole and fear of what she could be letting herself in for if she agreed.

What would she do if he tried to kiss her again, as he had almost done last night? She swallowed as she met his gaze and saw the banked-down flames of desire smouldering in his striking green eyes. A little tremor ran through her at the knowledge that he was attracted to her. Would it be such a disaster if she responded to him? her mind queried.

Her breath hitched in her throat as his eyes strayed down to the slopes of her breasts, visible where the edges of her robe had parted slightly. Time seemed to be suspended, and she was acutely conscious that her white dress, which was now being cleaned by Lanzo's housekeeper, had not required her to wear a bra. Her breasts felt swollen and heavy, and into her mind came the stark image of Lanzo pushing the robe over her shoulders and lowering his head to take one nipple and then its twin in his mouth.

'You would be a fool to turn me down, Gina.' His voice

jerked her back to reality and she tore her gaze from him, hot colour storming into her cheeks as she prayed he had not guessed her shocking thoughts. 'You need this job, and I need to appoint a temporary PA as soon as possible. I have excellent contacts, and when Luisa returns to work after her maternity leave I will recommend you to other company directors who may be looking for staff.'

It was an offer no sensible person could refuse. A golden chance to keep her flat, which was more than just a home but also a place where she felt safe and secure after two years of living on the edge of her nerves with Simon. She had hoped that buying the flat would be the start of a new chapter in her life—a mark of her independence now that she had escaped her violent marriage. She had vowed to take any job she could find to meet the mortgage repayments, she reminded herself. She was twenty-eight, no longer a naïve girl, and she was more than capable of dealing with her inconvenient attraction to Lanzo.

'All right,' she said quickly, before she could change her mind. 'I accept your offer.'

Lanzo was careful to hide the feeling of satisfaction that surged through him. He had realised when he had seen Gina on the yacht earlier tonight that his desire for her was too strong for him to be able to dismiss it. He wanted her, and his instincts told him that she was not as immune to him as she would like him to think. But he sensed her wariness, although he did not understand the reason for it, and knew that he would have to be patient and win her trust before he could persuade her into his bed.

'Good,' he said briskly. 'I'll pick you up from your flat at nine tomorrow morning, and my private jet will collect us from Bournemouth airport and take us to Rome. Luisa will come into the office for a couple of hours to run through everything with you.'

Gina gave him a startled look, doubts already forming thick and fast in her head. 'I'll need a few days to get myself organised. For a start I'll have to find somewhere to stay in Rome.'

'You can stay at my apartment. It will be ideal,' he insisted when she opened her mouth to object. 'I often work late in the evenings, and it will be useful to have you on hand. I hope you weren't thinking that this was going to be a nine-to-five job?' Lanzo said abruptly, noticing her doubtful expression. 'For the money I'll be paying you I will expect your full and exclusive attention twenty-four-seven.'

'Presumably my nights will be my own?' she replied coolly, stung by his tone. She was well aware that the job of PA to the head of a global company meant working extended hours, including evenings and weekends when required, but she would need to sleep!

Lanzo leaned back in his chair and surveyed her with a wicked gleam in his eyes. 'Certainly—if you want them to be, *cara*,' he murmured softly. Was she aware of the hungry glances she had been darting at him across the table? he wondered. Or the way the pulse at the base of her throat was jerking frantically beneath her skin?

Under ordinary circumstances he would not consider mixing his work with his personal life. Office relationships always created problems, which was why he never had affairs with his staff. But the current circumstances were not ordinary.

It had come as a bolt from the blue when his PA of the last five years had suddenly announced that she was getting married, and then a few months later revealed that she was pregnant. Of course he was pleased for Luisa—although somewhat surprised, because she had never given any indication that she wanted to settle down to a life of domestic bliss. But he resented the disruption her pregnancy had caused to his life. Two junior secretaries had jointly taken over organising his diary, but he missed Luisa's calm efficiency that had ensured his office ran as smoothly as a well-oiled machine.

His conversation with Gina's retired boss from Meyers had convinced him that she was ideally suited to fill the position of his temporary PA. But, more than that, it was a chance for him to get to know her again. She had lingered in his mind for a long time after he had returned to Italy ten years ago. They had been friends as well as lovers, and now it was perfectly natural for him be intrigued by her, he assured himself.

It went without saying that any relationship he might have with her would not involve his emotions. After the fire fifteen years ago had taken everyone he had loved he had felt frozen inside. His heart was as cold and hard as a lump of ice, and he was not sure than anything would ever make it thaw.

CHAPTER FOUR

'WHAT was the name of that little country pub in the New Forest that we used to go to?' Lanzo queried. 'Do you remember it? We went there several times.'

Of course she remembered, Gina thought silently. She remembered every place she had visited with Lanzo ten years ago. 'It was the Hare and Hounds, famous for its steak and ale pies,' she told him. 'You took me there for lunch on my days off from the restaurant.'

'Mmm—and afterwards we went walking in the forest.'

They had walked deep among the trees and made love in a little clearing, where the sun had filtered through the leafy canopy above and dappled their bodies. Gina inhaled sharply. 'Yes, we went on some lovely walks,' she murmured, pretending to clear her throat to disguise the huskiness of her voice. 'The New Forest is very pretty.'

'We made love in a little dell, hidden among the trees.' Lanzo stretched his long legs out in front of him and turned his head towards Gina, his mouth curving into a sensual smile when she blushed. 'Do you remember, *cara*?'

'Vaguely.' She affected an uninterested shrug. 'It was a long time ago.' She stared out of the window of Lanzo's private jet at the endless expanse of brilliant blue sky, and tried to ignore her fierce awareness of him. It wasn't easy when he was sitting next to her, his body half turned to hers so that her eyes were drawn to his face, and inevitably, to the sensual curve of his mouth.

She had only spent three hours in his company since he had picked her up from her flat that morning, but she was already losing the battle to remain immune to his charisma, she thought dismally. When he had taken the seat next to her on the plane she had assumed he would open his laptop and catch up on some work, but instead he had spent the entire flight chatting to her and reminiscing about the past.

To be honest she was surprised at how much he remembered of their affair. They had only been lovers for a matter of weeks, yet Lanzo recalled the places they had visited together, as well as those passionate sex sessions in the forest, which were branded indelibly in her memory but which she'd thought he had forgotten.

'How much longer until we land?' she asked him briskly. Perhaps once they were at the Di Cosimo offices in Rome she would be able to slip into the role of efficient PA, and her heart would stop leaping every time he smiled at her?

'We won't be long now. The pilot has just indicated that we should fasten our seatbelts,' he told her, his eyes glinting with amusement when she gave an audible sigh of relief.

Rome in late June was stiflingly hot; the temperature displayed on the information board at Fiumcino Airport showed thirty-two degrees Celsius, and Gina was glad to slide into the cool interior of Lanzo's waiting limousine.

'We'll go straight to the office,' he told her as the car moved smoothly into the stream of traffic heading in the direction of the city centre. 'Luisa is going to be there to hand over to you. This afternoon I'm holding a board meeting and I'll require you to take the minutes.'

As he spoke his phone bleeped, and he began to scroll

through his messages while simultaneously checking emails on his laptop. The powerboat racer playboy had been replaced by the powerful billionaire businessman, Gina mused. Dressed in a beautifully tailored dark grey suit, blue silk shirt, and toning tie, he was achingly sexy. She sighed and tore her eyes from him. She had barely slept last night, plagued by doubts over her decision to work for him. She had no qualms about her ability to cope with the demands of the job of his PA, but she was less confident about her ability to deal with the devastating affect he had on her peace of mind.

'I'm afraid my Italian might be a bit rusty,' she said worriedly. 'I spent six months working for an Italian company in Milan, but that was before...' She had been about to say *before I got married*, but she had no desire to talk about Simon—her marriage had been a bleak period of her life she preferred to forget. 'That was a few years ago,' she said instead. 'You'll have to ask your board members to be patient with me.'

'Don't worry about it. Di Cosimo Holdings is a global company and the board members are not all Italian. Meetings are usually conducted in English,' Lanzo explained.

Privately, he did not think the members of the board would be overly concerned with Gina's language skills and were far more likely to focus their attention on her curvaceous figure. Presumably her aim had been to look smart and efficient, in a pale grey suit teamed with a lilac-coloured blouse, but the pencil skirt moulded her derrière so that it swayed delightfully when she walked, and the cut of her jacket emphasised her slender waist and her full breasts. Long, slim legs sheathed in sheer hose, and high-heeled black stilettos completed her outfit, and the whole effect was one of understated elegance that could not hide the fact that Gina was a sexy and desirable woman.

Lanzo took a sharp breath. He had spent the entire flight fantasising about leading Gina into the bedroom at the rear of the plane and unbuttoning that prim blouse. He could see the faint outline of her lacy bra beneath it, and in the fantasy he had peeled the straps over her shoulders so that her ample breasts spilled into his hands. Patience was all very well, but his determination to take things slowly was already wearing thin, and he was wondering how quickly he could persuade her to lower her barriers. One thing was certain: he would have to subtly let it be known to his board members that his temporary PA was off-limits to anyone but him, he decided.

'I'm sure it won't take you long to settle in,' he murmured. 'Do you like pizza?'

'I love it—unfortunately.' Gina grimaced. 'I'm afraid my hips don't need any encouragement to expand.'

'You look in perfect proportion to me.' Lanzo subjected her to a leisurely inspection that made her feel hot and flustered. 'I agree you're not a bag of bones, in the way so many women seem to think is attractive, but you won't find any complaints here in Italy, *cara*. Italian men like their women to be curvaceous. At least…' He paused and trapped her gaze with his mesmeric green eyes. 'At least this Italian male does.'

He was blatantly flirting with her, Gina realised, irritated by her body's instinctive reaction to him. She wanted to tell him to back off—that the hungry gleam in his eyes was totally inappropriate when she was one of his employees.

What chance did she stand of resisting him when he turned on his full mega-watt charm? she thought despairingly. But Lanzo could not help flirting with women—all women. It was as natural to him as breathing, and it didn't mean anything. The best way to deal with it was to ignore it, she told herself firmly.

'Why did you want to know if I like pizza?' she said lightly. 'Were you going to recommend a good restaurant?'

'Agnelli's—it's a little place tucked away down a side-street, off the main tourist trail, and it serves the best pizza in Rome. I thought we could eat there tonight.'

'Please don't feel you have to entertain me,' Gina said quickly. 'I'm sure you have a busy social life, and I'm quite happy to do my own thing.'

His smile made her heart flip. 'But we are old friends, Gina,' he said softly. 'I want to spend time with you.'

Oh, hell! Did he have any idea how emotive she found the expression *old friends*? How it tugged on her heart and sent her mind spinning back to those few weeks many years ago when she had been so insanely happy? Perhaps the happiest she had ever been in her life, a little voice inside her head whispered.

The atmosphere inside the car suddenly seemed taut with tension. The rumble of traffic outside faded, and Gina was painfully conscious of the ragged sound of her breathing. Coming to Italy with him had been a mistake, she thought frantically. Yet she could not deny that she felt more alive than she had felt for a long, long time.

She could not tear her eyes from his mouth, and memories filled her mind of him kissing her with hungry passion all those years ago. His reminiscing over their affair had made her remember how gentle he had been with her the first time he had made love to her. Her ex-husband had rarely been tender, and had taken his own pleasure with selfish disregard for hers. Her unsatisfying sex life had been one of the first disappointments of her marriage, Gina thought ruefully. She had not known in those early days how much worse her relationship with Simon would become.

Every instinct she possessed told her that Lanzo was nothing like Simon and that he would never hurt her— not physically, at any rate. It was the threat he posed to her emotional security that worried her. When his mouth curved into a slow smile everything flew from her mind but her yearning for him to brush his lips over hers and then deepen the kiss until he obliterated all her fears.

She caught her breath when he leaned towards her, but then he stilled and she felt sick inside, knowing that he had noticed her scar. She had been in such a rush that morning, at the last minute frantically packing belongings she had thought she would need in Italy, and she had not taken as much care as usual to conceal her scar with make-up. She tried to jerk away from him, but he slid his hand beneath her chin and gently forced her to look at him.

'That must have been a nasty wound,' he said quietly. 'What happened?'

'I had an accident a year or so ago,' she muttered, pulling her hair around her face to cover the scar. She swallowed. 'It's horrible. It makes me feel so ugly.'

Lanzo gave her a puzzled look. 'What kind of accident— a car crash?' He hazarded a guess. The scar was a long thin line that ran down her face, beneath her ear and a little way down her neck. He could only think that she had been cut—perhaps by glass when a windscreen had shattered.

Gina shook her head. 'It's not important.' The matter of how she had gained her scar was absolutely off-limits. She never spoke of it to anyone—not even her family.

Lanzo hesitated, and then said matter-of-factly, 'It hardly shows, and it certainly does not make you look ugly, *cara*. Nothing could diminish your beauty.'

His smile deepened as she gave him a startled glance.

When she blushed she reminded him of the shy waitress who had had a crush on him years ago, who had responded to him with such sweet passion when he had kissed her. He wondered what she would do if he kissed her now. Probably she would jerk away from him like a frightened doe, as she had done when he had walked her home from the Di Cosimo restaurant in Poole. He would like to meet whoever was responsible for causing the fearful look in her eyes, Lanzo thought grimly.

The car came to a halt and Gina released a shaky breath as the chauffeur opened the door for her to step out onto the pavement. Minutes later she followed Lanzo through the tinted glass doors of Di Cosimo Holdings. She was acutely conscious of him as they silently rode the lift up to the top floor, and her hand strayed unwittingly to the long scar hidden beneath her hair as she remembered how he had told her she was beautiful *after* he had seen the unsightly bluish line.

Perhaps her overwhelming awareness of Lanzo was not so surprising. He had been her first lover, and sex with him had been utterly fulfilling. Was it so wrong to want to experience the pleasure of his lovemaking again? To revel in his hard, muscular body skilfully possessing hers, and to make love to him in return—two people meeting as equals and taking each other to the heights of sexual ecstasy?

The lift halted, and as the door slid open she forced her turbulent thoughts to the back of her mind. Now was not an appropriate time to be imagining Lanzo's naked aroused body. *Was* there an appropriate time? she wondered wildly. She had come to Italy to work for him, and she was determined to fulfil the role of his PA with quiet professionalism, she reminded herself firmly.

'Welcome to Di Cosimo Holdings. Come and meet my team,' Lanzo said smoothly. His eyes lingered speculatively on her flushed face, but, calling on all her acting skills, Gina gave him a cool smile and followed him into his office.

Despite being heavily pregnant, Luisa Bartolli was still incredibly elegant, as so many continental women were, Gina thought to herself. Lanzo's PA was also friendly and welcoming, and clearly relieved to meet her temporary replacement.

'Lanzo wasn't impressed when I told him I would be having a few months off to have a baby,' Luisa confided as she gave Gina a tour of the offices. 'I've been his PA for over five years, and I know how much he dislikes any disruption to his routine. But it can't be helped.' She shrugged. 'Until I met my husband I had no plans to marry or have children. But Marco was keen to have a family, and I'm so excited about the baby. I'm thirty-six, and I know I'm lucky to have conceived the first month we tried. I haven't dared mention it to Lanzo yet, but I'm already thinking that I don't want to come back to work full-time and put the baby in day care.' Luisa added. She glanced at Gina. 'I'm sure that with your experience as a PA you'll get on fine working for him. Perhaps you would consider job-sharing with me after my maternity leave is over?'

'I don't think so,' Gina replied hastily. She already had doubts about the wisdom of agreeing to spend the next six months working for Lanzo. She certainly did not plan to extend her time with him. 'I have a flat back in England, and I need to work full-time to pay my mortgage.' She smiled at Luisa. 'Everything seems straightforward, but thanks for saying that I can ring you if I have any problems.' She stared wistfully at Luisa's bump. 'When is the baby due?'

'Not for another six weeks.' Luisa grimaced. 'I feel fine,

but the doctor has told me to rest, and Marco won't allow me to do *anything*. He only allowed me to come into the office today after I promised to spend the rest of the day with my feet up.'

'Your husband is obviously determined to take good care of you,' Gina murmured, stifling a little stab of envy. Her marriage to Simon had been in trouble barely months after the wedding. The charming man who had wined and dined her for six months before he had whisked her away for a romantic weekend in Paris and proposed at the top of the Eiffel Tower had changed overnight, it had seemed, into a possessive husband of unpredictable moods who had been jealous of her friendships and subjected her to verbal abuse when he was drunk.

It was probably a good thing that she had failed to fall pregnant, Gina conceded. Simon's increasing dependence on alcohol meant that he would not have been a good father. She had tried to help him, but it was impossible to help someone who refused to recognise he had a problem, and in the end, for the sake of her sanity and increasingly her physical safety, she had left him.

After Luisa had left, Gina got straight down to business and quickly became absorbed in the pile of paperwork on her desk. It felt good to be back at work. She was not naturally idle, and had hated her enforced weeks of inactivity after she had lost her job in Poole.

She took the minutes of the board meeting, relieved to find that the board members were indeed a mixture of nationalities and everyone spoke English, so her fluency in Italian was not put to the test on her first day. Lanzo had further meetings booked for the rest of the day, but at five he called her into his office and told her that he had arranged for his driver to take her back to his apartment.

'You've done enough for today,' he said, when she

protested that she was happy to stay on until he had finished. 'Go and relax for a couple of hours and I'll meet you at home later.'

Trying not to dwell on the fact that she would be sharing his home for the next few months, she arrived at his penthouse apartment, close to the famous Spanish Steps, and was greeted by Daphne.

'I have unpacked for you,' the housekeeper explained as she led the way to the guest bedroom which, like all the other rooms in the apartment, was decorated in neutral colours. It was not a very homely home—more like a five-star hotel, Gina mused as she glanced around at the ultra-modern décor. Her thoughts must have shown on her face, because Daphne explained, 'Lanzo's real home is his villa on the Amalfi Coast. He only stays here when he needs to be at the head office. Would you like a cup of English tea? He told me to buy it especially for you, because he remembered that you always used to drink it.'

Don't read too much into it, Gina told herself firmly. She smiled at the housekeeper. 'Tea would be lovely, thank you.'

When Daphne had gone she made a quick inspection of her room and the *en suite* bathroom, and then stripped out of her work clothes and stepped into the shower. Ten minutes later she pulled on a cool white cotton sundress, collected her tea from the kitchen, and wandered out onto the roof terrace—a leafy oasis of potted plants with spectacular views across Rome.

She would find her grandmother's house while she was here, Gina decided. It was exciting to be in the historical city, and she was looking forward to playing tourist and visiting the ancient landmarks. For the first time in months she felt her spirits lift—and if her excitement stemmed mainly from the fact that she would be spending the next few months with Lanzo, then so be it, she thought defensively. She was a grown woman and she could look after herself.

An hour later she stirred at the sound of her name, and opened her eyes to find Lanzo standing beside the lounger where she had fallen asleep.

'You should have sat beneath the parasol,' he told her, hunkering down beside her and running his fingers lightly up her arm. 'At this time of the year the sun is still strong until late in the evening, and your fair skin could easily burn.'

'I didn't mean to go to sleep,' she mumbled, jerking upright and pushing her hair back from her hot face. 'I was going to finish typing up the notes from the board meeting.' She stared at him dazedly, her brain still fogged with sleep, and her heart rate quickened when she saw that he had changed into faded jeans and a tight fitting black tee shirt that moulded his broad chest. His hair was still damp from where he had showered, and his hypnotic green eyes gleamed with a hunger he made no effort to disguise. 'When did you get back?' she mumbled, unable to drag her eyes from the chiselled perfection of his handsome face.

'Ten minutes ago.' Lanzo did not add that he had been impatient for his meeting to finish so that he could come home to her. In her simple summer dress she did not look much older than she had at eighteen, he brooded, fighting the urge to tangle his fingers in her long, silky chestnut hair and tilt her head so that he could claim her mouth in a kiss that he knew would not be enough for either of them.

But the faint wariness in her blue eyes cautioned him to bide his time. Gina could not hide her desire for him, however much she tried, but something was holding her back, and he was prepared to wait until she had dealt with whatever demons were bothering her.

'Now that you're awake, are you ready to sample the finest pizza in Rome?' he asked lightly. He held out his hand and, after hesitating for a moment, she placed her fingers in his and allowed him to pull her to her feet. 'Let's go and eat, *cara*. I don't know about you, but I'm starving.'

As Lanzo had said, Agnelli's pizzeria was off the tourist track, tucked away down a narrow side-street that they had reached after a fifteen-minute walk through Rome. From the outside the peeling paint around the front window and the restaurant's air of general shabbiness was not inviting, but when they walked in they were greeted warmly by the staff. Signor Agnelli hurried out of the kitchen, the apron tied around his girth dusty with white flour, and pulled Lanzo into a bear-hug, before ushering them over to a table set in a quiet corner, which he clearly reserved for his close friends.

'Enrico and I go back a long way,' Lanzo confirmed when Gina commented that the restaurant-owner seemed to regard him as a long-lost brother. He did not add that Enrico Agnelli had been one of the first firemen to arrive at the di Cosimo home in Positano on the night of the fire, and that the fireman had almost lost his life trying to save Cristina and Lanzo's parents. The injuries he had received had meant that he had had to leave the fire service, and Lanzo had willingly given his financial backing to help Enrico move to Rome and open the pizzeria.

'That was truly the best pizza I've ever eaten,' Gina said as she finished her last mouthful and sat back in her chair with a contented sigh.

'I'll tell Enrico—he'll be pleased.'

Lanzo's smile made her heart lurch, and she took a hurried sip of her wine, but nothing could distract her from her acute awareness of him, Gina acknowledged ruefully.

He had ignored the cutlery on the table and eaten his pizza with his hands, his evident enjoyment of the food somehow innately sensual. She had been happy to follow suit, and as she'd licked a smear of tomato sauce from her finger she had glanced across the table and found him watching with an intentness that had sent heat coursing through her veins.

They wandered back to his apartment in relaxed silence, and as Gina stared up at the stars glinting in the velvet blackness of the sky she felt a curious lightness inside that she realised with a jolt of shock was sheer happiness. She hadn't thought about Simon and the miserable months when their divorce had become increasingly acrimonious all day. Instead her mind had been full of Lanzo. Sitting across the table from him in Angelli's, she had found herself imagining him *sans* his shirt and hip-hugging jeans, and had pictured the two of them naked on a bed, his bare golden skin gleaming like satin, his powerful arousal rock-hard as he lowered himself onto her...

As the lift whisked them up to the penthouse she could not bring herself to look at him, conscious that her cheeks were burning. Out of the corner of her eye she saw him lift his hand, and stiffened when he lightly touched her arm. Only then did she realise that the strap of her sundress and slipped over her shoulder, revealing a lot more of the upper slope of her breast than she deemed decent. She held her breath when he tugged the strap back into place, and his drawled, 'I'm sure you don't want to fall out of your dress, *cara*,' made her face burn even hotter.

What if, instead of pulling her dress strap up, he had drawn it lower, until he had bared her breast, then shaped it with his palm, stroked his finger over her nipple...?

Her legs felt weak as she followed him into the apartment. Get a grip, she told herself furiously. But she could not control her body's response to Lanzo. He evoked feelings inside her she had thought were dead, had awoken her sexual desires so that for the first time in almost two years she felt a hot, damp yearning between her legs.

'Would you like a drink?' he asked as he ushered her into the lounge. 'A brandy—or I can make you a cup of tea?' Lanzo's eyes narrowed speculatively on Gina's flushed face. Did she know that he could decipher every one of the thoughts that darkened her blue eyes to the colour of midnight? he brooded, hunger and frustration coiling in his gut when she quickly shook her head.

'I think I'll go straight to bed. It's been a long day.' And she was going to make a complete fool of herself if she remained with him for a second longer. 'Goodnight,' she mumbled, and shot down the hallway to her bedroom, closing the door behind her and finally releasing the breath that had been trapped in her lungs.

Things could not continue like this, Gina decided after she had changed into her nightdress, brushed her teeth and climbed into bed—only to find that sleep was impossible while she was imagining Lanzo in his room just along the hall, stripping out of his clothes and sliding into his bed. Did he still sleep naked, as he had done ten years ago? Stop it, she ordered herself, punching her pillows into a more comfortable shape for the umpteenth time.

An hour later she was still wide awake, and now she was thirsty. Knowing that she would never be able to sleep until she'd had a drink, she slid out of bed and stepped into the hall. Everywhere was in darkness, and she assumed Lanzo had gone to bed, but when she pushed open the kitchen door her heart jerked against her ribs at the sight of him leaning against the worktop, idly skimming through a newspaper. He was naked apart from the towel hitched around his waist, and droplets of water glistened on his shoulders and his damp hair, indicating that he had recently showered.

Dear heaven, he was gorgeous! He lowered the paper as Gina hovered in the doorway, his bright green eyes gleaming with amusement when she stared simply stared at him, her mouth open in a perfect *oh* of shock.

Dark eyebrows winged upwards. 'Did you want something, *cara*?'

She moistened her dry lips with her tongue, and the gleam in his eyes became intent and feral. 'I came to get a drink. I usually take a glass of water to bed with me,' she croaked.

'Lucky water,' he murmured, so softly that she wasn't sure she had heard him right. He took a glass from the cabinet, filled it from the tap, and strolled towards her. Her eyes hovered on his towel and she prayed it was securely fastened.

'Here.' He handed her the glass.

'Thank you.'

Leave now, her brain insisted urgently. But her senses were swamped by his closeness, the tantalising scent of clean, damp skin, the sensual musk of his aftershave, and something else that was irrevocably male and primitive that made every nerve-ending in her body tingle.

Green eyes meshed with sapphire-blue. 'Is there anything else you want, Gina?'

His breath whispered across her lips, and without conscious thought she parted them in silent invitation. Lanzo made a muffled sound deep in his throat as he lowered his head and grazed his mouth gently over hers.

It felt like heaven. Starbursts of colour exploded in her mind as he tasted her with delicate little sips, until he felt the little shiver of pleasure that ran through her and deepened the kiss. His lips were warm and firm, yet incredibly gentle, teasing hers apart, his tongue tracing their shape but not sliding into her mouth. Instinctively she leaned closer to him. He lifted his hand and threaded his fingers through her hair.

And then suddenly, from nowhere, Simon's image hurtled into her mind—a memory of him grabbing her hair and pulling several strands from her scalp during one of his drunken rages.

'No!' She jerked away from Lanzo so forcefully that she banged the back of her head on the doorframe. He frowned and lowered his hand. She could see the questions forming on his lips and she shook her head, silently telling him that she was not about to give an explanation for her behaviour. 'I can't.' Her voice was thick with misery. 'I'm sorry.'

She was still clutching the glass, and she spun away from him so urgently that water sloshed over the rim, soaking through her nightdress as she tore down the hall towards her room.

Lanzo watched her go, half tempted to follow her and demand to know what she was playing at. She had turned from soft and willing to tense and *frightened* in the space of a few seconds, and he wanted to know why. But he recalled the expression in her eyes—a silent plea for him to back off—and after a moment he switched off the kitchen light and padded down the hall to his own room, wondering what had happened in her past that had decimated her trust.

CHAPTER FIVE

GINA dreaded facing Lanzo the following morning, but to her relief he greeted her with a casual smile when she joined him on the terrace for breakfast, and made no reference to what had happened between them the previous night. If he was curious as to why she had reacted so badly when he had kissed her he did not allow it to show, and over coffee and the delicious herb and parmesan *frittatas* that Daphne served them he focused exclusively on work and the meetings planned for the day ahead.

A week later, Gina glanced around the quaint little courtyard tucked away down a side-street in the Campo di Fiori area of Rome, and then studied the faded photograph in her hand.

'I'm sure this is where Nonna Ginevra used to live,' she said excitedly. 'The fountain in the centre of the square is just the same, and that house over in the corner looks like the one my grandparents are standing in front of in the photo. It's amazing—this courtyard has hardly changed in over sixty years,' she murmured.

Lanzo peered over her shoulder at the photograph. 'Your grandfather is in military uniform, so I assume the picture must have been taken during the Second World War?'

Gina nodded. 'Grandad was stationed in Italy in the

war, and that's when he met Nonna. They married soon after the war ended, and she moved to the farm in Dorset with him, but she often spoke of her childhood home in Rome. It must have been hard for her to leave the place she loved, but she always said that she loved my grandfather so much that she would have lived on the moon with him if he'd asked her.'

It was hot in the enclosed courtyard, and she sat down on the stone wall surrounding the fountain, glad of the fine spray that cooled her skin.

Lanzo dropped down next to her. 'You were obviously very fond of your grandmother.'

'Yes, I was close to both my grandparents. After my mother left I spent a lot of time with them while Dad was busy on the farm. They died within a few months of each other, and although I was sad I couldn't help but be glad that they were together again,' she said softly. 'Even death didn't part them for long.'

Her grandparents' long and devoted relationship had epitomised all that marriage truly meant, she thought. Love, friendship, respect—the things she had hoped for when she had married Simon, until his drinking binges and increasingly aggressive behaviour had killed her feelings for him.

'I can't believe we've actually found Nonna's childhood home,' she said, refusing to dwell on dark memories when the sun was blazing from a cobalt blue sky. 'You seem to know every corner and backstreet of the city. Did you grow up in Rome?'

Lanzo shook his head. 'No, I was born in Positano, on the Amalfi Coast. I like Rome, and I spend a lot of time here because Di Cosimo Holdings is based here, but home is very much my villa on the clifftops, looking out over the sea.'

'I've heard that the Amalfi Coast is supposed to be one of the most beautiful places in the world,' Gina said, smiling at his enthusiasm. 'Do your family still live there?'

'I have no family. My parents died many years ago, and I was an only child.' Lanzo's tone was curiously emotionless, and his eyes were shaded by his sunglasses so that Gina could not read his expression, but something warned her that he would not welcome further questions about his family.

'I'm sorry,' she murmured. She remembered reading somewhere that he had assumed control of Di Cosimo Holdings when he had been only twenty—long before he had stayed in Poole ten years ago. Presumably he had taken over the company on the death of his father. No wonder he seemed so *detached*, she mused, trying to think of a suitable word to describe him. From the sound of it he had no one in his life he cared about, and perhaps losing his parents when he had been a young man had hardened him.

There was a proverb that stated 'no man is an island'. But Lanzo seemed to prize his independence above anything, and did not appear to need anyone. His housekeeper Daphne ran his various homes and took care of his domestic arrangements, and a ready supply of willowy blonde models satisfied his high sex-drive. She wondered if he had ever been in love, but when she darted a glance at his stern profile she dared not ask, feeling fairly certain what his answer would be.

'Now that we have found where your grandmother used to live, where would you like to visit next?' he asked after a few minutes. 'We're not far from the Piazza Navona, where the fountains are rather more spectacular than this one.' He dipped his hand in the small fountain and flicked water at her, grinning when she yelped. 'The square is world-famous, and the statues are truly worth seeing.'

'You don't have to be my tour guide all weekend,' Gina told him. 'You've already shown me so much of Rome.'

Her mind re-ran the past wonderful week. After her initial awkwardness with him that first morning she had slipped into the role of his PA with surprising ease, and a companionable relationship had quickly developed between them—although she was always conscious of the shimmering sexual chemistry simmering beneath their polite conversations.

Each evening they returned to his apartment to sample Daphne's divine cooking, and afterwards strolled around the city, admiring the exquisite architecture of the ancient landmarks and discovering secret little side-streets and courtyards where they drank Chianti beneath the striped awnings of some of the cafés.

Rome was a magical place, but in her heart Gina recognised that for her the magic was created by Lanzo as he walked close beside her, or smiled indulgently when she paused to study a pretty window box or peer into a shop window. It would be very easy to fall for him, she thought ruefully. And it was that knowledge which held her back from responding to the sultry invitation in his eyes each time she bade him goodnight every evening and went to her bedroom to sleep alone.

She was puzzled that, although he did not try to disguise the fact that he desired her, he had made no further attempt to kiss her. She supposed she should have felt reassured that he was obviously not going to pressure her in any way, but instead she lay awake every night, gripped by a restless longing as she imagined his muscular, naked body pressing down on her soft flesh, his dark head lowered to her breast.

'I've enjoyed showing you around,' he told her, his voice cutting through her erotic fantasy, so that she blushed scarlet and hastily avoided his gaze. 'We won't have another chance for a while. We'll be in St Tropez for most of next week, preparing for the launch of the new Di Cosimo restaurant, and after that I plan to spend some time in Positano.'

'I assume you'll want me to be here in Rome, to run the office while you are staying at your villa?' Gina murmured, trying not to dwell on how much she would miss him. He probably had a mistress in Positano, she thought bleakly, despising herself for the corrosive jealousy that burned like acid in her stomach.

'Of course not—I'll be working from the villa, and naturally I will require my personal assistant to be with me.'

Lanzo got to his feet and stared down at her, feeling his body stir into urgent life as his eyes were drawn to the deep valley between her breasts revealed by her low-cut vest top. After spending all week fantasising about the voluptuous curves she kept hidden beneath smart work suits and high-necked blouses, the sight of her in denim shorts and the clingy lemon yellow top at breakfast this morning had sent heat surging through his veins.

He could not remember ever wanting a woman as badly as he wanted Gina, he acknowledged, almost resenting her for the hold she seemed to have over him. He had told himself he would wait until she accepted that their mutual attraction could only have one inevitable conclusion, but he hadn't reckoned on her ability to shatter his peace of mind.

Lanzo took Gina's hand and drew her to her feet, but instead of leading her out of the courtyard he stood towering over her, so that she was faced with the choice of staring at his muscle-bound chest, and the tantalising glimpse of tanned flesh above the neckline of his shirt, or the chiselled perfection of his face.

'I want you to come to Positano with me,' he said, in

his rich-as-molten-chocolate voice that made the hairs on the back of her neck stand on end. 'And not just as my PA, *cara*.'

Her eyes flew to his, and she caught her breath at the feral hunger gleaming in his green gaze. Tension quivered between them, and the air in the courtyard was so still and silent that Gina was sure he could hear the frantic thud of her heart. 'You shouldn't say things like that,' she whispered. He had broken the unspoken promise between them—not to refer to their mutual awareness of each other—and she felt exposed and vulnerable.

'Why not—when it's the truth?' His arm snaked around her waist and he jerked her up against him, so that she could feel every muscle and sinew of his hard thighs pressing into her softer flesh. 'You must know that I want you,' he said roughly. 'And you want me too. Do you think I don't notice the hungry glances you give me, or the way you trace your lips with your tongue, inviting me to kiss you?'

'I don't—' Gina stopped dead, horrified to realise that she had unconsciously moistened her lips with the tip of her tongue even while Lanzo was speaking. But not because she wanted him to kiss her, she assured herself. Not because she longed for him to cover her mouth with his own and plunder her very soul.

His dark head blotted out the sun, and her heart beat faster as she saw the determined intent in his eyes. She should move, she thought desperately, but her body would not follow the dictates of her brain, and the soft brush of his lips over hers opened the floodgates of desire that she had tried so hard to deny.

Her common sense warned her not to respond, but already it was too late. She had no weapons to fight his sorcery. Her hands were shaking as she placed them against his chest, intending to push him away. The trembling that now affected all her limbs was not from fear, but from a fierce longing to press her body against the muscled strength of his and feel the thud of his heart echo the drumbeat of her own.

Lanzo tasted her again softly, carefully, as if he was aware that she was poised to flee from him. But the gentle pressure of his lips on hers tantalised her senses, and with a low moan she opened her mouth to welcome the erotic sweep of his tongue. And suddenly the dam broke, and he could no longer restrain the thundering torrent of his desire, kissing her with a blazing passion that had her clinging to him while he tangled his fingers in her long, silky hair.

It was Lanzo who finally broke the kiss, the functioning part of his brain reminding him that, although the little courtyard was deserted, they were in full view of the houses surrounding them. He lifted his head reluctantly and frowned. As the head of one of Italy's most successful companies he was a well-known figure in Rome. He never kissed his lovers in public, aware that paparazzi could be lurking anywhere. But yet again Gina had caused him to break one of his personal rules, he thought derisively.

He was unbearably tempted to take her back to his apartment and spend the afternoon making love to her, but once again the wariness in her eyes stopped him. He was sure now that some guy had hurt her in the past. She had brushed off his delicate attempts to probe into her romantic history, but her defensiveness told him there was a reason why she continued to pull back from him. Patience was a virtue, Lanzo reminded himself ruefully. Gina would be his soon, but he would not rush her.

'I leave it up to you to decide what we should do for the rest of the day, *cara*,' he murmured, forcing himself to ease away from her. 'We can go home and relax…' He paused, heat flaring inside him as he imagined removing her shorts and tee shirt and stroking his hands over her voluptuous curves. He took a ragged breath. 'Or we can visit the Pantheon, as we had planned to do.'

Gina stared at him in stunned silence, still reeling from his kiss. Part of her wished that he would make the choice for her, exert his dominance and whisk her back to his apartment so that he could take her to bed for the rest of the day. But she was afraid to admit her longing for him to make love to her. It was more than a step. It was a leap off a precipice. And her nerve failed her.

'I don't want an affair with you,' she said jerkily, cringing at her bluntness but needing to make it clear to him—to herself—that she was not in the market for a sexual fling.

His eyes narrowed, and she saw the effort he made to control his frustration. 'Why not?' he demanded. 'Don't think about denying the chemistry that burned between us when you responded to me so eagerly a few seconds ago. We were good together once,' he reminded her when she shook her head.

'Ten years ago you only wanted me for sex,' Gina reminded him shakily.

'That's not true.' It had started out like that, Lanzo admitted silently. He had been attracted to Gina, but he had assumed that once he had taken her to bed he would soon grow bored with her—as he did with all his mistresses. To his surprise his desire had increased with every week that they had been lovers. He had been drawn to her, and had wanted to spend all his time with her—until alarm bells had rung in his head and he had abruptly ended their affair, determined that he would never allow himself to become emotionally involved with any woman. He had learned that emotions hurt, and he was not prepared to risk going through the pain he had felt when he had lost Cristina ever again.

'It was not just sex. You meant something to me,' he said roughly.

'So much so that I never heard from you again after you returned to Italy?' Gina said bitterly. 'If you cared for me at all—' she could not believe he had '—why didn't you say so?'

'Because my head was messed up.' Lanzo exhaled heavily. 'I wasn't in a fit state of mind to contemplate a relationship. You were young and full of life. You deserved to meet a guy who would make you happy.'

Instead she had met Simon, Gina thought bleakly. 'Why was your head messed up?' she whispered. 'Sometimes I used to glimpse an almost haunted look in your eyes, but you never liked to talk about yourself.' She could tell from his shuttered face that things had not changed and he still would not confide in her. 'I never really knew you at all,' she said sadly. 'And now I don't want to spend a few more weeks as your convenient mistress.'

Lanzo stared at her intently. 'If I only wanted to satisfy a carnal urge there are any number of women I could call,' he said quietly. In truth he did not know exactly what he wanted from a relationship with Gina, but they had been friends as well as lovers ten years ago, and he saw no reason why they could not be so again now. His jaw tightened when he saw panic flare in her eyes. 'What are you afraid of, Gina?'

'I'm not...' The denial died in her throat when he gave her a look of frank disbelief.

'Does your nervousness stem from a previous relationship?' Lanzo voiced what he had begun to suspect, and knew he was near the mark when she quickly looked away from him.

'I don't want to talk about it,' she muttered, stubbornness creeping into her tone. As she pushed her hair back from her face Lanzo noted that her hand was shaking, and a feeling of tenderness swept through him.

'Maybe we both need to open up?' he suggested softly. He wanted to pull her close and simply hold her, until she felt with every beat of his heart that she could trust him. But as he moved towards her she stepped back and shook her head once more.

'What's the point? The only relationship I want with you is as your temporary PA.'

'Look me in the eye and tell me that,' Lanzo ordered, frustrated that he could not understand why she was determined not to give in to the chemistry that was a constant simmering presence between them.

Gina was glad that she had reached into her bag for her sunglasses. She slipped them on and met his gaze calmly, thankful that her expression was hidden from him. 'That's all I want,' she repeated firmly, desperately trying to convince herself as much as him, and before he could say another word she turned and walked out of the courtyard.

There was luxury, and then there was out-of-this-world breathtaking opulence, Gina thought as she stared around in awe at the new Di Cosimo restaurant in St Tropez. Nestled in the hills above the town, it offered diners spectacular views over the bay and the harbour, where huge yachts and motor cruisers—undoubtedly owned by the many multi-millionaires who flocked to the French Riviera during the summer—were moored.

The restaurant was all white marble floors and pillars, with wallpaper flecked with the kind of gold-leaf which also gilded the Louis XV style dining chairs and matched the gold cutlery set out on pristine white linen tablecloths. Stunning centrepieces of white calla lilies and orchids filled the air with their heavenly fragrance, adding to the restaurant's ambience of sumptuous elegance.

'Are you impressed?' Lanzo's deep voice sounded from behind her and she spun round, her breath catching in her throat at the sight of him looking breathtakingly handsome in a formal black dinner suit.

'I'm speechless,' she replied honestly. 'The décor is amazing. And the view from the terrace—those bright pink bougainvillea bushes and beyond them the sapphire-blue sea—is wonderful. I've never seen anything so beautiful.'

'I agree,' Lanzo said softly, not glancing at the view out of the window. Instead his eyes were fixed intently on Gina as he made a slow appraisal of her heather-coloured silk-chiffon dress. Floor-length and strapless, the dress clung to her curves and emphasised her slender waist. She had piled her hair into a chignon with soft tendrils left loose to frame her face, and her only adornment was the rope of pearls that had once been her grandmother's. The smooth, luminescent stones were displayed perfectly against her creamy skin.

'The view from where I'm standing is exquisite,' he murmured, watching dispassionately as soft colour flared along her cheekbones. Since he had kissed her in Rome their relationship had shifted subtly, and the tension between them was tangible. For the past week that they had been in St Tropez, Gina had been excruciatingly polite towards him, perhaps afraid that if they reverted to the easy friendliness they had shared since she had begun to work for him he would think she was willing to have an affair with him.

But despite her coolness Lanzo had been conscious of the fierce sexual chemistry bubbling beneath the surface, waiting to explode. He felt strung out and edgy, his body in a permanent state of arousal—and his patience was at an end. His concentration was shot to pieces, his thoughts dominated by his need to take Gina to bed, and he knew from the way her eyes darkened every time she looked at him that her longing was as great as his.

'Yes, well, everything is ready for the grand opening,' Gina said shakily, dragging her eyes from Lanzo's glinting gaze to glance at her watch. Her senses quivered as she inhaled the subtle scent of his cologne and she took a step away from him, terrified that he would notice her body's betraying reaction to him, her nipples jutting beneath the sheer silk of her gown. 'The guests should start to arrive soon.'

She had barely uttered the words when a sleek black limousine drew up outside the restaurant and moments later a well-known Hollywood star emerged from the car.

The guest list for tonight was chock-full of celebrities, and no expense had been spared to make the launch of the latest Di Cosimo restaurant an event that would hit the headlines around the world. Luisa had begun to organise the launch party before she had gone on maternity leave, but Gina had spent a hectic week finalising arrangements and dealing with last minute problems. Added to that, she had endured four days of the usual agony that accompanied her monthly period. She knew that the painful stomach cramps were a sign that her endometriosis was getting worse, and she was filled with an unbearable sadness that she was unlikely to ever have children.

The only good thing was that she had been so tired and drained at the end of each day that she hadn't had much time to think about Lanzo—although it had been difficult to ignore the escalating sexual tension between them. She did not know what to make of his assertion that he wanted her for more than just sex. If he did not want her for his mistress, what *did* he want? she wondered fretfully. She wished she had the courage to find out, but her marriage and subsequent divorce from Simon had been a bruising experience—and not just mentally, she thought ruefully, her hand straying unconsciously to the scar she had skilfully disguised with make-up. She was afraid to trust her judgement, afraid to give her trust to Lanzo, and now they seemed to be trapped in a strange stalemate which was dominated by their desperate physical awareness of each other.

She was dragged from her thoughts when Lanzo drew her arm through his. 'Duty time,' he murmured when her eyes flew to his face. 'We'll wait at the front entrance to greet the guests as they arrive.'

'Oh, but I thought that as you are the chairman of Di Cosimo Holdings you would prefer to do that on your own. Are you sure you want me…?' Gina trailed to a halt as he gave her an amused smile.

'I'm absolutely certain that I want you, *cara*,' he drawled, his eyes glinting when she blushed scarlet.

The launch party had been a great success, Gina mused hours later, stifling a yawn as she glanced at her watch and saw that it was almost midnight. The food had been divine, accompanied by a selection of the finest wines, and after dinner everyone had strolled out onto the terrace to enjoy the view and the endless supply of champagne served by white-jacketed waiters who wove through the throng of guests.

Inevitably some people had drunk too much—notably an English celebrity television presenter, who regularly featured in the gossip columns and was renowned for his rowdy behaviour. Finn O'Connell had grown increasingly brash and loud-mouthed as the evening progressed. He was swaying unsteadily on his feet, Gina noted, looking over to where Finn was standing with a group of people, including his pretty young wife. Miranda O'Connell was a talented stage actress, and like many people Gina wondered what she saw in her boorish husband.

Gina watched as Finn called to a waiter and demanded another glass of whisky—clearly he had moved on from champagne to neat spirits. His wife put her hand on his arm, as if to plead with him not to have another drink, and Finn reacted explosively, pushing Miranda away with such violence that she stumbled and fell. Gina heard the smash of glass on the tiled floor. As if in slow motion she saw Miranda fall, and memories instantly flooded her mind.

Dear heaven, no—not again, she thought as she flew across the terrace. She pictured Miranda landing on the broken glass, and it brought back the horror of feeling blood pouring in a hot, sticky stream down her own face. Finn O'Connell was shouting at the two burly security guards who had appeared out of the shadows and were gripping his arms. His wife was lying on the floor amid the shards of a broken glass, and Gina could barely bring herself to look, sure that Miranda must have been cut.

Lanzo got there first. He knelt by Miranda's side and spoke to her in a low tone before he gently helped her to her feet. There was no blood, Gina realised with relief. The young actress looked pale and shaken, but seemed otherwise unhurt.

'Stay with Mrs O'Connell while I arrange for a car to take her and her husband back to their hotel,' Lanzo instructed, glancing briefly at Gina. 'I'll tell a waiter to bring her some water—and black coffee for O'Connell,' he added grimly. 'He needs something to sober him up.'

'I'm fine, really,' Miranda said faintly as Lanzo strode away and Gina guided her to a chair. She bit her lip. 'Finn just gets carried away sometimes.'

'Fairly often, if the stories in the tabloids are even half right,' Gina said quietly. When Miranda did not refute this she murmured, 'You're not responsible for the fact that your husband drinks too much. And he has no excuse for lashing out at you—certainly not that he's downed too much whisky.'

Miranda gave her a startled look. 'You sound as though you're speaking from experience.'

Gina nodded. 'I am. Alcohol affects people in different ways; some become happy and relaxed, while others feel morose. My ex-husband used to become bad-tempered and aggressive.' She looked steadily at Miranda. 'I pleaded with Simon to seek help, but he refused to admit he had a problem. When his heavy drinking made him violent I knew that for my safety I had to leave him.' She hesitated, and gave the younger woman a sympathetic smile. 'It's not up to me to tell you how to live your life, but you need to take care of yourself—'

She broke off when Lanzo returned. 'Your car is waiting out front,' he told Miranda. 'I've taken the liberty of sending your husband back to your hotel in a separate car, accompanied by two of my staff. He seems more in control of himself now.' He did not add that Finn O'Connell's bravado had quickly dispersed when he had found himself sharing a car with the two burly bodyguards.

'I hope she'll be okay,' Gina murmured as she and Lanzo watched the hotel manager escort Miranda out of the restaurant.

'The security guards will make sure O'Connell behaves himself for the rest of tonight. Anyway, he's so drunk that he's probably out cold by now. Not that that's an excuse. Any man who hits a woman is a pathetic coward,' Lanzo said disgustedly. He glanced at Gina and frowned. 'Are you all right? You're deathly pale.'

'I'm tired. It's been a long day,' she said hurriedly, desperate to deflect any further questions.

'Go back to the hotel and get to bed. I'll call the driver to take you,' Lanzo said, taking his phone from his jacket. 'I have a few things to finish up here.'

She *was* weary—it hadn't just been an excuse, Gina realised. The upsetting events with Miranda and Finn had been the final straw, and so she did not argue, simply collected her shawl and allowed Lanzo to escort her out to his limousine.

They were staying just outside St Tropez, in a stunning five-star beach-front hotel. Some months ago Luisa had booked the luxurious Ambassador Suite for Lanzo, but she had not made arrangements for any staff who would be accompanying him. When Gina had later phoned the hotel to book a room for herself, and learned that there were no vacancies, she would have been happy to stay at another hotel. But Lanzo had insisted that she should share his suite.

'It has two bedrooms, each with *en suite* bathrooms, as well as an enormous lounge. It's ridiculous for you to stay somewhere else. After all, it won't be any different than us living together in my apartment in Rome,' he'd pointed out when she had tried to argue.

The gleam in Lanzo's eyes had warned Gina of his determination to have his own way, and from a work point of view sharing the suite made sense, she had been forced to admit. But tonight, as she crossed the spacious lounge and entered her bedroom, she locked the door behind her as she had done every night—although whether her actions were to keep Lanzo out or to stop herself from succumbing to temptation and going to him in the middle of the night, she refused to think about.

The night was hot and sultry, and from far out across the

bay came the distant rumble of thunder. Gina opened the French doors, hoping there would be a faint breeze blowing in from the sea, but the air was suffocatingly still.

The scene at the restaurant kept playing over in her mind, but she resolutely pushed it and all its associated memories away as she hung up her dress, washed off her make-up, and slipped a peach silk chemise over her head before she climbed into bed. She had been on her feet since six-thirty that morning, rushing around sorting out last-minute arrangements for the launch party, and she was grateful for the bone-deep weariness that swept over her so that sleep claimed her within minutes.

An hour later Lanzo entered the suite and made straight for the bar, where he poured himself a large brandy. It was his first drink of the night, for although the guests at the party had enjoyed unlimited champagne, he never drank alcohol while he was representing Di Cosimo Holdings. Nursing his glass, he strolled over to the French doors and opened them to step out onto the terrace. The sky was black, lit by neither moon nor stars, and the air prickled with an electricity that warned of an imminent storm.

As he stared out across the dark sea, lightning suddenly seared the sky, ripping through the heavens and illuminating briefly the white wave-crests as they curled onto the shore. His jaw hardened. The day had been intolerably hot and sticky, and hopefully a downpour of rain would clear the air, but he hated storms.

It was ironic that there should be one tonight, he brooded grimly. He hardly needed a reminder that it had been on this date fifteen years ago that lightning had struck his parents' house in Positano and set it ablaze. The fire had been so intense and had spread so quickly that the occupants had not stood a chance. His parents and Cristina had been killed by smoke inhalation while they slept, and when the blaze had finally been brought under control the fire crew had found their bodies still in bed.

He lifted his glass and drained it, feeling the brandy forge a fiery path down his throat. He could no longer see Cristina's face clearly in his mind; time had shrouded her features behind its misty veil and it was now Gina's face, her sapphire-blue eyes and her mouth that tilted upwards at the corners, that was burned onto his brain.

The sound of a cry dragged him from his reverie. It had been a cry of terror—a sharp, frantic cry of mingled fear and pain—and it had come from Gina's room. Pausing only to set his glass down on the table, Lanzo strode swiftly along the terrace, while above him the heavens grumbled menacingly.

CHAPTER SIX

THERE was so much blood. It was hot and wet, pumping all over her white dress and already forming a pool around her head. Gina tossed restlessly beneath the sheet, lost in her dream. She was amazed that she had that much blood, but she needed to stop it pouring out.

With a cry, she jerked upright and pressed her hand to her cheek. It was dark, so dark that she couldn't see, but as the dream slowly ebbed she realised that she wasn't lying on the hard kitchen tiles, and there was no smashed glass beneath her face, no blood seeping from her.

With a shaking hand she fumbled for the switch on the bedside lamp, and at once a soft glow lit up the room. Gina drew a ragged breath. It was a long time since she'd had the dream, and she knew it had been triggered by the events in the restaurant earlier, when Finn O'Connell had pushed his wife and she had fallen, her wine glass shattering on the ground seconds before she had landed. Miranda hadn't been cut, thankfully. But the incident had brought back memories of Simon, drunk and aggressive, hitting her when she tried to take a bottle of whisky from him. The bottle had slipped to the floor, spilling its contents. The smell of whisky still made her feel sick.

Afterwards, Simon had insisted that he hadn't meant to hit her, but whether by accident or design his blow to her temple had been so hard that she had reeled and fallen. She'd been shocked, and she hadn't had time to put out her hands. She had landed on the broken glass, which had sliced through her face and neck.

Pushing back the sheet, she jumped out of bed and fumbled to the open French doors, needing to escape the hot, dark room and the suffocating blackness of her dream. There was no moonlight, and she screamed when she walked into something solid. Hands gripped her arms as she lashed out.

'Gina!' Lanzo spoke her name urgently, shocked by her haunted expression. 'What's the matter, *cara*?'

It was the *cara* that undid her. Lanzo's voice was deep and soft, strength and gentleness meshed, so that she felt instantly safe. She felt instinctively that he would rather die than cause a woman physical harm. He was man of surprisingly old-fashioned values, who opened doors and gave up his seat, and considered it a man's role to protect the weaker sex. Female emancipation was all very well, but at this moment, when she was trembling and felt sick inside, Gina simply allowed him to draw her close and stood silently while he stroked his hand through her hair.

'What happened?' he asked gently.

'Nothing…I had a nightmare, that's all,' she whispered, unable to restrain a shiver as she recalled the details of the dream.

Lanzo gave her a searching glance, feeling a curious little tug in his gut when he saw the shimmer of tears in her eyes. 'Want to talk about it?'

'No.' She swallowed, and tore her eyes from the unexpected tenderness in his.

He sighed and tightened his arms around her, resting his chin on top of her head. No way was he going to allow her to return to her bed alone when she was still clearly upset about her dream. He knew about nightmares. He still suffered from them himself sometimes: tortured images of Cristina, crying out for him amid the flames, and of him unable to save her. He knew what it was like to wake sweating and shaking, afraid to go back to sleep in case the nightmare came again, Lanzo thought grimly.

Gina's hair smelled of lemons. He could not resist the temptation to brush his mouth over her temple, smiling when she gave a jolt but did not try to pull away from him. Gently he trailed his lips down her cheek and over the faint ridge of her scar. She immediately tensed.

'Was your nightmare about the car crash?' he murmured.

Gina drew back a little and gave him a puzzled look. 'What car crash?'

'I assumed you were cut by glass from a shattered windscreen.' It was the only explanation he had been able to think of. 'How *were* you injured, then, *cara*?' He frowned, feeling the tension that gripped her body. Something came into his mind—an image of Gina's terrified face when she had witnessed the incident in the restaurant earlier that night. When Finn O'Connell had lashed out at his wife Gina had looked as shaken as Miranda O'Connell.

A horrific understanding slowly dawned on him. 'Did someone hurt you?' he demanded roughly, feeling sick inside at the possibility. 'Did somebody do this to you, *cara*?'

Gina bit her lip when Lanzo ran his finger lightly down her scar. The compassion evident in his eyes was too much when her nightmare about Simon's brutality was still so real in her head. She felt desperately vulnerable, and her primary instinct was to retreat mentally and physically from Lanzo.

He must have read her mind, for he slid his hand from

her scar to her nape, massaging her tight muscles with a gentle, repetitive motion. 'I would never harm you in any way, *cara*,' he said deeply. 'You must know that.'

She recalled the year she had dated Simon before their marriage, when she'd had no inkling that he had a drink problem and seen no sign of his violent temper. Her wedding night had been memorable for all the wrong reasons, she thought ruefully. Simon had seemed fine after a couple of glasses of champagne at the reception, but on the plane he had ordered spirits, and numerous shots of neat whisky had revealed a side to his personality that had come as an unwelcome shock.

How could you ever know a person's true nature? Gina wondered. And yet she felt safe with Lanzo. She trusted him. And as that realisation sank in relief seeped through her. She had feared she would never feel confident enough to trust anyone again, but Lanzo *was* different from Simon—so different that it was hard to believe they were of the same species.

Lanzo watched the play of emotions on Gina's face, the faint tremor of her mouth before she quickly compressed her lips, and felt a hard knot of anger form in his gut at the idea of some guy hurting her.

'What happened?' he asked quietly, smoothing her hair back from her face and catching her fingers in his when she instinctively tried to cover the thin, slightly raised ridge that he had exposed.

She was under no obligation to tell him anything—so why did she feel a strong urge to share the memories that still had the power to evoke nightmares? He was so tall that she had to tilt her head to look at his face, and as she studied his hard jaw a wry smile tugged her lips. Strength and undeniable power meshed with the gentle expression in his eyes were a potent combination. She felt safe with Lanzo; it was as simple as that.

But it was still hard to admit the truth. Gina took a shaky breath. 'My husband…did this,' she said huskily. 'He was in one of his rages and he hit me.'

For a few stark seconds Lanzo went rigid with shock. 'You're *married*?' he demanded harshly.

'Not any more.' She managed a ghost of a smile that did not reach her eyes. 'My divorce was finalised just before I moved back to Poole, but I *had* left Simon a year before that. The night he did this—' she touched her scar '—was the final straw. I knew I had to get away from him before anything worse happened.'

'*Dio mio,*' Lanzo growled. 'How on earth did you end up married to such a monster in the first place?'

Gina bit her lip. It was a question that the few close friends who knew what had happed during her marriage had asked her. She felt a fool that she had been duped by Simon, and it was hard for her to talk about her marriage, but she acknowledged that she was never going to be able to move forward with her life until she had come to terms with her past.

'Simon was an investment banker. We met at a corporate dinner in the City,' she explained wearily. 'He was good-looking, charming, and successful—I guess he ticked all the right boxes, and we quickly became close. We were engaged six months after we met, and married six months after that. Our wedding night was the first time I had ever seen him drunk, but the next morning he was so apologetic that I put it down to the stress of the wedding.'

She sighed. 'Making excuses for Simon's drinking and his black moods became a regular occurrence, but I wanted our marriage to work and so I kept on ignoring the warning signs of his increasing reliance on alcohol.'

'I don't understand how you could have ignored it if he was violent towards you,' Lanzo said harshly. It struck him that Gina must have been madly in love with her husband to put up with his behaviour, and he was unprepared for the sharp stab of jealousy in his gut that the thought evoked.

Gina could see the shock in Lanzo's eyes and she hung her head, moving away from him to stare out of the window at the dark beach. 'I was ashamed,' she admitted in a low tone. 'I thought that I must somehow be to blame for Simon's drinking and his tempers. And I didn't know who to talk to. We were part of a large social group, but most of the people we met at dinner parties were Simon's business associates and I couldn't possibly have confided to any of them or their sophisticated wives that we were not the glamorous have-it-all couple we appeared to be.'

She twisted her fingers together, still not able to look at Lanzo. 'I know I was a fool, but I was clinging to my dream of having a family. We had agreed to try for a child as soon as we were married, and I hoped that a baby would magically make Simon stop drinking. Instead, I failed to fall pregnant, Simon lost his job in the banking crisis that hit the City, and things went rapidly from bad to awful because he spent all day at home drowning his sorrows.'

'Yet you still stayed with him?'

'I wanted to help him. I felt guilty that I didn't love the man he had turned into, but I was still his wife, and I felt it was my duty to try and support him. The trouble was Simon didn't want to be helped. During one of our many rows about his drinking I tried to take his bottle of whisky, and he reacted like a madman.' She swallowed, the memories vivid in her mind. 'He struck me, and as I fell I dropped the bottle I was holding. A piece of broken glass sliced through my face, and by unlucky chance through an artery in my neck. There was a lot of blood and confusion.

I needed numerous stitches, and was left with this lasting reminder of my marriage,' she said wryly, lifting her hand to trace the familiar path of her scar.'

'No wonder you looked so ashen when Finn O'Connell turned on his wife tonight,' Lanzo said harshly, feeling a fierce need to search out Gina's ex and connect his fist with the other man's face.

He noticed the glimmer of tears in her eyes and his gut clenched. Giving in to his own violent urges where her ex-husband was concerned would not help her, he acknowledged grimly. He sensed that it had taken enormous bravery for her to tell him about her marriage, and now she needed his support and strength. Suppressing his inner rage against her ex, he walked over to her and drew her into his arms.

'You were not to blame for your husband's drink problem any more than Miranda is responsible for O'Connell's behaviour,' he assured her firmly.

He bent his head and brushed his lips the length of her scar, the caress as soft as thistledown, causing a curious little pain in Gina's heart. He's simply being kind, she told herself sternly. Don't read more into it than that. She knew she should pull away from him, assure him that she had recovered from the nightmare and would be able to sleep now. Except that was a lie; she doubted she could fall asleep—not because of the bad memories of Simon, which were fading as the nightmare receded, but because of other memories, of Lanzo drawing her down onto the soft grass in that wooded glade many years ago, and making love to her with exquisite gentleness.

She swallowed when he lifted his head and stared down at her. Desire was still evident in his green gaze, but it was tempered with compassion and understanding, an unspoken vow that she was safe with him.

She sighed and felt the tension drain out of her, so that

she relaxed in his arms. Perhaps it was the knowledge that Lanzo would never hurt her as Simon had done, or the memory of his gentle caresses the first time he had made love to her all those years ago when she had been a girl on the brink of womanhood. Or perhaps it was simply that she could not deny her need for him any longer—a need that was mirrored in his hypnotic green eyes. All she knew was that when he slowly lowered his head she *ached* for him to kiss her, and instead of pulling away from him she parted her lips in readiness, her heart thudding with excitement rather than fear as he brushed his mouth lightly over hers.

Lanzo felt the tremor that ran through her, and was shocked to realise that it was not only Gina who was shaking. This moment had been building since he had first caught sight of her in Poole. He had known immediately that he wanted her, and a little later, when he had realised her identity—that she was *his* Gina, who had been his lover ten years before—his desire for her had intensified. He had not known then of the trauma she had suffered at the hands of her ex-husband, and now his desire was mingled with a need to show her that he would only ever treat her with the greatest care and respect.

He did not want to rush her. He wanted to savour every second, every soft sigh that whispered from Gina's lips as he drew her closer and deepened the kiss so that it became a sensual tasting that was both evocative and erotic.

Gina was aware of Lanzo's powerful arousal jutting against her pelvis, and she felt the drenching flood of desire between her legs. By choice she hadn't had a physical relationship with a man since her marriage had ended, but she was sure now that she wanted Lanzo to make love to her and obliterate the dark memories of Simon that still haunted her.

She knew she was risking her heart. Lanzo had ended their affair ten years ago, and from all that she had read about him since he still had an aversion to commitment. But nothing altered the fact that she wanted him. She yearned to feel his hands sliding over her naked body, the brush of his hair-roughened thighs pressing against her softer flesh. Dear heaven, the sensual tug of his mouth on her breast.

It was impossible to express her need in words, so she captured his face between her palms and drew his mouth down to hers, to kiss him with an unrestrained hunger that made him groan deep in his throat.

Passion exploded between them: wild, almost pagan in its intensity, and leaving no room for doubt. Without taking his lips from hers, Lanzo swept Gina up and carried her along the terrace to where the door to his bedroom stood ajar. He stepped inside and paused, looking down at her for long minutes, searching for an answer to his unspoken question before he gently lowered her onto the bed.

'You are so beautiful, *tesoro*,' he said thickly, his accent very pronounced. 'I swear I would never do anything to harm you.'

He dropped down next to her and threaded his fingers through her hair, which was spread like a curtain of chestnut-coloured silk around her shoulders. Tiny buttons secured the front of her chemise, and Gina snatched a breath when he deftly unfastened them and then slowly drew the thin straps down her arms until he had bared her breasts.

The air felt cool on her heated skin. She felt a dragging sensation low in her stomach when he stilled and allowed his gaze to roam over the creamy mounds of firm flesh that he had exposed, dark colour winging along his cheekbones, his eyes glittering with feral desire.

He leaned forward and slanted his mouth over hers, kissing her with a slow deliberation that could not disguise his barely leashed hunger. Only when her lips were softly swollen did he move his head lower, trailing a moist path down to her collarbone and then over the slopes of her breasts. Her nipples tautened in anticipation of his caress, her heart thudding, and she gave a little moan when he flicked his tongue delicately across one rosy crest and then its twin, back and forth, heightening her pleasure to fever-pitch until she curled her fingers in his hair and held him to her breast, sighing her approval when he sucked hard, sending starbursts of sensation shooting down to her pelvis.

This was where she wanted to be, Gina thought dreamily, watching through heavy-lidded eyes as Lanzo stripped off his shirt. His chest gleamed like polished bronze in the lamplight, his powerful abdominal muscles clearly defined beneath the whorls of dark hair that arrowed down over his flat stomach. He stood to remove his trousers, and she felt a mixture of excitement and trepidation when his boxers hit the floor and he stood before her, gloriously and unashamedly aroused.

He must have misinterpreted her expression, for he said fiercely, 'You want me, *cara*. Your body reveals what you might wish to deny—see…?' he murmured, as he cupped her breasts in his palms and rolled her nipples between his fingers until she gasped and arched her hips in frantic invitation.

'I don't deny it,' she choked with innate honesty, her eyes widening when he skimmed his lips over her stomach and gently pushed her thighs apart. 'Lanzo…' Shock drove words of protest from her mind as he stroked his tongue lightly up and down the opening of her vagina, the sensation so exquisite that she instinctively spread her legs a little wider and groaned when he discovered the tight nub of her clitoris.

Pleasure was building inside her, coiling, tightening,

until she was trembling and desperate for his ultimate possession.

'I know, *cara*,' he growled, his voice rough with need as he moved over her, his body tense and his erection rock-hard. With one hand he tugged the chemise down over her hips and settled himself between her thighs, supporting his weight on his forearms. Gina slid her arms around his back and urged him down onto her, desperate to feel him deep inside her, but suddenly he stilled and muttered an imprecation.

'What's wrong…?' she whispered shakily.

Lanzo cursed again and shook his head. 'I don't have anything with me,' he gritted, struggling to control his body's urgent clamour to sink his throbbing shaft into her. 'Condoms,' he elucidated when she stared at him uncomprehendingly. 'I hadn't planned on this happening—at least not tonight,' he added wryly, 'and I didn't buy any contraception.' He gave an agonised groan, 'I'm sorry, *cara*, but even in the heat of passion I'm sure that neither of us is prepared to risk an accidental pregnancy.'

A shudder of longing ripped through Gina. Still haunted by memories of how Simon had treated her, it had taken a great deal of courage for her to get this far. But Lanzo's gentleness had given her the confidence to lower her barriers, and she was desperate to make love with him and prove to herself that she was no longer affected by her marriage. Driven by instinct, she gripped his shoulders to prevent him from rolling away from her.

'There's no risk,' she muttered.

Lanzo frowned, his heart kicking against his ribs as fierce excitement quickly mounted. 'You mean you are protected?' he demanded, assuming that she meant she was on the pill. Never before had he broken his golden rule and had sex without taking responsibility for contraception, but the pill was regarded as the most reliable method available, his brain argued, and he could not bear another night of aching, agonising frustration. It was not only about sex, he realised. He wanted to obliterate Gina's memories of her violent ex-husband, and remind her that the passion they had once shared had not faded.

'Gina…?' he said urgently, his body shaking with his desire to ensure her pleasure. He sensed that it had been a long time since she had enjoyed making love in its true sense—a sensual experience shared by two people totally in tune with each other's needs.

Gina wondered if she should reassure Lanzo that the chances of her falling pregnant were non-existent. Not only was her endometriosis worse, but her period had only just finished, and she knew from all the months she had obsessively studied her ovulation chart, when she and Simon had been trying for a baby, that her one minuscule chance of conceiving was around the middle of her cycle.

But she did not want to discuss her infertility; she didn't want to waste time talking when her body was trembling with an intense yearning to take him inside her. The feel of his solid erection jabbing into her belly drove every consideration from her mind but her need to assuage the agonising, aching longing for him to possess her.

She touched the hard line of his jaw and traced her finger lightly over his mouth. 'I want you to make love to me, Lanzo,' she whispered, and heard his feral groan as he crushed her mouth beneath his in a possessive kiss. She felt his hand slip between her thighs and squirmed at the intimate probing of his finger as he parted her and stroked her until she was on the brink. 'Please…'

It was a cry from the heart, and he gave a rough laugh as he positioned himself above her.

'I intend to please you, *cara*,' he assured her. He could

feel that he was going to come at any second, but with a massive effort of will he controlled himself and gently eased forward, entering her carefully and oh, so slowly, pausing while her muscles stretched to accommodate him. He slid his hands beneath her and cupped her bottom, angling her so that it was easier for her to absorb his length, smiling down at her when she stared at him with stunned eyes. 'Good?' he queried softly.

Good did not come anywhere near it. There were no words to describe the intensity of pleasure that was beginning to build deep inside her as Lanzo withdrew a little and then drove into her, setting a rhythm that she eagerly matched. She clung to his shoulders, her lashes drifting down as she was swept away to a place where sensation ruled. Little spasms rippled across her belly as he increased his pace. She sensed his urgency and gasped his name, wanting the journey never to end. But the coiling inside her was growing ever tighter, and suddenly, cataclysmically, it snapped, and her cries of pleasure were muffled by his lips as he thrust his tongue into her mouth in erotic mimicry of the powerful thrusts of his body.

Lanzo could not hold back. The pleasure of feeling her body convulse around his throbbing shaft was too exquisite to bear, and he climaxed seconds after her, tensing for a few seconds as he tried to hold back the tide before he was overwhelmed, and then shuddering with the mind-blowing intensity of his release.

For long moments they lay, still joined, their mutual urgent need appeased for now, their bodies relaxing in the honeyed afterglow of lovemaking. It had never been like this with Simon—not even in those early days of their marriage when she had been sure that she loved him, Gina brooded. She had only ever felt this complete union, as if their souls as well as their bodies were one, with Lanzo.

But she did not kid herself that he felt the same way. He was a skilled and considerate lover who had taken her to the heights of ecstasy, but now, as he rolled off her, she sensed that his withdrawal was not only physical.

Should she get up and go back to her own bed? she wondered as she lay next to him, the silence between them broken by the sound of heavy rain lashing the windows. Some time during their frantic lovemaking the storm outside had broken, but she had been so swept away by passion that she had not even noticed. She pushed back the sheet, but as she eased away from him he curved his arm around her waist and pulled her up against his chest.

'Where are you going?' he growled, nuzzling the sensitive spot behind her ear so that she could not restrain a little shiver of pleasure.

'I was going to return to my room.'

Her answer should have pleased him, Lanzo brooded. He rarely spent the whole night with his lovers for once his physical needs had been satisfied he had no further need of them.

Through the open curtains the black sky was suddenly lit up by a jagged lightning bolt, and seconds later a deep rumble of thunder reverberated around the room, drowning briefly the sound of torrential rain. The storm had faded for a while, but now it was back to vent the full force of its fury.

The fire that had destroyed his parents' villa had raged out of control long before the rain had fallen during that devastating storm fifteen years ago. Perhaps if the heavens had opened as dramatically they had done tonight the flames might have been quenched and his parents and Cristina would have escaped, Lanzo thought heavily.

He did not want to be alone with his thoughts tonight. Ten years ago he had found solace and a few weeks of unexpected happiness with a shy young English waitress. He had never spoken to Gina about his past, but her gentle nature had soothed his ragged emotions, and when they had made love he had delighted in her unrestrained pleasure. Gina had made him forget briefly the pain inside him—and tonight he wanted to lie in her arms and focus on her silken skin and her soft, curvaceous body.

She had her own demons, too. Raw anger flared inside him as he thought of her brutal ex-husband. The fact that Simon had been an alcoholic did not excuse his behaviour, Lanzo thought savagely. He could not dismiss the image of her terrified face when she had stumbled into his arms, the horrors of her nightmare clearly evident in her eyes. He could not allow her to return to her room and perhaps be plagued once more by bad dreams. He wanted to hold her so that she felt safe for the rest of the night.

'Stay,' he murmured, trapping her against him by hooking his thigh over hers. Her bottom felt delightfully soft beneath his fingertips as he traced its rounded contours, before sliding his hands up to cup her breasts, and he heard her swiftly indrawn breath when he gently played with her nipples. He trailed one hand down over her flat stomach and slipped it between her thighs.

'Lanzo...?'

He ignored her breathless protest and carefully parted her womanhood, sliding his fingers between the slick folds and caressing her with delicate strokes that made her gasp and move restlessly against him.

'This is all for you, *cara*,' he whispered in her ear, when she attempted to turn round so that he could enter her.

Gina gave a little cry of pleasure when his clever fingers found her ultra-sensitive clitoris. She wanted him to share the experience, but he seemed determined to give her the ultimate in sexual enjoyment while unselfishly denying himself. The pleasure was too intense to withstand, and she sobbed his name as he took her to the edge, held her there, teetering on the brink, and then with a final stroke sent her tumbling over, holding her secure in his arms.

Afterwards he rearranged the pillows and settled her comfortably against him, feeling a curious tug on his heart when she gave him a sleepy smile.

'I imagine your experience with Simon has put you off marriage for good?' he murmured, unable to get the other man out of his mind.

Gina did not answer him straight away. She thought seriously about Lanzo's question. And discovered in those moments of contemplation that her hopes and dreams were still the same as when she had been eighteen.

'No,' she replied at last. 'My relationship with Simon was a disaster, but I still believe in marriage. I still hope that one day I'll meet the right person for me, just as Nonna Ginevra met my grandfather, and fall in love and marry again.' Her voice faltered a little. 'Have a family...' Maybe she would not be able have a baby of her own, but there were thousands of children who needed parents, and she would definitely consider adoption.

'I believe that just because something didn't go the way you planned it once, it's no reason not to try again,' she told Lanzo.

The expression in his green eyes was unfathomable. 'So you aren't afraid of having your heart broken again?'

By the time she had left Simon he had killed all her feeling for him, and the only emotion she had felt was relief that her marriage was over. There was only one man who had ever broken her heart, but wild horses would not drag the truth from her that that man had been Lanzo.

'Of course there's a risk that that could happen, but what is the alternative? To never allow myself to get close to anyone ever again? Never know the joy of loving someone for fear that it could end in tears? My heart might stay safe, but it wouldn't be much of a life.'

She paused, and then asked diffidently, 'Are you really content with *your* life, Lanzo? I know you have plenty of affairs, and technically you are never on your own when there is always another attractive blonde willing to share your bed, but I sense that you are alone,' she said softly. 'You don't seem to care about anyone.'

Lanzo had stiffened while she was speaking. There was a good reason why he refused to allow himself to get too close to anyone, he brooded. He remembered the savage pain that had ripped through him when he had been told that Cristina was dead—the disbelief that had turned to gut-wrenching agony when he had stared at the charred remains of his parents' house and realised that no one could have escaped such carnage. He never wanted to feel that kind of pain again, or sink to such depths of despair as he had in the months after the fire, when he had seriously wondered whether life was worth living without the woman he had loved. Fifteen years on he had forged a new life, and for the most part it was good. But he did not want to fall in love again.

'I like my life the way it is,' he admitted. 'I go where I please, when I please, and I answer to no one.'

He had not told her anything she did not already know, Gina acknowledged, trying to ignore the little pang his words had evoked. She had always known that Lanzo was essentially a loner—a man perfectly at ease in a crowd, but equally content with his own company.

How long would their affair last? A week? Months? she wondered, trying not to dwell on the inevitability of its ending.

She felt the need to take some control. Once his usual

PA returned to work, their professional *and* personal relationship would come to an end, she vowed. Their relationship could never be more than a brief interlude, and as long as she guarded her heart against him she would be content with that, she assured herself. For now she would enjoy every moment she spent with him, and she smiled as he drew her close and she felt the soft brush of his lips on hers.

CHAPTER SEVEN

THEY extended their stay in St Tropez for a few more days, spending lazy hours on the beach, and long nights of passionate lovemaking before falling asleep in each other's arms. Even in the early days of her marriage she had never felt this sense of completeness, Gina thought when she woke before Lanzo one morning, and lay studying his face. It seemed softer in sleep, reminding her of the younger man she had known ten years ago. Unable to resist, she leaned over him and brushed her mouth softly over his, stirring him so that he closed his arms around her and deepened the kiss into an evocative caress that tugged on her soul.

But it was not long before reality intruded. Lanzo's intention to fly back to Italy, to his home in Positano, was dramatically changed by news that the Di Cosimo restaurant in New York had been badly damaged by a fire.

'Arrange for the jet to collect us from Toulon-Hyres airport and take us direct to JFK,' he instructed Gina, after he had relayed the information he had received in a phone call from the manager of the restaurant.

'Has the restaurant been badly damaged?' she asked, remembering that the New York branch had recently undergone a major refit.

'I understand it's been gutted.' Lanzo shrugged. 'But

thankfully no one was injured in the blaze, and that's all that matters.'

Twenty-four hours after the fire, Gina stared around at the blackened walls and roof beams of the restaurant and shivered, despite the midday heat in New York. The fire had been caused by an electrical fault, and the damage was extensive—but, as Lanzo had said, thankfully every one of the diners and staff had escaped safely.

'Daniel Carter said he couldn't believe how quickly the flames took hold,' she said to Lanzo, after she had chatted with the restaurant manager who was clearly still in shock.

She glanced at him when he made no reply. From the moment they had arrived at what remained of the restaurant his expression had been unfathomable, but now he removed his sunglasses and she was shaken by the bleakness in his eyes.

'Fire is so appallingly destructive,' he said harshly. 'It consumes everything in its path and shows no mercy as it reduces everything to this.' As he spoke he kicked a pile of black ash, seemingly uncaring that his actions sent a cloud of choking soot into the air which fell back down and settled on his clothes.

Frowning at his obvious tension, Gina placed her hand on his arm. 'I know it's a terrible shame, but one of the fire crew told me that there is little actual structural damage, and although it looks like Armageddon the restaurant can be cleaned and redecorated.'

He gave a curious laugh. 'Sure—everything will be made shiny and bright again, and it will be as if the fire never happened.'

'Well, that would be good, wouldn't it?' she said slowly, trying to assess his mood. 'Six months from now the fire will be forgotten.'

Lanzo shook his head and moved away from her, so that her hand fell helplessly to her side. 'Some things can never be forgotten,' he muttered obliquely. 'Some memories haunt you for ever.'

'What do you mean?'

'It doesn't matter.' He swung to face her, his sunglasses back in place so that she had no clue to his thoughts. He seemed to give himself a mental shake and smiled at her, although she sensed that the smile did not reach his eyes. 'I'm talking rubbish, *cara*. It was just a shock to see how much damage the fire has caused. We'll go back to the hotel now. You must be feeling jet-lagged.'

Maybe Lanzo *was* feeling the effects of their frantic dash to the US and the six-hour time difference, Gina mused that night, when for the first time since they had become lovers he did not reach for her, but simply bade her goodnight and rolled onto his side of the vast hotel bed.

He was distant and preoccupied for the next few days, and when he did make love to her again the sex was urgent, and as mind-blowing as ever, but it lacked the intimacy that she had felt between them in St Tropez.

He soon returned to his usual charismatic self, but she sensed an edge of darkness beneath his easy charm which reminded her of how he had been when he had come to Poole ten years ago. Not for the first time she suspected that there were events in his past that he did not want to talk about.

They remained in New York for two weeks, while Lanzo dealt with the after-effects of the fire. On the Sunday before they were due to leave, Gina woke to find that he was already up and dressed.

'I'm spending the day out of town—a little place about sixty miles east of the city, near to the coast. Do you want to come?'

She pushed her hair out of her eyes and looked at him blearily, wondering how he could be so wide awake after a night of energetic sex and very little sleep. 'Okay.' It was stiflingly hot in town, and she liked the idea of a cool coastal breeze. 'When do you want to leave?'

'Twenty minutes.' He grinned at her dismayed expression. 'But I suppose that, seeing as I kept you busy for much of the night, I can give you half an hour.'

Two hours later Gina glanced around the flat airfield and then back at Lanzo. 'You seriously mean you've come here to *skydive*?'

'Certainly, *cara*,' he replied, looking amused at her horrified expression. 'Nothing beats throwing yourself out of a plane at ten thousand feet. I'm an experienced skydiver, and I can take you for a tandem jump if you like.'

'I'll give it a miss, thanks. I value my life.' She removed her sunglasses and gave him a searching look. 'Powerboat racing, skydiving, that super-powered motorbike you were telling me you keep in Positano—sometimes I get the feeling that you don't value yours, Lanzo.'

His own shades were firmly in place, disguising his thoughts, and he shrugged laconically. 'Life is more fun when it contains an element of risk, and I don't fear death.'

'No...' She sensed that was true. 'What you fear is allowing anyone to get too close.' She was frustrated that she only knew the man he allowed her to see, and that he never revealed his innermost thoughts to her. 'You don't mind risking your physical safety, but you refuse to put your emotional security in danger.'

She knew from the way his jaw tightened that she had pushed him too far. 'You don't know what I feel,' he said harshly. 'Do me a favour and keep your psychobabble to yourself, Gina,' he growled impatiently, and strode off towards the jump-plane waiting on the runway.

The following weeks were a hectic blur of planes, hotels, and occasionally brief trips to famous landmarks in whichever part of the world they happened to be in as they crisscrossed the globe, visiting various Di Cosimo restaurants and the new cookery schools which had proved to be a hugely successful project for the company.

Los Angeles, Dubai, Hong Kong, and Sydney blended into a kaleidoscope of images in Gina's head. She'd accompanied Lanzo to lavish parties, charity fundraising dinners, and the launch of his latest restaurant which had opened in Paris. Her previous job for the global retail outlet Meyers meant that she was no stranger to travel and socialising, and she was thankful that she had acquired a wardrobe of classic designer clothes which were now invaluable for her role as Lanzo's PA.

But while her smart work suits and elegant evening gowns were mainly from her days at Meyers, her nightwear was new—and bought for her by Lanzo. Skimpy lace negligees, delicate silk chemises, pretty bras, and matching thongs... Lanzo happily scoured lingerie shops for exotic and erotic underwear which he demanded that she model for him and then delighted in removing. Their desire for one another—far from waning as the weeks slipped past— was more intense than ever, and they made love with an insatiable hunger that left Gina secretly shocked by her unreserved response to Lanzo's bold demands.

And now at last they were in Positano, on the stunning Amalfi Coast, being driven by Lanzo's chauffeur along narrow roads with terrifying hairpin bends and spectacular views over an azure sea and the jagged rocky landscape.

Thank heavens Lanzo was not behind the wheel, Gina thought as she glanced out of the window at a hillside that fell in an almost sheer drop from the edge of the road down to the sea. She recalled those nerve-racking journeys in his car years ago, when he had driven her back to her father's farm after her she had finished her shift at the restaurant in Poole. If he were driving now they would no doubt be hurtling around the bends. Lanzo's love of danger had not changed, she thought ruefully. But their relationship was different from their brief affair when she had been eighteen; *she* was different—older, hopefully wiser, and determined that she would not give in to the clamour of her heart and fall in love with him again.

'It's so beautiful,' she murmured, awed by the pictur-esque view over the town. Dozens of terracotta-roofed houses clung to the cliffs which rose up majestically behind them, and in front of the houses the sea stretched into the far horizon, as flat and still as a lake, and crystal-clear.

'It's the most beautiful place in the world,' Lanzo agreed, his hard features softening a little as he drank in the familiar sights of the area where he had grown up. 'Around the next bend you will see my home—the Villa di Sussurri.'

'The villa of whispers,' Gina translated. 'Why is it called that?'

He looked away from her and stared at the sea, surprised by his strong urge to reveal that it was because he some-times felt that he could hear the voices of his parents and Cristina in the house, speaking softly to him.

'No particular reason. I simply liked the name,' he said with a shrug.

'It's not what I was expecting,' Gina admitted a few minutes later, when the car swung onto a gravel driveway and halted outside the villa.

'You don't like it?'

'Oh, no—it's breathtaking,' she assured Lanzo hurriedly. 'I just assumed that it would be an old house, built of local stone, like the houses in Positano.' Instead the Villa di Sussurri was square and ultra-modern, built on several levels, its brilliant white walls making a stunning contrast to the vivid blue sky above and the sapphire sea below.

Lanzo ushered her into a cool marble-floored hall, and Gina caught her breath when he pushed open the double doors in front of them to reveal a huge lounge, with glass walls on all three sides offering spectacular views over the bay.

'Wow! This is stunning,' she murmured, glancing around at the pale walls and furnishings in muted shades of blue and taupe. Elegant and sophisticated, the villa managed to combine style with comfort, and it felt much homely than his apartment in Rome.

'This is my home,' he told her when she said as much. He smiled at her enthusiasm. 'Come on—I'll give you a guided tour.'

An open spiral stairway at one end of the villa led to the upper floors, where many windows allowed light to stream in, giving glimpses of the sea from almost every part of the house.

'It's huge; I've counted five bedrooms, and there's still another floor above us,' Gina commented. 'Don't you find it rather a big house for one person?'

'I'm not alone here very often,' he said carelessly.

'No...I don't suppose you are.' Her steps faltered, jealousy burning like acid in the pit of her stomach as she thought of all the other women he must have brought here, and all the others he would bring in the future, after she had been consigned to the metaphorical graveyard of his ex-mistresses.

Lanzo wondered if she knew how expressive her face was. Probably not, he mused. Gina went to great efforts to act cool with him—except for in bed, where she responded to him with gratifying eagerness. He skimmed his gaze over her, noting the expert cut of her cream skirt and jacket, which emphasised her gorgeous curves, and he felt the predictable tug of sexual anticipation in his groin.

'Most of the time Daphne is here to run the house for me,' he explained. 'Luisa stayed for a couple of weekends before she was married, when we had a lot of work to catch up on, but you are the only other woman I've invited to the villa, and the only woman to share my bed here,' he admitted.

As he spoke he opened a door, and stood back to allow Gina to precede him into what she saw instantly was the master bedroom. Decorated in the same neutral tones as the rest of the house, the room was airy and full of the evening sunlight which streamed through the huge windows, but it was the vast bed in the centre of the room that trapped her gaze, and a little frisson of excitement ran down her spine when Lanzo closed the door and pulled her into his arms.

'*Cara.*' His voice was as soft and sensuous as crushed velvet. When he slanted his mouth over hers she melted into his kiss, no thought in her head to deny him. This was where she wanted to be—in his arms and soon, she thought with a little shiver, in his bed.

She could not hide her disappointment when he lifted his head after a few moments and stared down at her. 'How are you feeling now, after your dizzy spell this morning?' he murmured, noting the faint shadows beneath her eyes. She had looked tired for the past couple of days, and had seemed a little subdued, but now she smiled up at him and traced her lips with the tip of her tongue in a deliberately provocative gesture that ignited the flame inside him.

'I'm fine. This morning was just...' She shrugged, not sure why she had felt so curiously light-headed when she had got out of bed the last few mornings. 'It was nothing.' She began to undo his shirt buttons, and skimmed her palm over the satiny skin overlaid with whorls of dark hair that she revealed. 'But perhaps I should have a lie-down?' she suggested huskily, smiling boldly at him as her deft fingers unzipped his trousers.

'Witch.' Lanzo gave a ragged laugh, his own fingers busy with her jacket buttons. 'All day I've wondered whether you were wearing a bra beneath your jacket. And now...' His eyes narrowed, hot, urgent desire pounding through his veins. 'Now I know that you are not.'

Dio, she turned him on. He shoved the jacket down her arms, so that it fell to the floor, and cupped her breasts in his hands, testing their weight and kneading the soft creamy globes before he lowered his head and took one pouting pink nipple into his mouth. Her soft moan of pleasure shattered the last remnants of his restraint and he tumbled them both down on the bed, thrusting his hand beneath her skirt and inside her knickers, to find the betraying dampness between her legs.

He could not have enough of her, he acknowledged as he stripped her with ruthless efficiency and tore off his own clothes, pausing briefly to don a protective sheath as he had done every time they had had sex after that first night in St Tropez. He was even thinking that it would not be a disaster if Luisa decided only to come back to work part-time after her maternity leave, as he suspected she was thinking of doing. He was confident that Gina would not need much persuading to remain his secretary-cum-mistress. It was an arrangement that could continue indefinitely, he mused, smiling as he drove into her with one long, deep thrust, and crushing her soft cry of delight beneath the hungry pressure of his mouth.

Afterwards he found himself reluctant to ease away from her, and when he finally rolled onto his back he drew her against him and idly stroked her hair, feeling a contentment that he had not known since... He tensed, shocked at the idea that he had not felt like this since he had made love to Cristina, so many years ago.

He glanced at Gina and saw that she had fallen asleep. Her long lashes lay against her flushed cheeks and her mouth was slightly parted, so that she looked young and curiously vulnerable. The feeling inside him was *not* the same, Lanzo told himself again. But he was no longer relaxed and, muttering a curse beneath his breath, he slid out of bed, taking care not to wake her, and strode into the *en suite* bathroom to take a shower.

Lanzo's housekeeper, Daphne, smiled warmly at Gina the following morning. '*Buongiorno.* Would you like to have your breakfast out on the terrace?'

The mere thought of food was enough to turn Gina's stomach, despite the fact that she hadn't eaten anything since lunch on the plane yesterday.

'Not just now, thank you.' She shook her head, trying to clear her muzzy thoughts. 'I can't believe I've slept for fifteen hours solid.'

'Lanzo said you have been working hard recently, and that it would be better to allow you to sleep for as long as you needed to,' Daphne explained. 'That's why he did not wake you for dinner last night. Are you sure you don't want something to eat now? You must be hungry.'

Gina wasn't. She felt horribly queasy. 'I'll have something in a while, when I've woken up properly. Where is Lanzo?'

'In the garden.' The housekeeper's smile faded. 'He spends many hours there, and he does not like to be disturbed.' She darted Gina a sharp look with her bright black eyes. 'But perhaps he will not mind you searching for him. Go through the gate in the wall at the side of the house.'

'Thank you.' Gina followed Daphne down the hall, pausing in front of the two life-sized portraits hanging on the wall. 'Are these people Lanzo's parents?' she asked as she studied the painting of a middle-aged couple, struck by the strong resemblance between the handsome square-jawed man and Lanzo. The woman at his side was dark haired and elegant, with a kindly smile that spoke of a warm nature.

'*Si.*' Daphne nodded, but offered no further information as she continued down the hall.

'And the young woman in the other painting—who is she?' Gina queried as the housekeeper opened a door and was about to step into the kitchen.

Was it her imagination, or did Daphne stiffen before she slowly turned around? 'She was Lanzo's *fidanzato*,' the older woman said expressionlessly.

Lanzo's *fiancée*! For a second Gina felt the walls and floor tilt alarmingly, just as had happened during the dizzy spell she had experienced when she had got out of bed that morning. Thankfully normality returned almost immediately, but she was conscious of a dull ache inside her at the startling news that Lanzo, who eschewed any form of emotional commitment, had once been *engaged*.

She stared at the portrait of the woman, and acknowledged that *beautiful* was nowhere near an adequate description of her exquisite features: huge almond-shaped eyes, a shy smile, and glossy black curls that fell around slender shoulders. A girl on the brink of womanhood, Gina mused, and felt a sharp stab to her heart as she wondered if Lanzo had loved her.

She frowned and turned back to Daphne. 'Where is she now? Why didn't Lanzo marry her?'

'She is dead.' The housekeeper finally looked at the paintings of Lanzo's parents and his fiancée. 'They are all dead. Lanzo does not like to speak of it,' she added grimly, before she disappeared into the kitchen.

Gina had noticed the high wall running next to the side of the villa when they had arrived yesterday, and now, as she stepped through the gateway, she found herself in an enclosed garden of such breathtaking beauty that she simply stood and stared around in amazement. Green lawns were edged with a profusion of colourful flowers, long walkways held climbing roses formed into a floral arbour, still pools showed goldfish darting beneath the surface, and the spray of fountains glinted in the sunshine like thousands of tiny diamonds. And all this with the backdrop of a sapphire sea, stretching away to the horizon where it met the cobalt blue sky.

If there was a heaven, this was what it would look like, she mused, her senses swamped by the sweet scent of the lavender bushes, where industrious bees buzzed among the long purple spires. The splash of the fountains was the only other sound to break the cloistered quiet, and Gina found herself breathing softly for fear of disturbing the peace and serenity that seemed to envelop her.

It was ten minutes before she found Lanzo. He was sitting on a low stone wall that surrounded a pool, watching the fish swim among the water lilies.

'Daphne told me you were here,' she greeted him, when he swung his head round and saw her hovering uncertainly beneath an archway of jasmine and orange blossom. 'She also said you might not wish to be disturbed—so if you want me to leave…?'

She wished she knew what he was thinking, but as usual his sunglasses hid his eyes. Yet she sensed that his mind was far away—perhaps with his beautiful fiancée? Her heart clenched and she despised herself for her jealousy. The beautiful girl in the portrait must have died tragically young—but of course she did not know, because Lanzo had never spoken of her.

He seemed to drag himself from a distant place and smiled at her. 'Of course I don't want you to leave. What do you think of my garden?'

'There aren't the words,' Gina said simply. 'Being here, surrounded by the flowers and trees, it's like a little piece of heaven on earth.'

She flushed, sure he would mock her, but he was quiet for a few moments.

'That's what I set out to create,' he said slowly. 'A beautiful paradise secluded from the hectic world. A place to reflect and perhaps find peace.'

Gina waited, unconsciously holding her breath as she wondered if he would speak of the girl in the painting, perhaps reveal how she and his parents had died. But he said nothing more.

'Is the garden all your work?' she asked him, unable to hide her surprise at the idea that *he* had been responsible for the expert landscaping.

He laughed. 'Hardly—it covers two acres, and I employ a team of gardeners to tend it. But in the beginning I did a lot of the spadework.' It had been strangely cathartic, digging the soil where once his family home had stood. He had come here day after day and worked until he was physically exhausted, but nothing had banished the dreams where he heard Cristina's voice begging him to save her and their unborn child.

He saw that Gina was staring at him. 'Why are you looking at me as if I've grown another head?'

'I don't get you,' she admitted frankly. 'I can't equate the daredevil playboy who loves dangerous sports like sky-diving with the man who counts gardening as one of his hobbies.'

He shrugged. 'But I don't need you to understand me, *cara*.'

Gina knew he had not meant to be deliberately hurtful, and that made it worse—because his careless comment was deeply wounding. She had known from the start that he only wanted an affair with her. Just because sometimes in the aftermath of their lovemaking she felt closer to him than she had to any other human being it did not mean that he felt the same way.

Lanzo never revealed his emotions. But presumably he must have been in love once, and that was why the portrait of his fiancée was displayed in the hallway of his house—so that her face was the first thing he saw every time he walked through the door.

Gina had sat down on the wall near to Lanzo, but now she jerked to her feet, wishing she had the nerve to ask him about his past. But why would he confide in her when he regarded her as just another temporary mistress? she thought bitterly. And why did she care? It wasn't as if he meant anything to her. In a few months his usual PA would return to work for him, and once Luisa was back Gina would leave him and get on with her life.

Oh, *hell*. Why did that thought hurt so much? And why was her head spinning again? Or was it the ground beneath her feet that was moving, tilting so that she was falling into blackness?

'Gina!'

Lanzo's voice came from far away. And then there was nothing.

'I *do not* need to see a doctor. I can't believe you've called the poor man out when it's obvious I must have fainted because I haven't eaten for hours.'

Gina glared at Lanzo, infuriated when he gave her a bland smile and pushed her gently back down so that she was lying on the sofa.

'I'm surprised you didn't break your back, carrying me to the house,' she muttered. 'I'm no lightweight.'

'Stop talking and lie quietly,' he advised her, a nuance in his tone warning her that she was wasting her breath arguing with him. 'You've been feeling unwell for a week, and it's sensible to have a check-up. The doctor is here now,' he said, getting to his feet at the sound of Daphne's voice, followed by a deeper tone, coming from the hall.

To Gina's annoyance Lanzo did not leave the room while the doctor took her blood pressure.

'That all seems fine,' the elderly doctor assured her. 'You say you have never fainted before?'

'Never—' Gina said firmly.

'But Signorina Bailey has felt dizzy on several occasions during the past week or so,' Lanzo interrupted.

'There could be a number of causes,' the doctor mused, 'one of which is pregnancy. Is there a possibility—?'

'No.' Gina cut him off. 'No possibility at all.' The words of the gynaecologist she had seen when she had still been married to Simon echoed in her head.

'I'm afraid the scarring caused by the endometriosis means that your only real hope of having a child is with IVF.'

'It's out of the question,' she insisted, when Dottore Casatelli gave her a searching glance.

'Well, there are many other reasons for feeling faint—anaemia is certainly a possibility. I suggest you come to my surgery so that I can perform a simple blood test.'

Gina nodded, her mind only half concentrating on what the doctor was saying as she did some mental arithmetic. Her period was late—over a week late—and she was amazed she hadn't noticed. When she had been trying for a baby with Simon she had plotted the exact date, almost the exact hour, her period should start, and being even a day late had sent her rushing to buy a pregnancy test kit—only to have her hopes dashed every time. Undoubtedly this was just a blip in her cycle.

She glanced distractedly at Lanzo when he excused himself to answer a phone call. After he had left the room she smiled politely at the doctor as he stood and picked up his medical bag, but her smile turned to a look of puzzlement when he handed her a small package.

'I don't need to do a pregnancy test,' she insisted. 'I suffer from a medical condition that makes it virtually impossible for me to conceive.'

'And yet sometimes the impossible is possible after all,' the doctor said gently. 'Do the test, *signorina*, if only so that we can eliminate pregnancy as a reason for your dizzy spells.'

It was a complete waste of time, Gina thought to herself half an hour later, as she sat on the edge of the marble bath and waited for the required two minutes to tick past. Fortunately Lanzo was holding a conference call with his office in Japan, and she had slipped upstairs to carry out the pregnancy test without his knowledge.

It was stupid to feel nervous. It was habit, she supposed.

In the past she had carried out dozens of tests, and had paced the bathroom feeling sick with a mixture of excitement and desperate hope that she would receive the result she was praying for. Of course this time she hoped the result would be negative—or rather not hoped, but simply assumed that she could not be pregnant. She checked her watch and leaned forward to look at the test—and felt her heart slam against her ribs.

Pregnant 5+. Only she wasn't. The test was wrong.

Thankfully the kit contained a second test, but her hands were shaking so much that she fumbled to rip off the packaging and carry out the instructions. A sense of numbness settled over Gina as she watched the hand on her watch crawl round. This time the result would be negative, and that would be for the best—because she wasn't in a position to have a baby right now. As for Lanzo… Well, she dared not contemplate what his reaction would be—but it was ridiculous to worry because she *wasn't* pregnant. The gynaecologist had been very gentle when she had explained that both her fallopian tubes were blocked.

The two minutes were up. Taking a deep breath, she checked the test—and disbelief slowly turned to incandescent joy as she stared at the word 'pregnant' in the result box.

Lanzo had gone out on his motorbike, Daphne informed Gina after she had plucked up the courage to go downstairs and face him. Her sense of relief that she had been given a brief reprieve before she broke her astounding news soon turned to dread at the thought of him hurtling at breakneck speed along the narrow road that corkscrewed along the coast. What if he had an accident and was thrown over the cliff-edge onto the jagged rocks below?

Stop it, she ordered herself firmly. Lanzo knew what he was doing. But he had told her that he did not fear death.

She stared out of the window at the sea sparkling in the summer sunshine and felt a shiver run through her at the idea of Lanzo being injured—or worse. She would have to bring up her child alone. But perhaps she would be doing that anyway, her brain pointed out. She might be overjoyed about this baby, but there was a possibility that Lanzo would not feel the same way.

By the time she heard the throb of the motorbike engine almost an hour later her nerves were as taut as an over-strung bow. Wiping her damp palms down her jeans, she hurried out to the hall just as he walked through the front door, and despite her tension she did not miss the way his eyes went immediately to the portrait of his dead fiancée. Neither did she miss the fact that he looked lethally sexy in his black biker leathers, and she closed her eyes briefly, wishing he did not make her feel like an over-awed eighteen-year-old.

Lanzo studied Gina's pale face and frowned. 'Are you feeling dizzy again?' he demanded, concern sweeping through him. He was puzzled too, wondering why she seemed distinctly on edge, and he noted that she was carefully avoiding his gaze. 'What's wrong, *cara*?'

'I need to talk to you.' She swallowed and glanced at the painting of his fiancée. 'But not here.'

'Come into my study.'

Gina would have preferred the lounge; his study was too formal, somehow, to discuss something as personal as the fact that she had conceived his child. When he closed the door she felt a crazy impulse to wrench it open again and run away.

He rounded his desk and sat down, indicating that she should do the same. But she remained standing, and it struck her as she darted him a nervous glance how forbidding he seemed, with his hard jaw and slashing cheekbones, and those curious green eyes that at this moment were coolly assessing her.

'What is the matter, Gina?' he asked again.

Her heart was thumping, and she was sure it could not be good for the baby. Dear heaven, she thought shakily, the baby—she was going to have a *baby*. It still seemed unreal.

She took a deep breath and met his gaze. 'I'm...pregnant. The doctor gave me a pregnancy test—he said it would be a good idea to rule out the possibility,' she continued quickly, when Lanzo made no response. For once he wasn't wearing sunglasses, but she still had no idea what he was thinking. She wished he would say something; his silence was shredding her nerves. 'It...the test...was positive.'

Everything inside Lanzo rejected Gina's shocking statement. For a few seconds his brain simply would not accept it could be true, but common sense told him there was no reason why she would have made it up. His next thought was to acknowledge that he did not want it to be true. But it seemed that fate could not give a damn about what he wanted, he thought savagely.

She was watching him, and seemed to be waiting for him to say something. What was he supposed to say? *Congratulations?* he wondered sardonically. *How wonderful? Dio*, he felt as though his life had ended—and in a way it had, he realised grimly. Because, whatever happened now, his life was never going to be quite the same. If Gina was really expecting his child, he would be responsible for her and the baby.

He felt trapped by the situation that had been thrust upon him, and a feeling of mingled dread and panic filled him. Fifteen years ago he had failed to protect his fiancée and his unborn child. He knew he could not have prevented the fire, but if he had stayed at home with Cristina, as she had begged him to do, he could have saved all of them. He would have married the woman he had loved, his parents would have seen their grandchild, and his child would now be a teenager.

The familiar feeling of guilt that he had not been there for Cristina surged through him. The pain of losing her had almost destroyed him, and he had vowed that he would never allow himself to care for anyone else. He did not allow himself to feel emotions, and he was certain he would feel nothing for the child Gina had told him she was carrying.

'How could it happen?' he asked harshly. There had only been that first night when they had become lovers when he had not used protection, but she had assured him it was safe. 'You told me you were on the pill.'

'I...' Gina frowned, startled by his assertion. 'I didn't say that.'

'You said there was no risk,' he drawled, in a dangerously soft tone.

She had expected him to be angry, Gina acknowledged. He had a typical Latin temperament, and she had steeled herself for a blast of his explosive temper. Nothing had prepared her for this cold, controlled fury.

'I didn't mean that I was on the pill....' Gina bit her lip. 'When I told you there was no risk that I could fall pregnant I was absolutely certain that was true,' she said urgently. 'I believed I was infertile. I...I tried for over a year to have a baby with Simon, and when nothing happened I had various tests which revealed that I have a condition called endometriosis. It's a common cause of infertility, and further tests showed that my fallopian tubes were so badly scarred that my only hope of having a child was with medical intervention such as IVF.'

She pushed her hair back from her face with a shaky hand and stared at Lanzo, silently pleading for him to understand. 'This baby...' She swallowed the tears that clogged her throat. 'The fact that I am pregnant is nothing short of a miracle, and although I accept that the circumstances are not ideal, I have to be honest and tell you that I am overjoyed that my dream of having a baby might come true.'

He stared back at her, his face hard and implacable, his eyes still coldly accusing. 'It might be *your* dream,' he said harshly, 'but it is not mine. I do not want a child, and I have always taken scrupulous care to ensure that I would not father one. The fact that you have accidentally fallen pregnant does not alter how I feel.'

A child needed to be loved, but he had no love inside him, Lanzo brooded. All his emotions had withered and died the night of the fire, and it would be better for the child Gina carried to grow up without him instead of yearning for the father's love that he simply could not give.

Gina shivered, reaction setting in both to the astounding news that she was expecting Lanzo's baby and his insistence that he did not want a child. She did not know what she had expected from him. It was only natural that he was shocked by her news, but she had assumed that once he had grown used to the idea they would discuss how they would bring the baby up—together.

A wave of fierce maternal protectiveness surged through Gina. *She* wanted the fragile life nestled inside her, and she would love and care for her child on her own. Lanzo need not be involved in any way. But it was only fair to make clear to him that—fate willing—she *was* going to have this baby.

'I'm sorry you feel that way,' she said quietly. 'But the fact is that because of the endometriosis this is probably my only chance to be a mother, and nothing could persuade me to terminate my pregnancy.'

Lanzo jerked his head back as if she had slapped him. '*Dio*, I do not expect that,' he said, as shocked as he had been minutes earlier, when she had told him she was pregnant.

The idea was repugnant to him. But did that mean then that he *wanted* her to have his child? He could not think straight. His brain was reeling. He stood up abruptly, the sound of his chair legs scraping on the tiled floor shattering the tense silence.

'I accept that I am partly responsible for the problem,' he said tersely. 'When I come back we will discuss a financial settlement for the child.'

His stark words caused something inside Gina to shatter. 'Come back from where?' she asked shakily.

'I'm going out on the bike.' He had already snatched up his crash helmet, and did not look at her as he strode towards the door.

Fear that he would ride too fast turned to a slow-burning anger that he was prepared to walk away from his child.

'That's right—go and endanger your life for the sheer hell of it,' she said bitterly. 'That just about sums you up, Lanzo—you'd do anything to avoid a discussion that might in any way involve your emotions.'

He stopped dead and jerked his head round, his face so dark with fury that she took an involuntary step backwards. But as the silence stretched between them the expression in his eyes changed and became bleak, almost haunted. Without another word he strode out of the room, slamming the door behind him with such force that the sound echoed in her head long after he had gone.

CHAPTER EIGHT

RICHARD MELTON and his wife, Sarah—Gina's stepsister—lived in a recently built house on the outskirts of Poole. Lanzo parked in the narrow cul-de-sac and glanced at the six identical houses built in a semi-circle. The Meltons lived at number four. As he walked up the path to the front door he could see a baby's crib in the front living room, and he felt his heart give a curious little lurch, even though he knew that it was not *his* child sleeping within the wicker basket.

The Meltons' baby was two months old: a boy, so Gina had informed him during their one short telephone conversation, when he had struggled to hear her over the high-pitched wailing of a newborn infant. That had been pretty well all that she had said—apart from explaining that she had not answered his calls to her mobile because she did not want to speak to him.

There had been little point in him tracking down her whereabouts through her brother-in-law, she had told him coldly. For, desperate to find her, Lanzo had recalled that Richard Melton ran a company called Nautica World, and he had eventually persuaded the other man to give him a phone number where he could contact Gina, on the strict understanding that he did not upset her.

They had nothing to say to one another, she had continued, her voice stiff with pride. She was well, and there were no problems with her pregnancy—an early scan had shown that she was eight weeks pregnant—and she was managing just fine, thank you. She would appreciate it if he did not phone again.

What did she expect him to do? Twiddle his thumbs for the next seven months and hope she remembered to send him a 'baby's arrived' card? That was probably what she *did* expect him to do, he thought heavily as he pressed the front doorbell. Certainly he had not expected her to have left his home in Positano when he'd returned from racing his motorbike along the winding road that hugged the Amalfi Coast. He had only been gone for an hour, needing time to come to terms with her announcement that she was expecting his baby. His shock had receded now, but his fundamental feeling had not changed. He still did not want to be a father.

A harassed-looking woman clutching a toddler in her arms opened the front door.

'Yes, Gina's in,' Sarah Melton admitted begrudgingly, eyeing him with deep suspicion when he introduced himself. 'But I'm not sure she'll want to see you.'

'Why don't we allow Gina to decide for herself?' Lanzo said, polite but determined, edging his foot over the doorstep as he spoke. He frowned as the unmistakable sound of somebody being sick came from upstairs.

'She's in the loo—throwing up. It's a pretty regular occurrence,' Sarah said wryly. 'You'd better come in and wait.'

Gina wiped her face with a damp flannel, her whole body trembling from the effort of losing her lunch twenty minutes after she had eaten it. The same thing had happened after breakfast. At this rate she might as well cut out the middle man and simply flush her meals down the toilet, she thought dismally.

'Unfortunately a small percentage of women suffer from extreme morning sickness,' her GP had explained. 'And, as you are no doubt aware, it is not only limited to mornings. Your baby will be perfectly all right,' he'd reassured her, when she had been close to tears, terrified that she might miscarry the baby. 'All I can recommend is plenty of fluids, small meals, and plenty of rest.'

Out of the three, she was just about managing the fluids. Food of any type bounced back with tedious regularity, and as for resting—it was proving impossible to sleep when she was so worried about how she was going to manage as a single mother, and if she did manage to drop off in the early hours her dreams were haunted by Lanzo.

She opened the bathroom door and staggered along the landing to the tiny boxroom where Sarah and Richard had put up a camp bed for her, after she had fled from Lanzo's home in Italy and arrived back in Poole, homeless and distraught.

Golden late-September sunshine was streaming through the window, so that the tall figure standing by the bed was silhouetted against the light. But the broad shoulders and the proud tilt of his head were instantly recognizable, and she stopped dead in the doorway, acute shock causing her heart to beat so fast that she could feel it jerking against her ribs.

'What are you doing here?' she demanded, cursing herself for the distinct wobble in her voice.

'We need to talk,' Lanzo said steadily.

His deep, sensual accent tugged on her heartstrings, and she hated the fact that the sight of him, after three weeks apart, made her knees feel weak. It did not help that he looked utterly gorgeous, in black jeans and matching polo shirt, topped with a butter-soft tan leather jacket. His hair was shorter than she remembered, gleaming like raw silk in the sunlight, and his face was all angles and planes, softened by the beautifully shaped mouth that she had a vivid recall of moving hungrily over her lips when he kissed her.

From his shocked expression it was clear that kissing her was not on his agenda now, she thought grimly. She caught sight of her reflection in the mirror and saw what he could see—grey skin, dull eyes with great purple smudges beneath them, and lank hair scraped back in a ponytail.

'You look terrible,' he said bluntly, as if he could not hold back the words.

Despite telling herself she didn't care what he thought of her, tears stung her eyes. 'I doubt you would look so great if you were sick a dozen times a day,' she muttered.

Lanzo frowned. 'I know sickness is common in early pregnancy, but is it normal to be sick so frequently?'

'Do you care?' Pride was her only shield against the note of concern in his voice. He had made it clear that he did not care about her or the baby, she reminded herself.

He sighed heavily. '*Si*, I care about your well-being, Gina. That is why I am here—to make sure that you have everything you need.' He glanced around the cramped room, at the uncomfortable-looking camp bed and at her clothes piled on a chair and spilling out of her suitcase because there was no space to put a wardrobe.

'Your brother-in-law told me you are living here.'

'Temporarily,' Gina said shortly. 'If you remember, I rented out my flat when I started working for you, and the tenancy agreement runs until December.'

'So, do you then plan to move back into your flat? I thought there was a mortgage on it. How do you intend to meet the monthly payments when the baby is born and you cannot work?' Lanzo pushed for answers to the questions that had been circling endlessly in Gina's mind since her mad dash back to England. She avoided his gaze and sank weakly down onto the camp bed, which creaked alarmingly.

'I'm going to sell the flat and buy somewhere...' She had been about to say *cheaper*, but she refused to reveal her money worries to Lanzo and so mumbled, 'Somewhere more suitable to bring up the baby.'

He stared speculatively at her pale face and his stomach clenched. She looked so fragile, so unlike the strong-willed, confident Gina he was used to. His eyes dropped to her flat stomach. If anything she looked thinner than he remembered—perhaps not surprising, if she was being sick numerous times a day. He wondered if she was eating properly, getting the necessary vitamins and nutrients for the baby to develop. It was hard to believe that his child was growing within her when there were no outward signs of her pregnancy, he mused. Yet he sensed a difference in her—a vulnerability that filled him with guilt.

'Are you working?' he asked abruptly, thinking that her obvious tiredness might be because she was overdoing things.

Gina twisted her fingers together, tension churning inside her. 'Not at the moment,' she admitted. 'It's been impossible to look for a job when I'm constantly being sick. But hopefully I'll feel better in another week or so, and then...' She tailed off, trying to imagine how she would cope with holding down a full-time job when she had no energy and felt like a limp rag.

'So how are you managing financially?'

'I have some savings.' That were dwindling fast—but she was not going to tell Lanzo that. 'Look,' she said, jumping to her feet and immediately wishing she hadn't when the room swayed, 'I don't know why you're here...'

Her legs were so stupidly wobbly. She felt her knees give way, but before she fell Lanzo was beside her, sliding his arm around her waist to support her. The scent of his aftershave assailed her senses and she felt a crazy longing to rest her cheek against his broad chest and absorb some of his strength.

'I am here because it is my responsibility to help you,' he murmured.

She rejected his words violently, jerking away from him. 'No. I am *not* your responsibility, and neither is my baby. You made it clear that you don't want your child.'

Lanzo glimpsed the hurt in her eyes and sighed heavily. 'Sit down, *cara*, before you fall down.' He helped her back down onto the camp bed and hunkered down next to her. 'I did some research about the condition you suffer from, and I accept that you were convinced you were infertile because of the damage done by endometriosis,' he said quietly.

'I was about to start a course of IVF when I was with Simon, but our marriage was struggling as his drink problem grew worse and I knew it wouldn't be fair to bring a child into that situation,' she explained huskily. 'I believed I would never have a baby. But now I have this one chance, I'm terrified something is going to go wrong,' she whispered, her deepest fears spilling out. 'I know you don't want a child, but I don't think I could bear it if I lost this baby.'

Once again her vulnerability evoked an ache inside Lanzo, but he knew his limitations—knew he could not give her the emotional support she needed—and so he resisted the urge to take her in his arms and hold her close while he soothed her fears.

'I am not capable of being a father,' he told her harshly.

Startled blue eyes flew to his face. 'What do you mean? There's no question that this is your baby. You're the only man I've slept with since Simon—and that side of our marriage ended long before the divorce,' she added heavily.

'I'm not denying that you are carrying my child.' A corner of Lanzo's mind registered that he had been her only lover after she had ended her relationship with her abusive husband, and he wondered why the knowledge made him so inordinately pleased.

'I cannot love a child. I cannot love anyone—it is simply not part of my psyche,' he insisted, irritated by the flash of sympathy in her eyes. 'It's not a problem, *cara*. I like the fact that my life is free from the emotional debris that most people have to deal with. But I realise that a child needs to feel loved, and I'm sure you would agree that it would not be fair on this baby to grow up yearning for something I cannot give it.'

'But...' Gina stared at him, utterly nonplussed by his shocking confession. She had thought that he exerted iron control over his emotions, but according to Lanzo he did not *have* the normal range of emotions most people had, and it was impossible for him to love anyone—even his own child. 'Daphne told me that you were once engaged—to the girl whose portrait hangs in the hallway of the Villa di Sussurri. Didn't—didn't you love *her*?' she faltered.

His hard face was expressionless, but she sensed the sudden tension that gripped him. 'That was a long time ago. I was a different person then to the man I am now,' he said harshly.

Lanzo rose to his feet and took the two steps needed to cross the small room to the window, which overlooked the neat front lawn and the five other neat front lawns of the other houses in the cul-de-sac.

'Although I cannot be a proper father, I have a duty to

provide financial security for our child, and for you. Yes,'
he said firmly when Gina opened her mouth to argue. 'It
is the one thing I can give—the one part I can play in our
child's life. And you need my help.' He glanced at her, so
pale and strained, sitting on the precarious camp bed. From
downstairs came the sound of a baby crying, mingled with
the yells of two small children, and Gina's stepsister's raised
voice.

'It cannot be ideal living here—for you or your family.
I want you to live at my house on Sandbanks. You won't
be able to sleep on this contraption in a few months, when
your pregnancy is more advanced,' he pointed out, glancing again at the camp bed. 'There are five bedrooms at
Ocean View House, and a big garden for when the baby is
walking.'

'Walking! That won't be for a couple of years from now.'
Gina had a sudden image of a toddler taking his or her first
steps, and she felt a mixture of joyful anticipation and fear
for the future.

She still couldn't quite believe she was pregnant. Her GP,
who was aware of her medical history, had agreed it was
nothing short of a miracle that she had conceived naturally,
and she was acutely conscious that this could be her only
chance to have a baby. *Please let me carry the baby full-
term and let it be born safely,* she prayed silently.

But right now there were other problems to be dealt
with. She looked at Lanzo. 'I can't stay at your house all
that time.'

'It will be your house,' he told her. 'Yours and the
baby's—I have already instructed my lawyer to arrange for
the deeds to be transferred to your name. And naturally I
will cover all your living costs.'

'I don't want your money,' she said sharply.

'Cara...' He admired her stubborn pride, but she had

to accept that she needed him. 'Let me help you—for our child's sake. I've explained why I feel it is better if I am not involved in its upbringing, but I want you and the baby to live comfortably. You can't say you are doing that here— however welcoming your stepsister and her husband might be,' he said gently.

He had cleverly brought up the subject that was on her mind constantly, for there was no doubt that although she and Sarah had always got on well it was awkward staying here, and Gina felt that she was imposing on her stepsister's goodwill. It wasn't even as if she was much help with the new baby and her other two nephews when she spent so much time being sick, she acknowledged ruefully.

But how could she live in Lanzo's house and allow him to support her financially? It went against everything she believed in. She was proud of the fact that she had always worked since she had left school, and always paid her own way. She could not work at the moment, though. No employer would take her on when she had to rush to the toilet every half an hour.

'It would be a great help if I could live at Ocean View at least until after the baby is born,' she said quietly. 'But as soon as the morning sickness has passed I will look for a job.'

Lanzo frowned. 'There is no need for you to work.'

'Yes, there is. I don't really understand why you feel that you can't be a proper father to the baby,' she admitted, 'but I will love him or her enough for both of us. If you wish to support our child financially that's up to you, but I have never cared about your money, Lanzo.'

She pushed away the thought that she cared too much about *him*. If he could not love his own child he was hardly likely to fall in love with her. There wasn't much point in denying that she had secretly hoped he would, she thought bleakly. For whatever reason—and she suspected it had a lot to do with losing his fiancée—Lanzo believed that he was incapable of loving anyone, and she would just have to accept that fact.

To Gina's surprise, everything proved to be so much easier than she had expected. Lanzo helped her pack her clothes, and took her to his house on Sandbanks the same day he had turned up out of the blue at her stepsister's house. She did not know what he'd said to Sarah and Richard, but when she walked downstairs, clutching a carrier bag stuffed with hastily packed toiletries, they were chatting to him as if he were a long-lost brother—and she detected Sarah's relief that she was moving into his house, thereby freeing up the spare room.

'Daphne is going to stay here to cook and run the house,' Lanzo explained when the housekeeper greeted them at the front door of Ocean View, and led them into the lounge where she served a gorgeous tea of scones, jam and rich clotted cream.

'Maybe three scones was pushing my luck,' Gina said ruefully, emerging from the bathroom a short while later, after losing most of the meal.

Lanzo looked grimly at her wan face. 'You can't carry on like this. It's not good for you or the baby.'

'My GP assures me that the baby won't be affected, however many times a day I'm sick. It will take all the nutrients it needs from the small amount of food I manage to keep down. As long as the baby is okay, I don't care about me,' she said cheerfully, unaware that she resembled a fragile ghost to Lanzo's concerned eyes.

'Daphne will prepare you lots of small meals, and she is under orders to make sure you get plenty of rest,' he told her, the following morning as he was about to leave for a business trip. 'I'm going to New York to check on the progress of building work after the fire, and from there down to Florida, before I fly to Moscow. But I'll keep in contact.'

It was on the tip of her tongue to assure him that it was not necessary for him to phone her. She accepted that he did not want to have a role in their baby's life, and there was no reason for him to call her. But part of her—the silly, emotional part, she thought derisively—was glad that he intended to keep in touch...even if it was only through the occasional phone call. So she changed the subject and asked curiously, 'Are you planning to open a Di Cosimo restaurant in Florida?'

He slung his case onto the back seat of his car and glanced at her standing on the front steps of the house. 'No, I'm competing in a powerboat race in Miami.'

Gina bit her lip. Only recently the son of a well-known English multimillionaire had been killed when his powerboat had flipped over during a race. The story had been headline news, and she had felt sick when she had read it. It was stupid to wish that Lanzo would stay here with her, at his beautiful house overlooking the harbour, and wait for their baby to be born. He would probably die of boredom, she thought sadly. He was addicted to dangerous sports and he was not interested in the baby.

She bit back the words *be careful*, and said coolly, 'Have fun.'

Lanzo nodded and slid behind the wheel of the car, wondering why he felt a sudden urge to send one of his staff to New York. Gina would be perfectly all right with Daphne to take care of her, he reminded himself. Ocean View, like all his houses, had the most up-to-date fire alarm and sprinkler system fitted. Nothing could happen to her. But she looked so forlorn as she waved to him, and he was reminded suddenly of the day ten years ago, when he had dropped her back to her father's farm and told her that he was returning to Italy.

He recalled the shock in her eyes, the shimmer of tears that she had blinked fiercely to dispel, and remembered feeling the same hollow ache inside that he felt now. Of course he had known she was in love with him. It was one reason why he had decided to leave Poole, for he had not wanted to hurt her. It was only when he had brushed his mouth over hers in one last kiss and felt her tremble with emotion that he had realised he had probably broken her heart. But she was young—only eighteen and just starting out on life's journey—he had told himself as he had driven away. She would soon get over him.

And clearly she had—and had gone on to have a good career, get married... His jaw hardened when he thought of the scar on her neck caused by her alcoholic ex-husband. Gina was a beautiful person, inside and out, and she deserved a far better life than she had had with Simon. But instead she had conceived *his* child, and he had bluntly told her that he could not give her any emotional support. He had given her a house and an allowance, to appease his conscience, and was about to drive off and leave her to cope with her pregnancy alone.

What else could he do? he thought savagely as he swung out of the front gates and glanced back at her in his rearview mirror. There was an empty void inside him where his heart had once been, and it would be better for all of them if he remained a remote figure in Gina and the baby's lives. Maybe she would meet someone else in the future—some guy who would love her as she deserved to be loved. After all, he could not expect her to live the life of a nun, he reasoned.

The thought turned his mood to one of simmering black

fury, and when he reached the motorway he pressed his foot down on the accelerator pedal and shot into the fast lane.

Gina watched Lanzo's car turn out of the drive and then slowly walked back into the house, fighting the stupid urge to burst into tears. After his furious reaction when she had told him she was pregnant, she had left his villa in Positano within the hour and assumed that she would never see or hear from him again. She was still reeling from the shock of him turning up in Poole yesterday. Once again he had hurtled into her life like a tornado, and before she could blink she had found herself agreeing to live at his house on Sandbanks.

She could not deny that it was a relief not to have to worry about where she and the baby would live, but seeing Lanzo again had forced her to acknowledge that she had committed the ultimate folly and fallen in love with him. They had been friends as well as lovers, and the weeks she had worked for him and travelled the world with him had been the happiest time of her life, she thought softly, her heart aching as memories of laughter, long conversations, and nights of heady passion assailed her.

Now he had gone again, and part of her wished he had never sought her out—because for a few hope-filled moments she had assumed that he had come because he wanted her and the baby, and the realisation that the only part he intended to play in her life was that of benefactor had shattered her dreams.

She wandered aimlessly into the lounge and watched a fishing boat chug out of the harbour. A few minutes later Daphne came in, carrying a tray.

'I've brought you a snack. Hopefully you'll keep it down,' the housekeeper said with a sympathetic smile.

'Thank you.' Gina hesitated. 'Daphne, what happened to Lanzo's fiancée—I mean...how did she die?'

Daphne lively face instantly became shuttered. 'There was a terrible accident. Cristina and Lanzo's parents were all killed.' She hurried over to the door. 'Excuse me—I've left something in the oven,' she muttered, and disappeared before Gina could question her further.

Why was Daphne so reluctant to talk about what had happened? she wondered frustratedly. And why did Lanzo never mention his past? It must have been devastating to lose the woman he planned to marry and his parents, in one terrible event. She was sure that the accident was the key to understanding why he had locked his emotions away, but the only two people who knew what had happened refused to speak.

Lanzo phoned from New York and told her that the fire-damaged restaurant had been refitted and would open the following week. He phoned again from Miami, to say that he had won the powerboat race, and a few days later he called from Moscow, where he was planning to open another Di Cosimo restaurant.

As the weeks slipped by he settled into a pattern of phoning two or three times a week, and Gina looked forward to his calls. Lucky him, to be in the hot sunshine of the Caribbean when October storms were lashing the English south coast, she told him. And did he really expect her to be sympathetic because he was melting in the forty-degree heat in Perth, when she had woken up to find a white blanket of frost covering the lawn at Ocean View?

His husky laugh evoked a warm feeling inside her that banished the gloom of the cold November day. Somehow it was easier to talk to him when he was thousands of miles away. Released from her intense physical awareness of him, she was able to relax and chat to him with the easy friendship that they had shared when she had been his PA.

Her morning sickness gradually subsided, and as her energy levels shot up she was glad to find a part-time job as secretary to a local councillor.

'I'm not overdoing it,' she told Lanzo, when he sounded distinctly unenthusiastic about her new job. 'The most strenuous activity I do is walk across the office to the filing cabinet.'

'There's no need for you to work,' Lanzo growled as he stared out of his hotel window in Bangkok. He was tempted to catch the next available flight to England, to check that Gina really was as fit and well as she assured him. 'Why don't you use the money I've put into the bank account I opened for you?'

'I prefer to pay my own way,' she said crisply. She was determined not to touch his money, and it was lucky that she was earning again—because time had flown past and she was now nearly five months pregnant, with a sizeable bump. She loved wandering around the mother-and-baby shops, choosing maternity clothes as well as tiny newborn-sized vests and sleepsuits that she put away in the room she had decided would be the nursery.

She could not believe her pregnancy was passing so quickly, she mused, when she woke up on Christmas Day and ticked off another week on her calendar. Her due date was at the end of April, and she was finally daring to believe that the miracle *would* happen and she would soon be holding her baby in her arms.

She half expected Lanzo to call on Christmas morning, and delayed leaving for lunch with her family, hating herself for hovering near the phone. He had told her he was spending the festive period in Rome, mainly because his new PA—who was filling in until Luisa returned from maternity leave—lived in the city. He was snowed under with work at the moment, and Raphaella had agreed to come over to his apartment to help him catch up on paperwork.

She bit her lip. Maybe Raphaella, who had sounded incredibly sexy when she had answered Lanzo's mobile phone once, when Gina had called to tell him that her second scan had been fine, was helping him with more than his paperwork? He had a high sex-drive, and it was impossible to believe he had spent the past few months celibate.

The idea of him making love to another woman made her stomach churn, and she pulled on her coat and wrenched open the front door, desperate to be with people who cared for her, rather than alone with her jealous thoughts.

'Happy Christmas, *cara*.'

'L…Lanzo?' The disbelief in her voice caused his lips to curve into a lazy smile.

'Well, I'm definitely not Babbo Natale.'

'I guessed that by the lack of red suit and long white beard,' she said huskily, her heart thudding as her eyes roamed over his pale jeans and the chunky oatmeal-coloured sweater beneath his suede jacket. 'What are you doing here? I mean…' She flushed, remembering how she had imagined him getting close and personal with the sexy-sounding Raphaella. 'I thought you were in Rome.'

Lanzo had thought of half a dozen excuses for why he needed to come to England, but as he stared at Gina, struck by how beautiful she looked in a wine-coloured soft woollen dress that clung to the rounded contours of her breasts and the swollen mound of her stomach, he could not deny the truth.

'I wanted to spend Christmas with you,' he said simply.

Shock rendered Gina speechless, but a little bubble of happiness formed inside her, and grew and grew until it seemed to encompass every inch of her. She wanted to throw herself into his arms and kiss him, until he kissed her back and then carried her into the house and upstairs to bed. But the thought that he would struggle to carry her more than a few feet now that she had gained weight, combined with the fear that he would not find her pregnant shape attractive, stopped her. Instead she smiled, and her heart lurched when he smiled back, his green eyes gleaming as he walked up the front steps.

Reality caught up with her. 'I'm supposed to be having lunch with Dad and Linda. There's not much to eat here, because Daphne has gone to visit her sister for Christmas and I told her not to stock up the larder as I would be with my family.'

Lanzo shrugged. 'I don't expect you to change your arrangements for me. Go to your family, and I'll see you later.'

Gina shook her head. 'You can't spend Christmas Day alone.' She hesitated. 'You could come with me, if you like. I know my stepmother won't mind—she always cooks enough to feed an army anyway. Sarah and Hazel and their families will be there.' She gave him a rueful smile. 'It will be hectic, but fun. But if you'd rather not…'

It had been more than fifteen years since Lanzo had enjoyed Christmas with his parents and Cristina. He was glad he had not known at the time that it would be the last Christmas he would ever spend with them.

He pushed the memories to the back of his mind and smiled at Gina. 'I'd love to come,' he said softly. 'Does your father drink wine? I've got six bottles of a rather excellent burgundy in the boot of my car.'

CHAPTER NINE

GINA had fallen asleep on the sofa. It was hardly surprising after an enormous lunch and a noisy afternoon playing with her nephews and nieces, Lanzo mused. Christmas with her family had been as hectic as she had warned, but after an initial few minutes of awkwardness on all sides he had been surprised by how warmly he had been received by her father, stepmother, and stepsisters.

He stretched out his long legs and watched the twinkling fairy lights on the tree Gina had put up in the lounge at Ocean View. He never bothered with tinsel and baubles and all the other tacky decorations that came with the festive season. Whether he spent Christmas at his villa in Positano or at his apartment in Rome, the day meant nothing to him. It was a time of celebration, of families coming together, but he had no family.

He thought again of how welcome he had been made to feel by Gina's family. This time next year the baby would be here, but he would not come to England to spend Christmas with his child. It wouldn't be fair when he could not be a proper, loving father—like Gina's stepsisters' husbands were to their children. When he had watched Richard Melton cradling his infant son he had felt guilty, because he knew he would not love his child. Since he had lost Cristina he had hardened his heart and shunned any relationship that might involve his emotions. Nothing touched him, or moved him, and he liked the fact that his life was uncomplicated, he reminded himself.

Gina stirred and turned her head towards Lanzo, but she remained asleep, her long lashes lying against her cheeks and her chest rising and falling steadily. She had always been delightfully curvaceous, but pregnancy had made her breasts fuller—big and rounded beneath her soft woollen dress. The temptation to touch them and feel their weight was so strong that he inhaled sharply, his nostrils flaring as desire corkscrewed through him.

He had been too long without sex, he though grimly. It was months since he had made love to Gina, but he had no inclination to take another mistress. It did not seem right to sleep with another woman when his child was growing inside Gina. Perhaps when the child was born he would find it easier to distance himself from her. But right now all he could think of was peeling her dress down and baring those big, firm breasts. He wondered if her nipples were bigger too, and he shifted his position to try and ease the discomfort of his rock hard erection as he imagined sucking on each dusky crest.

'Lanzo... I'm sorry, I must have dropped off for a few minutes.' Gina opened her eyes, blushing when she realised that she had slid down the sofa so that her head had practically been resting on Lanzo's shoulder. 'You must be bored stiff, sitting here in the dark,' she mumbled, glancing around the shadowed room that was lit only by the colourful lights on the Christmas tree and the flickering flames of the fire.

One area of his anatomy was certainly stiff, he acknowledged derisively. 'I'm not bored, *cara*.' She was like a small soft kitten, snuggled up against him, and his heart gave a curious jerk as he lifted his hand to smooth her hair back from her face. 'It's peaceful, sitting here with you.'

After she had left Positano he had focused on work to prevent himself from thinking about her or the child she carried. Fifteen-hour days and constant travel around the world for Di Cosimo Holdings had allowed him little time to think about anything but business. But despite his self-imposed punishing schedule she had always been on his mind, and their long conversations when he phoned her from one faceless hotel or another had become addictive.

His desire for her had not faded in the months they had been apart. Memories of her gorgeous body had plagued his dreams, and now pregnancy had made her even more voluptuous and desirable.

The tick-tock of the clock on the mantelpiece was the only sound to break the silence. In the dusky dark of the barely lit room Lanzo's eyes gleamed with sensual intent, and Gina caught her breath when he slowly lowered his head. She knew he was going to kiss her, and she knew she should not let him, but she could not move.

Her lips parted.

'*Cara…*' His breath whispered across her skin, and that first brush of his mouth over hers was so sweetly beguiling that tears burned her eyes.

She could not resist him. And that, she thought ruefully, was the problem. She had fallen in love with him when she was eighteen, and deep down she knew that she had never fallen out of love with him.

He had missed her, Lanzo acknowledged, sliding his hand to her nape and angling her head so that he could deepen the kiss. Her lips were soft and moist, opening obediently to the firm probing of his tongue so that he could taste her. Heat flared inside him, and he groaned as hunger clawed in his gut, his body shaking with need. He cupped her breast and stroked his finger over the hard peak of her nipple, jutting beneath her dress, smiling against her lips when he heard her gasp.

Her need was as great as his. She had never been able to hide her intensely passionate nature from him, and her eager response increased his impatience to slide his throbbing shaft between her soft thighs. He moved his hand down and traced the curve of her stomach—and stiffened with shock when he felt a fluttering sensation beneath his fingertips.

'The baby is saying hello,' Gina murmured, feeling another, stronger flutter deep inside her. The sensation of her baby kicking was indescribably beautiful, and she held her hand over Lanzo's so that he could feel it again. 'Maybe he or she recognises their daddy,' she whispered. Her smile faltered when she saw his tense face. 'It's okay. It's quite normal for the baby to kick,' she assured him, thinking that he was worried something was wrong.

Lanzo jerked away from her as if he had been burned. The unguarded hope in her eyes had brought him crashing back to reality, and he raked his hand impatiently through his hair, cursing himself for allowing the situation to get out of hand. He should not have kissed her. But he had never been able to resist her.

'I've told you—I can't be the kind of father you want me to be,' he said harshly. 'I saw you watching your brother-in-law with his baby today, and I knew what you were thinking. But I will feel nothing for the child you are carrying when it is born—just as I feel nothing for anyone.'

'How can you be so certain?' Gina cried. 'When the baby is here you might feel differently.'

'I won't.' He stood up and snapped on one of the table lamps, the bright light it emitted throwing his hard features into sharp relief. He saw the hurt in her eyes and guilt gnawed at him. But there was no point in giving her false hope. 'I don't *want* to care for anyone,' he admitted.

'But why?' Gina ignored the painful tug on her heart. She had never realistically expected him to fall in love with her, but her baby would need its father to nurture and protect it, and most important of all to love it. She caught hold of his arm and clung to him when he would have pulled away.

'I know the way you feel is linked with losing your fiancée and your parents,' she said urgently. 'Daphne told me there had been an accident, but she won't talk about it.' She stared at him, willing him to talk to her and explain *why* he was so sure he could not love their child. But his expression was shuttered, and after a tense few seconds she allowed her hand to fall helplessly to her side and stepped back from him.

'I have to go,' he said roughly.

With stunned eyes she watched him stride over to the door. His jacket was lying on the back of a chair, and when he slung it over his shoulder the realisation sunk in that he was actually leaving.

'Where are you going? It's Christmas Day.' A day that had begun with such joy and hope and was ending in bleak despair. 'Surely there won't be any transport?'

'My private jet is on standby. I'll make a brief stop-over in Rome, before flying to Canada.' Work, as ever, would fill the void inside him. Discussions to open a new restaurant in Toronto would keep his mind occupied for several days.

Gina stumbled after him into the hall. His holdall was still there, where he had dropped it before they had gone to lunch with her family. He picked it up and opened the front door, so that a blast of icy air blew in.

She could not believe he was going. Surely he would turn back to her? Say something? He stepped out into the porch, and as he began to pull the door shut behind him her muscles unlocked and she ran forward.

'*Lanzo!*' She let out a shaky breath when he slowly turned his head, but the dull, dead expression in his eyes tore at her heart. 'Our baby needs you,' she whispered. She swallowed her pride and stared at him pleadingly. '*I* need you.'

He shook his head, as if to dismiss her words. 'I'm sorry, *cara*,' he said quietly, and strode down the steps to his car without looking back.

January brought snow to Dorset. Gina opened the curtains one morning to find that the garden had been transformed into a winter wonderland, and the sight of a red-breasted robin hopping over the white lawn brought a faint smile to her lips for the first time in weeks.

She told Lanzo about the snow when he phoned that evening. It was only the third time he had called since his abrupt departure on Christmas Day, and apart from his warning her not to drive the car if the roads were at all icy their conversation was stilted and painfully polite. She ended the call with the excuse that Daphne was about to serve dinner.

It was frightening how distant he had become, she thought dismally. The easy friendship they had once shared had disappeared, and it seemed as though they were strangers rather than two people who would become parents in a few short months. But Lanzo had been adamant that he would not be a father to their child. His only input would be to send regular cheques—presumably to appease his conscience, she thought bitterly.

The snow did not last for more than a few days before it turned to slush, and winter continued as grey and miserable as Gina's mood. And then one morning she woke to find that the bed was wet. Puzzled, she threw back the sheet—and for a moment her heart stopped beating, before she screamed for Daphne to come quickly.

'Explain to me exactly what placenta previa means?' Lanzo demanded, his jaw rigid with tension as spoke to the doctor in the hospital corridor outside the ward where Gina had been brought by ambulance earlier in the day.

'You are Miss Bailey's partner, I understand?' the doctor said, glancing down at his notes.

'*Si.*' Lanzo could not hide him impatience. 'I am the father of her child.' A father who had been hundreds of miles away in Rome when he had received Daphne's urgent phone call to tell him that Gina had been rushed into hospital because she was bleeding heavily, he thought grimly. He swallowed, and found that for some reason it hurt his throat to do so. 'There is no danger that Gina could lose the baby?'

'Fortunately the bleeding has stopped. But an ultrasound scan has revealed that your partner's placenta is lying partially across the cervix, which means that Miss Bailey will be unable to give birth naturally because of the risk of her haemorrhaging. She will need to have a Caesarean section,' the doctor continued. 'If there is no further bleeding, and Miss Bailey has bedrest for the next few weeks, I would hope that she can reach thirty-seven or thirty-eight weeks before the baby needs to be delivered.'

'I see.' Lanzo paused with his hand on the door to the ward. 'Will it be safe for her to fly to Italy by private jet, accompanied by a full medical team? I wish to take her to Rome to ensure that she rests properly, and I have arranged for her be cared for at a private hospital by one of Italy's top obstetricians.'

The doctor looked faintly startled, but nodded. 'Yes.

Ordinarily I would not allow her to fly, but with the arrangements you have organised for her care I think it should be okay. She can be discharged from here in the morning.'

'Then we will drive straight to the airport tomorrow,' Lanzo said in a determined voice.

Gina's eyes were swollen with crying, and at the totally unexpected sight of Lanzo striding down the ward more tears slipped silently down her cheeks.

'*Tesoro...*' His voice shook as he dropped down on the edge of the bed and drew her into his arms.

Gina did not know why he had come; she was still in shock from the nightmare events of the past few hours. All that mattered was that Lanzo was here. The horrible stilted phone calls of the past few weeks no longer seemed important as she clung to him and wept.

'I was so scared I was going to lose the baby. At first the doctor thought they would have to deliver early, but it's too soon—the baby is too small,' she sobbed.

'Shh, *cara*,' he soothed her, stroking her hair. 'You must stay calm for the baby's sake. Tomorrow I am taking you to Rome, so that you can be cared for by the best obstetrician in Italy.'

Gina eased away from him, suddenly conscious that she had cried all over the front of his no doubt exorbitantly expensive silk shirt. 'You don't have to do that. You don't need to be involved.' She fumbled for a tissue and blew her nose. 'My face puffs up like a frog when I cry,' she muttered.

Lanzo had never seen her cry like that before. To witness his strong, proud, beautiful Gina fall apart so utterly had evoked a terrible ache inside him, and his voice was gruff as he said, 'I've always liked frogs.'

Only Lanzo could make her smile when moments ago

she had been in the depths of despair. She needed his strength, but she dared not let him see how vulnerable she felt. 'I'll be okay. You don't need to take care of me out of some misplaced sense of duty,' she told him stiffly.

He winced, the familiar feeling of guilt clawing at his insides. 'Not because of duty,' he said. 'But because I want to.' She had told him that conceiving this baby had been a miracle—maybe her one chance to be a mother. 'I know how desperately you want this baby, *cara*, and I will do everything in my power to ensure you give birth safely,' he promised.

The last time Gina had been in Rome it had been stiflingly hot, but in February, although the sun was shining, the sky was a crisp, clear blue, and the temperature was twenty degrees lower than in the summer. Not that she had had much chance to walk outside. Her first two nights in the city had been spent at a private maternity hospital, where she had met the obstetrician who was to oversee her care.

'Strict bedrest, and I am afraid no sex,' Signor Bartolli had murmured when he'd come to her room to tell her that she could be discharged back to the apartment.

Agonisingly conscious of Lanzo's presence, Gina had blushed and carefully avoided his gaze, but she had felt a sharp pang of sadness that she was unlikely ever to make love with him again. He did not want to be a father to their child, and although he had surprised her by being involved now, her relationship with him would end once the baby was born.

'I don't think the doctor meant that I should spend every minute of the next few weeks actually in bed,' she'd argued the following day, after Lanzo had carried her through the apartment and deposited her as carefully as if she were made of spun glass onto the bed in one of the guestrooms.

'He meant precisely that—and so do I,' he said grimly, recognising the light of battle in her eyes. 'You are not to move out of this room, *cara*, and I plan to work from home to make sure you follow orders.'

'What about all your business trips?' Gina asked him.

'I have delegated them to my executives.' He sighed. 'Once again I am without a PA. Luisa has decided not to return to work after having her son,' he explained, 'and Raphaella only works part-time because she looks after her granddaughter two days a week.'

Granddaughter! So the exotic-sounding Raphaella was not some gorgeous young thing. The thought cheered Gina up no end. 'Why don't I fill in on the days Raphaella cares for her granddaughter?' she suggested. 'I can sit in bed with a laptop—that's hardly strenuous,' she pressed when Lanzo shook his head. 'I'm going to do as the doctor has told me—I'm certainly not going to do anything that might harm the baby—but I'll go mad if all I do is read magazines and watch daytime TV.'

'There *are* a couple of reports I need typed up,' Lanzo said slowly. 'I suppose it will be okay—as long as you promise to call it a day if you feel tired.'

For the first hour he trekked back and forth from his study to her room with various files, but eventually he brought his own laptop in and settled himself in the armchair near her bed. They worked in companionable silence.

'So, you're going ahead with the new restaurant in Toronto?' Gina commented, glancing down at the notes he had given her.

'Mmm—with a few changes to the menu. The chef wants to serve moose burgers.'

'*Really?*' She gave him a suspicious look when she saw his lips twitch. 'Are you kidding me?' she demanded, unable to hold back a smile when he grinned.

It was good to laugh with him again, she mused, tearing her eyes from the teasing warmth in his and staring at her computer screen. She had missed their friendship since they had argued on Christmas Day about his insistence that he did not want to be involved with their child.

The memory of his coldness when he had walked out of the house at Sandbanks caused her smile to fade, and she focused on the report in front of her.

With Lanzo and Daphne in constant attendance, Gina began to relax, and the trauma of being rushed into hospital in Poole, terrified that she was losing the baby, gradually faded. But two weeks later she woke in the early hours to find that she was bleeding heavily again. Her scream for Lanzo brought him hurtling into her room, and after that everything became a blur of paramedics, the wail of the ambulance siren, and nurses preparing her for surgery.

'I'm not due to give birth for another six weeks. Maybe the bleeding will stop, as it did before, and I can carry the baby for a little longer,' she begged the doctor when he told her she would have to undergo a Caesarean immediately.

But he shook his head, his face grave, and the last thing she remembered was Lanzo squeezing her hand and saying huskily, 'Everything will be all right, *cara*,' as she was wheeled into Theatre.

'Gina...'

Lanzo's voice sounded distant, and strangely muffled. Gina tried to open her eyes. Her lids felt as if they had been stuck down, but she finally managed to lift her lashes—and the first thing she saw was his tense face.

Her brain slammed into gear. *'The baby!'*

'A girl. You have a daughter, Gina.'

Even though her head was muzzy, she registered what he had said. *She* had a daughter—not we.

She licked her parched lips, feeling horribly sick from the anaesthetic. 'Is...is she all right?' He hesitated, and her heart stopped. *'Lanzo?'*

Lanzo heard the fear in her voice. 'She is fine,' he quickly sought to reassure her, 'but she is small...tiny...' Unbelievably tiny. The image of the little scrap of humanity he had seen briefly when a nurse had taken him to the special care unit was burned on his brain. 'She is in an incubator.' He hesitated once more, and then said gently, 'And on a ventilator to help her breathe, because her lungs are under-developed.'

Dear heaven. Gina swallowed, joy swiftly replaced by frantic worry. 'I want to see her.'

'You will soon, *cara*. But first the doctor is here to check you over.'

An hour later Lanzo wheeled Gina along to the special care baby unit.

'Why are there so many wires?' she asked shakily, blinking away the tears that blurred her eyes.

The moment she had first seen her little girl she had been overwhelmed with emotion. A tidal wave of love had swept through her, and now her hand shook as she touched the plastic side of the incubator. She longed to hold her child—but, as Lanzo had warned her, the baby was tiny. She seemed swamped by the nappy she was wearing, and surrounded by the tubes that were helping to keep her alive.

'But you're here, my angel,' Gina whispered, her eyes locked on her daughter's fragile body and mass of downy black hair. 'You are my little miracle, and I know you are going to make it.'

The paediatrician had talked of the potential problems that faced a premature baby born at thirty-four weeks and weighing under four pounds. Gina's face twisted when she recalled his warning of the high risk of infection and respiratory distress. The stark truth was that her daughter could not breathe without the ventilator that was giving her oxygen. In these early days her life would hang in the balance, but Gina refused to contemplate the worst.

She stared at her heartbreakingly delicate daughter, enclosed in the protective plastic bubble that was keeping her warm, and screwed up her eyes, determined not to allow the tears to fall. Crying wouldn't help, she reminded herself fiercely.

Lanzo could not bring himself to look at the child in the incubator. His one glance earlier had reinforced his belief that the skinny, wrinkled scrap had little chance of survival. He stood silently beside Gina, and the sight of her trying to hide her obvious distress evoked a dull ache inside him. He wanted to protect her from the pain of loss that he knew from bitter experience was almost unendurable.

'Try not to feel too deeply, *cara*,' he advised in a low tone. 'It would be better if you did not get too attached.'

Gina turned her head and looked at him blankly, unable to comprehend his words. Understanding slowly dawned, and she recoiled from him. Emotions swirled through her, the strongest of which was incandescent fury.

'*Don't get too attached?* She is my child—part of me—and part of you too, only you don't have the guts to face up to fatherhood,' she told him with withering scorn. 'Do you think that if I don't love her it will hurt less if she…?' She struggled with the words. 'If she doesn't make it? Is that what all this is about, Lanzo? I know your fiancée died, and your parents at the same time, and I don't doubt that must have been devastating for you—but you can't cut emotion from your life like it's a cancer that has to be removed.'

She took a shuddering breath. 'You are a coward. You might act the daredevil—taking part in dangerous sports like skydiving and powerboat racing—but you don't fear the risk to your personal safety. The real danger is to feel emotions—to put your heart on the line and take the chance of being hurt again, as you must have been when you lost your family. But that's a risk you're not prepared to take. Your baby is fighting for her life, and you refuse to *feel too deeply* because you don't want to deal with messy emotions like love and maybe...' her voice shook '...loss.'

Lanzo looked as though he had been carved from granite, but before he could respond a nurse pushed aside the curtain that had been drawn around them to allow some privacy, and announced that she had come to take Gina back to bed.

'I'm sure you must need some pain relief so soon after the Caesarean,' she said, smiling sympathetically when she saw Gina's drawn face. 'Then I will help you to express your milk, so that we can give it to your baby through the feeding tube until she is strong enough to feed from you herself.'

'I don't want to leave her,' Gina said thickly. She was determined to ignore the painful throb of her stitches and stay at her baby's side.

'You need to rest,' the nurse told her firmly. She smiled cheerfully at Lanzo. 'And her *papà* is here with her.'

The silence screamed with tension.

'He's just leaving,' Gina said dully, and did not glance at him again as the nurse pushed her wheelchair out of the SCBU.

CHAPTER TEN

LANZO raked a hand through his hair, shocked to realise that he was shaking. Gina's outburst had forced him to accept some bitter home truths, and he felt raw and exposed, as if she had peeled away layers of his skin.

He could not deny any of the accusations she had thrown at him, he acknowledged grimly. A coward? *Dio*, yes—she had been right to call him that when he had turned his back on her for most of her pregnancy and insisted that he did not want to be a father to their child.

He turned his head slowly towards the incubator, and felt his heart slam against his ribs when he found his tiny daughter gazing at him with big, deep blue eyes that were the image of her mother's. His breath caught in his throat as he took a jerky step closer to the incubator, and as he studied her perfect, miniature features the trembling in his limbs grew worse.

Utterly absorbed, he barely noticed the arrival of a nurse until she spoke. 'You can touch her,' she said softly. 'Put your hand through the window of the incubator—see?'

She was so tiny she would fit in his palm. Her skin was so fragile it was almost translucent. But she felt warm and soft, her chest rising and falling almost imperceptibly with each breath of life she took.

An indescribable sensation was unfurling deep inside

Lanzo. He gently stroked his daughter's tiny hand, and unbelievably she opened her minute fingers and curled them around his finger, her eyes still focused on his face as she clung to him.

Santa Madre, he was breaking apart. His throat was burning as if he had swallowed acid, and he tasted salt on his lips. Tears ran into his mouth.

'Here.' The nurse smiled gently and handed him a tissue. He couldn't stop the tears seeping from beneath his lashes, and he scrubbed his eyes with the tissue just as he had done when he had been a small boy who had grazed his knee and run to his mother for comfort.

He had cried after the fire—at the funerals of his parents and Cristina. But his grief had been agony, and he had learned to bury the pain deep inside him. For fifteen years he had locked his emotions away, but now, as he stared at his frail little daughter, it was as if a dam had burst and the feelings he had sought for so long to deny cascaded through him.

Gina had called the baby her miracle, but she was *his* miracle too—a tiny miracle who had unfrozen the ice around his heart. He did not have a choice of whether or not to love her, because love was seeping into every pore of his body—and he knew without even giving it conscious thought that he would give his life for his child.

'What do you think her chances are?' he asked the nurse gruffly. 'Do you think she will be okay?'

She nodded. 'I'm sure of it. She's a fighter, this little one. I've worked with premature babies for many years, and I sense she has a strong will.'

'She gets it from her mother,' Lanzo murmured, and sent up a fervent prayer of thanks that his daughter had inherited her mother's feisty nature.

* * *

Gina managed to contain her emotions until she was back in her private room and had obediently swallowed the pain-killers the nurse had handed her. But once she had been left alone to sleep the tears came—great, shuddering sobs that she tried to muffle by pressing her face into the pillow.

Her hormones were all over the place, she told herself when the storm finally passed, leaving her with a headache and hiccups. One of the things she had learned from life was that crying never solved anything, so she blew her nose and gingerly lay back on the pillows, wincing with the pain from her Caesarean wound. She needed to sleep and regain her strength so that she could care for her baby—because they were on their own now. No doubt Lanzo had left the hospital after the terrible things she had said to him. She had always known she was going to have to be a single mother, and for her baby's sake she had to stop feeling sorry for herself and get on with it.

It was early evening when she woke up, and she was horrified that she had slept for so long. The Caesarean had left her feeling as though she had been flattened by a truck, and she was relieved when a nurse told her it was too soon for her to try to walk yet, and wheeled her down to the special care baby unit.

She hadn't expected Lanzo to be there, sitting close to the incubator, his eyes never leaving the baby. He was still dressed in the jeans and black jumper he'd worn when she had been admitted to the hospital twelve hours earlier, and she had a strange feeling that he had been there all the time she had been asleep. He looked round when the nurse parked the wheelchair next to the incubator, an expression in his eyes that Gina could not define. She bit her lip, not knowing what to say to him, and he seemed to share her awkwardness for he quickly dropped his gaze to the book of baby names she had brought with her.

'I thought you had chosen a few possible names?' he murmured.

'None of them are right for her.' Gina's heart melted when her daughter gave a little yawn. It hadn't really sunk in until this moment that she was a mother, and a fierce wave of protectiveness swept through her. 'We can't keep on calling her "the baby".'

'What about naming her Andria?' Lanzo suggested. He hesitated, and then added softly, 'It means love—and joy.'

She threw him a sharp glance, but his green eyes were focused on his daughter and his thoughts were unfathomable. Hand trembling, she reached into the incubator and stroked the baby's silky black hair. 'Andria...it's perfect,' she whispered. Now it was her turn to hesitate. 'What was your mother's name?'

'Rosa.'

'Oh—that was Nonna Ginevra's second name.' Her eyes met his in a moment of silent agreement.

'Welcome to the world, Andria Rosa,' he said deeply, and to Gina's shock he put his hand into the incubator and placed it over hers.

Her heart jerked. She did not understand why he was here when he had been so insistent that he could not be a father, and especially after the things she had said to him, she thought ruefully. Dared she hope that he had had a change of heart? She was too afraid to ask, but a sense of peace settled over her as they sat in silence, two parents watching over their newborn daughter.

As the nurse had predicted, Andria Rosa was a fighter. She grew stronger day by day, and her cry became shriller. Gina did not mind. The sound of her daughter's voice filled her with utter joy and thankfulness for her miracle baby.

Every day brought a new landmark: the day Andria came off the ventilator, the first time Gina managed to walk to the SCBU rather than shuffle along in agony from her Caesarean scar, the first time she was able to hold her baby in her arms without all the tubes that had been keeping her alive, and breastfeeding her for the first time.

Gina recovered quickly, and was discharged ten days after the birth. Going back to the apartment without her baby was the one occasion when she wept, but Lanzo drove her to the hospital every day, and invariably stayed with her and their daughter in a private room.

'I know you must be busy with work.' Gina finally broached the subject she had been skirting around for days. He had been so adamant that his only role in their baby's life would be to provide financial support, and she was confused by his continued presence in Andria's life. 'You don't have to stick around,' she told him bluntly. 'You made it clear that you never wanted to be a father.'

A nerve flickered in his jaw, and he stared down at his daughter sleeping peacefully in his arms for long moments before he spoke. 'I honestly believed I did not want a child,' he admitted in a strained voice. 'You were right to accuse me of being a coward. I chose to live my life on my terms—selfishly only pleasing myself, refusing to allow myself to get too close to anyone—because it was easier that way, less complicated, and with no danger of ever being hurt.

'But then you conceived my baby, and for you it was the miracle you had believed would never happen. At first I was angry—determined that I would have no part in the child's life apart from to honour my financial responsibility. And then Andria was born.' He exhaled heavily. 'A tiny scrap who fought so hard to cling on to life. I feared that if you loved her you would be heartbroken if she lost her battle. I was trying to protect you,' he said, a plea for understanding in his voice as he met her startled gaze.

'You shamed me,' he told her roughly. 'You rounded on me like a tigress defending her cub, scornfully refusing the idea of withholding your love from our baby. You knew there was a danger she might not survive, but you loved her more—not less. You were not afraid to risk your heart, and I was humbled by your bravery, *cara*.'

There was so much more he needed to say to Gina, Lanzo acknowledged, so many things that were only now becoming clear to him—emotions that he could no longer deny. But after so many years of burying his feelings in the deepest, darkest reaches of his soul he was finding it hard to reveal what was in his heart.

She pushed her long hair back from her face, and his gut clenched as memories of running his fingers through the fall of chestnut silk assailed him. 'I'm not sure I understand what you're saying,' she mumbled, and Lanzo knew he could not blame her for sounding guarded after the way he had been.

'I'm saying that I want to be part of our daughter's life. I am her father, and I intend to devote myself to fulfilling that role—caring for her and protecting her.' His voice rasped in his throat as he thought briefly of how he had failed to protect Cristina. He pushed the thought away, determined to focus on the future. 'And most important of all loving her.'

Shock robbed Gina of words. She sensed Lanzo was waiting for her response, but she did not know what to say. Throughout her pregnancy she had prayed he would have a change of heart and accept his child, but now that he had she could see many problems ahead. Presumably access arrangements would have to be made, perhaps with solicitors involved, and decisions taken on where she and

Andria would live. Maybe Lanzo would want them to live in Italy, so that he could visit regularly, but she had expected to be a single mother and had planned to return to Poole so that she'd have the support of her family.

Andria stirred, and made the little snuffling sound that Gina instantly recognised as the sign she needed feeding. Her breasts felt heavy with milk, and she held out her arms when Lanzo brought the baby to her, maternal instinct taking over so that everything else faded from her mind but the intensity of love she felt for her daughter. One thing was certain: she would never agree to be parted from her child—which meant that if Lanzo wanted to be part of Andria's life he would have to be a continued presence in *her* life too.

The future was impossible to envisage, and so she stopped trying and focussed her attention exclusively on the little miracle in her arms.

They took their daughter home five weeks after her traumatic birth. Now weighing a healthy six pounds, Andria still seemed scarily tiny, but her demanding cry proved that there was now nothing at all wrong with her lungs. She was as pretty as a doll, with her blue eyes and mass of black hair, and Gina was utterly besotted with her.

Instead of taking the baby to the apartment, Lanzo explained that he had arranged for them to fly straight to the Villa di Sussurri in Positano.

'We'll have to buy a crib, and a pram,' Gina fretted, wishing that she had discussed living arrangements with Lanzo. She could not stay in any of his houses as a long-term guest. Andria needed a permanent home. But at the moment she did not even know whether she should plan to buy a house of her own in England or Italy.

'Everything has been taken care of,' Lanzo assured her.

'Daphne is already at the villa, and is desperate to meet the new addition to the family.'

But they weren't a family, Gina wanted to point out. Nothing was sorted out between them about how they were both going to be parents to Andria. And now a new problem had sprung up, she thought dismally as Lanzo lowered himself into the seat next to her on the jet, after checking that Andria was securely strapped into a special baby carrier. For the past weeks she had been enveloped in the haze of hormones that accompanied new motherhood, and her sudden acute awareness of Lanzo was unsettling.

If only the doctor at her postnatal check-up a few days ago had not mentioned that she could resume normal sexual activity whenever she felt ready. That very evening she had felt a tightening in the pit of her stomach when Lanzo had strolled bare-chested into the sitting room at the apartment, faded jeans hugging his lean hips and his hair still damp from his shower, and joined her on the sofa where she had been skimming through the TV channels. Then, as now, the scent of his aftershave had teased her senses, and she had been horrified to realise that she would be happy to 'resume normal sexual activity' right there on the sofa.

She had mumbled the excuse that she was tired and fled to her room, mortified by the amused gleam in his eyes that had warned her he had read her mind. Now, trapped in her seat as the jet sped down the runway, she tore her eyes from his handsome face and stared out of the window, every cell in her body tingling with awareness of his potent masculinity. He had said that he wanted his daughter, but had given no indication that he hoped to resume his relationship with *her*, Gina reminded herself. But, as she knew too well, he had a high sex-drive and it was likely he would soon take another mistress—perhaps he already had, she thought, jealousy searing her.

Lost in a labyrinth of dark thoughts, she gave a jolt when he reached out and closed his hand over hers. Her eyes flew to his, and for a second something flared in his green gaze that she could not define. His eyes narrowed; she recognised desire in their sultry gleam and hurriedly looked away, her heart thumping. Did he want them to be lovers once more? she wondered, her mind whirling. If so, how long would his desire for her last? And what would happen when he tired of her but still wanted to see his daughter?

The future loomed, an uncertain spectre, and she could not help thinking that it would have been easier if Lanzo had stuck to his original intention of turning his back on fatherhood—because that way she might have eventually got over him.

The white walls of the Villa di Sussurri gleamed in the spring sunshine, and although it was only April, pink roses were already blooming around the front door. Daphne greeted them with a beaming smile, her black eyes glowing as she cooed over the baby.

'I never thought I would see Lanzo look so happy,' she confided to Gina when Lanzo excused himself to make a brief business call. Gina was startled to see tears in the housekeeper's eyes. 'Cristina was the love of his life, and when she died his grief nearly destroyed him. But you and the *bambino*—you have brought joy to his heart once more.'

'You told me that she died in an accident. What happened to her?' Gina asked, seizing the chance to find out more about Lanzo's past.

But Daphne made no reply and hurried out of the room, leaving Gina with a host of unanswered questions. She wandered out to the hall and stared at the painting of the beautiful Italian girl Daphne said had been the love of Lanzo's life. The thought evoked a sharp pain inside her, a yearning for what could never be—for if Cristina had been his one true love, he was not likely ever to fall in love with her.

'Come and see the nursery,' Lanzo invited when he emerged from his study. He took Andria from her, and led the way upstairs and along the landing to a room that Gina knew was next to the master bedroom.

When she had stayed at the villa with him he had used this room as a dressing room, but now it had been transformed into a haven of powder-pink walls, carpet, and curtains, with a collection of fluffy toys on a shelf and a motif of cute white rabbits hopping around the room. Gina's eyes were drawn to the crib, with its exquisite white lace drapes. The nursery had been designed with loving care, but she did not understand why.

'Don't you like it?' he asked, when he saw her troubled face.

'It's beautiful—just the sort of nursery I would have planned,' she admitted, recalling how she had studied paint charts and debated colour schemes when she had been living at his house on Sandbanks. But she hadn't actually started to decorate a room for the baby because she had decided that she could not stay permanently in Lanzo's house—and she still felt that way now. 'It just seems such a waste to have gone to so much effort when Andria and I won't be staying at the villa for long.'

Lanzo placed his daughter tenderly in the crib and stood watching over her for a few moments, his heart aching with love for his child. The knowledge that he had been prepared to distance himself from her life chilled him to the bone. He had come so close to losing his precious little girl because he had been afraid to love her, and it was only thanks to Gina that he had seen sense.

He frowned as her words sank in. 'Of course you and Andria will be here, *cara*. I have decided that it will be better for her to grow up in Positano, rather than in Rome. The Amalfi Coast is so beautiful, and she can have a freedom here that would be impossible in the city.'

Gina felt a spurt of temper. Sometimes Lanzo could be so irritatingly arrogant and high-handed. 'What do you mean, *you've* decided? Surely the subject of where Andria will spend her childhood is something we should discuss together? We need to start planning how we can both be parents to her,' she said huskily. 'If you would prefer me to live with her in Italy rather than England then I am prepared to do that. I understand that you will want to visit her often—'

'I have no intention of *visiting* her,' Lanzo interrupted sharply. 'I told you—I want to be a proper father to Andria, which means living with her permanently as she grows up, having breakfast with her every morning, and tucking her into bed every night.' He paused and then dropped the bombshell. 'That is why I think the most sensible solution is for us to get married.'

Gina opened her mouth, but no words emerged. Lanzo's suggestion of marriage was utterly unexpected, and, although it was something she had long dreamed of, the reality did not evoke the slightest feeling of joy inside her. He had sounded so prosaic when he had offered his 'sensible solution', and those two words had shattered any faint hope she'd had that they could have any kind of a future together.

His eyes narrowed as he sensed her tension. 'We both want to be full-time parents to our daughter,' he reminded her.

'We don't have to get married to do that.'

'But it would be far better for Andria to be brought up by two parents who are committed to her and to each other.'

She could not deny it. She had always believed it was best for a child to grow up as part of a stable family unit. Marriage and children had been her holy grail. But not like this, she thought painfully. Not because it was a convenient solution to their living arrangements.

'I don't believe it would be a good idea to marry simply for Andria's sake,' she croaked, swallowing the lump that had formed in her throat.

'But it would not only be for that reason, *cara*.' Lanzo walked towards her, heat flaring inside him as he trailed his eyes slowly over her.

She had regained her figure remarkably quickly, and looked slim and sexy, her tight-fitting jeans moulding her bottom and her simple white tee clinging to her voluptuous curves. Many times when he had watched her feeding the baby he had felt a tug of desire that he had quickly stifled, but he could no longer fight his longing to bare her breasts and shape their swollen fullness with his hands.

'The chemistry still burns—for both of us,' he insisted softly, his eyes focusing on the faint tremor of her mouth. 'Did you think you could hide your awareness of me, when I know every inch of your body and recognise its every instinctive reaction to me? You cannot hide your desire for me, *cara*, any more than I can pretend that I am not burning up for you.'

His words, his tone, were beguiling. It would be so easy to give in and follow her heart rather than her head. But her head was urgently warning that he would break her heart, as he had done when she had been eighteen. She shook her head. 'That's just sex,' she muttered.

'It was always more than the slaking of a physical urge. We both know that,' he said deeply.

He had been aware from the beginning of their affair that she was the one woman who could make him break his promise to Cristina. Maybe it had started even further back than then, when she had been a plump, awkward eighteen-year-old, with a shy smile that had tugged on his heart?

Could she really believe that their sexual relationship meant something to him? Gina wondered bleakly. All the time she had been his PA he had never given any hint that he saw her as more than a temporary mistress.

'You wouldn't have considered marrying me if I hadn't had your baby,' she said stiffly.

There was no point in denying what they both knew to be the truth, Lanzo acknowledged grimly. But he was a different man now; Gina had changed him and made him see things differently.

'There is every reason to believe we could have a successful marriage. Added to our mutual desire to do the best for our daughter we share friendship, laughter...' he shrugged '...and, yes, good sex. What more is there?'

She swallowed the tears that clogged her throat. 'Well, if you don't know, there's not much point in me spelling it out. But the one thing missing from your list is presumably the most important reason why you asked Cristina to be your wife. Daphne said she was the love of your life,' she said, when he looked puzzled. '*Love* is the missing ingredient in our relationship, Lanzo, and that's the reason I won't marry you.'

He was staring at her intently, reading the emotions that she could not hide, and humiliation swept through her as understanding slowly dawned in his eyes. 'Gina?'

She could not bear to break down in front of him, but tears were filling her eyes, threatening to overspill.

'*Gina…*' he said again, his voice urgent.

She saw him take a step towards her, and with a choked cry she spun round and ran out of the nursery and down the stairs, her breath coming in agonising gasps as she paused before the portrait of his beautiful dead fiancée. *His one love.* The words pounded in her head, and, hearing his footsteps tearing down the stairs, she pulled open the front door and kept on running.

He found her in the walled garden, sitting by the pool, watching the goldfish darting between the lily pads. The realisation had hit her as she had fled down the drive that she could not run away from Lanzo because she had left Andria behind in the nursery, and nothing on earth would separate her from her baby.

Lanzo's footsteps slowed as he approached her. She could not bring herself to look at him, and after a few moments he came nearer and stared into the green depths of the pool.

The garden beds were ablaze with bright yellow narcissus, waving their heads in the breeze, and through the trees Gina glimpsed the dense blue of the sea. A curious sense of peace settled over her and she sighed. 'This is a beautiful place.'

'The garden was built over the site of my family home,' Lanzo told her, his voice harsh as he struggled to control the emotions storming inside him. 'The house was burned to the ground by a fire.' He paused. 'My parents and my fiancée were unable to escape.'

'Oh, God!' Gina felt sick. When Daphne had mentioned that Lanzo had lost his parents and fiancée in an accident, she had immediately thought of the narrow, winding road along the Amalfi Coast and imagined that they had been involved in a car crash. Not that it would have been any better, she thought with a shiver. But to be trapped in a burning building was truly horrific. 'What happened?' she whispered.

He turned to face her, and she caught her breath at the raw pain in his eyes. She had believed once that he was hollow inside, incapable of feeling the normal range of emotions other human beings felt. But she saw now she had been wrong.

'There was a storm one night and the house was struck by lightning. It was an old house, built in the seventeenth century, and the dry timbers in the roof caught alight instantly. Within minutes flames had engulfed the top floors where my parents slept.' A nerve jumped in Lanzo's cheek. 'My mother and father both struggled with the stairs. I had nagged them to move to a bedroom on one of the lower floors, but my mother loved the view from the top of the house. They didn't stand a chance,' he said heavily. 'The fire crew told me later that the flames had been fanned by high winds and the house went up like tinder.'

'So you weren't you here when the fire happened?' Gina murmured.

'No.' His voice rasped in his throat. 'And I have never forgiven myself. I should have been here. Cristina had begged me not to go to Sweden for a business meeting.' He closed his eyes briefly, the memories still hurting even though so many years had passed. 'She had just told me that she was pregnant,' he revealed huskily.

His mouth twisted when Gina could not restrain a gasp of shock. 'I'm ashamed to say that I reacted badly. We were both very young, and had agreed not to start a family for several years so that I could concentrate on preparing to take over the running of Di Cosimo Holdings when my father retired. I didn't feel ready to be a father,' he admitted. 'I stormed out like a spoiled child. But while I was away my common sense returned. I knew we would manage, knew that I would love our child, and I was impatient to get back to Positano to reassure Cristina that I was pleased about the baby.' His jaw clenched. 'But my meeting overran, I missed my flight, and I had to wait and catch the first flight home the next morning—by which time it was too late to tell Cristina anything,' he said grimly.

'You couldn't have known what would happen,' Gina said gently. 'You can't blame yourself.'

His jaw tightened. 'But I do. I knew nothing about the fire until I arrived at Naples Airport and was met by Cristina's father. When he broke the news that she and my parents were gone I knew that it was my fault. I could have saved them,' he insisted harshly when Gina shook her head. 'If only I hadn't gone away I would have got them out of the house—even if I'd had to carry both my parents down the stairs.'

Gina shivered again as she pictured the terrible scene. 'Was Cristina's room at the top of the house too?' She could understand why Lanzo's elderly parents had been trapped, but the portrait of Cristina showed that she had been young and able-bodied, so why hadn't she escaped?

'She was asleep in my room, on the floor below my parents. Daphne was in the staff quarters on the ground floor and was awoken by the sound of the fire alarm. She knew Cristina would not have heard it, and she tried desperately to reach her, but the stairs were already alight and the smoke was too thick.' Lanzo sighed. 'Poor Daphne has never forgiven herself for escaping and leaving the others. She cannot bear to speak of the events of that night.'

'But—*why* didn't Cristina hear the alarm? *Why* didn't she try to get out?'

He let out a ragged breath. 'She was profoundly deaf.

She'd had meningitis as a child, and lost her hearing as a result of the illness.'

'*Oh, Lanzo.*' Gina stood up and walked over to him. 'I'm so sorry.' The words sounded banal. Driven by an instinctive need to comfort him, she wrapped her arms around his rigid body. For a moment he did not move, and then he lifted his hand and threaded his fingers through her hair.

'Cristina was my childhood friend,' he explained quietly. 'We grew up together and I had always taken care of her. I was looking forward to doing so for the rest of my life. Sometimes she used to get upset about her deafness, and worry that that I would want to be with someone from the hearing world, but I promised her that I would never love another woman, only her. If I had not gone off in a temper and left her she would not have died,' he said raggedly. 'I failed to take care of her and the child she had just conceived, but standing at her graveside I repeated the promise I had made to her that I would never replace her in my heart.'

Gina understood, she truly did, but even though she now knew why he could never love her it did not make her heartache any less, she thought sadly. She guessed that Lanzo had never grieved properly for the people he loved, but had buried his pain deep inside him. She understood why he had refused to risk his emotions. It must have been hard for him to open his heart to his baby daughter, but he loved Andria and wanted to be her father.

After all he had suffered, how could she deny him his daughter? But how could she marry him when she knew that his heart belonged irrevocably to the girl whose beautiful smile still greeted him in the hallway of his home? Feeling suddenly awkward at the way she was clinging to him, she loosened her arms and took a step backwards.

'You didn't fail Cristina. Fate was cruel that night, but

you could not have changed it, and I don't think that the woman whose love for you shines from her face in that painting would have wanted you to spend the rest of your life consumed with guilt.' Gina blinked back the tears that blurred her eyes. 'I think Cristina would have wanted you to find happiness again,' she said huskily.

She half expected Lanzo to deny that he could ever be happy again, and she was startled when he closed the gap between them and drew her against his chest, holding her so close that she could feel the hard thud of his heart.

'How wise you are, *cara mia*,' he said gently. 'Whereas I am a fool who has taken far too long to accept what I know in my heart is true. I know that Cristina would not have wanted me to grieve for ever, but I used the promise I made at her grave as a shield. I never again wanted to suffer the pain I felt after the fire, so I clung to that promise and used it as an excuse for why I could not fall in love.'

He eased back from her a little and stared into her face, the expression in his eyes causing Gina's heart to miss a beat.

'I can't hide from the truth any more, or deny how I feel about you any longer,' he said, his deep voice shaking with emotion. 'I love you, Gina, with all my heart and soul and everything that I am.'

She stared back at him wordlessly, scared to believe it could be true. She had seen him look at Andria with tender adoration blazing in his eyes, and had wished with all her heart that he could look at her the same way. It seemed that her heart had been granted its dearest wish, but her vision was blurred with tears and she was afraid to accept what her eyes were telling her. She thought about his broken promise and bit her lip.

'Even if it's true, you can't feel happy about…loving

me if you feel guilty that you have betrayed Cristina,' she whispered.

Lanzo smiled and tilted her face to his, wiping away the tears that slipped down her cheeks with unsteady fingers. 'It *is* true, and loving you makes me the happiest man in the world, *tesoro mio*.'

He glanced around the garden that he had created as a memorial to the woman who had been his first love. He would always have special memories of Cristina, but Gina had taught him to love again. She had given him his precious daughter, and a future that he hoped to share with her for the rest of his life. His heart overflowed with his love for her.

'You are my life, Gina,' he murmured. 'You and Andria are my reasons for living, and I will no longer risk my life by taking part in dangerous sports.'

She managed a wobbly smile, joy unfurling tentatively inside her. 'You mean you're giving up skydiving and powerboat racing?' It was difficult to believe that the daredevil playboy would be content with a quiet life. 'How will you satisfy your need for excitement?' she asked doubtfully.

'You are all the adrenalin rush I need, *cara*,' he murmured, his green gaze glinting as he pulled her against him and watched her eyes widen when she felt the hard ridge of his arousal.

'Lanzo...' His mouth was a sensual temptation she had been denied for too long, and a tremor ran through her when he brushed his lips over hers in a gentle kiss that tugged on her heart. She wanted more—needed the fierce passion that was so intrinsic to their relationship—and her mouth quivered when he broke the kiss and lifted his head.

'There is something you can do for me. Marry me— please, *amore*. Not for Andria's sake,' he said urgently as she bit her lip, 'or for any reason other than that you are the love of my life and I want to spend my life making you happy.' He lightly touched the scar on her neck. 'You deserve to be happy, Gina, and I promise I will never do anything to hurt you.'

He was nothing like her first husband. She had always known that. 'You did hurt me once,' she admitted softly. 'I fell in love with you when I was eighteen and you broke my heart. And then, to add insult to injury, you went away and forgot about me.'

He shook his head. 'I never forgot you. Over the years I was drawn back to Poole, although I did not acknowledge that it was because I was looking for the girl with a shy smile. And then, when we finally met again, I did not realise at first that the beautiful, elegant Ginevra Bailey was *my* Gina.'

'*Your* Gina?' she questioned, startled by the depth of emotion in his voice.

He nodded, suddenly sombre. 'I started to fall in love with you ten years ago, but when I realised that you were a threat to my heart I ran for the hills. I was afraid to love you,' he admitted. 'But I am not afraid any more.'

He stroked his fingers through her long hair and Gina was puzzled by the sudden uncertainty in his eyes.

'I wouldn't mind knowing how the girl who was in love with me ten years ago feels about me now,' he said roughly.

She smiled then, although tears were not far away. Maybe dreams really could come true. 'Oh, she still loves you. Deep in her heart she never stopped,' she told him softly.

He swallowed, welcoming the tidal wave of emotion that swept through him rather than trying to fight it as he had for so long. 'And will you be my wife, *amore mio*, and stay with me for ever?'

'I will.' It was a promise from her heart.

He kissed her with exquisite tenderness, and then, as passion overwhelmed them, with a hunger that she shared. His hands roamed feverishly over her slender body as he crushed her lips beneath his, and he slid his tongue into her mouth, deepening the kiss until she was trembling—or was it him?

She smiled at his obvious pleasure when he drew her tee shirt over her head and unclipped her bra, so that her breasts spilled into his hands. He tugged her jeans over her hips and knelt to draw her knickers down, before slipping his hand between her thighs and caressing her with infinite care until she gasped and squirmed and begged him to make love to her.

'With my body and my heart,' he assured her as he stripped off his own clothes and drew her down onto the camomile lawn that enveloped them in its sweet fragrance.

He entered her slowly, afraid that he would hurt her when they had not made love for months, but she welcomed him eagerly into her and lifted her hips to meet each gentle thrust, until he could not hold back and took them both swiftly to the pinnacle of pleasure.

'*Ti amo*, Gina, always and for ever,' he groaned as they climaxed together and fell back down to earth safe in each other's arms.

She captured his face in her hands and pressed her lips against his damp lashes. It had been a long journey for both of them, but finally they had found each other—and a love that would last for eternity.

'Always and for ever, my love,' she agreed.

EPILOGUE

THEY were married a month later, in the church in Positano. All of Gina's family flew out for the wedding, and the ceremony was a joyous affair, full of love and laughter. The bride wore a simple ivory silk gown and pink roses in her hair, and the groom looked impossibly handsome in a dark grey suit. The tender smile on his face when he kissed his new wife caused Daphne to burst into tears, but the smallest guest stole the day—for it was also Andria Rosa's christening. The baby looked angelic, in a froth of white lace, and smiled and gurgled happily unless her father tried to put her down, when she squawked indignantly.

'Our daughter might be small, but she is very determined,' Lanzo murmured when he placed Andria in her mother's arms and she immediately snuggled into Gina's neck. 'I wonder where she gets it from?' he added dryly.

They held a reception in the walled garden, and later, when all the guests had departed and Daphne had taken charge of Andria, Lanzo swept Gina into his arms and carried her into the villa.

'Where is the painting of Cristina?' she asked, noticing immediately the space on the wall where the portrait had hung.

'I've taken it down and put it away. You are my wife, *cara*. The Villa di Sussurri is your home, and I did not think you would want to have a reminder of my past on display.'

Lanzo's green eyes were no longer shadowed, Gina noticed, but clear and blazing with emotion as he stared down at her. She had not been his first love, but she had no doubt now that he loved her with all his heart—just as she loved him.

'Cristina was a special person in your life, and I know you will never forget her—nor would I want you to,' she told him softly. 'She is part of your past, and she belongs here. Put the painting back, Lanzo.'

'Have I told you how much I love you, Signora di Cosimo?' Lanzo said deeply as he carried her up the stairs to their bedroom.

Her smile stole his breath. 'Many times. But you can tell me again—and show me,' she invited huskily when he laid her on the bed.

'I intend to, *cara*,' he promised. 'For the rest of my life.'

MILLS & BOON®

Need more New Year reading?

We've got just the thing for you!
We're giving you 10% off your next eBook or
paperback book purchase on the Mills & Boon
website. So hurry, visit the website today and type
SAVE10 in at the checkout for your exclusive

10% DISCOUNT

www.millsandboon.co.uk/save10

MILLS & BOON®
By Request

RELIVE THE ROMANCE WITH THE BEST OF THE BEST

A sneak peek at next month's titles…

In stores from 20th February 2015:

- **Royal and Ruthless** – Robyn Donald, Annie West and Christina Hollis

- **At the Tycoon's Service** – Maya Banks

In stores from 6th March 2015:

- **He's the One** – Cara Colter, Barbara Hannay and Jackie Braun

- **The Australian's Bride** – Alison Roberts, Meredith Webber and Marion Lennox